The Texas Gun Club

To Bob,

Enjoy !

Cheers,
Mark
Bawlin

The Texas Gun Club

Commander Mark Bowlin, USN (Ret.)

The Texas Gun Club

Copyright © 2010 by Mark Bowlin

This is a work of fiction.

Cover art, artwork by Keith Rocco for the
National Guard Heritage Series.

Manufactured in the United States of America.

For information, please contact:

The P3 Press
16200 North Dallas Parkway, Suite 170
Dallas, Texas 75248
www.thep3press.com
972-248-9500

A New Era in Publishing™

ISBN-13: 978-1-933651-55-2
ISBN-10: 1-933651-55-5
LCCN: 2009910232

Author contact information:
Commander Mark Bowlin, USN (Ret.)

www.markbowlin.org

The Texas Gun Club is dedicated to my parents,
Stan and Zee Bowlin, who instilled in me a love of
history and reading—and you can't do
much better than that.

Foreword

The Texas Gun Club is an adventurous novel about the perilous experiences of a group of Texas National Guardsmen participating in the first Allied invasion of Europe, in the Salerno area of Italy during World War II. Although the characters and their specific stories are fictional, the big picture of the historic invasion is authentic. This combination makes for a sequence of exciting and continuing events, which CDR Bowlin presents with great skill.

The soldiers are all members of the 36th Texas National Guard Division, and their family stories and military experiences are blended together well. It isn't long until the reader feels like one of the group.

This is an engaging tale of high adventure, emphasizing patriotic devotion to one's division, state, and country.

Fred L. Walker, Jr.
Colonel, USA (Ret.)

Acknowledgments

First and foremost, I need to thank Susan and Alex for their support during the writing of *The Texas Gun Club*. Their love, understanding, and encouragement made the transition from naval officer to writer much easier than I had any right to expect.

Many generous people offered technical advice and editorial suggestions—they share no responsibility for the mistakes this sailor may have made concerning ground operations. Others, including strangers, offered help in a thousand different ways. I would like to thank my father, Stan Bowlin, as well as COL Fred Walker, Jr., USA (Ret.); COL Eric Stanhagen, USA (Ret.); CDR Bob Rose, USN (Ret.); CDR Rob (2-Bit) Hoar, USN; Lt Col Frank Chawk III, USMC; LCDR Jim Ford, USN; Capt Fin Jones, USMC (Ret.); LT Tony Jamison, USN; Cynthia Stillar; Stacy Schoolfield; Bob Wranosky; Ann Bishop; Bruce Makous; Kay and Harry Bernardi; William Medico; Jeff Hunt and the Texas Military Forces Museum; and, of course, the blood-thirsty ladies of the Excellent Point Book Club of Flower Mound, Texas.

Chapter One

September 14, 1943
1305 hours
East Slope, Mount San Chirico
Italy

They had returned to die with the company, but the killing had already begun.

The lieutenant knew he'd made a bad decision. *One of many*, he reflected bitterly. As the jeeps skirted up the highway, he'd taken a shortcut. A road to nowhere. He'd been told Able Company was on the other side of the mountain, but to drive around it would take too much time. Besides, he didn't know who controlled the roads. They'd been gone too long.

Against the backdrop of the smoke-filled sky, the lieutenant took in the horror of the battlefield. Massive clouds of flies marked the dead while vultures and ravens gorged on the unexpected bounty. Broken, listless soldiers sat in ditches praying for the end, praying for salvation while others moved forward towards the smoke and noise of combat. It wasn't over yet.

There was no road leading down the eastern slope. It ended on a flat, rocky plateau where a shattered wooden cross lay strewn across the rocks. It might have been a beautiful place to pray once, but not today. He wasn't seeking salvation. There was no sense looking for what would never be granted.

The lieutenant spotted American soldiers on the crest. By God, he was tired. If they'd been German soldiers he would've been dead by now. *Perhaps they'll know where Able Company is*, thought the lieutenant as he led the jeeps to the far rim of the crest, where a small group of officers had gathered to watch the battle unfold. For the first time in ages, fortune had smiled on him: he knew these soldiers.

The lieutenant climbed out of the jeep and made his way towards a short, bull-necked lieutenant colonel with dark tired eyes: his battalion commander.

"Sir," he said. He nodded but did not salute.

The colonel glanced at the lieutenant, turned and silently counted the soldiers in the jeeps. Some were missing, but he couldn't remember how many there had been in the beginning. Was it eight? Or ten? He turned his gaze back to the action at the base of the mountain, looking over the lieutenant once more in the process: he'd changed. Gone was his cocky confidence. He didn't look injured, but he was covered in dried blood and smelled like a slaughterhouse.

Without taking his eyes off the battlefield, the colonel asked the only question that mattered, "Are they going to help?"

"No, sir. They're movin' too slowly. They won't be here for days."

The battalion commander let out a long sigh. "Well, that's it then. It's just us."

"Yes, sir. It's just us." The words were chilling, but the lieutenant didn't care. He needed to get back to his company.

He walked to the edge of the crest and looked down. He'd been gone from the Salerno plain for days, and although the war had by no means passed him by, this was different—less personal—than the killing he'd seen. The killing he'd done. There was enough of a breeze off the water to push the haze around, granting brief glimpses of the battle below. It looked no better from this side of the mountain.

A burst of fire erupted several hundred yards below where the mountain sloped to a ribbon of flat land that lay between the base and a small creek. Beyond the water lay a farmer's pasture where water buffalo or perhaps cattle had grazed in happier times. On this day, the pasture had become a field of carnage as the battle reached its culmination. The lieutenant knew the little bridge over the creek was the key to the beachhead, to the battle. *If the Allies hold the bridge, they inexorably build up and move inland. If the Germans win the narrow strip of wood and iron, it would make Dunkirk look like a weekend at the shore.*

"Sir, I was told we've been ordered to evacuate to the ships. Is that true?" The lieutenant had heard the rumor only yesterday and had driven through the night to return. It had been the worst night of his life.

"It was a stupid order. Never give an order you know cain't be obeyed. We ain't goin'. . . ," The battalion commander was interrupted by the sound of cheering. Through a hole in the smoke, they watched as a salvo of naval gunfire destroyed a tank and a squad of panzer grenadiers who'd been using the tank as a shield.

"Sir, where's Able? I need to get back to my platoon." The lieutenant thought it a damn odd thing cheering the deaths of a score of men, but then thought maybe the

Germans had been praying for an end as well. Perhaps their deaths were . . . what was the phrase? Sweet and fitting. *Dulce et decorum est pro patria mori.* The old lie.

Reading the anxiety and need for haste on the lieutenant's face, the colonel said, "Your cousin's fine. That's them straight down—in front of the bridge. There's a goat path to your right, it's the best way . . ." The colonel stopped talking as German artillery found the bridge's defenders. The mountain shook as a ton of explosives hit the hillside. The concussion from the blasts and the falling debris forced the watchers away from the edge and down into foxholes or behind rocks—except for the colonel and the lieutenant. The colonel looked defiant, yet resigned to the inevitable. He had the same look seen on the faces of men at more memorable places like the Alamo and Rorke's Drift and, more recently, Dunkirk and Dieppe. "You and your boys are my battalion reserve. No one's left. Y'all head on down now. I'm going to direct Baker to send a platoon from their defenses, and then my staff and I'll be right behind you."

"Thank you, sir," said the lieutenant, even though he wasn't feeling remotely grateful. He turned and motioned to his soldiers, who grabbed weapons and packs before starting grim-faced down the path to join the remnant of their company.

Chapter Two

September 7, 1943
0545 hours
Onboard USS *Thomas Jefferson*
Oran, Algeria

The tall, muscled officer watched from the taffrail of the ship, his hands resting on the steel cables, as distant Africa emerged from the shadows of the early morning. First Lieutenant Sam Taft had been on deck since the *Thomas Jefferson* had moved out of the Oran harbor in the early morning hours and begun to roll on a gentle swell from the northwest. He'd spent almost every summer on the water and, unlike many soldiers, he'd never had to wait for his sea legs. As the ship moved, he instinctively shifted his weight to keep his balance. The motion made him think of happier days spent riding his favorite horses. The memory elicited a loud sigh. Sam knew if it was in his power he'd gladly trade all the ships at sea to spend just one more day on his ranch back in Texas.

Sam was careful to stay out of the way of the busy sailors. As soon as the ship had completed its sea and anchor detail, he'd found a solitary place on the fantail where he could look back at where they'd been. The busy activity of the soldiers and sailors irritated him. A few had ventured aft to see the view but had quickly moved away after seeing the hard look on the huge officer's face. When the ship gathered speed and found its station in the massive convoy, Sam took a long look at the continent he was leaving behind. Africa seemed more beautiful from a distance; although Sam was glad to say he'd been here, he had few regrets about leaving it behind.

He'd been told they would learn their mission in a few hours, but the battle mattered less than getting it over with and moving on to the next battle and the one after that. Within a day or two, the division would be in combat for the first time in this war—Sam would be one step closer to finishing this chapter of his life and getting home. They'd come a long distance, he knew, but there was such a long way to go.

"I knew I'd find you here!"

Sam was joined by another tall lieutenant, this one with a broad smile on his face. Sam looked at his cousin, Perkin Berger, with a mixture of amusement and cynicism. "Is that right?"

"Uh-huh. Everyone else is looking forward to seeing where we're goin'. I knew you'd be lookin' back." Perkin said, equally amused.

"Is there any land up there to look at?" Sam didn't want to talk but knew Perkin had walked the length of the ship to find him, so he felt the need to at least be civil and attempt small talk.

"No."

"Then what's the damn point?"

Civility had run its course.

Perkin laughed but said nothing. He leaned over the taffrail and spit into the ship's wake, then smiled happily at his cousin. He knew Sam's mood would soften. Sam just didn't like change much, and he liked the army even less. Perkin stretched and yawned, then spit again. He reveled in the sea air, loved being surrounded by soldiers and sailors, and felt privileged to be part of the greatest moment in human history. Although few of the soldiers who embarked on the army transport ship were happy about the prospect of this unknown but inevitable battle, Perkin was delighted the division was finally on the move. True, he was apprehensive about the days to come, but he was eager to test himself in battle and anxious to get the first fight out of the way.

Perkin had found a home in the army; he was debating whether to stay in after the war or go back to academia. For Sam, there was no question. As soon as he completed his service, he would resign his commission and head home to Texas and his wife Margaret. Although Sam hated the disruption in his life, Perkin recognized that his cousin was one of the best officers in the regiment and as tough as any soldier Perkin had ever met. Sam was uncomplaining to all but Perkin, with a work ethic forged on one of the largest ranches in Texas. He had a natural authority and had been in charge of hard men long before coming into the army. Perkin knew Sam would be a good combat leader, but he was a little disappointed that he didn't share his enthusiasm for the army or his appreciation for the spirit of the times.

"Don't you want to know where we're goin'?" Perkin asked.

"No."

"You ain't afraid, are ya?" Perkin knew his cousin wasn't afraid. Simply put, teasing and tormenting each other had been elevated to an art form between the two young men who'd been raised as brothers.

"Ain't there some sailor you can go bother? Why don't you go ask the captain next time we're at general quarters if you can drive the boat again? Maybe that'd give you your fill of conversation. I seem to remember he had a lot to say to you then."

"You know that was a misunderstanding." Perkin squirmed at the unpleasant memory; as a new thought crossed his mind, he brightened and grinned at his cousin, "Besides, different boat, different captain. Maybe this one's a little more reasonable. Look, we're finally underway for combat. In a day or two we're gonna embark in those landing craft over yonder and be chucked onto some distant shore. I thought it might be nice to spend this historic moment with family."

Sam looked away from Africa, straightened up and glared at his cousin. "It ain't. Now go away." He was nearly two inches taller than the six-foot three-inch Perkin and about fifty pounds heavier, but unless Sam was really angry, his size had never intimidated Perkin.

"You used to be fun, Bear. When'd you get so old?"

"Go away and don't call me that."

"Fine. I'm headin' to the fo'c'sle. That's up at the pointy end of the ship where all the other company officers are. While you're looking backwards, maybe you could spend some time thinking about how it was your idea that got us here in the first place. It's what you get for talking me into skippin' church on Easter." Perkin walked quickly away without looking back, a smile on his face. Sam would grouse for an hour or two, and then he'd be back to his normal happy self.

Sam was only partially paying attention to Perkin's chatter; when the last jibe sunk in, he whipped around— but Perkin had already moved behind some landing craft and was out of sight.

"My idea?" Sam snorted as he thought back to that Easter Sunday in 1939.

It had been one of those stunning South Texas spring days, warm and clear with only the hint of a storm building far past the islands. Back in those easy days, fishing was life for these two cousins. Even the mild disapproval of family and the inevitable hard looks from neighbors couldn't compel them to attend church on such a fine day. Still, South Texas was South Texas, and people were expected to be in church on Sunday mornings, especially if that Sunday was Easter. But both men had been in their early twenties at the time and felt independent enough to take such risks, both thinking they'd spent enough Sundays in church to last a lifetime. Had it been raining, they would have gone to Portland's sole Presbyterian church and prayed and sung along with the truly devout, but on this day the bay was calm, the winds were gentle from the southeast and— word was—the speckled trout were biting.

The young men walked to the water's edge, tossed their gunny sacks of live shrimp into the bay, and knelt to make the final adjustments to their tackle. Wordlessly, they handed hooks, sinkers, and corks back and forth until both were ready to go, each unconsciously checking their implements of good fortune. Sam's was a lucky straw hat he'd worn on one particularly triumphant day of fishing. Perkin's was a well-worn 1915 Liberty Head half-dollar. After ensuring that they'd done all they could to entice lady luck, the two cousins waded out to a sandbar running parallel to the shore and began to sin in earnest. Their favorite fishing spot was a stretch of Corpus Christi Bay between Portland and Indian Point. Shimmering across the bay lay the low silhouettes of Mustang and Padre islands.

Both men reached into the small gunny sacks trailing behind them in the water and pulled out small brown shrimp. Expertly hooking the live shrimp, Sam and Perkin threw their lines out into deeper water and settled down for a couple hours of fishing. There'd been many a day when, as boys, they'd caught a trout on the first cast, but despite the optimistic forecast, this particular Easter Sunday had started slowly.

After several tries without result, the cousins waded several hundred yards to another sandbar. "So, catch me up with what's going on in the world," said Sam as they pushed through the greenish-brown water. "I've been working on fences for the past two weeks and I ain't had much time for the news."

Sam's family had been involved in local ranching since the turn of the century. His grandparents had acquired the dominant interest in what had once been known as the Coleman-Fulton Pasture Company. The ranch had adopted Sam's family name and been known as the Taft Ranch for years until it was broken up and sold in 1929 at the expiration of the ranch charter. In its heyday, the ranch was over three hundred thousand acres, and Sam's father, Raymond, had retained the best sixteen thousand acres for himself after the dissolution of the ranching company. Raymond Taft had died of a heart attack during Sam's junior year at Texas A&M, and Sam had left college to run the remaining Taft holdings in South Texas.

"Local, national, or international?" asked Perkin. This was a time-honored ritual between the two. Perkin was a graduate student in history at the University of Texas who could argue politics and current events with anyone—usually without an invitation to do so. He'd long been a conduit of information for his cousin. Sam occasionally read the papers and frequently listened to the radio, but he considered Perkin a more reliable source.

"I assume that nothin' of significance is goin' on locally or I'da heard about it from Lupé." Lupé, his cook, was the town gossip and married to one of Sam's top hands. "Besides, nothin' noteworthy happens here anyway."

Perkin nodded. "Well, nationally, there's Marian Anderson. She'll be on the radio this afternoon. Wanna listen with me?"

"I might," said Sam. "Who is she?"

"The colored girl who's singin' at the Lincoln Memorial today."

Sam shrugged and shook his head.

Perkin explained, "The DAR denied her the use of some hall for a concert because she's a Negro. After that, she couldn't even find a high school in DC that'd let her in, so Roosevelt is letting her use the National Mall."

At the mention of Roosevelt's name, Sam rolled his eyes and spit. "Thanks, but I ain't interested. You know I don't care for nigra music. You keep trying to get me to listen to that stuff, and I keep telling you I don't like it. And an endorsement from Roosevelt don't help much neither."

"Nah, she doesn't sing jazz. She's an opera singer."

"Aw, for the love of Pete, that's even worse. I'd rather sit on Old Perkin's porch in a heat wave, watchin' him spit t'bacca juice at the cat all day than listen to opera for five minutes. If we ain't going out for a beer tonight . . . oh right, it's Sunday. Anyway, come out to the ranch and we'll put on some Bob Wills or maybe that old Skillet Lickers record . . . ," Perkin made a face at the thought but said nothing as Sam continued, ". . . that's real toe-tappin' music and bound to put you in a good frame of mind before you talk to Old Perkin. That's why you came down this weekend, ain't it?"

"Well, I didn't come down to get drunk while you sing, 'Ya Gotta Quit Kickin' My Dog Around,' over and again like last time. I'll grant you it's toe-tappin' music, and I particularly like it when you bark and howl, but once is enough." Perkin laughed at the memory and then smiled mischievously at his cousin before saying, "Maybe I came down to ask the librarian's daughter out. If you ain't got the juice to do it, maybe I should. Someone ought to 'cause a girl that pretty is just going to waste down here."

Sam scowled and then blushed but said nothing as he looked across the bay at the distant islands. The dark clouds lying low on the horizon were becoming more visible but they didn't interest Sam. The librarian's daughter did— he'd been working up the courage to ask Margaret out. A stunning redhead with dark green eyes, she was best known for her intellect, humor, and sharp tongue.

Perkin used his pole to push a small jellyfish towards Sam. "Seriously, ain't you gonna ask that girl out? She's too good lookin' to wait around. Do ya need me to do it for you? I have no problem talkin' to pretty girls."

Neither did Sam—except for when it came to Margaret. He was preparing an insult of his own, but what came out instead was: "Aaaah! Jesus Christ, that hurts!" The jellyfish had brushed against his arm. As he pushed it back towards his cousin he said, "So, other than the fishin' and the promise of a Skillet Lickers tune and the threat of askin' out the girl for me, why'd you leave the city comforts of Austin? Are you gonna talk to Old Perkin or what?"

"Yeah. I came down to talk to him. My mind's mostly made up. I'm joinin' the army at the end of the semester. Hey! Careful with that Man o' War, someone could get hurt."

"It ain't a Man o' War, and that somebody's me. Now, about this army stuff, Old Perkin ain't gonna like it."

Perkin shrugged and said, "I could go without tellin' him. Is that what you'd have me do, Sam? Run off without telling him?"

"I ain't sayin' that. I ain't sayin' that at all. But he won't support you and you know why." Sam paused, "Listen, Perk, let the matter drop. Y'all are headin' for a fallin' out. It's your life . . . but I don't want you to do it either."

Perkin looked back out at the bay as the water surrounding their corks began to explode with shrimp. He felt a sharp tug on his line—a school of trout was directly underneath them. He set the hook and began to work the trout in. He was glad for the distraction and used the time to think through what Sam had said.

After they'd both brought in several fish, Sam was the first to break the silence. "Tell me again why it can't wait 'til after you're done with your doctorate. Hitler ain't goin' away anytime soon, and if he does, well, all the better."

Perkin nodded and began to speak in the persuasive debater's tone he'd honed in graduate seminars. "Sam, you know what's goin' on in the world. First it was the Japs in Manchuria in '31 and then came the Germans again. In just the last six years, the Nazis have seized power in Germany, usurped their parliament, rearmed, destroyed the free press, reentered the Rhineland, and annexed Austria. And the countries sworn to uphold Versailles did nothing—absolutely nothing. This year, the Germans essentially did the same thing to Czechoslovakia, but this time it was worse 'cause the democracies helped. And now Germany is making noise about reclaiming Prussian lands in Poland and the little Baltic states. Every time we turn our heads and ignore their aggression we take another step towards a global war—a world war that would be worse than the great one."

Sam had only a vague notion of what the Baltic countries were, but he understood the rest of Perkin's argument. Riding fences or not, it was hard to escape the dramatic events unfolding in Central Europe. Germany had repatriated the Sudetenland Germans by annexing the territory and then declared that the rump Czech state was a German "protectorate."

Perkin abandoned his scholarly tone as his anger rose. "You know, it really bothers me that there was one true democracy in that part of the world and Chamberlain and Daladier gave it away to the lowest kind of trash imaginable. And the worst part is that the British and the French have been holding four aces since before the Rhineland and Hitler, who had a pair of sixes, still managed to bluff them."

Sam took a fish off his hook, placing it on a stringer tied to his wet overalls. He looked over at his cousin, "Guess they thought that Hitler had a straight flush, but I ain't convinced it has squat to do with us. So what happens next?"

Perkin considered the question for a moment and then said emphatically, "Poland! And that's the point that I'm trying to make. I've come to the conclusion that another European war is inevitable. 'Peace in our time with honor'? Don't count on it. Speeches ain't gonna stop Hitler. Know why? 'Cause he's never been held accountable, not one damn time, for his actions since comin' to power. And you know what else I think?"

"What?"

"He despises us for it. You take one look at him and you can just see the contempt he holds for us. He ain't gonna stop. He has no reason to."

"You have a point there, that fella looks angry all the time. He should take up fishin'."

"Yes, he should," Perkin said with a smile. The mental image of the German dictator with waders on made him laugh. "In place of that, someone needs to stand up to Hitler—but they won't until it's too late."

"Why do you say that?"

"After pretty much overturning Versailles, he's a national hero." Perkin cast his line out and continued,

"You asked what's next? I'll bet you a case of Shiner that he causes an incident over Poland before this month is out."

"I'll take that bet. Hitler can't move that fast." said Sam. "Think about it, Perk. He's gotta be cautious after carving up the Czechs. Even if Hitler ain't done thievin' by half you think he'd lay low, brand his new stock, and make like he's done, even if he ain't. Otherwise, he'll embarrass the Frogs and the Limeys so bad that even Chamberlain will have to act." Sam shook his head at the thought of the British prime minister. "So what happens if the Poles stand their ground and the British and French hang tight? What happens then?"

"Good question. Wish I knew." Perkin said. "On a good day, they kick the bejesus out of the Germans. Everyone knows the French have the best army in the world, and the British Empire has good soldiers. But then, so do the Germans. On a bad day, it's 1914 all over again. That's what's got me worried. If the British and the French can't deal with it, then it becomes our problem again."

"Aw, that's bullshit, Perk. Just the worst kind of liberal crap imaginable. Listen, it ain't our problem. Besides, you said so yourself: the French have the best army in world. They can take care of themselves. They don't need us, and it ain't like Germany can build a world-class army to threaten us overnight. Or the Japs for that matter. We have a better shot at being invaded by Mexico than Japan or Germany. They're too far way and they just can't hurt us."

Perkin cursed as he lost a fish. "No. You're wrong. The world has changed, and we can't hide behind the oceans anymore. Nor should we. If there is any lesson to take away from this decade and the depression, it's that we need the rest of the world in order to get along: for trade, security, and moral support. I'm tellin' you, if the democracies don't stand together then we'll be picked off one at a time."

Sam, looking stubborn, was preparing to tell his cousin that America didn't need anyone when Perkin preempted him. "Let's leave off that for a moment and, for the sake of argument, assume I'm right . . . as usual. What do we do about it? Let the Alvin Yorks of Appalachia fight our fight for us? The Iowa farm boys? Or do we recognize that we have a stake in this and do our part?"

"Well, I ain't close to concedin' that you're right, 'cause you ain't. But if the day comes when you are, then I'll do my part. But in the meantime, I ain't going anywhere. I don't know why you'd ever want to leave South Texas, let alone the state." Sam looked over at his cousin with a grin, "Besides, you never know, I might feel the urge to ask out the librarian's daughter someday, and I can't do that from the Philippines or Camp Lewis or any other dumbass place I'd end up. One Taft in the Philippines per century is enough."

Perkin snorted. "Your sense of service moves me. You know, if your destiny hinges on asking out Margaret or joining the army, I'd say that there's a better chance of you becomin' a Mexican general than having a date with that girl." He paused while Sam was stuck between taking a trout off his line and preparing a retort. "There's one last thing, Sam. I know it won't carry much weight with Old Perkin, but I don't just want to read about history, I wanna be part of it. I just don't think that I'll contribute much on that account from either Portland or Austin."

Sam was silent while he put his fish on his stringer, then said thoughtfully, "You give history too much due and Portland not enough. You can't swing a dead cat in the Taft family without hittin' someone historical. But so what? D'ya think Uncle Billy was a better man than you or me just because he was president? At least Grandpa Charlie made a meaningful contribution to mankind: he owned the Cubs. Your history's overrated."

Perkin started to laugh, "Put in that light, perhaps it is, but history has taught me a thing or two. For example, the saying that 'there's not enough room to swing a cat' refers to a cat-o'-nine-tails, not a . . . uh . . . a postmortem feline. That's a navy term by the way."

Sam laughed. "Well, ain't you just the Perkin of Menlo Park? Actually, I was using an Indian phrase. Old Perkin told me that swingin' a dead cat was a ritual in Comanche weddings." He shrugged. "I kinda figured it was an Indian aphrodisiac or something. You ever heard of Spanish fly? This is Indian cat. That's the phrase I was using. I don't see no point to yours."

The cousins laughed and joked awhile before Sam, taking a look at the building clouds on the horizon, said, "We ought to wrap this up. We've got more fish than we can eat. I must have fifty or so, what do you have? Two? Three? Let's head back to the shore and let go the little ones—those would be yours—and head over to Old Perkin's to fry up the rest. You can run your plan past him, but don't be lookin' to me for help. Maybe you're right about where Europe is headin', but I don't like your solution."

"Sam? Sir?" Second Lieutenant Ed Brown's soft voice brought Sam back to present and the fantail of the *Thomas Jefferson*.

Sam looked at the young officer from Dallas and grunted, "What?" before saying, more politely, "What's up, Eddy?" The short, thin officer had been a student in the School of Commerce at Southern Methodist University at the time of Pearl Harbor. He enlisted the next day, using family connections to get assigned to the Texas division. Sam found Ed to be one of the most thoughtful and kind soldiers he'd met in the army.

"Cap'n Spaulding asked me to give you a fifteen-minute heads-up. He wants all company officers to meet in the wardroom for breakfast, and then we'll get our mission briefings." The young lieutenant hesitated and then grinned, "Perkin said you were fixin' to jump overboard and swim back to Texas. He wants to know if you left him anything in your will in case you get eaten by a leviathan."

"What's a leviathan?"

"It's a sea monster in the Bible." Brown, one of many deeply religious soldiers in the division, closed his eyes before quoting Psalms, ". . . here is the ocean, vast and wide, teemin' with life of every kind, both large and small. See the ships sailin' along, and Leviathan, which you made to play in the sea." Brown smiled as he looked out on the scores of ships surrounding the *Thomas Jefferson.*

Sam couldn't help himself. He smiled back at the young officer. "It don't sound too tough. Tell Perkin that if he has any more dumbass questions he can come ask them himself. See you in the wardroom." Sam looked back at the ship's wake and, instead of thinking about sea monsters, his thoughts returned to the fish they'd caught that Easter four years earlier.

The cousins had waded back to the beach; they'd released the smaller trout and red fish but kept the six largest trout, including a beautiful six-pounder that Sam had caught. They threw the fish into a large metal ice chest in the back of Sam's Model A pickup, toweled themselves off and put on dry overalls.

"Before we go, let's say a quick prayer for 'em. I suppose that they'd like that on Easter," said Sam.

The two young men walked down the bay another fifty yards, turned inland, and bowed their heads. They were facing what had been the temporary internment site of their mothers; a mass grave for the victims of the September 1919 hurricane.

Neither Perkin nor Sam had a living parent remaining, a void largely filled by Perkin's grandparents. Sam's father had died while Sam was in college, and Perkin's father, an army officer, was killed at the Battle of the Marne on July 15, 1918. The blood kinship between Sam and Perkin was through their mothers, twin sisters named Natalie and Elizabeth Granberry. After more than a year of Elizabeth mourning Captain Berger, the two sisters decided to spend a weekend on the beach at Mustang Island. They left both boys with Elizabeth's father-in-law, Old Perkin, who taught the four-year-olds how to spit that weekend, and borrowed his keys to a small cottage he owned in Port Aransas.

There were reports that a powerful hurricane was active in the Gulf but was headed for the Louisiana or Mississippi coast. Inexplicably, the storm was "lost" at sea; by the time anyone knew it would make landfall in South Texas, it was too late to evacuate the outlying islands. Elizabeth and Natalie's bodies were two of hundreds that washed ashore in Corpus Christi and Nueces bays. They were buried on that remote beach south of Portland. Neither cousin had a clear memory of his mother, so the time praying along the beach was somber for only a moment. As they drove back into town, Perkin mused, "I wonder how things would've been different if they'd lived."

"Maybe with a female influence you wouldn't pick your teeth at the table or spit t'bacca juice at that old cat with your grandfather."

"I have Anna," Perkin said of his grandfather's second wife. "I don't know what I hate more, tobacco or that nasty old cat, although to be fair to Old Perkin, the spittin' affair was accidental. He remarried; why do you think your dad didn't?"

"The cat remarried? I didn't know that. Naw, I've thought about it over the years. Dad wasn't much older than we are now when Mom died. I don't think there would've been a lack of interested women given his name and money. He didn't pine away or nothin', he just never got married again. I wish he had for his sake. Besides, it would have been nice havin' a woman around the house other than Lupé. All I got outta that was an appreciation for tamales for Christmas. Well, that and my Spanish is better than yours."

"You keep bringin' this up, but once again, *estás equivocado*," Perkin said before switching back to English. "I speak Spanish. You speak border Mexican. Ain't the same thing."

"Just keep pattin' yourself on the back there pardner. I'm the only one of us who can actually communicate in the language that some folks speak down here. It ain't like you're headed to Spain any time soon, and most of the Mexicans think you're puttin' on airs."

The truck pulled up to Old Perkin's house, set on a bluff overlooking Corpus Christi Bay. Old Perkin liked to brag that his house held the highest point on the Gulf Coast, which seemed a minor point to his grandson as its elevation above sea level was barely thirty feet. Still, as South Texas is easily the flattest place on God's earth, the vista from any altitude could be impressive. As boys, Sam and Perkin had never tired of watching the sunlight sparkle off the waves in the bay. They could have easily waded out from the backyard and fished there; it was equally good fishing, but it was also good to get away from town—especially when playing hooky from church on Easter. They sat down in the shade of a mesquite tree and began the less-than-glamorous side of fishing: cleaning the fish.

Sam finished his first fish, tossing the filets into a large pan of water. The carcass of the fish went into a bucket and quickly became the subject of interest to Rufus, Old Perkin's ancient tomcat.

"Get outta here, you nasty old thing!" Perkin kicked at Rufus but missed, muttering to Sam, "Goddamned cat. I'd like to take his ass to a Comanche wedding." They'd never been on easy terms, and the relationship had taken a decidedly downward turn when Rufus sprayed Perkin's bed some years back. Perkin gladly would have sent the battle-scarred cat on a one-way trip to kingdom come except that Old Perkin was terribly fond of the beast.

"Who's swearin' at my cat?" A deep voice rumbled from behind the cousins.

Perkin and Sam both turned, smiled and said in unison, "Hey Pop!" Nobody called him Old Perkin to his face.

"Ya missed a great morning out in the bay. We let a dozen or so go, but we kept some good ones. Thought we'd fry 'em up if that's okay," said Sam.

"Good. I told Anna not to make a big fuss with Easter dinner. I knew you boys would come through, although there would have been hell to pay if you hadn't. She's makin' cornbread muffins, we got some good potato salad and we're gonna try some Kentucky Wonders as well." At the blank look on Sam's face, he explained, "Snap beans. I tried to get away from church and come with y'all, but Anna thinks that at my age I need some more interaction with the Almighty."

Old Perkin sat facing his grandsons—he regarded Sam as one, although there was no blood kinship between them. He opened up a large pocket knife, which he kept razor sharp, pulled a trout off of a stringer, and flipped it over on its back. He slit open the fish's underbelly and dropped its insides into the bucket. He then ran the knife along the backbone, cutting off a nice filet that he skinned on a flat rock kept under the tree for just that purpose. The whole fish was cleaned in less than a minute.

"So boys," he said. "What's going on?"

"Perk was just bad-mouthin' your old cat there. There's some bad blood between 'em, and I think they're gonna get into a serious scrap one day." Sam added with a wicked smirk at Perkin, "My money's on Rufus."

Pop picked up Rufus, and the old cat began to purr, an honor he bestowed only on Old Perkin. The old man scratched the cat's remaining ear, "Could be he's got the edge. Could be Perkin does." With a wicked grin of his own, he said, "But don't force me to choose between my cat and my grandson. There are some choices an old man shouldn't have to make. Besides, I reckon there's glory enough coming my way no matter who wins. But would you look at this old boy?" he asked them admiringly. "He ain't never lost a fight, and there ain't a dog on the Gulf Coast that can take him, even if the poor old fella lost his ear to Jasper's shepherd. And just look at them doodads!" Old Perkin exclaimed proudly. He held up a suddenly twisting and snarling Rufus as an exhibit. "You don't see nuts like that on just any old cat. He's probably sired half the cats in South Texas." The cousins had seen Rufus's considerable testicles before, and the volume of foul-looking orange cats in Portland supported Old Perkin's theory. Although they were past the age of giggling, every time Old Perkin brought up the subject of the cat's reproductive prowess, they couldn't resist laughing like a couple of kids.

"Would you put that poor cat down, please? For Pete's sake, why do you do that?" Anna had walked out to survey the three men in the backyard. In some ways, she thought, Sam and Perkin looked so much alike they could have been brothers. They'd been frequently mistaken as such when they were small boys, but they'd grown into distinctly different men. Both were very tall by the standards of the depression era, but Perkin was shorter and lean, while Sam was taller, heavier, and more muscular. In their own ways, they each resembled their mothers, who were both striking brunettes with pale blue eyes, but Sam's eyes were matched with a fair complexion and sandy hair. Perkin shared the Berger family's odd combination of black hair, a dark complexion, and piercing blue eyes. When they were teens, the boys had been wild, running all over South Texas as if it was a fiefdom and they were the lord's only heirs. Going to separate colleges had been good for them. Sam had matured more quickly, and Anna acknowledged that he was the steadier of the two young men. She still worried about Perkin. He was impetuous, and his happy-go-lucky personality lacked direction and, in too many ways, discipline.

She walked over to the mesquite tree, kissing Sam on the cheek to say hello. "Hey, Sam! It's good to see you. We missed you at church. You boys should have been there, the sermon was about sacrifice. The Almighty sacrificed his only begotten son for us. Perhaps you boys could have learned a thing or two about what it means to give of yourselves." Anna had plenty more to say about the boys skipping church, but she checked herself before venting her full disapproval. Understanding that it might be a trying day for the family, she smiled instead. "Now, I'm going to take this fish from you. If I had to wait for men to cook, I'd never eat. Why don't you give me a half hour then come wash up."

Old Perkin looked up at Anna before turning to Perkin to say, "Perk, would you carry them fish up for Anna? And on your way back, bring us some cold beers."

As Perkin and Anna walked to the house, Old Perkin looked at Sam. "Well, did he bring it up?"

Sam looked back thoughtfully at the elder Perkin. "Yep. It's why he came down this weekend. Well, that and the bay's finally warm enough to fish. Part of him thinks that it's his duty to follow in his daddy's footsteps and join the army and, you know, that whole sense of adventure thing too. But don't be fooled, another part of him truly wants to go into academia like you. He ought to—he's made for it—but I don't know if I can talk him out of the army, or if I should even try." Sam paused and pointed out a huge brown pelican that was diving for fish before continuing, "Perk's most likely right. We're definitely headed down a bad road, and it's just a matter of time before this manure from Europe gets splattered on us. Or, as Perkin tells me, maybe it'll come from the Orient first. I understand that the British are fixin' to reinstitute conscription by the end of this month. I reckon Washington can't be far behind. So maybe Perk ain't the only one thinking along those lines."

Old Perkin locked eyes with Sam. "I lost one boy to the army. I couldn't bear the same fate for you or for Perk."

Sam sympathized with the older man but didn't back down. "Pop, if he's set on it, there ain't a durn thing you and I can do to talk him out of it. Given my druthers, I'd never spend a goddamned day in uniform. I had enough of that nonsense in the Corps at A&M and I'm completely content working my ranch and fishin' from time to time. But I'm thinking that maybe neither of us has a good choice in the long run. Besides, someone has to take care of Perk." Sam paused again to watch the pelican try for the fish a second time. "We spent the whole morning talkin' about the state of affairs in Europe. He didn't even talk about Olivia de Havilland once, so he must be concerned. Shoot, he didn't even bring up jazz other than to tell me about some colored woman who's singin' in DC today."

"She's a contralto."

Sam waved away a mosquito and shrugged. "Oh, I thought he said she was colored. Anyway, I might have a middle ground for the two of you."

At this point, Perkin walked up with three opened bottles of Shiner Bock. Portland was outside the Spoetzl

Brewery's delivery range and was a dry town in any case, but Old Perkin had taught the boys that the good things in life were worth the effort, so they occasionally made the drive to Goliad, a town inside the critical seventy-mile delivery radius. It was worth it to get the best beer made in Texas. Shiner Bock was their favorite, and this was a special treat as it was only available during Lent.

"What are we talking about?" Perkin asked, although he knew the answer judging by the serious looks he saw on their faces.

Old Perkin replied as he took a beer, "Thanks. Sam and I were talking about the army." Old Perkin stopped talking but the boys said nothing. They knew it was a momentary pause while he collected his thoughts, and the old man got very irritated if people interrupted him when he wasn't speaking. After a minute, he started up again, "I know your position. I respect your instincts and your analysis of what is transpiring in Europe. You're probably right about these fuckin' Germans, but I don't want you to go into the army."

Shocked, Sam and Perkin looked at each other. Although they'd heard that word plenty of times, they seldom used it themselves and certainly had never heard it uttered by their grandfather.

"That's right. You heard me. Goddamned fuckin' Germans. It ain't enough that they took my boy—they'll take my grandsons as well. I know it's not fair and it's a stupid thing for an old man to say, but this ain't the time to go into the army." Old Perkin's eyes had gone watery and he looked out over the bay towards Corpus Christi, as if seeking guidance.

Perkin didn't hesitate, firing back at his grandfather, "When is a good time, Pop? After the war starts? Do you want me to wait and end up a conscript on a battlefield with six weeks of training? Look, I think it's gonna happen no matter how we feel about it, and both Sam and I will be drafted for certain. I'll tell you something else, if the United States goes to war against either Japan or Germany, it'll be the defining event of our lives—and I'm not sure that I'd want to sit on the sidelines and just watch."

"Your daddy told me something similar when I let him talk me into West Point . . . and he died in the most pointless war in the history of mankind. Perkin, you don't understand what this means. You're the smartest young man I've ever known, but you ain't seein' this clearly. Let me tell ya something. When you were four or five, I took a sabbatical from the college, and Anna and I went to Europe—you stayed with your Uncle Raymond. It was important enough for me to leave you for six weeks, because I wanted to see what my boy had died for. Nothin'. He died for nothin'. Two years after the war to end all wars, Europe was just as corrupt and venal. It still is, and all them millions of boys died for nothin'. By God, I could see this moment coming from way back then." Emphasizing each word, Old Perkin said, "Don't you boys buy into this nonsense of the new world steppin' in to save the old. It isn't worth it. It wasn't then, and it ain't now." The old man wiped his eyes with the back of a trembling hand, "Perk, I went to the riverbank where your daddy died. I had to see it for myself and, two years later, the destruction was still incomprehensible. It was a wasteland. I can't describe it as anything else, just a wasteland. There wasn't a tree standing, the ground was all tore up; there were no buildings left, no farm animals. The farmers can't even grow crops there no more 'cause the ground is poisoned. And I couldn't bear it, standin' there thinkin' how terrified my boy must have been in his last moments. It broke my heart all over again." Old Perkin fixed his eyes on his grandsons. "Boys, I'm here to tell ya that war

ain't glory. It is pain and it is tragedy and it ain't nothin'
else. How any of them boys lived through it back then is
beyond me—and war don't get less lethal with time."

"Pop, Dad died doin' what he wanted to do . . ."

"Yes, he did." There was truth in what Perkin said.
Captain Berger had loved the army and believed deeply in
the righteousness of the Great War. But the old man said
firmly, "I don't expect a young fella like you to understand,
but that still don't make it right. And you are so like him
that it frightens me as much as it delights me . . ."

Sam looked at his cousin. He saw that Perkin's jaw
was clenched and that a fire was building in his eyes. His
grandfather was just as set; and Sam knew, with great
sorrow, that the conflict building between the two men
would lead to a breach between them as sure as the storm
over the islands was heading their way. Sam couldn't allow
that breach. They were the only family he had left.

"Perk," he said quietly, "I was tellin' Pop that there's
a middle ground. We ain't discussed it yet, but I think
that I know a way to compromise." When he had the
attention of both men, Sam took a sip of his beer and
continued, "Instead of the army, why not the National
Guard? I don't want to be a full-time soldier, I couldn't
go into the army without giving up the ranch, but I
could consider the guard, and I could do it with you. If
we stay at peace, it's not gonna take us away from what
we ultimately want to do: you can go back to Austin and
finish your doctorate, and I can keep building the ranch.
We could join a unit that's somewhere midway, like San
Antonio, and drill together."

Perkin started to object, "The National Guard's just a
weekend gun club . . ."

Sam raised a hand and stopped him. "The guard serves
the governor first and, if is there is a disaster, they're the
first on the scene. So, we'd be doing something for the

people around us, and if the worst happens—like we were talking about today—well, then we're all gonna be soldiers anyway. For my money, I'd rather soldier with our boys, with the Texas gun club, than the regular army."

He looked at Perk, who looked back at him thoughtfully.

"I don't know, Sam. I hadn't really considered it before. I'm not sure I want to sign up for the guard and then end up roustin' strikers or pickin' up after twisters."

"Perkin," his grandfather said, and then he paused again, ". . . maybe Sam is right. You can soldier on the weekend, and if something big happens, well, you might go anyway. As for picking up after a tornado: you should remember that it was the guard that buried both your mothers." A spasm of guilt crossed Perkin's face. He had forgotten about his mother only an hour after praying at her burial site. "I think," his grandfather continued, "Anna and I can live with this compromise."

On the ship, four years later, Sam thought about his grandfather's reminder about their mothers. That was what had sealed the deal for Perkin. A month after that Easter, Sam and Perkin had met in San Antonio and joined the 141st Infantry Regiment of the 36th Division, Texas Army National Guard. They had served in the guard less than two years before the United States instituted its first peacetime draft in September 1940. Two months after conscription was instated, the 36th Division was federalized for national service, making them full-time soldiers. As Sam walked to the wardroom, he couldn't help but think that after all that time, it really made no difference whose idea it had been to skip church that day.

0815 hours
USS *Thomas Jefferson* at sea

Breakfast completed and the dishes cleared from the table, the officers of the *Thomas Jefferson* surrendered their wardroom to the staff officers of the 1st Battalion of the 141st Infantry Regiment and the officers from the battalion's companies. Captain Lockridge, the battalion intelligence officer, kicked off what turned out to be several hours of meetings and discussions. Lockridge was a serious, thin, athletic man with a receding hairline whose wire-rimmed glasses hid alert, intelligent eyes. He picked up a wooden pointer, cleared his throat, and began the briefing.

"Good afternoon, Colonel, gentlemen, Aggies." A few officers laughed out loud, but most looked around a little nervously. The colonel in question was Lieutenant Colonel Robert Wranosky, the battalion's commanding officer, and he was still an unknown, having come over from the regular army to take command in the past month. "For those of y'all who don't know me, I'm Jim Lockridge—1st Battalion's S-2. Colonel Wranosky asked me to start by giving an overview of what's been named Operation Avalanche. I'll then turn the briefing over to the navy metoc officer for the weather considerations, and then I'll cover the intel portion. Major Turner, S-3, will follow me and cover company missions. We'll break for chow and then review communications and logistics. The overall classification of the briefings you'll receive is secret."

Lockridge stood in front of a map of the Italian peninsula and said, "Okay, first off—who's who in the zoo." Wranosky coughed pointedly. "Pardon me, sir. Command and control. Operation Avalanche is a combined operation assigned to the Fifth Army commanded by Lieutenant General Mark Clark. Fifth Army is comprised of two corps—VI Corps and X Corps—and as I suppose you know, we are attached to VI Corps under Lieutenant General Ernest Dawley.* For now, VI Corps is all American, and the only other division in the corps is the 45th—the Guard division from Oklahoma, but additional divisions will be added as shipping permits. As I mentioned, it is a combined operation and the British element is X Corps, commanded by Lieutenant General Richard McCreery. The forces under Sir Richard include the British 46th and 56th Infantry Divisions, British commandos, and the U.S. 2nd Ranger Regiment. So, the initial assault force ought to be easy enough to remember . . . the going-in divisions are the 36th, 46th, and 56th followed by the 45th, which brings us to the question: going in where?"

Lockridge stepped to the side, turned, and pointed at the map of Italy, "Paestum. Or I guess I should say the greater Salerno plain."

Perkin leaned over to Sam and groaned, "Paestum. Shit. Who won the pool?"

Sam whispered back, "Private Kulis."

Lockridge continued, "The assault is set for September 9. X Corps lands to the north near Salerno itself with the two British divisions, commandos, and Rangers going ashore on D-day. VI Corps lands some twenty plus miles south near the ruins of Paestum—and the 36th is alone and unafraid on D-day. Although the geometry of the beachhead mandates more troops than one division in our corps sector, there isn't enough shipping to support the initial landings of a full corps in our sector and a

---

*Generally speaking for the Allies in World War II, an army consisted of two or more corps. Each corps had two or more divisions, with each U.S. infantry division having approximately 15,000 soldiers, about a third of whom were infantrymen. Each division had three regimental combat teams, which were formed around three rifle battalions (plus numerous other units). These in turn were comprised of three rifle companies and a heavy weapons company. Each company had three rifle platoons and a weapons platoon.

full corps in the British sector in addition to supporting Montgomery in the south."

Colonel Wranosky interrupted; the short, bull-necked officer stood up and faced the gathered soldiers, "Let me jump in for a minute. Captain Lockridge is dead-on target. The Salerno geometry is pretty goddamn big, and there will be at least a ten-mile gap between U.S. and British forces. Jim will get to that in a minute. Our requirement is to establish a beachhead ten miles wide by six or seven miles deep and to protect the flanks of the British. I can tell you now that VI Corps ain't gonna have enough troops ashore for nearly a week to manage that—even when the 45th comes ashore, it's only landing two regiments. Their third regiment won't land for nearly a week. I don't want to minimize the British role, they're going to have their hands full, but we're going to take it up the ass if the Germans attack our beachhead and we can't reinforce because Monty is holding shipping in reserve."

Wranosky started turning red in the face, and his Alabama accent became more pronounced. "Yep, y'all heard me right. We cain't land all the troops we need for the U.S. sector because of Montgomery. The Eighth Army landed at Reggio on the third of September, and while their crossing at the Messina Strait and their movement up the peninsula has been unopposed—well, mostly unopposed—it's been slow because of blown bridges. Monty's demanded that amphibious shipping be held in reserve to support his maneuver—and that's enough shipping to preclude the 45th from landing alongside us on D-day. In theory, our landing should allow us to encircle and annihilate the German forces in all of southern Italy, but I suspect that they'll withdraw so much faster than Monty advances that they'll have plenty of time to swing by and say how-do to us on the beach on their way north. Let's face it, if we're waiting for that slow-assed son-of-a-Brit Montgomery to take the pressure off of us, we might wanna bring our winter clothes." Wranosky stopped and took a deep breath. "Okay, Jim, enough of that. Back to you."

"Yes, sir. The objective is to secure the beachhead and establish a lodgment, permitting the landing of follow-on forces. By the way, this will be the first permanent Allied presence on the European mainland since Dunkirk three and a half years ago. Fifth Army will engage and destroy the German forces in the area and prepare for subsequent operations for the taking of Naples and then Rome. The timeline for consolidation of the beach and then onward movement towards Naples is three or four days."

Captain Lockridge talked for a few more minutes, concluded his overview, and then passed the pointer over to a massive navy lieutenant, a meteorologist, whose name Sam didn't catch. "The weather will not impact the landings. High pressure should dominate for at least another two to three days, meaning clear skies, moderate temperatures, and dry weather. No guarantees beyond the weekend. Average daytime highs will be the same as we'll have during this underway—in the low eighties. Nighttime temperatures will be in the upper sixties. Sunrise is at 0535, but it should start getting light about 0500. There will be no moon for the September 9 landings—it sets at midnight, about the time the assault wave begins embarkation. The moon is nearly three-quarters full and rises on the ninth at 1500; it sets on the tenth at 0055 local. Sea states should be negligible with waves at one to two feet in the outer and inner transit areas and below one foot for the landings with minimal surf on the beach. This supports all phases of operations for landing craft and assault shipping. DUKW operations will not be impacted." A discussion between the senior staff officers and the navy ensued on tides, expected sea state for follow-on forces, beach gradients, and other technicalities of amphibious operations. Sitting in the audience, Sam was particularly concerned with the shrugs he saw from the naval officers when asked if the waters would be completely swept of mines before the landing craft began their assault runs to the beach. He had heard from the squids aboard the *Thomas Jefferson* that mines had sunk more shipping so far in the war than submarines and surface action combined, and the thought of being blown up at sea irrationally concerned him much more than the same action occurring ashore.

As the navy linebacker sat down, Lockridge began to speak again, "Okay, gentlemen. Now let's take a look at what we are facing. The battlefield, as we've mentioned, is pretty large. The shore side of the Gulf of Salerno is like the box end of a canyon—it's got the Amalfi coast boxing it in at the north and this headland down here boxing it in at the south." He continued to point at the map as he described the geography of the battlefield. "Avalanche's battlefield begins at the north with the village of Amalfi in the X Corps sector. This is near where our Rangers will land. And the southern limit pretty much ends with the village of Agropoli—this is one of the objectives of our battalion. The S-3 will cover that in a moment. So we go from Amalfi to Agropoli. That is a span of about thirty miles as the crow flies, but more like forty plus road miles along the beach itself. The depth of the battlefield varies as Amalfi is literally carved out of the mountains as they drop nearly vertically into the gulf. Further over in the British and American sectors, there is a range of five to ten miles from the water's edge to the mountains. Where we will be landing in the south, there is a coastal plain of several miles, then foothills transforming into mountains in the three-thousand- to four-thousand-foot range. Artillery sited in the foothills and the mountains will be able to fire on our landing beaches, and German observers will have a clear view from the mountains of the entire battlefield."

He paused momentarily to let that point sink in. "The key line of communication is Highway 18, which is the main thoroughfare from north to south through the battlefield. Complicating the battlefield is the riparian geometry—there are three east-west rivers, which will complicate our communication with X Corps, and one large north-south stream to contend with. That, and there are numerous creeks, drainage ditches, and marshlands as well. The main river is the Sele River, which merges upstream with the Calore River—see, they kind of form a 'Y.' If you look at the upper 'Y' here, I've heard this combined river system, specifically the land between the rivers, referred to as the Sele-Calore corridor. By the way, the Sele is the nominal dividing line between the U.S. and British sectors; however, neither of us have enough troops to protect the ground from our landing sites to the corps boundary at the river. So it doesn't take a great deal of imagination to see the threat that this gap poses for us: there is an expanse of ten miles or more between us and the Limeys and no way to fill the gap until the follow-on forces arrive. The Germans can pick a side of the river, come screaming down it like Comanches in panzers, and then hit our flanks using the river to protect their own."

Lockridge paused and took a drink of coffee, "What in God's name does the navy put in their joe?" Grimacing, he set the cup down. "It's as thick as sorghum and tastes like tar—catches me off guard every time I taste it. Okay, what do we expect of the Germans in the area? Unfortunately there is no real intelligence consensus of the German order of battle and capabilities in southern Italy—defined as south of Rome. Realistically, there are at least two German corps within a hundred miles of Salerno. Of the five-plus divisions in those two corps, most are under strength and are refitting following combat operations in Sicily. To add to the equation, there are rumors floating around, I think to be taken seriously, that Italy will surrender to the Allies by the time we land, and, in effect, switch sides. I honestly don't know if that helps us much or not. So if the Italians desert their posts, how quickly can the Germans fill the Italian coastal defenses? Your guess is as good as mine, but if the Italians don't have the presence of mind to spike their guns and blow their depots, well, I guess the Germans can take over pretty quick. My money is on the Italian soldiers just fading away, never to be seen again. I think that we'll be fighting Germans in hasty-to-prepared defense, but my opinion is in the minority."

Lieutenant Colonel Wranosky stopped his intelligence officer and spoke again, "I'm with the deuce on this. There is a hell of a lot of wishful thinking on the part of General Clark's staff. Our boss, General Walker, hasn't shared his opinion with me, but I suspect that Walker's going in pretty sober and expecting a scrap. That is what I want you to convey to your boys—hope for the best, but be prepared for the worst."

He nodded over at Lockridge and said, "Jim, give 'em the worst case as you described it to me."

"Yes, sir. The Germans undoubtedly know that we're at sea but may not know where we're heading. The counter-intelligence guys assess that our operational security has been pretty good so far. So the Germans probably have something like Able Company's pool going as to where we will land."

Wranosky interrupted, "Able Company has a pool? Bill, who's your winner and what's the pot? Make sure battalion gets a cut."

Captain Spaulding was all innocence itself, "What pool is that, sir?"

Wranosky grinned and said, "Uh-huh. I thought so." He then waved to Lockridge to continue.

Lockridge, smiling, said, "Sorry, Bill. I assumed that you had already contributed to the battalion slush . . . I mean, the 'Widows and Orphans Fund.' Anyway, the Germans are alert to the movement of two Allied corps, and even if they don't have hard intelligence on our intentions, they can do the analysis as well as we can. Assuming that they've ruled out the unlikely venues like southern France or the Balkans, that pretty much leaves Italy. There are only a limited number of assaultable beaches in Italy that have military utility. It makes sense to land in southern Italy to be positioned to support Monty and vice versa. Salerno was chosen because it's within the combat radius of aircraft operating out of Sicily—other Italian beaches like Gaeta and Formia aren't. The Salerno plain has good beaches and quick access to Naples. If I'd been allowed in Able's pool, I'd picked Salerno as most likely. My point is that if I could figure it out, so could the Germans."

Lockridge sat down on the edge of a table and looked at the assembled officers before speaking, "Here's the worst case. Their analysis indicates an Allied Army landing in the vicinity of Salerno. We know that there are at least elements of one division garrisoned in the area—the 16th Panzer Division. They can't be positive, so they can't mass all their forces there, but it is reasonable to expect reinforcement of the 16th Panzers. Let's say maybe elements of two under-strength divisions are available on the first day, plus the Italian coastal artillery manned by Germans—or by the Italians if the rumors are wrong. Okay, that doesn't sound too bad—we have three divisions landing and a division-minus in reserve on

D-day. The problem is, of course, that we can't land at once—we have to come ashore piecemeal with riflemen being the totality of the first assault waves. So if they can establish two to three battalion-sized panzer or panzer grenadier task forces and hit us on the water, they stand a good chance of seriously disrupting our landing. We'll find out soon enough whether they want to hit us on the beach or try to destroy us inland, but my belief is that the geometry—particularly the gap between us and X Corps—offers enough of a possibility to drive us back into the water for it to be worth their while."

Chapter Three

September 8, 1943
1500 hours
USS *Thomas Jefferson* at sea

The bosun's mate of the watch blew long and hard on his bosun's pipe into the microphone of the ship's 1MC intercom. Aware of what the captain's announcement was to be, he wanted to greet it with as much fanfare as possible. It was the best news the bosun's mate had heard since joining the navy in 1941.

"Attention all hands. Standby for an announcement from the captain." The grinning bosun's mate stood aside for the captain, a prewar merchant sailor with a master's ticket who also happened to be a reserve lieutenant commander from Los Angeles.

"Good afternoon, this is Captain Grumby. I have good news to share with you. Italy has agreed to terms of armistice with the United Nations and, therefore, is no longer a belligerent state in the war." Despite himself,

Grumby looked around the bridge, grinning at his sailors. *There was so much left to do in this war, but there's nothing wrong with celebrating good news.* There had not been much to celebrate since Pearl Harbor. Over the whoops of delight and the laughter and applause, Grumby continued, "My army counterparts have asked me to pass along to you that it does not change your mission tomorrow morning. Expect opposition and be prepared for the worst. Good luck to you and God bless you all."

Despite the skipper's admonition, the cheering continued for several minutes. Several of the Texans onboard the *Thomas Jefferson* danced impromptu jigs. Smiles and handshakes were exchanged between the sailors and soldiers. Even the officers, who suspected that there might be more to the story, let out a deep sigh of relief. The cracks in the Axis were widening around the world and, even though many sailors wished that it had been Japan or Germany to go first, the news was welcome.

"Listen up! Listen up!" Perkin's commanding voice cut through the cheering, and in a moment he had the full attention of his platoon of forty happy soldiers. They'd taken over a cramped corner of the ship's hold to receive their mission briefing from Perkin and Captain Spaulding, the Able Company commander. Perkin was under no illusions. The surrender of Italy was wonderful, but in many ways it would clear the way for Germany to take complete control of its former ally.

As Captain Spaulding walked away to spend time with the other platoon commanders and their soldiers, Perkin turned to his attentive men. "Gentlemen, I'm here to tell you that's concerning news . . . in addition to freeing the Germans' hand in Italy, it also means we're gonna have to change the platoon motto."

"I beg your pardon, sir, but what motto is that?" Milton Evers, the platoon sergeant, was a new addition to the

division and had come to the 36th after recovering from
the dubious honor of being one of the first American
casualties at the Kasserine Pass. If there was a platoon
motto, he thought he ought to know it.

With a grin, Perkin said, "Never let a Dago by." The
platoon laughed. Even a cheap pun was funny after an
announcement of that magnitude. As the laughter died
out, Perkin continued, "That's the best news we've had for
ages—let's all understand it is a direct result of American
and British successes in the field. But we cannot take the
pressure off of the Germans for a second. It's critical that
we hand them a decisive defeat quickly after the surrender
of their oldest ally. That's where we come in. So, I'd like
to say a few words about our role in this coming battle
and why what we here do is so important. First, I want
you to always remember who we are: We are Texans and
we are guardsmen. I know that the division is only about
three-quarters Texan at this point, but to paraphrase
Shakespeare, those who fight with us today will forever
be Texans." Perkin looked over at two more vocal but
popular privates from New Jersey and said dryly, "Except
for Michaels and Fratelli. No matter how hard I try, I just
can't see them boys in boots and Stetsons."

When the platoon stopped laughing and exchanging
insults, Perkin continued. "Remember we are part of the
141st Infantry Regiment, the famous Alamo Regiment,
which traces its lineage back to those ill-fated defenders
of liberty. Those men had a simple but glorious dream—
just one motivating idea that kept them going through all
the hardships. And that idea, to which all modern Texans
owe so much, is: 'If we take the land from Mexico, then it
belongs to us.' God bless 'em, what a vision! Their followers
took an unpromising land of mosquitoes and mesquite
trees and turned it into a true paradise of mosquitoes,
mesquite trees, and cows. Thank God those early pioneers

wouldn't give up!" In his best Groucho Marx voice, he said with a grin, "And unfortunately for the boys in the Alamo, neither did the Mexicans." The soldiers laughed, again hurling insults back and forth.

"Now, I'm sure that even Corporal Pena and Private Martinez will join me in hoping for a little more success for the regiment this time around, which brings me to another point I want to emphasize. I have undying faith in Colonel Jamison, who commands this great regiment, but let's face the cold hard fact of our present situation: 1st Platoon of Able Company is the glue that holds the Alamo Regiment together. We all know it's true. Shit, we've been carrying the weight of this regiment around on our shoulders since the Louisiana maneuvers! And that's not all. Our impact may not even stop at regiment. I don't know if I should tell you this, because I haven't been able to confirm it before now, but I heard that the division commander was in our area the other day seeking advice from Private Kulis."

Private Edwin Kulis, a shy, diminutive, bespectacled rifleman from Rosebud, Texas—one of Perkin's favorite soldiers—looked up, surprised. "Well, that ain't true, sir. I've never even met General Walker."

"Well, thanks for clearing that up Kulis. I think it's his loss though, because I bet he could have learned a thing or two from this platoon, such as how to roll up a defensive line."

"Yes, sir, I could have told him that one. Hit 'em on the flanks."

"Right. And how do you do that?"

"You get 'round them and bring fires to bear on the end of the line. And if you cain't do that, you have to breach the line and make your own flanks."

Perkin continued, "Goddamn, Kulis, you're as sharp as razor soup, no matter what the sergeants say about you. One more question: who guards our flanks at Salerno?"

"Why, I guess it looks like we do, sir. We're the end of the line."

"Yep. It's us. Thank you, Private." Perkin turned to the rest of the platoon and said, "For the first day, at least, we are the end of the line. And as I'm sure Kulis here was about to tell you, we're gonna be just like Joshua Chamberlain and them Yankee boys at Little Round Top. We will hold the line. No one gets around us, no one gets past us, and no one brings fires to bear on the end of our beachhead while 1st Platoon guards the flank! As of tomorrow morning, the German troops we'll be facing will be the second best in Europe, but if they turn our flanks here, we may easily lose our lodgment and that, folks, is the end of Operation Avalanche. Meaning the war is set back at least a year, maybe two." Perkin smiled grimly. "That's why 1st Platoon, the glue of the regiment, is there. We were obviously chosen by a higher power to be at this critical place at this critical time because we're the best."

"God is putting us there, Lieutenant?" interrupted Private Martinez.

"Not God, Martinez. Eisenhower. But close enough. One last thing, this division is in the spotlight. Everyone is looking at the 36th to see how the National Guard performs in this war. We aren't the first guard division to be committed to battle, but we are the first to be given the kind of responsibility that we will bear at Salerno. Let's think about that for a moment. We are the assault force, the vanguard, for the United States on mainland Europe, and everyone back home is going to pay close attention to our achievements and failures. When we succeed, all the folks back home will say, 'Of course they won, they're Texans.' But if we get kicked off this beachhead, then the goddamned 4F warriors will say, 'Well, what do you expect? It's a National Guard division. We should have let the professionals handle it.' Well, to those shitbirds I say, fuck them and the horse they rode in on!"

He turned to Sergeant Bill Kenton, one of his squad leaders and easily the largest man in the company next to Perkin's cousin Sam. "Sergeant Kenton!"

"Sir?"

"That's your job."

To the great amusement of the platoon, the large redheaded sergeant pulled a small green notebook from his pocket and said slowly as he wrote, "Fuck ... the ... horse. Right. Sir? Do we know how big this horse is?" Following a string of insults from the other soldiers, Kenton grinned and said, "Well, I don't want to complain, sir, but them Arab ponies in Africa were just too small."

After the groaning and laughter had subsided, Perkin lowered his voice and looked each of his soldiers in the eyes. "Fifth Army G-2 says that there aren't likely to be many Germans in the area, and they won't be able to organize quickly. I sincerely hope they're right, but the battalion S-2, Captain Lockridge, thinks that with the Italian surrender that we just heard about, the Germans will expeditiously man Italian coastal defenses. I've known Jim Lockridge since my days at UT—for those of you who don't know him, he's a West Texas boy from Kermit, and Kulis notwithstanding, he's the smartest man in the gun club. If Lockridge is concerned ... well, let's say I'm concerned. I'd rather have fought Italians than Germans, but you play the cards you're dealt. Whether the Germans resist or not, there is no doubt in my mind that we'll succeed here. I want you boys to remember that we're better trained and equipped than the regular army was when we got federalized three years ago and, most importantly, we're Texans. The toughest, smartest, and at least in my case, best-lookingest sons-a-bitches in the army!" Boos and catcalls from the platoon followed this last statement, and Perkin, momentarily basking in the derision, struck a recruiting poster pose for his soldiers.

"Okay, gents. We all know our assignments for tomorrow, but here are my priorities: when we get there, plant the Lone Star flag on our beach and keep moving. I want everyone to know whose property it is. Then 1st Squad under Sergeant Kenton goes right, determines our distance to the Solofrone River, and protects our flanks. I also want 1st Squad to do several soundings of the Solo-frone because I want to know how difficult it may be for armor to ford—and I want to know that ASAP. Take a Handie-Talkie and, if that doesn't work, send back a runner with the information.* Captain Spaulding needs to know quickly. So will battalion. Remember, we'll be moving inland so make sure the runner adjusts his return accordingly. Sergeant Kenton, use your best judgment whether he retraces his steps or moves to intercept us. Scout it out well and take multiple soundings, 'cause that river is a helluva big question mark. The Solofrone looks narrow in the aerial photos, but I'll feel a damn sight better if armor can't cross without bridging first. Infantry we can deal with, but I'd prefer to have the rest of the regiment in if there are panzers coming at our flanks. After your assessment of the river, first squad comes up the north bank and we meet up at the railway bridge. We do those three things—flag, river recce, and link-up, and everything else will fall into place. Squad leaders: everyone should be set for tomorrow. Let's get a few hours sleep before embarking at midnight. Y'all carry as much water as you can and get a good meal in before embarkation. Take care of each other out there and listen to your sergeants. I'll see you on deck when we embark—good luck and God bless you all. Dismissed."

---

*The handheld transceiver popularly known today as the "walkie-talkie" was known then as the SCR-536 "Handie-Talkie." The longer range back-mounted SCR-300 transceiver was known then as the walkie-talkie.

1835 hours
USS _Thomas Jefferson_ at sea

Captain Bill Spaulding handed out cigars to all of his officers—even Perkin accepted one—before surveying the five soldiers. Perkin and Sam were the most senior officers. They were both first lieutenants and would make captain before long. Both were extremely talented soldiers and, over the months, Spaulding had fought many a battle with the executive officers at battalion and regiment to keep them assigned to Able Company. He knew the cousins wouldn't stay long at Able Company after the battle. If they lived, they would get commands of their own. Ed Brown was also likely to be promoted soon. It was hard to believe, but he'd been with the company for almost a year. Brown would do well in combat. Spaulding felt extremely fortunate to have three excellent platoon commanders.

It was a testament to Spaulding's humility that he didn't see that the outstanding traits of his officers and NCOs were largely due to his own qualities as a leader. There had been a time when no other commander would have coveted Perkin for his own command. Perkin's restless energy had not always been constructively directed before Spaulding took command of Able Company. Spaulding's other two officers were shave-tails—junior second lieutenants. Len Anderson was the weapons platoon commander and Frank McCarter was a supernumerary lieutenant assigned to Perkin's 1st Platoon. They were good men but inexperienced, and on several occasions Captain Spaulding had witnessed Lieutenant McCarter start to address Master Sergeant Hawkins as "sir," only to catch himself.

"Gentlemen, I've been savin' these cigars for a momentous occasion. I thought about breakin' 'em out when Perkin told me that Lenny lost his virginity in Oran, but that event didn't seem to rise to the occasion. This does." Spaulding cupped his hands to protect his lighter from the winds whipping over the fantail of the *Thomas Jefferson* and lit each officer's cigar in order of reverse seniority—saving his own for last.

"I'm not one for speeches, but I prepared one for today." Spaulding stood upright and faced his officers. "I want to say that I'm proud of all y'all, and I expect that we'll do jes' fine tomorrow. Now that my speech is over with, Sam's brought us all a little surprise."

Looking over his shoulder to make sure that no senior officers or sailors were about, Sam reached into his jacket and pulled out a pint bottle of T.W. Samuel's bourbon—one of many he'd successfully nurtured, preserved, and protected since leaving the States so many months before. He pulled out his huge bowie knife and cut the wax off the top. As he did so, Perkin passed out paper cups stolen from the ship's wardroom. Sam poured a shot into his company commander's cup, "Go ahead, sir."

Spaulding grinned, "You want me to break the law first, is that it?"

"No, sir. If that was my concern, I'd give the bottle to Perkin. Besides, what are they gonna do to us? Shave our heads and send us into battle? No, sir. You just deserve the first swaller is all."

The other officers nodded, but Spaulding shook his head, "No, let's do a Texas roister. Like you said, what are they gonna do to us?"

Sam poured out shots for the rest of the officers, corked the bottle and tucked it away in his jacket. He took his cup from Perkin. Bill Spaulding served as the master of ceremonies. Familiar with the Texas roister, the group stood in a circle and held their cups together in the center with their wrists bent outwards.

Spaulding cleared his throat and said, with just a touch of emotion, "To God." The soldiers repeated the toast, but instead of taking a drink, they lifted their cups to their ears as if they could hear the sounds of the bourbon's old Kentucky home.

The hands placed back in the center of the circle, still held at that odd angle, Spaulding continued the ritual. "To country," and the young officers repeated the toast and the movement of the drinks to their ears and back.

"To Texas!" rang out the emphatic refrain from the Able Company officers. The yell caught the attention of a nearby sailor, who nudged a shipmate and gestured towards the Texan soldiers' antics.

The last toast was an improvisational one, and Spaulding thought for a second before saying, "Remember this, boys: if ya ain't cheatin', ya ain't tryin'. To success . . . at all costs!" The surrounding officers seconded, "To success!" As one man, they finished the toast with a loud rolling "Roiiiiisssster!" and downed their shots before throwing their cups over the fantail.

Sam put the bottle back into circulation without ceremony as the five warriors on the eve of their first battle finished their cigars, silently watching the sun set over the ship's wake.

Chapter Four

September 9, 1943
0300 hours
Gulf of Salerno

September 9, 1943, was the first American D-day on the European mainland, and the Texas Army—as the 36th Infantry Division was sometimes called—had the honor of being the first U.S. Army division to land. Once he'd heard this news, Perkin, the former history student, was determined to be the first U.S. soldier to set foot on the continent proper and was therefore profoundly dissatisfied with the tedious speed of his landing craft.

He dropped his pack, then squeezed and pushed his way aft through his crowded platoon and said to the navy coxswain who was steering the craft. "Jesus Christ, Chief! Quit dick-dancin' around and put your goddamn foot on it! We paid you good money, and I want us on the beach first. Cain't you hear the other landing craft? They're pullin' ahead of us." That may or may not have been true. He had no idea where the other boats were; it was pitch black, and he couldn't hear a thing over the engine of his own landing craft. Still, he thought it best to leave nothing to chance, and a little forceful encouragement of the sailor couldn't hurt. In this, Lieutenant Berger had the support of most of 1st Platoon. The idea of becoming history makers appealed in general to the soldiers, as they'd been told that the landing was unlikely to be opposed. To forward this great cause, his sergeants had each contributed to the "tip" for the sailor ferrying them to the beach. The sergeants had devised a sure-fire plan which, in addition to the tip for their own driver, also included bribing the coxswains of the crafts carrying the 2nd and 3rd Platoons of Able Company to keep their landing crafts just a little behind their own. Although some of Lieutenant Berger's troops had severe reservations about speeding into battle, most were caught up in his infectious enthusiasm. All wanted to survive, first and foremost, but if they were also able to claim that they were the first soldiers to liberate Europe— well, that was just icing on the cake.

"L.T." Chief Petty Officer Jim Duncan patiently began, "I ain't . . . uh . . . dick-dancing around. I'm happy to get you fellas there first, but . . ."

Whatever reservations Chief Duncan had remained unexpressed as the British naval barrage opened up to the north on German targets ashore. The Fifth Army commander, Lieutenant General Mark Wayne Clark, had wanted to achieve tactical surprise by conducting the landings without a preliminary barrage on the beach defenses. Much to the dismay of the soldiers of the American assault wave, this is how they would land. But the British had insisted on naval gunfire preceding their assault, and while the British warships were a considerable distance from the American landing craft, the lights and sounds were impressive and captivating.

Dragging his eyes away from the lights on the horizon, Perkin continued to urge the sailor: "Chief, listen to that. Those are the British battleships opening up. You could hear that racket back in Austin. We ain't gonna surprise anyone. Every fuckin' Kraut with a gun or tank is headin' down to the water to see what's what. We're a lot better off getting there before they do, and that goes for you as well. If we beat them to the beach, you can drop us off and return to the ship before anyone is in a position to shoot at you. Come on now and hurry it up!" Duncan shook his head but increased the throttle on the landing craft.

Perkin pushed his way back to the bow, stopping along the way to chat with his soldiers and to encourage his squad leaders. The seas were not high, but the flat-bottomed landing craft pitched and rolled enough to make the soldiers nauseous, some even outright sick. Those soldiers who were ill got either a word of encouragement or gentle teasing from Perkin as he made his way through the landing craft, until he stopped to shake Second Lieutenant Frank McCarter's hand. "We're going to do it, Frank. I think we're gonna be first on the beach. I reckon that Sam is at least thirty yards behind us, but I can't make out where Eddy is. Remember, if we're unopposed, plant the flag on the beach, make sure the sergeants get everyone organized, and start moving inland. If we're opposed, well, plant the flag quickly—then you, me, and the sergeants will just keep dragging everyone's ass on forward."

Frank grinned and nodded. He was preparing to say something about the inevitability of success but coming from East Texas, Frank's speech was a little slower than most, and Perkin had already moved on before he could formulate his first word.

Perkin smiled to himself. Despite Frank's slow speech, he thought the East Texas boy was a promising young officer—even if he was obsessed with thoughts of women. On the verge of the greatest landing in Europe to date, Perkin rightly believed that Frank's thoughts had wandered back to his favorite subject—Marlene Dietrich. He'd recently seen her perform in Algiers and couldn't stop talking about the experience. Perkin shook his head as he pushed his way forward. He'd never understood the appeal of that skinny German woman.

0310 hours
Gulf of Salerno

As Lieutenant McCarter's thoughts drifted between women and war, Sam's thoughts were exclusively on his immediate future. He could make out the wake of his cousin's landing craft some ways off the starboard bow and he suspected, rightly so, that Perkin had manipulated events to somehow be first on the beach. Other than a concern for his cousin's well-being, that was fine with him.

Whereas Perkin was excited to test himself in battle, Sam found the army to be stupid, tedious, and restrictive. Recalling their argument from two days before, Sam reflected that he didn't really blame Perkin for his being in the army, although he was piqued at Perkin being promoted to first lieutenant before him. Perkin had told him that seniority among junior officers was "like modesty in a whorehouse—it really doesn't count for much," and it wasn't Perkin's fault that Sam's promotion had been slower. For now, they were both first johns, but Perkin would almost certainly get a company command first. It wasn't that Sam coveted command, because the truth was that he didn't, but the thought was still a minor burr under the saddle of his ego. This irritation was tempered by his concern that once Perkin did get a company, the odds were good that they'd go their own ways in the division and only see each other infrequently at best.

Sam longed for Texas. Although he was surrounded by Texans, it just wasn't the same. He missed his ranch and his horses, fishing in the bay, the familiar food, his friends and family. Mostly though, he missed his wife, Margaret—the librarian's daughter. They'd been married for over two years now, and as the circumstances permitted, she'd followed him from Texas to Florida to Virginia to Massachusetts before his deployment overseas. Sam felt fortunate that he had the means to move Margaret around; she'd gone back to the ranch after the division embarked for Africa. Many junior officers had no more money than the army provided, deciding to keep their families at home. Sam knew officers in the regiment that had not seen their family for over a year, and many of the enlisted troops were in even worse shape.

As the landing craft rode over the waves, the operations and intelligence briefings that they'd had about Operation Avalanche began to run in a loop through his mind. He was frantically trying to remember every detail. Whereas Perkin took a lighthearted approach to the army, as he did with life, Sam felt the press of an officer's responsibilities heavily. Mistakes on his part could cost his soldiers their lives, and he wanted to make sure he'd done everything in his power to get his boys home safely. He knew enough about warfare to know that most of the battle would be out of his hands, and that concerned him as much as those things he could influence. Of all the aspects of the coming battle he'd heard of from Jim Lockridge, none concerned him so much as the discussion of the gap between the British and American divisions on the beach. *Who made that decision?* he asked himself with trepidation.

0315 hours
Gulf of Salerno

While Sam Taft mentally recounted the intelligence briefings and Frank McCarter thought of Marlene Dietrich, Perkin returned to the front of his landing craft, trying hard to focus on the mission at hand. He, however, was having less success than Sam. His thoughts were continually interrupted by a song running through his head. No matter how hard he tried, he couldn't dismiss the words: "With a ha-ha-ha, and a ho-ho-ho, and a couple of tra-la-las—that's how we pass the day away, in the merry old land of Oz." While he thought his internal soundtrack was somewhat ironic, he yearned for a little more clarity of thought. The song, which did not come close to meeting his high musical standards, brought forth an old memory of Texas.

It was Labor Day weekend in 1939, and he'd returned from graduate school in Austin to spend a long weekend fishing in South Texas with his cousin and grandfather. The three of them had gotten up early on the Friday morning and spent the day fishing in Corpus Christi Bay. It had been a fantastic day, with all three men catching and releasing trout almost as quickly as they could pull them in.

It was Perkin's first trip back to the Coastal Bend since the beginning of summer. He enjoyed Austin and thought from time to time that he might like to settle there if he could get onto the university faculty. There was fishing at several of the nearby lakes, which were new public works creations on the Colorado River, but he thought bass fishing on a lake a poor substitute for trout fishing in the bay. When presented with a beautiful day out with Sam and Old Perkin, he made the most of it.

That evening, he and Sam had gone to Corpus Christi on a double date to see *The Wizard of Oz*. The movie had been out for a week, and the word was that it was a bit of a kid's movie, but Sam had been persuasive. Perkin liked to see the rare color movie and—also rare—the theater was air-conditioned, which was definitely welcome to a sunburned fellow in South Texas on the first day of September. Mostly, he had gone to see it because Sam had finally scored a date with the librarian's daughter and was in dire need of moral support. Almost four years later, and riding into his first battle in a landing craft, Perkin laughed out loud at the memory of Sam's nervousness as they were getting ready for the evening. "I can't believe she agreed to go out with me. Maggie is far too beautiful for someone like me," Sam had said.

"Nah, that's not really the issue." Perkin had replied. "She's too smart for someone like you. It's not the looks but the brains that pose a challenge, but now that I think about it, her looks are out of your league as well."

Ignoring the withering glare that Sam had shot him, Perkin continued, "I guess I don't get it either—maybe her boyfriend is sick and her backup is out of town. Oh, by the way—you probably ought to stick with 'Margaret.' 'Maggie' may be too familiar. Try and keep it more formal than usual and chew with your mouth closed. She's smart but may be uninformed about the culinary folkways of Aggies." Perkin continued to offer unsolicited advice. "Just relax though. While I think the standard advice for a situation like this is to 'just be yourself,' that poses obvious problems for you, so maybe you should . . . you should . . . well shit, Sam." Perkin looked away from the mirror where he'd been combing his hair and smirked at his cousin. "I can't really think of a way for you to come out of this wrapped in glory with the beautiful girl on your arm. Perhaps you should go ahead and start planning for the inevitable humiliation of failure. Yes, that might be best . . ."

"You know, your help ain't helpful. As usual." Sam had muttered.

Perkin had borrowed his grandfather's Ford sedan and they'd stopped for dinner before the movie at a place called Old Larry's World Famous Barbeque. Perkin's date, a stunning brunette named Alice, was a friend of Margaret's from Rockport. As the girls carried most of the conversation, Perkin entertained himself by watching the interaction between his cousin and the librarian's daughter. It was obvious that Maggie either didn't worry about the culinary folkways of Aggies or at least liked big strong ranchers—she seemed as smitten with Sam as he was with her. The four of them made it through dinner with only one major incident—when Sam's first foray into conversation had ended prematurely when he'd knocked his Dr Pepper onto the lap of Perkin's date. All things considered, reflected Perkin in the landing craft, it had been a successful dinner and had gone far better than he'd expected.

So it was that at least three of the party entered the movie theater in a good mood. Alice, unhappy and embarrassed, was trying to be as good a sport as a girl can be on a blind date with a soda-soaked dress. She didn't understand Perkin's sense of humor and her feelings were hurt when he laughed as Sam spilled his drink on her. Although she found him to be very good-looking, she thought his name was ridiculous. She'd resolved before they even made it to the theater that he would have to show much more promise if there was going to be a second date.

Sam was a stickler for being on time to an event and, consequently, they got good seats at the theater. While Maggie and Alice went to powder their noses and see what they could do for Alice's sticky dress, Perkin and Sam settled back to review the evening. "I am such an idiot," said Sam. "How is it that I can't git through an evening without ruining it?"

"Oh no, don't think that!" Perkin replied. "You're more entertainin' than usual."

"I wasn't really concerned about your entertainment."

"Well, I find that a little disappointing since you invited me. However, I wouldn't worry about Margaret either. I reckon she digs your chili."

"Oh, for Christ's sake, what language do they speak in Austin? I don't even know what that means," said Sam irritably.

"It means, cousin, that I think she likes you. Look, she's smart and pretty—we knew that already—but she's still here after you humiliated her best friend by dumping an ice-cold drink on her crotch. Oh, and ruining her best dress by the way. That shows perseverance. I think there's nothing to worry about—but there's only one way to be sure if she's really interested."

"And what's that?" asked Sam warily.

"Spill coffee in Alice's lap later tonight. If Margaret hangs around after that, you know you're the man of her dreams."

The cousins were still laughing when the girls walked up to the table. "What's so funny?" asked Alice suspiciously.

"I was just telling Sam that I was going to get you a cup of coffee so you could get your revenge on him," said Perkin as he stood up to let the girls in to their seats.

"Isn't that just the sweetest thought? Make it hot," said Alice with a genuine attempt at a smile as she sat down between Sam and Perkin.

Perkin was about to crack another joke at his cousin's expense when the cinema manager walked to the front of the theater. "Could I have your attention, please? As usual, we'll start our feature film after the news reel and tonight's cartoon, but I thought you might appreciate an update on today's events in Europe."

Sam leaned over to Perkin and whispered, "What's going on in Europe?"

Perkin whispered back, "It's gotta be Poland, but I haven't heard any more than you have today."

The manager continued, "The German Army attacked in force across the Polish frontier early this morning. The German government issued a statement to the effect that the attack on Poland was in retaliation for a Polish attack on a radio station on German territory on Wednesday. The Polish government has denied any participation in the attack on the radio station and is appealing to the western democracies for assistance. London and Paris are both calling for a German withdrawal from all Polish territory and have warned the Third Reich that they would honor their security guarantees to Poland. Polish forces have been hit hard by the German attack, and there are reports of heavy civilian casualties resulting from air raids on Polish border towns, but the Poles are reportedly still holding their ground. I'm afraid that's all we know right now, but I believe that some people probably hadn't heard about the war. I'm sorry to bring you folks the bad news, but our news reel is already out of date. Good night and enjoy your show."

Sam leaned over Alice and said to Perkin, "Shit. Sorry." The apology was to Alice for swearing. "You've called it right all along, Perk. Hope you ain't right about the rest."

Alice looked at Perkin, "What's he mean? What's the rest, Perk?"

Perkin noticed her use of the diminutive Perk and liked how she'd said it. "I think this means a general European war—and that it has a good potential to bring us into it. But I think that it's equal odds that the British and French finish off this Hitler fella once and for all. Let's hope so."

Alice shuddered and said, "I hope so too. Maggie told me that y'all are soldiers. Do you think it will affect you?"

Sam replied as the cartoon began to run, "We're guardsmen, not full-time soldiers. This has a long way to go before it involves us. I guess there's plenty of time for you to get your revenge." Secretly, Sam was very pleased about Alice's comment. In his limited conversations with Margaret, the subject of the National Guard had never come up, so she'd done some checking up on him as well.

It was during the song about the merry old land of Oz, the song that Perkin would not be able to get out of his head some four years later, that he'd looked over and saw his cousin and the librarian's daughter holding hands. Perkin had smiled—thank God, he'd thought, *that's a start*. He'd despaired of his cousin ever asking out Margaret. Despite the teasing, the cousins' favorite pastime, he wished the best for Sam. His cousin was normally not shy with girls, but when it came to Margaret, he was tongue-tied and, as poor Alice could attest, all thumbs. As Perkin turned back to listen to the music and the marvel of Technicolor, his thoughts turned from his cousin back to the news from Europe, and the smile disappeared.

The news itself was disturbing but not unexpected. The big unknowns were whether or not the British and the French would keep their commitments, and if they did, how their armies would perform. He'd spent a large part of the summer in Austin debating these issues with his friend and fellow graduate student, Jim Lockridge. Perkin had a fascination for all history, but his emphasis of study was the early American frontier. Jim's was European military and diplomatic history, and his nearly complete dissertation was on Bismarck and the Hohenzollern candidature for the throne of Spain. Over many beers in the jazz and blues bars of Austin, the two history students agreed that a German attack on Poland was probable, a Polish defeat inevitable, and an Anglo-French counter attack possible-to-likely. But it was over the question of how the western democracies would fight that Jim and Perkin diverged. As he'd discussed with Sam some months earlier, Perkin maintained that everyone knew that France had the best army in the world and that the United Kingdom had the Royal Navy and the immense resources of the empire. Perkin believed that Germany was overreaching with Poland and, at best, would face swift defeat. At worst, there would be another stalemate reminiscent of 1914.

Jim Lockridge was not nearly as sanguine about the Allies' prospects. "Look," he would say. "National Socialism is a malignant philosophy, but it's also dynamic and electrifying to those who've suffered through a depression worse than our own and who believe that they were cheated and betrayed at Versailles. To the mystics in the Nazi Party, and there are a lot of them, Hitler cannot be defeated. He's promised the Germans a thousand-year empire, and they fuckin' believe it. My point is that the Germans have bought into this crap hook, line, and sinker. They believe that they will win and will fight to win. The French don't care enough about democracy and their own miserable leaders to fight. Britain isn't much better."

On the landing craft, it was to the quick defeat of the democracies and Dunkirk and then finally back to Salerno that his thoughts drifted. The thought of a Dunkirk happening to the 36th, and all the implications that followed, chilled Perkin deeply. His imagination took him to a beach where Texans were frantically re-embarking on transports while under attack from German airplanes, tanks, and artillery. The world was a different place now, and he knew the Germans could be beaten, but he was still scared of failure. Unlike many soldiers, Perkin had a good understanding of the big picture and what this landing meant to the Allied war effort. He was objective enough to recognize that that his pep talk the day before was largely showmanship—bravado to pump the boys up and have a few laughs before the laughing stopped—but he'd meant what he said about the consequences of failure. It could set the war back at least two years, maybe indefinitely, and he thought it might be too much to ask of a National Guard division that hadn't seen combat for twenty-five years. He shook his head as if to clear his mind and decided that, as they said back home, they were "fixin' to find out."

0320 hours
Paestum, Italy

Amphibious landings are the most complex operations that any military can conduct. During the course of the war, both the United Kingdom and the United States became expert practitioners of expeditionary warfare. Yet even for the best in the world, as they surely were, it was still a complicated and messy business that was equal parts science and art.

To the staff officers who considered the charts, tides, friendly and enemy dispositions, logistics, communications, and a thousand other variables, planning an amphibious landing called for a scientific and methodical approach. However, to the sailors, soldiers, and Marines who had to execute the plan, throwing a land army ashore from the sea is nothing less than pure art.

Ensign Eugene Evans was known as "Double E" to his Naval Academy classmates. He never was certain if it was a complimentary takeoff of his name or reflective of the hated Electrical Engineering course at the academy. In any case, Ensign Evans was not thinking of the subtleties of art and science in expeditionary operations, nor was he reminiscing about Annapolis. He was desperately trying to establish a fix on the medieval tower that the ancient inhabitants of the coastal village of Agropoli had ironically built to warn of invasion from the sea, but neither he nor his bosun's mate could see the tower in the dark.

Ensign Evans was in command of the control craft that would guide the Texan assault force of the 1st Battalion of the 141st Regimental Combat Team ashore onto the strip of sand designated as Blue Beach. His dilemma was that he'd established a single line of bearing from a similar tower to the north at the ancient ruins at Paestum, but he needed at least one more line of bearing, preferably two more, to establish a fix on his position. Without these, he could only guess where he was and could easily direct the assault craft in his sector to the wrong beach. He was where he thought he was supposed to be but, at the same time, he knew that he did not know with certainty where he was. Time was up. Evans turned on his blue light and directed it out to sea for the coxswains to follow in to Blue Beach.

Perkin and the platoon swayed to their left as Chief Duncan saw the blue light far off his starboard bow and brought the landing craft around to line up with the control craft. H-hour of D-day was upon them. It was time. Perkin knew they had to be close. The landings were scheduled for 0330 hours and, although sailors lived in an alien world to the soldiers, he was confident the navy would get him to the beach on time. For the first time in about an hour, the annoying song from *The Wizard of Oz* had left his head, only to be replaced with the sound of his heart beating—rapidly. Although he was, at best, a casual Presbyterian, he crossed himself in the dark before looking around to see if anyone had noticed. *It can't hurt,* he thought, and grinned. Perkin pulled himself up to look over the bow ramp of the craft. There it was. Surf.

Perkin grasped his Thompson submachine gun tightly and turned back to his platoon. "This is it, boys! Get ready. Keep your heads down and move fast." He yelled back to his coxswain. "Chief, thanks for the ride and good luck!" As he turned back and faced the bow ramp, the soldiers from Texas heard an accented voice on a bullhorn calling from the dunes: "Soldiers! Come on in and surrender! We've got you covered!"

In the best tradition of infantry officers, Perkin was preparing to call out, "Follow me," but what came out instead was: "What the fuck?" Then the landing craft slid to a hard stop. Chief Duncan had brought it in fast and, as the keel of the craft grounded on the beach, Perkin's helmet and face slammed into the bow ramp of the landing craft. As Perkin was adjusting his helmet and several soldiers were reestablishing their footing, the ramp dropped and the 1st Platoon of Able Company landed in knee-high surf on the shores of Europe.

It was only ten yards to the water's edge, and Perkin was the first American soldier to land on the beach—at least as far as he could see. The triumphant moment was short-lived as a flare went up from behind the dunes to their left. Perkin and every soldier in the platoon, except one, instinctively followed the flare upwards with their eyes and watched as it burst into brilliance. "Goddamn it, you fuckin' morons! Don't look at the flare. Keep moving!" Perkin realized guiltily that Sergeant Kenton's words applied to him and he then added his voice to the sergeant's: "Follow me! Keep moving! Get to the dunes!"

As Perkin and his troops surged forward, the first shots were fired on the Texans. Although Perkin had heard the MG-42—the German frontline light machine gun—many times before in training, it sounded different when directed at him. It was, he thought, a rather unpleasant sound. He grabbed Private Kulis and pulled him forward and, out of the corner of his eye, saw Kenton do the same with another soldier.

0330 hours
Paestum, Italy

Within thirty seconds of the call to surrender, the landing craft was emptied and Chief Duncan began to reverse away from the beach. Sam Taft observed this from his own landing craft, which grounded about the same time Duncan began reversing. As Sam mirrored the actions of his cousin and began to move out towards the dune, pulling his soldiers behind him, he saw Second Lieutenant Frank McCarter plant a huge Texas flag on the beach, which began to flap immediately in the off-shore breeze—*only Perkin would think of doing that*. McCarter then sprinted towards the relative safety of the dunes kicking sand up behind him as he ran. Sam was amazed, as Frank wasn't known any more for quickness of action than he was for quickness of speech. Sam saw from the tracer rounds that the incoming fire was not perpendicular to their landing site but was offset further to the left, meaning his platoon was closer than Perkin's to the MG-42. Third Platoon, which he couldn't yet see, would be landing virtually in front of the machine gun. He'd observed in that single second that 1st Platoon had taken casualties—he saw two soldiers fall—but had also begun to return fire.

Jack Younger, Sam's platoon sergeant, was taking shelter at the edge of the dunes. "Younger! Get 1st Squad working over to the left—let's get that MG-42. They'll tear 3rd Platoon apart." Younger nodded and grabbed the squad leader, who in turn motioned to his team. They set off together working their way back through the small sand dunes. Sam watched them go, then turned his attention back to the battlefield.

All of Salerno Gulf had lit up at once. Sam could see at least half a dozen flares burning over several hundred yards of waterfront. By their light, he could see that the first wave of the Blue Beach assault force had come in largely together, but that there was a large gap of empty space on the beach where the adjacent force landing on Yellow Beach should be. Either that entire wave was late or someone landed in the wrong area. With a sinking heart, Sam began to suspect that his company was landing too far south and were now exposed on both their right and left flanks. Although many soldiers had identified the sound of the MG-42, Sam was the first to grasp its significance: they were fighting Germans, not Italians, and the Germans had been expecting them.

Perkin was coming to the same conclusions. He'd noted that there was a small stream to their right which, by his map, suggested they were too far south by at least five hundred yards. That would pose problems, not the least of which was where the subsequent assault waves would land. Each wave was to come in at a seven-minute interval; his company commander and the Headquarters Platoon were due to arrive any minute. More importantly, he thought, the third wave would begin the landing of the heavy equipment—artillery, mortars, machine guns, tanks, and trucks. But would they come in at the right beach or the wrong one? It appeared to Perkin that he was in the wrong spot, but so were scores of other soldiers. Another problem beginning to crystallize in his mind was the terrain. The beach exit from Blue Beach was supposed to be good dry ground, but if he was where he thought he was, then the land on the other side of the dunes was comprised of marshland and drainage ditches.

The machine gun shifted its fire to the north, and Perkin took the opportunity to run the short distance back to the beach, where two of his men were down. One of them was Perkin's platoon sergeant, Milton Evers. Thankfully, neither man had a life-threatening injury, but both would have to be evacuated. Evers had been shot in the leg; Perkin thought he could see bone through the mangled flesh of his thigh. Perkin grasped Evers' hand, the sergeant's grip tightening as a bolt of pain shot through him. Only a few words were passed between them, "Good luck and see you later." Perkin made room for his medic and knelt beside the other wounded soldier, a draftee from Tennessee, and also wished him good luck.

As he ran back to the dunes, the loss of Sergeant Evers struck Perkin. Evers was a recent transfer from the 1st Division and had seen combat with the Big Red One in North Africa. He was a good leader, and Perkin had been counting on his battle experience in the days to come. Lieutenant McCarter would have to serve in that role and, assuming they made it through the battle, Sergeant Kenton would become the platoon sergeant.

Perkin was preparing to have Sergeant Kenton and his squad head south to the Solofrone River when additional flares began to appear overhead on either side. He motioned to Kenton. "Let's wait. There's no point in you running a gauntlet to get down to the river just yet. It looks like they have forces over to the right, so let's keep you and your squad here in case we have to defend this flank." Perkin turned to Frank McCarter, "Get scouts moving to the southeast and straight in as well. We need an idea of how heavily this is defended and we'll need answers quickly. I don't think we're where we're supposed to be, and if the rest of the assault waves come in north of us instead of on our position . . . well, it might get kinda lonely down here."

McCarter nodded and moved off. He sent two different two-man teams forward through the dunes. Even as Sam's 2nd Platoon silenced the MG-42 on their left, a burst of machine gun fire to Perkin's right caused the scouts to drop to the ground. They began to crawl back to 1st Platoon's position while other scouts continued to work their way forward into the dunes.

Perkin noticed the inbound fires were increasing. *I guess we woke the rest of them up*, he thought. Adding to the automatic fire, the first mortar rounds began to land on the beach, and the soldiers from Texas began instinctively to move towards the relative safety of the dunes. Seconds later, German artillery opened fire from the foothills two miles away, and their situation worsened.

0345 hours
Gulf of Salerno

Captain Bill Spaulding, the commanding officer of Able Company, drew his Colt .45, pulled the hammer back one click, and pressed it hard into the forehead of his coxswain. "Get this boat in there. Now!"

The coxswain, a twenty-year-old petty officer from Vermont, turned the craft back towards the beach but did not increase the throttle. "Sir! There's no way we can make it through that. We need to go back to the ship. Just look at it—that beach is fucking exploding!" The young sailor had a point. Spaulding looked towards the shore. Great columns of water were rising from the sea as German artillery rounds began to fall on the beach and into the water. As if to emphasize the sailor's argument, a landing craft two hundred yards off their port beam struck an unswept mine. Even at that distance, the force of the explosion rocked their landing craft. Mercifully, in the darkness Spaulding's soldiers and crew were unable to see the landing craft vaporize.

Spaulding didn't want to go to the shore any more than the sailor did, but a line from a book came to mind, "This whole act's immutably decreed. 'Twas rehearsed by thee and me a billion years before this ocean rolled. Fool! I am the Fates' lieutenant; I act under orders." Spaulding had no choice. Taking a deep breath, he pulled himself up close to the terrified coxswain, leaving Melville behind in his mind. "What the fuck did you expect, sailor? Roses and champagne? It's not as bad as it looks and sounds. Trust me. Now, you're taking me to that beach or I'll drive this craft myself. Those are my soldiers and they're dead without reinforcement. Our second wave is already late—the third should be landing now. Get moving."

The coxswain shook his head as Spaulding turned away in disgust. He couldn't shoot the sailor, though he was tempted. He holstered his pistol, pulled one of the landing craft's two gunners out of his turret and said, "Get this fucking boat to the beach."

The sailor, younger even than the coxswain, looked at the angry Texan and said calmly, "Aye, aye, sir. Don't worry, I'll get you there. We're about ten minutes out, but I'll see if we can do better." He turned to the coxswain and pulled him gently from his station, "Come on, Danny, I'm driving."

Exactly five minutes later, Captain Spaulding and the Headquarters Platoon stormed ashore at Blue Beach. Spaulding's intuition was right—the artillery was actually not as bad as it had appeared from the seaward side. He could see that the beaches to the left, the north, were being hit harder than his own. Spaulding looked for a beachmaster, saw none, ran in a crouched position over to a soldier and asked, "Where's Able Company?"

The soldier, a private from Baker Company, was about to say, "How the hell should I know?" when one of Spaulding's soldiers from 3rd Platoon ran out from the dunes.

"Cap'n, we're over here. Lieutenant Brown is dead."

Spaulding was speechless for a second. *So Eddy was the first. The poor boy died in the first minute of his first battle.*

"I'm very sorry to hear that, Mendoza. Please round up Lieutenants Berger, Taft, and McCarter and have them meet me over there." Captain Spaulding pointed to a relatively large dune that appeared to offer some shelter. He ran hunched over with Master Sergeant Robert Hawkins, the company first sergeant, to the dune. Kneeling in the sand, Spaulding lit a cigarette, offered one to Hawkins and, as Sam and Perkin had done only a few minutes before, began to take stock of the situation.

In the few moments before his officers arrived, Captain Spaulding and Sergeant Hawkins concluded that the fire really wasn't as severe on Blue Beach as it appeared on what they could see of the Yellow, Green, and Red beaches to the north. Spaulding wondered if that was just an illusion based on seeing things from a distance, or if the other battalions had landed in a more heavily defended area. His battalion, the 1st of the 141st Regiment, had the waterfront designated as Blue Beach. The 3rd Battalion of the 141st was assigned to land on the adjacent beach to the north, Yellow Beach, and the 2nd Battalion was being held in regimental reserve. The 142nd Regimental Combat Team had Green and Red beaches and the third Texas regiment, the 143rd, was being held in divisional reserve. Why there was such a large gap between his battalion and the 3/141st?*

"Hooray for Captain Spaulding, the African Explorer!" sang Perkin as he and Frank ran crouched over to their company commander. Perkin was a big fan of the Marx Brothers. "Good to see you, sir."

---

*In 1940, the 36th was reorganized from a square division of four regiments to a triangular division of three regiments (141st, 142nd, and 143rd). The 144th was broken off from the 36th and spent the war performing continental defense and training duties. The remaining regiments each had three rifle battalions, and each battalion had three rifle companies, a heavy weapons company, and a HQ company. Perkin and Sam were part of Able Company of the 1/141st, which is to say, the 1st Battalion of the 141st Infantry Regiment.

"Good to see you too. I'd do my Groucho dance for you, but it seems a little undignified in front of the first sergeant. Perk, have you heard anything of Eddy?"

"No, sir, d'ya want me to send a runner?"

"Not yet. We need to be quick. Where's Bear?"

Perkin was about to say that he hadn't seen Sam either when the big rancher slid belly first over the sand dune behind them. Sam immediately squatted down, handed his M-1 Garand to Perkin, took off his pack and began to shake sand out of his uniform.

"Howdy, Bear. All right?" It was seldom safe to use Margaret's pet name for Sam to his face, but Spaulding believed he could indulge himself under the circumstances. The company commander said, "Sorry I'm late, boys. It was a bit of a chore to convince the navy to drop me off here. I don't know if you've heard—Ed Brown is reported KIA. Can y'all confirm that? No? Frank, check it out when we're done here. If it's true, take command of 3rd Platoon. Perk, Sam, what's your assessment?"

As Frank motioned to an NCO and whispered in his ear, Perk began to speak rapidly, "First and foremost, we are on the wrong beach. I estimate that we landed about five hundred yards south of Blue. That puts a considerable gap between us and 3rd Battalion. I don't know, maybe seven or eight hundred yards. I recommend getting with battalion or regiment and requesting that they close that gap. That could pose a lot of problems later on if, when, the Germans counterattack. Second, they were expecting us. They called on us to surrender before we even landed. As you can see, this beach is more heavily defended than we expected and by Germans . . . not Italians." He looked over at Sam for confirmation, who nodded. "Third, there are interlocking machine guns, MG-34s or 42s, there and there, say, about a hundred and fifty to two hundred yards inland." He pointed north and south of their position.

"I've also heard MGs firing inland, so this is likely just the first line of defense."

Sam interrupted. "Yeah. We took out the crew on the northern nest—not a full team, just two men in a hastily prepared position. I don't think this sector is heavily defended, at least not this close to the waterfront."

"I agree," Perk said. "Fourth, we're getting some mortar fire but not at a high cyclic rate. There may just be a single mortar crew in this area, and they haven't been very accurate to this point. We received artillery fire a few minutes before your arrival, but as you can see it seems to be shifting to the northern beaches. Maybe they have something else planned for us. Fifth, we've found landmines from the high-water mark up to the dunes. We've not hit any yet and we've marked the handful we found. So we're demining and taking down the barbed wire to establish a corridor towards the beach exit, wherever that might be. We'll turn all that over to the engineers when they get here. Finally, I've sent scouts straight ahead and to the right, but I've not sent the team to the river. I thought it best to wait and see what we're up against here. Is that okay?"

Spaulding thought for a moment, "Yeah, we'll see. I want to know about that river and our flanks, but if this sector is heavily defended, it could have been trouble for your squad. Wait until the scouts come back and we'll see then. Anything else?"

"Yes, sir. Two casualties—both nonlethal but bad enough for evacuation. One was Sergeant Evers. I don't think he'll be coming back anytime soon."

"Shit. Sorry to hear about that. Sam? Anything to add?"

"No, sir. I think that about sums it up. I'd like to say, again, I don't think this is heavily defended and we should be able to push on through, although it was kind of interestin' for a moment. Second Platoon has one casualty—Williams. He doesn't require evacuation. Any word on the third wave? They should have landed by now."

The five men turned and looked out at sea. There was no sign of additional inbound shipping in the dark and for good reason—they were looking in the wrong place.

Ensign Evans had completed his fix during the first wave's landing as the shore-based flares gave him enough light to identify fixable landmarks. Swearing as he realized his mistake, he sailed his small control craft through mined waters to the proper position and began to direct the third assault wave to the proper Blue Beach. Some of the second wave craft, milling about in indecision and fear, followed him and his blue light as he traversed northwards and landed with the third wave some five hundred yards north of the first landing site. The 1st Battalion was now split between two beaches, with the southernmost contingent comprised only of riflemen.

Captain Spaulding lit his third cigarette since arriving in Italy. He offered the pack, but only Lieutenant McCarter took one. With the cigarette between his fingers, Spaulding pointed to a map of the landing sites.

"We need to get moving and head onwards to our objectives. Frank, take 3rd Platoon on our left. I'm sorry about Eddy. I know he was your best friend. Maintain contact as much as possible with Baker Company. No telling what percentage of Charlie and Dog companies will land here or on the proper Blue Beach—let's call it Blue Beach North—and this one, Blue Beach South. Sam, I'll go with you and 2nd Platoon in the center. First Platoon will stay to our right and, once over the dunes, will take out the MG-42, sending a squad down to recce the Solofrone. One last thing, Perk is senior man, so he takes command if anything happens to me. Any questions?"

"Does your Victrola come with the job?" asked Perkin.

"No, but since you brought it up—I've decided to leave it to Frank; he never annoys me. Okay, let's move out."

Perkin unstrapped his Thompson and whispered to Sam as the group broke up, "I wasn't joking—that's a really nice record player." He paused for a second before saying, "Good luck."

Sam whispered back, "What about me? Frank has no taste in music." He offered his hand, "Good luck to you too." They shook hands, and as they went their separate ways, Sam watched Perkin motion to Sergeant Kenton to round up the platoon.

0410 hours
Blue Beach South

Perkin was lying face down in the sand behind the short row of dunes, mentally willing himself to be flatter. He was breathing rapidly and trying unsuccessfully to control his fear. The one time he rose up on his elbows to look around, the MG-42 had fired at him. He was in the smallest of depressions in what was otherwise the flattest of grounds. His little dried-up puddle had kept him alive so far, and he was quite willing to remain in place until the firing ceased for good. He knew that Sergeant Kenton had a squad working its way to the side of the German gunners, and he fervently wished that they would hurry up.

They'd been creeping along in relative darkness towards where they thought the German machine gun nest was when the Germans fired another flare. They were much closer to the gun than Perkin had expected and his scout had reported. As the Germans opened fire, he dove to the right as the rest of the squad he was with scattered to the left into some brush. He could hear the sounds of his soldiers firing at the Germans but was no longer inclined to see how the fight was going.

Shortly, or interminably, from Perkin's point of view, a squad member crept close enough to lob a grenade into the German machine gun nest. Following the explosion, Perkin looked up in time to see Private Kulis calmly walk up to the nest and shoot two stunned and wounded German soldiers in the chest. He then ran his bayonet through the back of the third member of the team. Perkin watched, fascinated, with his heart nearly pounding out of his chest as the small rifleman quickly propped his M-1 Garand against a stack of sand bags and began to look through the Germans' possessions. He took a small leather box from one dead soldier and a wristwatch from the other. Perkin looked over and saw that Sergeant Kenton was also watching, equally fascinated. They looked at each other and shrugged.

A moment later, Kulis jogged over to Perkin in the dwindling light of the flare and said, "A present for you, Lieutenant." He handed Perkin the leather box, which had belt loops on it. The lieutenant opened the box to find a set of German field binoculars—a very nice present indeed.

"Thank you, Kulis. You don't want to keep them?"

"No, sir, I don't want to carry the extra weight. But I was looking for a new watch. My dad gave me his Waterbury, and I'd like that to survive the war intact." In the light of a fresh flare off to their north, Kulis checked out his new watch. "It says . . . Jaegar-Lecoultre." The rifleman pronounced the words as Jaguar La Cooter. "Never heard of it, but it sure looks nice."

Still breathing heavily and trying to come to terms with the fact that the bookworm rifleman was actually a calm killer and his savior, Perkin said, "Yes it does. Hey, um, Kulis . . . we take wounded soldiers prisoner."

"Oh, yes, sir. I thought about that. These fellas were dying from the grenade—the one yonder was nearly dead and the others weren't far behind him. I thought it better for 'em."

"Oh, well, uh, let's let the medic look at 'em first next time. But thanks again, and, uh, good work with that machine gun."

"Yes, sir," Kulis said with a grin. "It was nothin'—just like training."

Perkin walked over to Sergeant Kenton, who said, "That was very clever of you, sir—keeping the Krauts occupied for us like that."

"What? Oh . . . yeah." As his heart rate began to normalize, he mumbled dryly, "It's your turn to be clever next. Shit. Thought I didn't stand a Chinaman's chance back there." Perkin nodded at Private Kulis, who was showing off his new watch to Private Fratelli. "So, how 'bout your boy Kulis there?"

Kenton laughed softly as he motioned the platoon to move forward again, "Yeah, how 'bout that? You know, he's the youngest of four brothers, and he told me that they did everything short of killing each other. I thought he meant shooting rubber bands or something like that."

"Yeah, he seemed kinda casual about it, didn't he? Go figure. Okay, back to business. You're the platoon sergeant until I fire you. Send a runner to Captain Spaulding and tell him we took out the nest, no casualties. I'm gonna have Corporal Pena take 1st Squad to our right and check out the river like we planned. I want him to hustle along, and we'll rendezvous at the bridge. Let's move out quickly and get there first. Oh, and I've decided to keep Kulis next to me as my bodyguard."

0430 hours
Blue Beach South

An hour after the first elements of Able Company had landed in Italy, they'd advanced some six hundred yards from the water. A trickle of stragglers joined the company as a few landing craft landed at Blue Beach South. Most welcome among those who came in late was the Able Company Weapons Platoon led by Second Lieutenant Leonard Anderson. Three mortars, three bazooka teams, and two .30 caliber machine gun sections. Also welcome were Lieutenant Colonel Wranosky and his battalion staff, who came running up hard behind Able Company.

As Wranosky walked along in company with his platoon, Sam shamelessly eavesdropped on the conversation between his battalion and company commander. After asking Spaulding how he was getting along, Wranosky said, still breathing hard, "What a snafu—the navy landed you guys too far south."

"Yes, sir, maybe by five or six hundred yards. It opens up a terrible gap between us and 3rd Battalion, doesn't it?" said Spaulding.

"It sure as shit does. It gets worse. Our radio don't work and we can't reach regiment or the ships to let them know about the gap, and I doubt that they've figured it out yet. What about yours?"

Spaulding reached for a cigarette, couldn't find the pack, and instead tucked a wad of tobacco into his cheek from a pouch that he kept in his jacket pocket. "Sir, we've tried radio checks but haven't reached anyone. We can hear that the net is full of users, just no one's answering us. It's like the Tower of Babel."

Wranosky took a drink of water and spat. "Well, no one is reaching heaven this way either. Keep tryin' and we'll settle for regiment. Anyway, it's pretty confusing off the coast; the squids are redirecting traffic everywhere but where it belongs. I had a good sailor who took us down here, but I guess I lost about half the battalion staff in the process—including the XO and Ops. They'll catch up sometime later, don't know when. The real Blue Beach is being hit hard by artillery and there ain't nothin' landing there. It's a mess. So they've closed Blue Beach and Yellow Beach. Looks like Green and Red are the only ones receiving traffic. This will screw up our augmentation and the reception of heavy weapons. We were supposed to have the regimental cannon company ashore by now, but I don't think they'll make it for hours. The Shermans and the tank destroyers were supposed to be landing at daylight, but we probably won't see tank support until noon—who knows? All right, I'm taking a couple of your riflemen and heading left to Baker Company when we're done here. Take what I have of my staff with your company and we'll site my headquarters on the south side of the Solofrone by the bridge. Oh, one other thing. With comms the way that they are, if you need me, send a runner. Good luck."

"You too, sir. We'll see you at the bridge in about half an hour," said Spaulding.

0435 hours
Blue Beach South

As he continued to push inland, Sam was beginning to question the wisdom of leaving the beach. He was walking through ankle-deep stinking and stagnant water. Each step awoke a thousand mosquitoes. Back on the ship, James Lockridge had told him that first the ancient Greeks and then the Romans had forsaken this part of the Italian coast because of the mosquitoes. The Texans had been issued a cream reputed to repel the insect, but Sam was beginning to believe that the cream merely served to shore up their footing. Coming from South Texas, Sam was no stranger to the creatures, but his familiarity with the problem did not lend itself to nostalgia.

Sam stepped out of the pool he was in and gratefully stood on dry ground. He heard and partially witnessed Perkin's firefight, hoping that his cousin was okay. He'd seen Kulis move into the machine gun nest and had heard the rifle shots, although in the light he was unclear which soldier had taken the nest. He could also see 1st Platoon moving to catch up on his right. All of these observations were done in the strange light of the battlefield. When he was on the landing craft, it had been pitch black. But now there was a dim glow over the whole area and the low clouds slowly drifting over Paestum were reflecting the light from all the fires and the flares. He couldn't have read a compass or seen a watch with it, but it was enough light to move by.

Jim Lockridge, who had been part of the staff that had landed with Colonel Wranosky, fell in next to Sam. "Where's Perkin?" he asked.

Sam pointed over to his right, "First Platoon is that way. He was in a firefight earlier. Would you mind checking on him?"

Jim nodded and said, "I was headed that way anyhow. See ya."

Beyond Able Company, Sam had no conception of how the fight was progressing, but Colonel Wranosky's read on the battle was pretty grim. He was greatly concerned about the soldiers who had landed at the other beaches and knew they were catching hell. There was a great deal of noise coming from all directions as German artillery fire mixed in with the sounds of the big naval guns to their north. The mountains ringing the Gulf of Salerno echoed the sounds back onto the warriors in such a way that it became difficult to tell from what direction the firing originated. It was disorienting, but at least there was no one firing at his company.

Able Company came to a concrete drainage ditch running northeast to southwest—almost perpendicular to their path. As Sam was lowering himself into the ditch, he heard the chilling cries: "Armor! German tanks approaching from the north!"

The call was echoed by other soldiers along the ragged line of Texans. "Tigers! Tigers coming in from the north!" Sam looked to his left and then ahead but saw nothing. Over the sounds of the fighting on the beaches, he could hear the creak and squeal of moving armor. The noise was distinctive and one the soldiers had heard many times before—in training.

"Perkin! First Platoon!" Sam heard Bill Spaulding's strong voice booming over the marsh, "Armor coming in—maybe to the north or northeast." Without waiting for a reply, Spaulding turned to Lieutenant Anderson. "Len, get one bazooka team over to 3rd Platoon. Keep the other two here in the center. See that your machine guns get placed to cover our left and front. Remember—they'll have infantry in support of the tanks. First Sergeant, give 'em a hand and get the mortars sited further back towards the dunes. Everyone else—in the ditches!"

An airplane droned overhead and Sam's hopes rose momentarily for air support, but it was not to be. The German aircraft began dropping flares at several thousand feet over the length of the American beachfront. As ground-fired flares climbed into the sky and turned the battlefield into a surreal and shadowy version of daylight, Sam jumped out of the ditch and looked around. The land was nearly as flat as South Texas, with only scrub brush growing in its sandy soil. There was no protection at all except for the drainage ditches. All around him, soldiers were hitting the dirt or scrambling for a ditch. To his

right, Perkin's platoon was doing likewise. He turned to
help site the machine guns and the mortars.

0440 hours
Blue Beach South

Perkin had heard Captain Spaulding's warning of armor,
and like his cousin, he tried to see where the threat axis
was. He also started to look for cover for his troops, but
except for the small network of drainage ditches, there was
none. Perkin heard the sounds of tracks for the first time.
He turned towards the noise, staring hard to his north.
Emerging from the darkness and into the light of the flares
were four tanks. Still several hundred yards distant, the
tanks were moving along the south bank of a small stream,
effectively the northernmost boundary of 1st Battalion.

"There they are!" Sergeant Kenton yelled, pointing at
the tanks.

"Looks like the Germans found the gap between
battalions," said Perkin to his grim-faced platoon sergeant.
"Which way will they go? Towards us and our little group
or head to the beach and go after the landing site?"

"If I was them, sir, I'd tidy us up first and then move
to the big prize. They don't want us behind them. God
damn, they got here fast. They found our weak spot in an
hour in the dark. I reckon they sent the varsity to play."

Perkin took a deep breath, looking around to see what
else needed to be done. He was bouncing on the balls of
his feet as he looked over the battlefield and answered
Sergeant Kenton out of nervous habit. "What a match—
the Wehrmacht versus the Texas Gun Club! I almost feel
sorry . . . oh crap, here they come! Get the boys ready.
We're going to have to fight with grenades and rifles."

Kenton shook his head, swore, and moved off to see to
the troops.

The German tanks had indeed shown their hand. Four tanks turned left, spread out into a line and moved directly towards B Company to the left of Able Company. Behind the first tanks, Perkin could see another four panzers emerge onto the battlefield and behind them rumbled another three. Perkin turned to Jim Lockridge, moving with 1st Platoon, and said, "Jim, those ain't Tigers. I make them out to be Panzer IVs, you agree?"

"Yep, those are the new ones—complete with a long-barrel 75 millimeter main gun and two MG-34s." As if to accentuate Jim's point, the lead tank fired its main gun at a target to Perkin's left. "This ain't good, pardner. Any thoughts?"

"I was thinkin' about gettin' some breakfast . . . in Austin."

"Don't you wish. Look there. D'ya see there's no infantry with the tracks? I bet they don't have enough to go around yet and they're rushing the armor into the battle."

"I don't mind waiting."

The second set of tanks split off and crossed the stream to their right. Third Battalion was going to be hit as well. The remaining three panzers turned left, crossed 1st Battalion's front and headed for the Solofrone River. Several soldiers from the left side of the battalion line got up from the ground and started to sprint towards the south and possible sanctuary in the river. Simultaneously, the first set of tanks and German MG-42s sited four hundred yards away from the American line opened up. There was another and more extensive line of German defenses between the Texans and their objectives. The soldiers were cut down quickly and the volume of the fire coming from the tanks and the shore defenses was immense and intimidating.

0515 hours
Blue Beach South

Daylight was coming slowly to the battlefield. The sun was not yet up, but there was enough light to herald its imminent arrival. The fight was largely one-sided but not entirely. The four panzers worked over the northern end of the line pretty severely, and Sam was certain that there would be little left of Charlie and Baker companies. Able Company had lost contact with Frank McCarter's platoon as he'd moved left to get into ditches in the B Company area. So far, the other three tanks had just completed a quick recce of the river and then simply taken up position several hundred yards east-southeast of the company. Although Sam couldn't understand why they were not in the fight, he had no complaints. He knew that Perkin had sent a squad over to the river but had not heard any firing from his right, assuming that the squad was hugging the river bank for safety.

Without the Shermans or the M-10 tank destroyers, there was little in the riflemen's arsenal that was effective against tanks. The bazooka, their best weapon, was still fairly new to the battlefield and not considered very accurate at a range over one hundred yards. The soldiers had antitank grenades—handheld and rifle-fired—but these weren't effective against the armor on the Panzer IV without precise placement of the grenade. Still, for soldiers with limited means against armor, the Texans were fighting back bravely. At least one bazooka had made it into the fight, and Sam believed it was the team that had been sent to 3rd Platoon. He didn't see its launch but reacted to the whoosh of the rocket as it fired. The shaped-charge round hit a panzer at an angle on the turret with no apparent effect other than driving the tank out of range towards the German line. Other soldiers threw handheld antitank grenades at the armor and fired nonstop but ineffectually at the German armor with their rifles.

German mortars opened fire at this point, targeting past the American lines and then working back towards the soldiers in the ditches. Sam thought they were trying to flush the Americans out of their trenches for the tanks to finish them off. The Able Company mortars were responding in kind, but in the dim light and with the distance, the mortar crews had a hard time gauging the fall of their rounds. All the while, the tanks continued to go back and forth across the front of B and C Companies, firing machine guns and occasionally a main gun round. The panzers methodically swept the scrub brush with machine gun fire and tried to do the same with the irrigation ditches but with less success.

The soldiers of Able Company were trapped, and it was only a matter of time before German infantry arrived to support the armor. Once that support was gained and the antitank weapons of the Texans were eliminated or suppressed, the tanks would move. If the T-Patchers, as the Texans were known, tried to push forward towards their objectives, they would be cut down by the MG-42s deployed along the railway.* If they tried to get to the relative safety of the Solofrone, the tanks would easily catch them in the open. Only the lines of communication back to the beach remained open. Once the Germans decided to encircle the trapped troops, the battalion would be annihilated.

Inexplicably, the four panzers had not come far enough down the line to Able Company's position before turning back, but Captain Spaulding still kept yelling for his troops

---

*The Texans were called T-Patchers in reference to their divisional unit patch – a downward pointing arrowhead with a "T" for Texas centered in the arrowhead. The arrowhead represented Oklahoma, as the 36th was originally formed from the guard units from both states for service in WWI. After that war, the division was organized from Texas units.

to keep down. Most soldiers watched anyway. Spaulding himself had tried to make his way over to 3rd Platoon's ditch, but to get there he had to cross open ground. The German machine guns to the rear opened up on him immediately and he hit the deck, rapidly slithering back into his ditch.

The remaining three tanks from the first group withdrew to join the tank hit by the bazooka, which had taken up position behind the railway line. The sun was up, but as the Salerno plain was ringed by mountains to the east, long dark shadows accentuated the dimly lit region. Sam could see the railway bridge and the rail line—they were maybe five or six hundred yards from their first objective. When the tanks had retired from the battlefield—it was hardly fair to say they had retreated—the three tanks parked on the bank of the river began to move westerly along the bank of the Solofrone.

0630 hours
Blue Beach South

"They're movin', Lieutenant."

Sergeant Kenton's words were hardly necessary. As soon as the other tanks had withdrawn, the company's attention turned to the remaining three tanks. Perkin saw immediately what they intended to do—they were going to go down the river and then turn sharply onto his position. Unlike the other four tanks, which had cruised back and forth in front of the American positions like battleships on a gun line, he believed that these tanks would attempt to roll up the Texans by coming from the end of the line. Such an approach would allow them to fire directly down the length of the trench.

For the first time, the geography worked in the Texans' favor. The tanks did as Perkin expected and turned directly in line with 1st Platoon, but they had not gone more than twenty yards before the lead tank nosed into a marsh. The driver immediately tried reversing out of the marsh, but his left track spun wildly, throwing up mud but not moving the tank. The panzer was stuck. The second tank in line did not hesitate but swung out to the far right, avoiding both the stuck panzer and the marsh. The third tank moved cautiously in behind the first, and a crewman jumped out of the first tank. They were going to attempt to connect a cable and tow the stricken tank.

"Mortar! Get mortar fire on those tanks—kill the tanker! Cap'n Spaulding, we need a bazooka team! We can kill the stuck one, maybe both! Hurry!" yelled Perkin, as loud as he could. Every soldier in 1st Platoon opened fire, either at the stuck tank or at the approaching one. They really didn't have a good angle on the tank crewman who was frantically pulling the tow cable off the front of the third tank, but that didn't matter—they had something to shoot at. Perkin looked at the incoming tank, turned to see a bazooka team working its way up the ditch, then looked back at the stuck tank and its would-be savior. He was coming to a decision and needed to time his actions just right.

"Riflemen! Suppressing fire on the machine guns! Leave those tanks alone and keep the gunners' heads down." He turned to Sergeant Kenton. "Get the bazooka on it quick and keep the suppressin' fire on the MGs. Be right back."

Perkin shrugged off his pack, picked up his Thompson, and sprinted out of his ditch towards the inbound tank. As he ran, he felt the outside of his jacket pockets for grenades. He had two. He ran up to the left side of the panzer, matching its speed. There was an exterior open box welded on to the side of the tank below the turret that the crew used to store water jugs. Perkin grabbed the side of the box and swung himself onto the main deck of the tank.

For now, he was unnoticed by the other tanks— otherwise occupied—and so was hidden from view of the machine gunners. Breathing hard, he debated quickly between a grenade and his Thompson—he chose the Thompson. He flipped the safety off, stood up, grabbed the handle on the commander's hatch on the tank's turret, and pulled hard. Nothing. It was secured from inside the tank. He tried one of the side hatches to the panzer's turret. Nothing. Cursing, he tried the commander's hatch on the tank's turret, but it would not open. He looked around the panzer for a place he could wedge a grenade, not seeing one. Then he saw the tools clipped to the side of the tank—an axe, a sledge hammer, and a giant crow bar. Perkin slung his Thompson over his shoulder and pulled the heavy ten-kilogram sledge hammer from its clip on the side of the tank. Walking quickly to the front of the moving tank, he stood with one knee on the turret and one foot on the tank's deck. The Texan raised it high above his head and, with great violence, brought the hammer down hard on the driver's visor. The thick glass of the visor shattered and, amid shouts from inside the panzer, the tank immediately spun wildly to the right and began to head back towards the other tanks. Perkin dropped the hammer on the deck of the tank and pulled his Thompson off his shoulder. He slammed the barrel of the weapon into the cracked visor and pulled the trigger and held it down. The Thompson bucked hard in his hands—the barrel was wedged into the visor and wasn't going anywhere. When the magazine emptied, Perkin could hear screaming and more shouts from inside the tank. He also noticed he was now exposed to the German gun line. As the German gunners saw him on the tank and began to fire at him, he slung his Thompson, grabbed the sledge again and scampered over the turret to the right side of the tank. He smashed the massive hammer down hard onto the coaxial machine gun. He thought that the barrel bent slightly from the force of the hit, although he knew that was unlikely—one more to go. He was about to smash the other machine gun when he heard the commander's hatch opening. Perkin spun around and saw a hand with a Luger in it begin to emerge from the open crack of the hatch.

As the Luger fired wildly, Perkin swung the sledge hammer down again, this time hitting the hatch lid as hard as he could. The tank commander screamed and dropped his pistol, his hand nearly severed at the wrist. Perkin dropped the hammer on the deck of the tank and began reaching for a grenade—but he was too slow. The tanker, rightly believing that his crew's survival depended on quickly securing his hatch, withdrew his mangled hand and slammed the hatch shut. Perkin grabbed the Luger and stuffed it down the front of his jacket before reaching for the handle of the sledge hammer. He was losing time; they were getting to the end of the American line and too close to the other tanks. He turned and slammed the other MG-34 protruding from the turret. He could not see any damage to its barrel, but the gun slew wildly on its mount. Grinning fiercely, he bid *auf Wiedersehen* to the German crew by pounding the sledge once more against the commander's hatch. He hopped off the tank and, as a parting gesture, tossed the German sledge into the main gear of the tracks sprinting back to his ditch. As he ran towards his platoon, his eyes tracked a bazooka round as its rocket sped towards the stuck tank. There was a small explosion followed instantly by a much larger one as the shaped-charge penetrated the tank's hull and detonated the onboard ammunition. The force of the explosion knocked Perkin off his feet, sliding

him headfirst into the safety of the American trench.
The third tank quickly reversed behind the smoke and
flames, and the two remaining tanks left the battlefield.
This time, they retreated.

0715 hours
Blue Beach South

Lieutenant Colonel Wranosky had watched Perkin's
battle with the panzer from the Baker Company trench
and was absolutely delighted with its outcome. But like
the other spectators, he hadn't expected Perkin to survive.
He sprinted over the gap in the ditches to Able Company
just to be able to express his feelings to the lieutenant in
person.

"You are the dumbest son of a bitch I ever met," said
Lieutenant Colonel Wranosky with a broad grin. "If
I live through this war, I'll dine on this story for years.
The day I saw a German tank forced off the battlefield
with a sledge hammer. Ha ha! Jesus Christ." He turned to
Bill Spaulding, still shaking his head, "That's what your
team is gonna be known as from now on, 'The Hammers.'
Goddamn! That was fine work. Perk, you sit yourself
down and recover. After they lick their wounds, they'll be
back. Bill, let's talk about what's next."

Captain Spaulding slapped Perkin on the back before
he and the battalion commander huddled in the trench.
Perkin was being congratulated by his troops, but the
exhilaration was wearing off and he was a little nauseous.
His hands were shaking and he couldn't stop them, so he
sat down in the ditch with his back to the wall, crossed
his arms, and hid his hands. Jim Lockridge came over and
sat down next to his friend but said nothing. After a few
minutes of silence, he asked with a kind smile, "Still want
some breakfast?"

"I ain't hungry anymore."

"By the way, what did you think of my briefing the other day?" asked the intelligence officer.

"I'm sorry, what? Your briefing?"

"Yeah, my briefing. Maybe you haven't been paying attention to the war, but I think it's fair to say it was the highlight of the campaign so far. Nothing else has really caught my eye yet, how 'bout you? That's what gonna win the war for us—application of precise intelligence, not brute force. I watched you beat that tank nearly to death with your little mallet. That's such a nineteenth-century approach. Never win a war like that today." Jim laughed, "Jesus Christ, Perk, you scared the shit out of me! No one back in Austin will believe it, although if that little blond coed you liked so much had seen it, she might finally lift her skirt for you. There seems to be a hammer analogy there as well, but it escapes me."

Perkin smiled back at his friend, "I doubt it. I think she's tougher than the Germans. Certainly meaner. I gotta say though, it scared the shit out of me too. Look." He held up his still shaking hands for Jim's examination. "I'm shakin' like a dog trying to shit a peach pit. Oh, and since you asked, that was a fine briefing. I'm sure that the tribal elders in Kermit will pass the story down around the campfire for generations, but I hope you ain't trying to tell me this is an intel success story here."

"Well, we know that there are only two assessments about any battle: an operational success or an intelligence failure. Jury's still out here. What do you have in your rations? I have a can of brown stuff and a can of green stuff—got another color to trade?"

Sam had watched Perkin's assault on the tank and was appalled at the risk he took. He knew that it came with the job, but watching his cousin on the tank had filled him with an anxiety worse than his wedding day—a day on which he shook almost as severely as his cousin had after the tank attack. At the same time, he was terribly proud of Perkin. He knew that Perk had turned the tide of that skirmish, but he also knew they weren't done yet.

"Lieutenant?"

Sam looked over and saw Sergeant Younger. "What's up?"

"The battalion CO and Cap'n Spaulding want to see all A Company officers. I'll scoot over there and see if I can find Lieutenant McCarter." The standards were changing quickly; ten minutes prior it would have been unthinkable to sprint between ditches.

Sam worked his way down the shallow trench, not even ducking as a mortar round exploded forty yards ahead of the company line. In the span of a few hours he had become an expert in judging the proximity of an incoming round. Several had come close, but so far his platoon had not taken any casualties since leaving the beach. He didn't expect it to remain that way.

As Sam reached the provisional company command post, which happened to be wherever Bill Spaulding was standing, he saw the colonel, Bill, Jim, and Perkin all crouched and talking. He squatted next to Perkin and offered his hand and a smile. "So, heard any good jokes lately?"

Perkin's face lit up at the sight of his cousin. "Well, as a matter of fact I have. Two Aggies and a nun walk into a bar . . ."

To Sam's great disappointment, what happened to the two Aggies and the nun would remain a mystery. A burst of machine gun fire heralded the arrival of Lieutenant McCarter, who had sprinted the distance from the B Company position, where his platoon had taken shelter. Of all the Able Company officers present, Frank looked the worst. He was pale and had blood smeared on his jacket but appeared uninjured. He moved to the other officers, careful not to present a further target to the German machine gunners.

"Sir." He nodded to Colonel Wranosky and looked around at the group of officers.

"Welcome to modern maneuver warfare, boys," said Wranosky dryly. "We cain't move out on this here ground until those machine guns are eliminated. There's just no cover between us and them, so we stay put. There'll be no goin' over the top nonsense if we can avoid it. I'd bet Perkin's paycheck we're gonna get hit by another counterattack soon. So we're going to set up our own little fort and defend this ground as if it were sacred. Perkin, what's your hometown? We'll name our fort after it."

"Oh, thank you sir," Perkin replied. "But how about naming it after one of the homes of the enlisted guys? I've got a soldier that took out an MG-42 nest single-handedly, and he saved my life in the process."

"Perfect—where's he from?"

Perkin avoided eye contact with Bill Spaulding, who was trying to wave him off. "I can't remember sir," he said innocently. "He's right over there. Kulis, come here for a moment."

As Kulis was crawling over to the officers, Lieutenant Colonel Wranosky mildly took Perkin to task. "You should know where every one of your soldiers comes from. Ah, Private Kulis—I understand that you took out a Spandau this morning."

Kulis, thinking that he was in trouble with the battalion commander for killing the wounded soldiers, squirmed but gave the only possible answer. "Yes, sir."

Wranosky smiled benevolently and said, "Great work, son. We're gonna name our little outpost here after your hometown in your honor. Would that be okay?"

Kulis smiled shyly and said, "Oh, yes, sir! The folks back home will think it's a real hoot. I mean, they'd . . . I'd . . . be really pleased."

"All right then, on behalf of the 1st Battalion, 141st Infantry, I proclaim this to be Fort, uh . . ."

"Rosebud, sir."

Wranosky's smile faltered slightly. "Rosebud?"

"Yes, sir. It's in Falls County," Kulis added helpfully.

"Yes, of course." Wranosky debated with himself for a moment about telling Kulis he couldn't ask soldiers to die defending a fort named Rosebud, but after looking at the boy's hopeful face, he decided he would keep the proclamation of Fort Rosebud confined to Able Company. "Well, Fort Rosebud it is then. Good work, soldier."

After Kulis had left, Wranosky turned on Perkin. "You asshole. You set me up, didn't you? If you hadn't earned your pay this morning, I'd have you digging my latrine and wiping my ass for the rest of the war." He started laughing. "Rosebud? Ah, shit. I have to say that's damn funny and just the kind of smartass crap I pulled as a lieutenant." He looked Perkin squarely in the eye and, as he quit laughing, said, "Let's hope this day goes better than the first Battle of Rosebud." At the questioning look on Perkin's face, Wranosky said with an air of friendly superiority, "Ain't you the historian? Appears you're not as smart as you thought. Look it up and get back to me." He turned back to the rest of the officers, saying dryly, "Alright, if Lou Costello here is done making jokes at the expense of the man who holds his life in his hands, then let's get to it. Bill, how many bazooka and mortar rounds left?"

"Three and four respectively, sir. What about the other companies?"

"Charlie's Weapons Platoon caught up to them. Baker's did not. I don't know where Dog Company is. I suppose that Charlie's in the same boat as Able. I'm gonna go down with the S-2 when we're done here and we'll find out. This is what I want you to do: save the mortar rounds for next time they come in case they bring infantry. Preserve our .30 cals for the same. Don't fire the bazooka rounds until the tanks are close enough that you can't miss. Try and get some boys back to the beach and bring up ammo, particularly mortar and bazooka rounds. They'll have to crawl most of the way so get 'em going soon. If our position is completely overrun, try and make it to the river and cross over. Any word from your squad?"

"No, sir," replied Captain Spaulding.

"If they radio in, have them see if their sniper can start working on the German gunners from the bank of the Solofrone, otherwise have them scout out Agropoli." Wranosky became more formal. "Okay, I need to go, but give me a rundown on casualties. Lieutenant Berger?"

"None since the beach, sir. There we had two evacuees. Again, no word on 1st Squad."

"Lieutenant Taft?"

"Three wounded, none requiring evacuation."

"Lieutenant McCarter—you have 3rd Platoon now?"

"Yes, sir. Counting Lieutenant Brown, six dead and fourteen wounded. At least a third of those require evacuation. We were with Baker Company—well, you were there, you know. They're in about the same shape." Frank, close to tears, couldn't bring himself to look Colonel Wranosky in the eyes. His head was down and he was staring at his leggings.

The other officers were silent for a moment as they wondered which soldiers might have been killed or wounded. As the 36th was a National Guard division, most of the men had soldiered together for years—in some cases for more than a decade. Although the war and the call-up for federal duty had brought an influx of outsiders—

some of whom were conscripts from other states—these casualties might be friends, neighbors, or kin from back home. Wranosky himself was an outsider—he was regular army and from Alabama. Although he'd never been in combat before, he understood the relationship that soldiers have with each other and had a feel for the dynamics of the National Guard. To him, the common state ties and bonds of kith and kin were both the greatest strength of the guard and its greatest weakness. Unconsciously echoing a thought of Sam's from several years before, Wranosky believed that the men enjoyed being with fellow Texans and wanted to share their experiences with friends and neighbors. Wranosky had found the *esprit de corps* of the 36th Division to be incredible—much higher than most regular army units he'd been in—but he'd always been concerned with what would happen when the Texans started taking casualties.

"Frank," Wranosky said, not unkindly. "You head on back with me now. The men are going to be looking to you to set an example, so don't take this loss personally or as a reflection of your leadership. War is like this, and good folks get killed. Your boys can take care of the dead and dying as best they can while you focus on preparing them for the next attack. There'll be one." He turned back to Captain Spaulding. "Bill, you and your Hammers help me hold Rosebud. There ain't much we can do against panzers if they actually decide to punch through, but if all you've got is a hammer, well, then all the world looks like a fuckin' nail, don't it? I'm gonna send runners from the other end of the line to the beach, looking to secure artillery support and ammo as well, but get yours going. I'll be back later to check on you." With that, Wranosky motioned to Frank McCarter and Jim Lockridge, and they began to work their way up the line to Baker Company.

0755 hours
Yellow Beach

When three soldiers of Able Company, led by Sergeant Bill Kenton, got to the beach seeking artillery support and ammunition, they nearly turned back to the relative safety of Fort Rosebud. Kenton sighted the still-standing Lone Star flag and, had he been a literary man, might have viewed it as the ensign flying at the gates of hell in lieu of Dante's sign warning those who enter. Once past his company's landing site, the carnage on the beaches was horrific—and the slaughter was continuing. German artillery alternated between targeting the landing craft and shelling the beaches. Destroyed landing craft rocked back and forth in the surf; some of the Higgins boats—scorched and still smoking—had shattered bow ramps and shredded and perforated hulls. They passed a steady stream of wounded men working their way to the beach from 3rd Battalion, while yet another, much smaller stream of soldiers headed inland. Kenton saw dozens of soldiers wounded and seated on the edge of the dunes, some taking care of each other, and some lying listlessly, waiting for help. A glance at a long line of boot soles showing from underneath tarps indicated the number of dead Texans.

As they made their way up the beach, Kenton spied a medic sitting in the water next to a destroyed landing craft with his head in his hands. Kenton almost moved past the soldier, but the image of the boots under the tarp made him stop.

"Mac, you gotta get up. There's people here who need you." Kenton said as he squatted down next to the medic.

The soldier looked up at him, and Kenton saw streaks of tears cutting lines through the grime on his face. The soldier nodded but didn't make a move. Thinking perhaps the soldier was shirking, Kenton asked him where his platoon was. The soldier took a deep breath, pointed his thumb behind him at the landing craft, and said, "Sarge, we beached right in front of a machine gun nest." Kenton's head turned toward the dunes, but he saw nothing. "When they dropped the ramp, I could see the German gunner's face. He was that close. I thought I was dead. But you know what he did? He pointed to his helmet, then at his sleeve, and waved me off the boat." The medic fingered the Red Cross armband on his left sleeve. "When I was out of the way, he opened fire on my platoon."

Kenton walked to the front of the landing craft and looked in—there were too many bodies to count. The sailors were dead at their stations in the back of the craft, the soldiers had fallen backwards and were stacked like fallen dominoes. Kenton turned away and vomited. He'd never before seen the effects of machine guns on human bodies; the destruction was beyond anything he'd imagined. The twisted and tangled young American bodies would become a snapshot of war forever burned into his memory. After he spat the bile from his mouth, he stopped his two soldiers from looking in for themselves. Kenton realized he had to keep going, or he too would end up sitting down and crying.

"I'm sorry, buddy. What happened to the gunner?"

"He was hit by his own artillery right after this. He was too close to the beach."

Kenton got the soldier standing, put his arm around the medic's shoulders, and used his body to block the soldier's view as he walked him past the landing craft and his dead friends. When they had moved up the beach another fifty yards, Kenton steered the medic towards an aid station, where medical personnel were sending the severely wounded out to the ships on returning landing craft. The walking wounded were being patched up and returned to their units. "Get in there and help them out, you can find your company later. Good luck, Mac."

Amid the chaos—the continued German shelling, the rifle fire, and the shouts and the cries—Kenton began to get oriented to the battle. Blue Beach North remained closed, and there was virtually no activity left at Blue Beach South. Yellow Beach was also closed and being shelled regularly. From what Kenton could gather from his vantage point, the beach he supposed was Green Beach was open but under so much fire that most assault shipping was turning further north to Red Beach. Only Red Beach appeared to be fully open.

Out to sea, Kenton watched as an American destroyer pulled within two thousand yards of the beach and opened fire at targets ashore. Although he was over a mile away from the ship, he was awed by its power. Until, that is, a British monitor joined the firing line. Then Kenton got a soldier's appreciation for what is perhaps the purest application of sea power. The monitor, HMS *Abercrombie*, was a slow-moving gunship with a single main turret mounting two 15-inch battleship guns forward of its superstructure. The ship slowly moved into position and turned parallel to the shore. Even at twenty-five hundred yards, Kenton could make out the barrels of the main battery. As the big 15-inch guns opened fire, the sergeant could feel the force of its guns even from where he was standing on the beach. Kenton fancied he could follow the rounds as they screamed overhead, and he turned inland to see if he could mark where the rounds landed. There was no question that he could as a mountainside exploded in fire and smoke. Kenton and a thousand soldiers cheered as the fire quickly slackened on the beaches—not because Abercrombie had destroyed a German battery; it would have been extremely lucky for its first salvo to take out a German position—but because German artillery immediately shifted fire to the warships. Kenton was unaware of this and believed that the monitor was making short work of the enemy artillery, and it was with growing optimism that he and his soldiers walked up to the 141st RCT's command post. The vision of the landing craft was compartmented away for now.

"God bless the navy," he said to another sergeant who was also watching the ships' fire.

"Not our navy, buddy. That's the Royal Navy making all the noise. The destroyer is ours though."

"No shit? Well, God bless his royal highness, King George the Third. Where's the ops officer?"

The sergeant was on the verge of explaining that the sovereign of the British Empire was actually three Georges later, but after looking Kenton over, said, "Ops is busy, you can talk to him." He pointed to a captain sitting at a small fold-up desk under camouflage netting. The captain stood up with a leather-encased thermos in his hand as Sergeant Kenton approached, a stack of papers on the desk behind him held down by the magazine from the officer's M-1 carbine. He moved to walk past Kenton, but the large sergeant sidestepped to stand directly in front of him.

"Move, sergeant. I need to get some coffee," the captain said.

Kenton looked the captain over. He saw a square jaw, black eyes, a thin black mustache, and straight white teeth. He was, Kenton observed, one of the few soldiers almost as tall as himself. The officer had movie star looks and resembled a matinee idol in his impeccable uniform. Kenton immediately marked him as a candy-ass—one of those officers who try to get close to the front so they can say they were "there" but not so close that he might actually have to fight. *He must be feeling quite inconvenienced today*, thought Kenton.

"Sir, I'm Sergeant Kenton from Able Company. I have a message from Colonel Wranosky, and I need to see Colonel Jamison or the operations officer."

"Need? What you need to do, Sergeant, is get out of my way. It's been a long morning, and I *need coffee*."

"Please sir!" Sergeant Kenton was insistent. "1st Battalion is pinned down and under repeated armor attack. They need the tank destroyers or at least artillery support and immediate resupply!"

"Look," the officer said, sighing dramatically. "I'm not used to explaining myself to sergeants, but you can see our situation here. The assault wave hasn't done its job, and we'll have to evacuate the regimental headquarters if we don't get a break. I am aware of Lieutenant Colonel Wranosky and 1st Battalion's problems, but the whole damned beachhead's in danger of collapsing. I'm afraid there's nothing we can do. Now, get out of my way!"

Furious, Sergeant Kenton spun around and began calling at the top of his lungs: "Colonel Jamison! Colonel Jamison!"

"Over here!"

Kenton looked up the beach some thirty yards and saw his regimental commander and the operations officer standing next to another table—this one covered with a large map. The operations officer was yelling into the handset of a walkie-talkie but was evidently having trouble establishing contact with his party. He slammed the handset down and shook his head at Jamison.

Colonel Jamison looked up as the large sergeant approached his desk. Both Kenton and Jamison had red hair and florid complexions, but there the physical similarities ended. Jamison was of medium height and as slender as the sergeant was large, but he looked every inch a soldier. Kenton had met the regimental commander only once before. When he'd been promoted to sergeant, Jamison had shaken Kenton's hand and told him to set an example for his soldiers and always do what he thought was right.

The operations officer, a major, tried to head off Sergeant Kenton, but Kenton brushed past him heading for the regimental commander.

"Sergeant," Jamison said impatiently. "What's up?"

"Sir, Kenton from Able Company. I'm here as a runner for Colonel Wranosky and Captain Spaulding."

Jamison relaxed visibly and said, "Thank God. We've had no contact with 1st Battalion since the landing—we were just trying again to reach them. Give me what you've got and then let's take a look at the map. We'll figure out how to support your boys." He looked over and saw the tall captain standing in the background and said with evident distain, "Ebbins, if you don't have anything better to do, get the sergeant and me some coffee."

Kenton smiled, deciding to stir the pot a little, "Sir, I take it then that you're not going to evacuate your headquarters?" He inclined his head towards Captain Ebbins.

"What? Hell no! Is that what that fuc . . . er, um, the captain . . . excuse me, Sergeant." Jamison turned to take a message handed to him by an orderly. He took the message over to his ops officer and turned back saying, "Third Battalion is under armor attack on its right flank again. We need to make this quick, Kenton."

"Yes, sir. We were landed in the wrong place, so there is a gap of several hundred yards between 1st and 3rd battalions. This morning, they sent fifteen or so Panzer IVs down the gap, and then some turned in and hit 3rd Batt; some turned out and hit us. If this attack is on 3rd Battalion's right flank, I bet 1st Battalion is getting hit again as well!"

0930 hours
Fort Rosebud

Sergeant Kenton was right. The Germans counterattacked, were driven off, and then counterattacked again for a second time within the hour. This time, they sent five tanks directly against the center of the 1st Battalion line. Again, the line held and four tanks left the battlefield, but not before Baker Company and the 3rd Platoon of Able Company sustained additional casualties. It took two bazooka shots from Able Company's Weapons Platoon to destroy the one tank and a third round fired at another tank missed altogether. Ammunition was running short where it counted—the bazooka rounds. Nothing else could penetrate the panzers' armor—certainly not the rifles or machine guns, nor even the rifle-fired antitank grenades. The bazookas had definitely caught the attention of the panzer troops, but the diminished rate of bazooka firings told them that ammunition must be running low.

The four tanks did not quit the battlefield entirely. After withdrawing several hundred yards, the tanks turned and faced the American positions. The message was clear—no one would get past the German tanks. They were positioned to charge into the battalion's line at a moment's notice.

Sam looked at the tanks and walked over to Private Pfadenhauer, his second squad sniper and the best in the company, perhaps the entire regiment. Pfadenhauer came from a third-generation German-American family from a small German-speaking community in the Texas Hill Country northwest of San Antonio. In addition to being an outstanding marksman, he was one of the company's four German speakers.

"Howie," Sam used Pfadenhauer's nickname. Like every other slow-talking Texan, he found it more expedient to avoid the private's surname. "What do you reckon is the distance to those tanks?"

The soldier squinted at the tanks, looking at each one through his rifle's scope. "This 'un here is closest. About five hundred yards. The others are more. That 'un down yonder is just shy of six hundred yards I think. They've moved back past where the machine guns had been." Between assaults, the Germans had relocated their machine guns further back and closer to the railroad. Sam hadn't seen any need for the Germans to do so, and he suspected that artillery would be coming soon; they wanted to avoid being caught by a short-falling round. That still did not give much advantage to the Texans; the land was flat and, following a morning of fighting, was devoid of cover except for the drainage ditches. Quite simply, the riflemen of the 1st Battalion remained pinned down in the middle because they had no place to go until the Germans were driven away.

"Feel like a little bet?" Sam asked.

Pfadenhauer grinned, "Yes, sir." The platoon saw Sam as an easy source for cigarettes as he frequently bet or traded the pack from his rations for chewing gum.

"Here's what I think: the Germans will get bored in a few minutes, and one or all of them will pop the hatch so they can smoke. Maybe even come out of the turret to taunt us a little. Here's the bet, no make that bets. First, that they'll do just that. Second, that you can't hit 'em when they do."

Pfadenhauer thought for a second and said, "Well, there's a problem there, sir. If they come out, I owe you a pack, and if I hit 'em, then you give it back to me. That don't seem like much incentive."

Sam closed his eyes and mentally traced the wager. Pfadenhauer was right. "Ah yeah, I see your point. But if we don't have the first bet, there's no reward for me."

"Except for the knowledge of a job well done, sir." Pfadenhauer had been waiting for a long time to throw one of the lieutenant's favorite sayings back at him. "That ought to be reward enough for any officer. Here's my counteroffer: if he pops his head up and I miss, I'll give you my gum. If I get him—and I'm sure you understand this is a shot that Sergeant York would decline—I get two packs of smokes. Deal?"

Sam agreed to the terms and Bill Spaulding took out his field glasses and spotted for the sniper. Meanwhile, Pfadenhauer placed his pack on the side of the ditch and rested his beloved 1903 Springfield on the little mound. Pfadenhauer moved his crosshairs back and forth between the tanks and waited patiently.

At the same time, Sam took his M-1 and began to turn the elevation knob on the sights—counting the clicks as he went. It would be a fairly long shot for the scoped Springfield and an exceptionally long shot for the M-1 through aperture sights, but Sam was an exceptional marksman and had been one long before he joined the guard. Growing up, he and Perkin had spent countless hours on the Taft Ranch with small caliber rifles shooting at everything from tin cans to armadillos (which they called "Hoover Hogs"), and Old Perkin had taken the boys hunting for deer and javelina countless times. Both Bergers were good shots, but Sam was something special with a rifle, and Perkin had long since quit trying to compete with his cousin. In all modesty, Sam believed that there was not a better shot in the regiment—except perhaps Pfadenhauer. He'd toyed with the idea of taking the Springfield away from his sniper and trying it for himself, but he didn't want to undermine the young private. Besides, he had the Garand—the weapon he believed would win the war.

Two years earlier, he'd been a volunteer evaluator during an army competition between the M1941 Johnson semiautomatic rifle and the M-1 Garand. He loved the Johnson and thought it to be a marginally superior weapon, but he recognized that the Garand made more sense as it was already in production. Despite having

written Captain Melvin Johnson, USMCR (Inactive) two
letters asking him for an M1941 rifle to keep, a request
which remained unfulfilled, he was also a big fan of the
Garand. It packed a serious punch, was very accurate, and
could be loaded and reloaded quickly by someone with
thorough training and a calloused thumb. It was, he had
always believed, far superior to the other options available
to him as a platoon leader—the lighter M-1 carbine or
Thompson submachine gun. Had he chosen either of
those two weapons, the shot he was planning to make
would not have been possible.

The minutes drifted by, and the attention and interest
of the platoon began to wane. Some soldiers took
advantage of the lull in the fighting to pull out canned
rations and eat for the first time since chowing down on
the ship the night before. Other soldiers inspected their
weapons and checked and rechecked their ammunition.
Everyone fought a battle with the mosquitoes; Sam had
expected them to diminish once the sun was out in force,
but they did not. *Maybe they like the taste of the newcomers,*
he thought. His father had once hosted British guests
at the ranch, and they were absolutely savaged by what
some called the state bird of Texas, while the Texans went
largely unmolested.

While the warriors on both sides at Fort Rosebud took
a breather, the fighting beyond their immediate battlefield
continued unabated. The soldiers in the drainage ditches
noted for the first time the presence of combat aircraft
over the battlefield. The sound and the sight of aircraft
brought a spike in their morale as they had been promised
air support—surely it was only a matter of time before
the P-38 Lightnings made short work of the Germans
blocking their advance. The lift in morale was only
momentary as the German aircraft swooped down over
the beaches and bombed and strafed the soldiers there.

"On my command, suppressing fire!" Captain Spaulding called out. One of his sharp-eyed soldiers had just pointed out a platoon-sized party of American soldiers working their way to the company position from the dunes. He wanted to be prepared to suppress the machine guns if necessary, but not tip the Germans that more troops were inbound.

"Cap'n! I have a target!" Pfadenhauer had seen the hatch open on the most distant tank and was sighting in on the tank commander as he stood up in the tank turret, binoculars in hand.

"Take him!"

Pfadenhauer fired first. The .30-06 caliber bullet hit the tank commander in the chest, passing through his heart. A split second later another .30-06 round fired from Sam's M-1 tore through his throat as the already dead tanker was sliding back into the tank through the hatch.

Most of the soldiers could not see the result of the shot, but they exulted as the tank reversed and quickly crossed over the railroad. The soldiers laughed as they saw Lieutenant Taft reach into his pack and pull out two packs of Raleigh cigarettes that he'd been saving for barter. He tossed them to the young private, who rather than thanking the rancher, set to complaining to his platoon commander.

"Oh, come on, sir—I had him. There was no need for you to shoot. I got him clean through the heart. That was a great shot, but there was no need for you to shoot his head off," he repeated.

"I know. I saw the whole thing. That's why I gave you the smokes. If I'd *had* to shoot, you'd be giving me your gum now," Sam said untruthfully. As good as Sam's eyesight was, he was not even sure whether the first round hit or not, and he did not really care. He had intended to ensure that the tank commander paid a price on behalf of the panzer corps for that morning's slaughter of the Texans.

1005 hours
Fort Rosebud

Lieutenant Colonel Wranosky read the handwritten note from Colonel Jamison, which had been handed to him by Sergeant Kenton. The soldiers that came up behind Able Company were led by Kenton and included his two original soldiers and about thirty "lost" soldiers from various companies that he had rounded up on the beach. Each soldier carried additional ammunition or water, and for the time being, 1st Battalion was flush with new bazookas and bazooka and mortar ammunition. He figured Wranosky would be happy to make his apologies to the soldiers' parent units later on.

After reading through the note once, Wranosky read the abbreviated message aloud for the Able Company officers: "Bob, understand 1st Battalion situation. Hold Rosebud! Ha, ha. Advance objectives when possible. Fight stabilizing, but 141st focus of enemy effort. My priority is 3rd Battalion right flank. 2nd Battalion has landed on left flank. 143rd landing. Cannon company landed, operational soon. Will request naval fires on enemy posit vicinity railroad ASAP. Kenton swell G.I. See you this PM. Good work/luck, Tony."

"Sergeant Kenton?" Wranosky waved him over.

"Sir?"

"Good work. I owe you one. Thanks. And thanks for the coffee—it's mighty welcome."

On his return, Kenton had given the note and a leather-wrapped vacuum flask filled with steaming coffee to the battalion commander, mumbling something about "courtesy of the regimental staff." Wranosky had been around the block a time or two and he knew when to ask sergeants questions and when not to. He mused inwardly that it might be best to tuck the thermos away from regimental view in the future, but he thought he might just hang on to it as a memento of this historic day. Kenton had also informed the battalion commander that on his own initiative, he had solicited an aid station and stashed another dozen walking-wounded volunteers back in the dunes with two bazookas as insurance against a German run on the beachhead. A not-quite-walking lieutenant from 3rd Battalion with bloody bandages covering his head and his right eye volunteered to go along, and two other soldiers helped carry the wounded officer. Kenton also had "acquired" two Handie-Talkies, leaving one with the group in the dunes, but the battalion was still unable to establish comms with regiment.

Wranosky divided the thirty soldiers up between the companies, with Baker Company getting the lion's share. "I'm not waiting for the navy to hit these assholes. I want to open mortar fire in five minutes on the Kraut machine gun nests—use no more than half the rounds. Let's see if we can tempt the tanks in to shut us up and we'll bag a few more with the new bazookas. If not, we'll begin to advance and force the issue."

Five minutes later, the mortars were prepped and ready to fire. So were the bazooka teams—the little trap was set. Wranosky gave the command and the battalion's four remaining mortars opened fire from the dunes. The German gunners returned fire momentarily and then fell silent.

Perkin watched the challenge unfold with his new field glasses—they were truly excellent binoculars. The German nests were not eliminated though; one crew of two soldiers picked up their weapon and ran to the far side of the railroad. A second crew of three soldiers quickly followed suit. Once behind the embankment, Perkin could no longer see the German soldiers, but he assumed that they were setting up to fire from the other side of the tracks. The decision was made to force the issue.

Able Company's 1st and 2nd Platoons advanced first. Captain Spaulding waved the company forward, and both platoons sprinted forward thirty yards to the next drainage ditch. The panzers opened fire with their machine guns but stayed in place. No one was injured. Perkin looked about and saw little different about his new position other than it was closer to the Germans. *Not really* an improvement, he thought. The machine guns had moved back some fifty yards, but then the company moved thirty yards closer. The move also did not bring the Germans appreciably closer to bazooka range. Until the rest of the battalion moved up, Able Company was more isolated and vulnerable than before.

"Kenton, why aren't the panzers coming for us?" Perkin asked.

"Probably had their fill of the bazookas, sir."

"Let's hope so, but I wonder . . ."

"Wonder what, Lieutenant?"

"Well, they've had us pinned all morning. So, why not just come in and finish us off? The answer is that they're waitin' for something—but what? Are the panzers going to withdraw and then hit us with artillery, or are they waiting for infantry?"

As happens so frequently in war, the moment a question is formulated, the answer is given. The Germans were waiting for infantry support. The Texans had enjoyed a slight advantage as long as their antitank ammunition held out and the Germans only mounted lukewarm attacks. That advantage was negated when enemy infantry joined the fight in support of the armor because the infantry could eliminate or suppress the bazooka teams while engaging the Americans in the ditches.

As Perkin watched with his German binoculars, at least two platoons of panzer grenadiers—elite German infantry assigned to armor or mechanized infantry divisions— joined the tanks. He twisted around to look at the rest of the battalion behind him. "This is it," Perkin said to no one in particular. "We can suppress the infantry, but we'll have to come out of the ditch to do it."

"Hold your fire! Let 'em get close! Rifles on infantry, bazookas on armor." Bill Spaulding ran crouched over along the Able Company ditch. "We'll be hit first, let's make it count."

The three tanks pulled slowly ahead of the infantry, which trotted behind. A squad of soldiers split from the rest and headed towards the bridge paralleling the railroad. As they approached the river, they turned right and began to work their way along the tree line on the river bank. The fourth tank reappeared over the railroad and moved up to shield the infantry along the tree line. Together, they would block any exit to the river, and when the opportunity presented itself, the Germans would try to turn the flank of the American line.

1025 hours
Right Bank, Solofrone River

Corporal Roberto Pena had been in the weeds lining the river bank of the Solofrone River for almost an hour when he heard the soldier splashing down the river. It seemed like a lifetime ago when he and the other ten men of his squad had completed their reconnaissance of the river. They had discovered that the river was fordable by soldiers, but would be difficult for armored vehicles to cross. It was about three feet deep and had steep banks.

The squad had been preparing to return to the company when the first German armored assault against the battalion began in the darkness, provoking a fierce argument among the soldiers of the squad. Some wanted to join the fight against the tanks, even though the heaviest weapon in the squad was a Browning Automatic Rifle, called a BAR by the soldiers. Others, including Pena, felt that they would not contribute much to the fight in the field and thought that they should continue on to their objectives.

Pena was not shy about exercising his new authority as squad leader. He could see no infantry in support of the German attack—the only target they could reasonably engage—and therefore he decided that they should move on. He took his squad across the Solofrone, soaking his Handie-Talkie when he stumbled midstream in the process, and came to another decision. Pena had been told to meet the platoon at the bridge, but he also knew that Agropoli was its ultimate objective. He reckoned, however, that Agropoli was about three or four miles from his crossing site, and he did not want to be that far away from the company. So he made an internal compromise. There was a high hill that they could climb—from there he could see both the fate of his company and possibly check for Germans in the village.

On the other side of the bridge, the railroad took a sharp turn towards the sea and before long it curved back south around the hill and ran through Agropoli. As the squad approached the tracks, they came across the unmistakable signs—tread marks of armor and the detritus of soldiers—of a recently abandoned laager, but they did not see any German soldiers. *Perhaps,* Pena thought, *this was the bivouac site of the panzers that attacked the company.* They very cautiously crossed first the railway and then the road connecting Agropoli to Highway 18.

They began the climb up the wooded hill; although it was small by Italian standards—rising about eight hundred feet from its base—it was high by a flatlander's standards. Pena came from Cuero, Texas, which has few hills and none this high. The corporal nevertheless set a punishing pace that had the soldiers sweating and breathing hard. It was to be the first of many such climbs for the Texans in Italy.

Once at the summit of the hill, the 1st Squad of the 1st Platoon of Able Company had the best view of any Allied soldiers of the first American battle on the mainland of Europe in a quarter of a century. They had reached the top after sunrise, and before them stretched out the panorama of the Salerno plain and the varied battlefields. Pena and his soldiers were amazed at the sight of scores of ships in the gulf, the hive of activity on the beaches and the noise echoing off the mountains. That the Texas Army was having a tough time was apparent from the hilltop. German artillery continued to crash down at the water's edge, destroying landing craft and ships, machinery and men.

Pena did not have a set of binoculars, so he took the squad's sniper rifle from Private Froman and watched the battle through the rifle's scope. He looked to the mountains to see if he could identify the German artillery sites. Occasionally, he thought that he could see flashes that corresponded in timing to the report of the guns, but he was not sure. The German powder propellant for artillery was mostly smokeless, and there was such a heavy haze over the coastal plain that it did not make much difference in any case.

Pena watched in silence for several minutes, and his soldiers were likewise mute. He was quite disturbed by what he saw, and the soldier in him felt ashamed that they were not in the fight. He believed that what the squad was doing was the correct course of action, but it was still not to his liking. Pena turned and faced towards the sea and marveled again at the shipping. He watched as HMS *Abercrombie* opened fire, and he asked himself why hadn't there been a preliminary bombardment— surely much of the pain of the landing could have been avoided. Pena watched the duel between the ship and the German gunners, then twisted further to his left and looked at Agropoli. He did not have a very clear vision of the village as it was still over a mile and a half distant, but he could see well enough to note that there were no visible concentrations of troops or armor in the village, or between the village and the battlefield. For now it looked as though the southern flank of the American line was secure from this quarter at least.

Corporal Pena handed the Springfield back to Private Froman and pointed at two responsible soldiers, "You and you. Stay here and watch for German movement on this road. If you see any, you've got about five minutes to get down the hill and across to the river bank before they are at the bend here." Pena traced the line of the road with his finger to the bend around the hill. "So don't fuck around. You can find us where we crossed this morning. If there are no Germans, stay here and we'll come get you tonight."

The rest of the squad set off for the river. As they moved down the mountain, Pena recounted his decisions mentally and felt fairly comfortable in what he had done. He was hoping that he would get to keep the squad and knew that he would have to justify his actions to Sergeant Kenton and Lieutenant Berger. His squad was now down to nine soldiers counting himself. Kenton likely would not come back to the squad, and he had just left two soldiers back on the hill. That gave him seven soldiers with M-1 Garands counting himself, one soldier with a BAR, and one sniper with a bolt-action Springfield. *Maybe I should have left just one soldier on the hill,* he thought. He didn't have much firepower left should it come to a scrap.

The squad returned to the river bank at 0930 and was in place to watch the five Panzer IVs attack the battalion. It was clear to Pena from the volume of American fire that there was now more than Able Company in the fight. He found his fist clenching and unclenching involuntarily during the fight, and he shook his head as he watched a bazooka round strike a panzer too low to penetrate the hull. But the tank had thrown a track and was helpless. Thirty seconds later, Pena whistled softly as another bazooka round penetrated the turret, and the tank exploded and caught fire. He did not relax until the other four tanks withdrew. Pena contemplated a quick sprint to the Able Company position, but did not want to run the risk of being shot by those he called Anglos—whether they were German Anglos or trigger-happy white-boy Anglos from Texas.

As time passed, he was getting bored and anxious simultaneously. He heard the rifle shots as Private Pfadenhauer and Lieutenant Taft shot the unfortunate panzer commander, but he did not know who was firing or at whom. The rifle fire did suggest a course of action to him though, and he turned and waded upstream in the Solofrone to where Private Froman was eating his emergency ration chocolate bar. "Froman—move towards the bridge until you can take a shot at the German gunners. Wait until the next fire fight before opening fire. Kill any officers you see."

Private David Froman, a butcher's son from Chicago who was a draftee, not a guardsman, nodded and asked, "Can I take someone with?" Although he was trained to work alone, he preferred to work with other soldiers to act as spotters and to provide security.

"No." Pena turned and started wading downstream.

Froman gulped, his Adam's apple bobbing up and down. He looked at the corporal's back, started to say something and then changed his mind. Finally, he called out in a low voice, "Okay. Just don't leave me hanging out there." The private turned and waded up the river as the bank was too steep to get much traction. He moved slowly and noiselessly as he had been trained to do until he was within one hundred yards of the railroad bridge. Froman selected a site where he could maintain his position on the bank and which had good cover behind him and from the bridge. He slowly slid his rifle forward and looked through the scope—it was a good spot. He could see the machine gun teams and the three tanks, and he decided to target the MG nest farthest from himself. *An easy shot*, he thought, and he waited.

He did not have long to wait. As he was sighting in the MG-42's loader—he did not have a clear shot on the gunner—Lieutenant Colonel Wranosky was giving his orders to prepare the mortars to open fire. Five minutes later, they did.

The first salvo caught Froman by surprise. He did not fire, even though the German gunners opened up in response. But Froman surmised correctly that more rounds would be falling, and as the next mortar round exploded some thirty yards away from his target, the sniper gently let out his breath, squeezed the trigger and fired. The bullet from the Springfield caught the loader behind his left ear—his head was the only part of the soldier that was visible to Froman—passed through the German's helmet and killed him instantly. The bullet exited through the soldier's right temple and just missed hitting the gunner.

Without hesitation, the gunner picked up his weapon, shouted to his spotter to follow him, and ran hard through the mortar fire to relative safety behind the railway embankment. When the second MG-42 crew saw him decamp, they followed quickly behind. Private Froman could have taken several more shots in this time, but his hands were shaking so badly that he could not aim his rifle.

The Germans responded to the mortar fire. German mortars started dropping rounds where they suspected the Texas mortars were, which fell silent in any case when the machine gunners decamped. Lieutenant Anderson, who was back in the dunes with the mortar teams, relocated his mortars to the alternate pits that his soldiers had dug in the sand. Private Froman was unaware of the mortar movement and would not have been very interested in any case—he had just noticed the arrival of the two platoons of panzer grenadiers. Within seconds an internal debate was raging—open fire or not? Head back to the squad or stay put?

Froman decided quickly when he saw the squad break away and head towards the river. He picked up his casing, sliding it into his pocket, and waded as quickly as he could towards Corporal Pena and the rest of his squad.

"Bobby!"

"Shut up!" Corporal Pena hissed. Pena was usually amused when the Anglos called him "Bob" or "Bobby," even though his name was Roberto. He was even more amused when the Anglos tried to roll their "Rs" when saying Roberto in the Mexican style. Only Lieutenant Berger could do it justice. But he was not amused to see his sniper come pushing his way down the river and making noise. Besides, Pena was a squad leader now and he was not sure that he wanted some teenage private from Chicago calling him "Bobby."

"There's a Kraut squad coming down the river bank."

"You think we don't have fucking eyes? Get your ass downstream and get in position to shoot. You can explain

later why you left your post. We're going to hit these
fuckers when they get even with us. Go!"

1025 hours
Fort Rosebud

Perkin poked his head up and pulled it back down
quickly. The tanks were approaching the American line,
their machine guns sweeping an arc of fire back and forth
across the drainage ditch. It looked like the first three
tanks and their supporting infantry would hit the rest of
the battalion, and the tank and soldiers coming along the
river would take on Able Company. Perkin was tracking
that tank, which was masking the movement of the panzer
grenadiers. *Soon,* he thought, *we will have a shot at both the
tank and the soldiers.* The tank was still over two hundred
yards away when Perkin heard the BAR open up from
the river bank. That was followed quickly by the sound of
rifles firing—all American as far as he could tell. *Pena!*

The tank continued to move towards the Able
Company position, but the turret slewed around towards
the river. The barrel depressed and the main gun fired.
Perkin watched as the force of the explosion threw dirt,
water, and brush up into the air. The turret began to turn
to its forward position and accelerated towards the Able
Company ditch.

He turned to the bazooka team. "Okay, now."

The bazooka team sprang up from their crouched
positions, and the bazooka operator took careful aim and
fired. The rocket streaked towards the tank and hit the
panzer just below the still-turning turret. The three-and-
a-half-pound shaped charge entered the tank, filling the
inner compartment with molten metal. The crew was
instantly killed, but the work of the bazooka round was
not finished. So quickly as to be virtually indistinguishable
from the impact of the round, the panzer's ammunition

cooked off inside the tank. The resulting explosion was so forceful that the turret of the tank was lifted off the panzer, and so loud that Perkin felt as if a rifle was fired next to his ear.

"Holy crap," Perkin said to no one in particular. He tried to see Pena's squad but could not see through the smoke of the wildly burning tank. Perkin turned to the bazooka team to tell them to reload, but they were already busy getting the bazooka ready to fire again. "Get to the other side—go!" He yelled at the deafened team. The other tanks were continuing on to the left and center of the American line, and Perkin hoped to get a shot at them as they passed abeam of Able Company. He also thought it might be a good idea to have the team at the other end in case the tanks turned left.

He was about to turn his attention to Pena's squad when he heard the unmistakable sound of incoming artillery. "Incoming! Everyone down!" He yelled. No one needed to be told as all the soldiers of Able Company ducked below the rim of the ditch. Consequently, Able Company missed seeing the effects of the first American artillery rounds landing in support of the 1st Battalion.

What had eluded the riflemen of the 1st Battalion over the course of the morning was achieved in less than five minutes by fires from two antiquated French 75-millimeter cannons mounted on American M-3 halftracks, which were coordinated with fires from USS *Philadelphia*—an American Brooklyn-class light cruiser. Together, they forced the tanks and the panzer grenadiers from Fort Rosebud.

Lieutenant Anderson of the Able Company Weapons Platoon, back in the dunes, had finally established tenuous communications with the 3rd Battalion of the 141st RCT, which was in turn in communications with regiment. Anderson passed the Handie-Talkie over to the wounded officer who had volunteered to join the 1st Battalion team in the dunes, and Anderson began to develop the fire mission. He then read his coordinates to the wounded officer, who passed them to 3rd Battalion, who passed them to a regimental radio operator, who in turn handed them to a naval liaison officer assigned to the regiment. The navy officer was in direct communications with USS *Philadelphia*, using navy communications gear, as the army could not speak directly to the ship.

Six thousand yards from Fort Rosebud, the fire mission was received and prepared on the *Philadelphia*. The ship turned its number two turret, which housed three 6-inch guns, and fired a single high capacity round. Seven seconds later, the round impacted the battlefield four hundred yards east of the battalion, between the Texans and the railroad. Although relatively distant from the American soldiers, it was apparent that this form of artillery was in a completely different league than any other that they had seen during the course of the long morning. The exploding round brought flames and dirt high up into the air, leaving a large crater where it impacted. Many soldiers were unaware that this was friendly fire and were dreading being on the receiving end when the fire was adjusted. Some, however, had noted the direction of the fire.

"That's ours! The heavy stuff must have landed!" Perkin yelled at Sergeant Kenton.

"No, sir. That's the navy." Kenton replied with confidence. "Just wait until they get registered."

Lieutenant Anderson was in the process of assisting just that when the halftracks opened fire. They were close enough to the fight that they were firing over open sights as they passed through the dunes to the northwest of Fort Rosebud. The first rounds landed in the vicinity of the tanks, although there were no direct hits on the armor.

The effects on the German infantry were devastating as the shrapnel ripped through the panzer grenadiers.

This was the first inkling the tankers had that they were in serious trouble; they knew that American artillery had come to the battlefield, but they did not know that halftracks were close enough to engage. For a brief moment, the thought crossed the tankers' minds to accelerate into the American lines to seek safety from the artillery, but they had gained enough respect for the bazookas that this was not a feasible option. The lead tank spun hard on its tracks, followed quickly by the other two panzers. The surviving panzer grenadiers were already headed back to the railroad when the adjusted fire from *Philadelphia* came to the battlefield. This time the cruiser devoted nine of its fifteen 6-inch guns to the defense of Fort Rosebud. Over the span of the next few minutes, the cruiser fired nearly four tons of munitions at the battlefield fronting Fort Rosebud.

The combined artillery barrage lasted only briefly, but time had seemingly come to a halt for those combatants on the battlefield west of the railroad. The din was incredible, the ground shook from the explosions, and dust, dirt, and smoke blackened the sky. To the few Texans watching— most of the soldiers were curled up and praying in their respective ditches—it was finally apparent that there would be no repeat of the Alamo at Fort Rosebud.

When the firing stopped, Perkin raised his head above the lip of the ditch and looked for the tanks. In addition to the burning hulk near the river, two more panzers were completely destroyed and burning furiously. There were no infantry to be seen. The fourth and final tank was damaged—it had thrown a track—and its crew was scrambling out of the stricken panzer. "Make 'em pay!" someone yelled, and a score of rifles from Able Company opened up on the fleeing tankers.

As the soldiers of the 1st Battalion poured out their collective hatred and vengeance onto the German soldiers—and many soldiers kept firing long after the five tank crewmen had been killed—the 75-millimeter cannons opened fire again. This time, Len Anderson was directing the Cannon Company gunners to the machine gun positions on the far side of the tracks.

1100 hours
Fort Rosebud

As the soldiers of the 1st Battalion climbed out of their fighting position in the drainage ditches for the first time in six hours, they saw a scarred and burned battlefield. The field had been mostly barren before the battle, but there were no remnants of life in the field save the Texans. At first the soldiers came out one at a time, and when no one shot at them, the others climbed onto the flat land in groups of three and four.

When Sam looked around at his comrades, he saw mud, dirt, and blood on their faces. Some had broad smiles on their faces—they had been in their first skirmish of the war and were exhilarated by coming through the experience unscathed. They clapped each other on the back, and said things like "Did ya see that?" or "Guess they won't mess with us again." For others, the first taste of battle was less redeeming. These soldiers did not talk. Although the American shelling had been a lifesaver for the Texas soldiers, it had also been terrifying and traumatic for the many soldiers whose nerves had already been stretched thin by the repeated attacks by the tanks. Although he did not expect to find it, Sam looked closely at some soldiers to see if he could identify some of the signs of shell shock, or as the army was now calling it, "battle fatigue." It looked as though a few soldiers had been crying, but the tracks through the dirty faces could also have been streaks from sweat. Everyone in his platoon looked whole to Sam—a few cuts and scrapes, but nothing serious.

He looked over to check on Perkin, who was doing a quick head count of his troops. Perkin looked okay to Sam, so Sam turned to Sergeant Younger and said, "Let's get a muster, but all things considered, I think that we're okay."

Captain Spaulding had sprinted over to the 3rd Platoon position as soon as it had been safe to do so. He came walking back to Sam and Perkin shortly afterwards, shaking his head and looking very upset. It was a disturbing sight for Sam to witness—Bill Spaulding never showed any emotion except for humor and occasional irritation. "Third Platoon is nearly gone. They got hit far worse than we did in our ditch; Frank is down to about ten guys." He sat down on the side of the ditch he had recently left, took his helmet off and ran his fingers through his black hair then wiped his eyes with the back of his hand. "Shit," was all he had to say.

Sam turned to his platoon, sighted one of his medics, and called out, "Kaufman, round up the other medics. Head over to 3rd Platoon and see if you can help." He turned back to Bill Spaulding and asked, "What are your orders, sir?"

Spaulding held his hand out, and Sam pulled him up. Spaulding's brown eyes looked back at Sam tiredly and said, "I haven't talked to the colonel yet, but let's get movin' to our objectives. Whatever we do, I want to get off this open ground as quickly as possible. I'll have Len see if he can get through to the beach and get trucks, jeeps, whatever to carry our badly wounded boys back to an aid station and evacuation if necessary. Have the walking wounded—the capable soldiers—prepare to move out with the company. We might need them again before today is out."

Sam nodded and passed his orders down to Sergeant Younger. He thought of something he wanted to get from their first position in the ditches. Sam jogged back towards the trenches and surveyed the scarred earth. There it was. He picked the object up and looked at it. The handle had been chewed off by the track of the panzer to about a third of its original length, but the head and foot-long shaft remained in good condition. He slipped off his pack, looked at the object again, and shaking his head he snorted and then laughed. Sam slid Perkin's hammer inside his pack and went back to join his company.

Chapter Five

September 10, 1943
1400 hours
1st Battalion HQ
Agropoli, Italy

Lieutenant Colonel Robert Wranosky and Captain Bill Spaulding shared the same foul mood. They had been tasked to execute a mission that originated with the Fifth Army staff, and they did not want to do it. In their considered opinion, it was a pointless mission that would strain valuable company resources. But in the manner of armies immemorial, the Fifth Army had tasked VI Corps; VI Corps passed the tasking down to the 36th Division; 36th Division had tasked the 141st Regiment; and the regiment had tasked the 1st Battalion. Wranosky, as the battalion commander, was in the process of tasking Able Company.

"This is how Colonel Jamison explained it to me," began Wranosky. "He said that 'Old Lady Clark'—his words, not mine—was getting nervous and wanted to encourage Monty to accelerate his drive here but without appearing anxious."

"What's Clark nervous about?" interrupted Spaulding.

"Just a case of the vapors. Let's hope he'll settle down. But I'm afraid that Clark sees these German counterattacks as a prelude to another Gallipoli or Dieppe. Shit, what'd he expect the Germans to do? I ain't worried about it though, Walker knows his business. If we keep moving outward, they won't be able to come inward and destroy our lodgment. The boss has been in the muck before, and it looks to me like he has this fight in hand. Having said that, I don't know about old Dawley—Colonel Jamison said he looked pretty ragged. Anyway, here is the task. Able Company needs to put together a reconnaissance patrol to head down the peninsula and make contact with Eighth Army. No more than ten guys and three jeeps. One of your platoon leaders heads this up—either Berger or Taft. McCarter and Anderson are too green. I'd rather not let anyone go, but I'm giving this to Able because your company had the lightest casualties in the battalion. Sorry, but that's the way it is." Wranosky took a drink from his canteen, "I'll leave your company organization to you, but I recommend that you divide up one platoon's squads and flesh out 3rd Platoon for the time being. Hopefully by the time the patrol gets back we'll have our first set of replacements in and we can fully reconstitute Able Company, as well as the rest of the battalion."

The conversation continued for several minutes, and then Wranosky stressed two points. "Here's the kicker, Bill," he said. "This patrol cain't engage the Krauts unless absolutely necessary. I want 'em in and out quickly, and they'll be upwards of two hundred miles behind the enemy line. The other thing is . . . when they make it to

Monty, they are not to go in like supplicants beseechin'
the king for favors. The last thing I want is for it to
appear that we *need* help. Walker wants to talk to the
patrol leader before they go, and I bet he's gonna tell 'em
the same thing. By the time they get there, Monty will
have a greater appreciation of how the Salerno battle is
going than our patrol. So their job is to demonstrate that
there is a route that Monty can use that is unimpeded by
the Germans."

"What if it ain't?" asked Spaulding.

"Are you familiar with FAWOMO?" asked Wranosky.

Spaulding shook his head with a grin. He thought he
knew most of the army acronyms, but this was a new one.

"I heard it from a squid officer from a minesweeper. It
means, 'Find a Way or Make One.' I like it. That is what
I expect our boys to do."

Twenty minutes later, Spaulding was in the lobby
of Agropoli's sole hotel, not surprisingly named Hotel
Agropoli, looking for his platoon leaders. He did not have
far to look. Perkin was sprawled on the lobby's sofa and
Sam was snoring on the floor beside him. Len and Frank
were at a small table on the hotel bar's balcony drinking the
first espressos of their young lives. They were able to do so
because the 1st Battalion had been placed in regimental
reserve and was expected to be off the line for at least
a day. Able Company had been moved into Agropoli, a
charming little seaside village on the cliffs overlooking
the Tyrrhenian Sea. The young officers had seen to the
billeting of their men, and then each had pursued his own
priorities. Perkin and Sam opted for sleep; Len and Frank
for food. They all knew better than to drink alcohol before
it was authorized by Captain Spaulding, but they had
quickly secured several bottles of Italian wine for later,
and Perkin had been persuaded to buy a bottle of a local
specialty called limoncello.

"Len, wake up the sleeping beauties over there," Bill ordered as he spied his officers. "Be careful with Bear, he can be a little grouchy on comin' out of hibernation."

"Here, let me do it. I've had a lifetime of practice." Perkin said as he yawned and stretched on the sofa. He stood up and then walked to the bar and poured a glass of water from a pitcher on the counter. "Stand over there outta the way." He pointed at a spot past the sleeping Sam's feet. As Len complied, Perkin walked around the sofa and stood behind Sam's head. In one fluid motion he poured the glass's contents onto Sam's face, then quickly flung the glass at the startled Lieutenant Anderson, who instinctively caught it with one hand. Sputtering, Sam roared awake. He saw Len standing at his feet with an empty glass, assumed the obvious, and before Len could take a step backwards, the angry rancher was on his feet and had gripped Len's jacket front in his two giant fists.

He glowered down at Len's mortified face and demanded, "What the hell did you do that for?" He shook the unfortunately mute lieutenant and roared, "Answer me, goddammit!"

There was absolute silence in the hotel, and Sam finally noticed the rest of the people in the lobby. Frank was smiling for the first time since landing in Italy, and Bill was watching with an exasperated look on his face. The manager of the hotel, on the other hand, had an extremely anxious look on his face—he had never seen anyone as large as Sam and was certain that the American giant was going to destroy his hotel. The idea that something was wrong was becoming apparent to Sam. Where was Perkin? Sam spun around. Perkin was near the lobby door looking innocently at a painting of a seaside village along the Amalfi Coast. Perkin looked over at Sam and raised his eyebrows as if to say, "What's all the commotion about?" They made eye contact and Perkin shot out the door with Sam hot on his heels.

Minutes later, they were back inside with Sam holding Perkin bent over in a head lock. "Apologize!" Sam demanded, and he force-walked Perkin over to Len Anderson.

"Sorry, Len," Perkin said to the lieutenant's shoes.

Perkin was dragged over to Bill Spaulding, "Again."

Perkin apologized to Bill's shoes as well, but Sam still did not let go. "Now, the rest of it," Sam said, and he tightened the head lock.

"Old Rufus is smarter than me."

Sam tightened his grip and said, "All of it."

"No, I can't! My tongue will catch fire!"

"Say it!" Veins popping out of his neck from the exertion, Sam squeezed Perkin's head even more.

"Christ! Okay, okay! God bless Texas A&M," Perkin grunted. Sam let go and Perkin scowled at him as he rubbed his temples.

"Who's Rufus?" Bill asked. He stood up and stretched. "It don't matter as you're both idiots; God bless North Texas State Teacher's College. 'Only the educated are free,' you know, and it seems that both you morons could profit from more learnin'. Lenny! If you're done stirrin' up trouble, get us a bottle of wine out of my pack and some glasses, please. Let's sit out on the balcony."

Len returned with a bottle of red wine and five glasses. Captain Spaulding took the bottle from him, pulled the cork with the corkscrew on his Swiss Army knife and poured out the entire bottle of wine evenly between the glasses. "Here's to Eddy and all our lost boys." He lifted his glass, clinked it with the other soldiers, and took a long deep drink of his wine.

"Sir, what's the word on the rest?" asked Len. Able Company was still down a dozen soldiers from the

Headquarters Platoon and the 3rd Platoon. They were sharing a landing craft with two squads of soldiers from Baker Company.

"No word, Len. And the more time that passes, the more concerned I am for them. When we were coming in on our assault run, there was a large explosion to the left of us. A landing craft hit a mine or was hit by artillery, I don't know. I hate to even voice the possibility, but I'm thinking that might have been their boat."

The officers sat in silence for a moment. Captain Spaulding spoke first. "We've been given a special job by General Clark—Able Company has to send a patrol to find Monty. We're looking at ten men or less, jeeps, and a round trip of four to five days. Colonel Wranosky has ruled out the butter bars, so Sam and Perkin—one of you boys will lead this patrol. Do either of y'all want to take it?"

Sam and Perkin looked at each other. They remained silent for a minute, then Perkin spoke for both of them. "Well, sir, given our druthers, we'd both like to stay with the company and our platoons."

"Understood, and I respect that, but one of you is going. Whoever goes, his platoon's gonna be divided between 3rd Platoon and, uh, whoever doesn't go. We'll be down to two rifle platoons until the patrol returns and we get our first levy of replacements. The patrol leader will take a senior NCO, an Italian translator, and a German translator and can make his case to me for any soldier he wants from the company. So, do you boys want to choose, or do you want me to decide?"

"Hang on," said Perk. He and Sam walked to the railing of the balcony. As the others watched, the cousins discussed the subject in low but animated tones. It was apparent that there was going to be no easily arrived at consensus. Therefore, they were not surprised when Sam and Perkin put their hands in front of them and began conflict resolution in the more peaceful of the traditional Berger-Taft methods. Sam's paper beat Perkin's rock on the first round; Perkin's scissors won out over Sam's paper on the second round; and Sam's scissors decided the issue when Perkin chose paper in the final round.

They walked back to the table and Perkin said, "I volunteer."

2100 hours
Hotel Agropoli

Perkin joined his cousin and Captain Spaulding at what had become the officer's table on the hotel balcony. He had been to a meeting with the division commander and his team had spent the afternoon locating and securing three jeeps—two of which had mounted M1919 Browning .30-caliber light machine guns—and enough supplies for four days. Every soldier would carry his own weapons, and Perkin had scrounged a bazooka and four rockets. On the advice of their hotel manager, each jeep had extra jerry cans full of American fuel—they should avoid impure Italian gasoline if they could help it. Also, the helpful manager had recommended taking extra soap and cigarettes for barter—"Italians love to haggle," he told the Texans. "Never take the first offer."

Perkin's plan was to take seven soldiers plus himself. He had soldiered with these men for a long time and knew exactly who he wanted to take. Sergeant Kenton would be the senior NCO that he was allowed. In addition, he was taking part of Corporal Pena's squad with the replacement of Private Pfadenhauer for Private Froman. Pfadenhauer spoke German, and besides, Froman was claiming deafness following the run-in with the panzer the morning before. For his Italian speaker, he was taking a draftee from New Jersey named Vincent Fratelli from his second squad.

Perkin got a kick out of the Jersey attitude of the private, and he was a good soldier. Additionally, he was going to take Private Kulis, who was also from 2nd Squad. Perkin liked the little Texan—he was as smart as any soldier he had met, and he had already proven his worth in battle.

After the hotel manager brought Perkin a gin and tonic (the manager assumed all English-speaking people liked the drink, but it was another first for the lieutenant), Perkin described his meeting with General Walker.

"Walker's headquartered at Casa Vannula, a tobacco farm over the highway from Red Beach. He was pretty busy, but he gave me a few minutes. All he wanted was to impress upon me the need to be diplomatic with the British. It was the same piece that you heard from Colonel Wranosky. Don't appear anxious; just ask them to 'hurry yourself along please.'"

Perkin had not given Captain Spaulding the complete rundown about his meeting with Walker. He would share it later with Sam, after he had run it through his mind a few times, but the truth was that he had been more than a little surprised by his first encounter with his division commander. He had walked into Walker's headquarters—a tobacco barn that was marked by a huge Lone Star flag flapping in the sea breeze—and not unexpectedly, Perkin was told to wait.

While he waited, Perkin looked around the barn. It was unlike any barn that he had seen in Texas. It was taller than a standard farm barn, with no hayloft or manger, just row after row of beams up to the rafters. Walker's master sergeant saw Perkin looking around and joined him. "Ever been in a t'bacca barn?" When Perkin shook his head, the sergeant said, "I'm from Weston, Missouri. We grow some burley there, same as here. These beams are to hang the 'backy out from so they can dry. In the fall, you'll get a bunch of fellers walkin' round up there, hanging the stalks. It's damn hard work." As Perkin was looking up to the ceiling, imagining walking around on the beams, squatting down, and hoisting up the tobacco, the sergeant said, "I think the old man is ready for you now, sir."

Perkin headed over to a corner of the barn, where the general was leaning against a chest-high built-in worktable covered with maps. Walker was of medium height and build. He was older than most of the current crop of George C. Marshall's generals, but he looked tough, alert, and capable to Perkin.

"Come over here, Lieutenant, and let's talk about your trip down the peninsula," Walker said as he waved Perkin over.

Perkin was nervous as he walked up to the general. He was trying to remember the specific protocol for meeting a general officer. Walker was Perkin's first, and he decided that when in doubt, salute and sound off. He stopped several paces from the general, came to attention, knocked out a parade ground salute and said, "First Lieutenant Perkin Berger, Able Company, 141st, reporting as ordered, sir."

Walker automatically started to return the salute. Then he hesitated, looked puzzled for a moment and finished the salute. "What did you say your name was, Lieutenant?"

"Berger, sir. Perkin Berger. I was told to report here . . ."

"Was your father a soldier? Are you from South Texas?" Walker interrupted Perkin's unnecessary explanation.

Perkin paused before answering. He began to run through what he knew of General Walker's past. Walker was not a West Pointer; he had been commissioned through college in Ohio. He had been in the Great War and had been awarded the Distinguished Service Cross. That was it, Perkin guessed. Walker knew his father from the war.

"Yes to both questions, sir." Perkin replied. "My father was also named Perkin. He was in the 30th Infantry, 3rd Division, and was killed at the Marne."

"Yes, I know. By a German 75-millimeter shell. That was a terrible day." Walker himself looked a little shook up as he examined Perkin from head to foot. "You have a rather unique name, but I think I would have known you in any case. I knew your father well in North Carolina and then in France. I was his immediate superior; I was the 1st Battalion commander in the 30th, and he had one of my companies. Boy, you look so much like him . . . but I don't remember him being as tall as you. Now that I think about it . . . ," Walker turned to make sure his master sergeant wasn't listening in, "Now that I think about it, I know I bounced you on my knee once or twice over at your father's house at Camp Greene. You must have been one or two at the time that your dad introduced me to the fine art of smoked brisket—although he was always ranting about having to use hickory instead of mesquite. How is your mother? I wrote to her when your father died and again after the war but never heard from her. She seemed to drop out of army circles. I hope she's well?"

"She died a year after my father during a hurricane. If she had kept your letters, sir, they were destroyed then as well . . ."

At that point, the master sergeant walked up and interrupted the conversation. "Sorry sir," he said. "I just got word that Generals Clark and Dawley are en route to the Casa to talk to you. They should be here in the next five minutes or so."

Walker looked at the young lieutenant. "Perk—that's what your dad went by—I have to wrap this up. Do you have a route planned out?"

"Yes, sir. The quickest, most direct route is down the center of the peninsula along the main north-south highway. But that, of course, is what the Germans are defending. We're going to stick to the coastal roads and shoot into the mountains if necessary. This will be a party of eight total—seven riflemen, including myself, and a medic. Of the riflemen, I'm taking one BAR and one sniper, who are also my Italian and German speakers respectively. We've got three jeeps laid on, two with mounted .30 cals."

Walker nodded. "Good. I'd prefer to send a patrol from the 36th Reconnaissance Troop, but they're going to have their hands full as we continue to push the Germans back into the mountains. When you make contact with the British, suggest diplomatically that they can move quicker than they are, and then offer to show them how. Don't be surprised when they tell you they're moving as fast as they can and they don't need your help. Don't take unnecessary risks. Just get there and back." Walker offered his hand, which Perkin took. "You have an open door here, and when we get the chance, I'd like to tell you what a great soldier your father was."

"Thank you, sir. I'd like that very much."

When Perkin had left, the master sergeant and the major general walked back to the table of maps. Walker turned to his sergeant who had been with him for years, "Lee, talk about a ghost from the past. If Lieutenant Berger comes back in here again, he gets whatever he wants. His father was one of the bravest soldiers I knew, and when the 3rd Division earned the name 'Rock of the Marne,' I think they had him in mind. I sure hope this boy's not as crazy as his daddy was though, or he'll never make it through this war."

2230 hours
Hotel Agropoli

"By God, I could sure come to appreciate this drink if given half a chance," Sam said to Perkin, Bill Spaulding, and Jim Lockridge over his fourth gin and tonic.

"I know what you're saying. Just throw a lotta ice in it and make it quart-sized so a Texan can enjoy it, it'd be just fine. This may be the best argument yet in favor of empire!" Spaulding was in complete agreement over the merits of a gin and tonic.

The boys were preparing to order another round when the regiment's British liaison officer, Captain Waller Finley-Jones, walked into the lobby of the hotel. He went immediately to the desk and spoke to the hotel manager in Italian, obviously trying to get a room. Perkin watched as the manager shook his head. The hotel had filled up hours ago. Finley-Jones pulled a bill from his pocket placed it on the counter and asked again for a room. The manager still shook his head but less vehemently. The British captain put two more bills and a pack of cigarettes on the counter and received a key from the smiling manager's pocket.

Turning, Finley-Jones spied the soldiers at Perkin's table. They had gotten to know the eccentric British officer well in Africa. "Seeing you there has me thinking of Shakespeare!" Finley-Jones said in a singsong Welsh accent. He then tried a Texas accent with little success, "May I join you cowpokes? Sheee-it, boys. Howdy, howdy!"

Grinning, Bill nodded and pulled a chair over from another table. "Well said, Waller. Now, how on earth can we make you think of Shakespeare?"

"To be truthful, it's not you so much as something relevant to our situation here that I've just learned."

"And that would be?"

"Good Christ! Is that a gin and tonic? Who would have thought the wogs, pardon me, the wops as you Americans say, would have gin and tonic. I need one of those. Jamison saddled me with an absolutely dreadful officer to nursemaid—just managed to ditch him. But I think as long as I remain close to fighting soldiers that there is little danger he will find me again. Perhaps a drink courtesy of President Roosevelt's finest would go a long way towards easing my feelings towards your fellow countrymen."

Sam said to the Welshman, "If FDR were here, I'm sure that he would be happy to dip into the socialist security slush fund to buy you a drink. In lieu of that, I'll buy you one. So, whaddya know pardner? Is the regiment moving?" Sam waved the hotel manager over and ordered a round for the table.

"Oh hell no, it is much more important than that. Who can keep track of that nonsense? Regiments come and regiments go. Besides," Finley-Jones grinned, "they never tell me that kind of stuff anyway. Let me ask a question of you then. What famous line from Shakespeare is most appropriate to our situation just now? The one I have in mind is perhaps the single-most cogent line in all of literature. Something so meaningful that Sam has likely shouted it out to his cows back 'home on the range,' as you say. But now that I think of your abysmal knowledge of anything other than cows or baseball, if anyone gets the correct line, the next round is on me."

Bill Spaulding replied, "Hell, Waller, it ought to be anyway. It's a Texas tradition that the British always buy the next round. But, since you brought up baseball, I'm bettin' on the Cards, in case you were wondering." He tipped his chair back, took a deep drink, thought for a moment and then a big smile spread across his face. Spaulding asked, "Is the line, 'To err is human, to forgive bovine'?"

The Welshman laughed, "That's not Shakespeare, 'twas almost Pope though. I'll give you points for substituting a cheap pun in lieu of classical literature . . . one more shot."

"'To be or not to be?'"

"Let me guess, that's the only line from Shakespeare that you've heard. Well, it's not only wrong but lugubrious. Who's next?"

Sam scratched his head and asked the collective group of soldiers, "Does anyone else know what lugubrious means? Nope? Guess, it's just you and me, Cap'n, and I ain't sharing with this lot."

"Me neither," said the British officer.

They all gave up on "lugubrious" and pondered the question. Jim went next. He stood up, extended his left arm outward and put his right hand over his heart. "'I would speak with Clarence and I come hither on my legs,'" quoted the intelligence officer in a dramatic stage voice. The four other men stared at James, then Captain Finley-Jones said, "Afraid not, old boy. But I must say that I find it unnerving to think of Sam reciting that to his herd. Nice try though. Who else wants a go?"

"'Once more unto the breach dear friends?'" tried Sam.

"Ironically close in sentiment, but the wrong play. Sorry, try again."

"'Out, out damn spots?'" asked Perkin looking down at his uniform. "'Cry havoc and let slip the dogs of war?'"

"Wrong as well," said Finley-Jones laughing. "It's clear that you Americans don't understand Shakespeare. I mean truly understand Shakespeare—the truth is that he was a filthy-minded old bugger. Shall I tell you what it is then? Alright, the line that *Leftenant* Taft nearly hit on comes from *King Lear*, not *Henry V.* It is, as the Bard said . . . 'Let copulation thrive!' I've found a brothel . . . let's go thrive, shall we?"

Chapter Six

September 11, 1943
0500 hours
Hotel Agropoli
Agropoli, Italy

Although it was less than four miles from the fighting, the Agropoli Hotel somehow seemed remote from the troubles of the Salerno plain. As Bill Spaulding and Perkin talked in front of a jeep, they could hear the continuous and distant firing of rifles, tanks, artillery, and naval guns, but they paid no attention to the sounds. Occasional trails of antiaircraft fire snaked up to the sky, and the clouds above reflected the violence below, yet Agropoli remained quiet and peaceful.

Most soldiers needed little encouragement from their noncommissioned officers to get food and sleep. They expected to enter the line again within the day, and they knew that sleep would then be at a premium. Even the salaciously intrepid Captain Finley-Jones had a good night's sleep, alone, in the manager's personal apartment at the Agropoli Hotel. By the time he had rounded up a party to accompany him to the brothel, there was an accumulation of soldiers waiting at the door to a run-down house that might have been built during Caligula's reign. The line of soldiers did not deter Finley-Jones. He intended to pull rank: "All's fair where love and war coincide," he told the others. Determined as he was, however, graffiti scrawled on the sides of the dirty building convinced him and his party that this might not be the ideal venue for their carnal pursuits. Jim translated the first from German as, "An hour with Venus, a lifetime with Mercury." Underneath it in fresher paint was an announcement by the Wehrmacht medical corps stating, "Off-limits to German personnel." The other warning, written in Italian, had been painted over but had bled through; it was known to Finley-Jones: "Abandon hope, all ye who enter." The newest addition to the wall was not a warning, just an announcement that Kilroy had visited the brothel.

One soldier was not deterred, not because he purposely ignored the warnings—as the first customer of the day, he hadn't waited in line and therefore hadn't seen them—but because now that he had seen war firsthand, Private Kulis was determined not to die a virgin. That was one of two secrets he had kept to himself since becoming a soldier sixteen months earlier. The other was that he would be turning seventeen in a couple of weeks. He was no longer ashamed of his virginity, as it was no longer relevant, but he aimed to keep his age discreet for some time to come.

Kulis had no complaints with soldiering. He liked the platoon, was surprisingly capable of taking care of himself in the company of rough men, and most importantly from his perspective, he had more food in the army than he had ever seen in his life. The depression and drought had been severe for Rosebud. His life had been hard but so had everyone else's and he was not the type to complain. Still, the army was an improvement, and he was grateful his parents had looked the other way when their bookish youngest son used his brother's birth certificate to enlist.

Private Kulis was to be the jeep driver for Lieutenant Berger, and he was drifting in and out of sleep at the wheel waiting for the word to begin. His waking thoughts were on last night, and he smiled wide to himself in the dark. He had few dreams of love in his life, but physically it was even better than he had imagined it to be. He was hoping for a short patrol so he could visit the brothel again. The prostitute, whose name was Rita but went by the trade name Paola, had deflowered virgin soldiers of many nationalities before, but never had she known clients quite as enthusiastic and methodical as Kulis. He had spent all of his invasion pool winnings, most of one month's pay, and a considerable amount of Paola's time, learning and practicing the basic positions of lovemaking. Three additional positions were those of his own devising—two of which had proven quite successful, but the third sadly required an athleticism and flexibility that Paola had not possessed even when she was a young woman.

"Listen, Perk," Captain Spaulding's low tones interrupted Kulis's reverie. "You're like a brother to me, and I'm going to give you some brotherly advice. The next step is an order, but let's not go there now. You have to cut the immature shit out. This war isn't for your amusement, you have terrible timing with your jokes, and you are going to piss off the wrong guy sometime. And for God's sake, don't antagonize Wranosky anymore. He's one of the good guys." Spaulding pulled a pouch of chewing tobacco from his pocket and patted down his other pockets to confirm that he still had his cigarettes. As he stuffed a chaw into his cheek, he said, "These troops look to you as how to behave, and I want them to see maturity and judgment, not a prankster. Now, not later. If you outlive me, you'll likely be the next company commander; and you'll see that there is more responsibility in the job than you think."

"Bill, I'm sorry if I've gotten you in any trouble with the colonel . . ."

"You haven't, and that ain't the point." Spaulding spit a stream of tobacco juice into a bush in front of the hotel. "I've been meanin' to talk to you about this for awhile, but I'm tellin' you this now because I had a nightmare last night about this trip to find Monty. I woke up in a cold sweat and didn't go back to sleep thanks to you. In my dream, you got in an argument with Montgomery and threw a goddamned gin and tonic in his face. You pissed off the British Empire to the point that Churchill personally wrote me a letter telling me what a prick you are and what a failure as a leader I am. To top it off, he sent a carbon copy to General Marshall and a second to my mother. Since I don't have the time to correspond with either the prime minister or the chief of staff, behave yourself. It ain't funny, so stop laughing. You're a good soldier, now be a good officer."

Perkin was highly pleased with Bill's dream. "Yes, brother. Just don't tell Mom and Dad. Sorry if I've been difficult. Now I'd like to say something."

"This should be interesting. Go ahead," said Bill dryly. He rolled his eyes as he sensed Perkin's imminent transition away from his short-lived contrition.

Once again imitating Groucho Marx, Perkin sang:
"Hello, I must be going.
I cannot stay, I came to say, I must be going.

I'm glad I came, but just the same, I must be going.
Tra-la."

"I don't know why I bother," Bill said, shaking his head, but smiling nonetheless. "Get back quick—us Hammers will need you. One last thing—keep a log. Jot down notes about bridges, tunnels, road conditions—that kind of stuff. It might be useful to your friend Jim."

"I've already got one. I stole the ledger from the hotel to use."

Bill shook Perkin's hand even as he shook his head, turned, and headed back into the Agropoli Hotel to see if he could go back to sleep. Sergeant Kenton and the other soldiers of the patrol were waiting by the other jeeps. Perkin sat in the front of his jeep, and Kenton squeezed in the back among the supplies they were taking.

Perkin looked for Sam and thought that he might have to leave without saying good-bye, but then he saw his cousin coming out of the hotel with something in his hand. A bleary-eyed Sam walked up to Perkin's side of the jeep and handed him two pint-sized bottles of T.W. Samuel's Bourbon. "Hey."

Perkin replied in the usual way, "Hey yourself."

"Trade one of these with the Limeys for some gin. We seem to have drained Agropoli's supply last night. The other's for you."

"Thanks. Gin. Hmm . . . right. Have you cleared this with Bill? I gather he ain't comfortable with me drinking gin and tonics around the British. Ask him about it. What about tonic?"

"It seems the hotel has enough tonic for another Texas division, just no gin to put in it."

Sam offered a somewhat shaky hand, which Perkin took. "Poor planning. Take care, Perk."

"You too, Bear."

0605 hours
Castellabate, Italy

An hour after leaving Agropoli behind, the patrol had only covered five out of the two hundred miles that lay before them. There was difficulty in clearing their own roadblocks, and Lieutenant Berger had to order an engineering detachment not to blow a bridge leading out of town until the patrol had passed.

Once outside of American lines, the patrol proceeded cautiously. In Perkin's opinion, the Agropoli-Castellabate highway was not as much of a highway as what he assumed a glorified goat path would be like. The occasionally paved road weaved in and out of the hillocks that lined the snaking valley between the two small towns. Each curve brought an anxious moment, not only because some curves worked around steep embankments that most frequently lacked rails, but also because the Texans expected to round a bend and come face-to-face with a German roadblock.

Jim Lockridge had discussed the possibility of such an encounter with Perkin. "Fifth Army staff thinks there are two German divisions between us and Monty. I don't know what that assessment's based on, but I can't contradict or affirm it. There are two possible courses of action for the Germans between us and Eighth Army. By the book, they either mass against Monty or mass against us with the preponderance of mass being determined by terrain and operational requirements. That says to me that we'll be the Germans' primary target and Monty is secondary. They can hold him up along the main inland highways by blowing bridges in the mountains. That'll let them concentrate their mass against us, while a smaller force delays the Limeys. What I'm gettin' at is that they may be sending forces north along the coastal road while you and your boys are leisurely headin' south along the same scenic highway. I've looked over the map and theoretically you can do back roads through the mountains almost all the way down the peninsula—I think that it'd take you days to do it, and you'll run out of gas before you get to Eighth Army. My advice is to proceed along the good roads, namely the coastal highway, and duck into the mountains if you have to."

That was what Perkin intended to do, and this plan was reinforced by their slow pace over the "good" road. After following the valley floor, the road began to climb sharply; Castellabate was built on a small mountaintop overlooking the sea. When the road crested the mountain, they found themselves on a ridgeline heading to the southeast and into Castellabate. Outside of Agropoli, they had not yet seen any Italian towns, but the sight that faced them would become familiar to the Texans.

As they approached the village, Perkin stopped several hundred yards out and took a look through his German binoculars. He saw the top and one side of an ancient town of a hundred homes or more stacked impossibly on top of one another and seemingly hanging by magic off the side of the mountain. Surely, he thought, one of these infamous Italian earthquakes would send this village down the mountain and into the sea. But defying gravity and volatile geology, Castellabate had successfully clung to the side of the mountain for countless centuries.

They proceeded slowly into the town. Corporal Pena's jeep, which had a .30 caliber Browning machine gun, went first. Perkin's jeep was second with Sergeant Kenton sitting in the back, the bazooka across his lap. The third jeep, driven by Private Fratelli, brought up the rear. The patrol drove into town and parked in a square facing the Texans' first castle—seemingly guarded by an unbelievably large and hungry-looking tan-and-black dog, alert to the Americans' every move.

"D'ya reckon it's a church or a castle?" asked Sergeant Kenton.

"I think it's an Anatolian Shepherd. Ha, ha. A bit of both I think. Cap'n Lockridge told me that Castellabate means the 'Abbot's Castle.' You wanna go pound on the door and see if that hound's master is home?" said Perkin with a grin.

"Not really—do you want me to?"

"Not really," Perkin replied. "It was a test of your bravery. You failed. Well, I guess we keep going. I'd like to see if there is a *Carabinieri* post here, but it looks as if the whole town is still asleep."

"Excuse me, sir." Fratelli had joined the conversation. "I doubt if anyone other than Germans and Americans are awake in Italy now. People here stay up late then sleep late—they don't even have their evening supper until nine or ten at night. We might find a baker or someone like that up though."

"All right, mount up and let's look this town over quick and keep moving."

They had not driven more than two hundred yards before they found what they were looking for—a small café which was either open for the early risers of Castellabate or had not closed from the night before. Perkin and Fratelli walked in and a tall, uniformed Italian with a heavily scarred face and forehead rose up from his seat, clicked his heels together, and saluted Perkin.

"Sergente Rossi, Tenente," the tall Italian said to Perkin.

Perkin returned the salute and shook hands with the military policeman as Fratelli explained, "He's the local *Carabinieri* here, sir, rank of sergeant. His name is Rossi."

"You don't say." Perkin turned to the Italian sergeant, "Do you speak English?"

"Un po'." A little bit.

Perkin found out that a little bit meant "not really,"

so he had Fratelli order three espressos and a three-way conversation ensued. On the auspicious occasion of the arrival of the American Army, the barista dug deep into his cabinet and brought out actual espresso beans and carefully ground them—for over a year most Italians had been drinking ersatz coffee. Although Perkin understood and appreciated the magnanimous nature of the gesture, he thought the espressos were as harsh as the navy coffee that Captain Lockridge had complained about only a few days prior on the ship.

As Perkin discovered, Rossi was intelligent and was used to operating independently. He was awake because of the distant noise of war echoing through the mountains; he was a combat veteran of Italy's ill-fated support to Germany on the Eastern Front and had not had a good war. Rossi had been severely injured northwest of Stalingrad in the summer of 1942, and his current post in sleepy southern Italy was considered a convalescent tour. The sergeant was in charge of the small Castellabate post and was responsible for policing the town and numerous smaller outlying hamlets that reported to him. Sergeant Rossi, who had never shared a coffee with an Italian or German officer, was honored to sit down and have one with an American officer. Rossi approved wholeheartedly with the armistice and was generally delighted that the Americans had arrived. He told Perkin through Fratelli that he had family in Buffalo, but he did not mention that he and all Italians were deathly afraid of German reprisals if the Americans were defeated. He had seen the Germans at work firsthand during his tour on the Eastern Front, and he shuddered at the thought of Teutonic justice set loose on Italy. Still, he saw the Americans and the British as the only hope that the Italian monarchy would be saved from the fascists and the Nazis. Like all *Carabinieri*, his loyalty lay with the House of Savoy. The King said support Mussolini, and they supported Mussolini. The King said arrest Mussolini, and the *Carabinieri* arrested Mussolini. *Allora*. In response to Perkin's questioning, he reported that there had been Germans in the area at platoon strength several days ago, but he had seen none since the Allied landings.

"May I offer a suggestion, Tenente?" asked Rossi.

"Absolutely. Please do."

"Let me call the *Carabinieri* post in a neighboring village and ask them if there are Nazis or fascists in control there, or if they know of German patrols in the area. There is no need to tell them why. You can then adjust your plans accordingly. When you get to their village, ask them to do the same thing for you. I assume you are heading south; the roads offer many chances for German ambush. The *Carabinieri* will help, I am sure of that."

Perkin paid for the espressos with a dollar; there was no complaint about the currency from the Italians as he had already given cigarettes to everyone at the café. Rossi and the two Americans left the café, and Rossi nodded approvingly when he saw the machine-gun-equipped jeeps. "Brownings. Very nice," he said in heavily accented English.

When they got to Rossi's station house, which was really a small office with a single jail cell, Rossi went to a map on the wall and pointed at a village further down the coast named Acciaroli. "I will call there—it is another post like mine, although smaller. He answers to me. It is twenty kilometers away and should not take you long to get there." He picked up the earpiece and cranked the handle to the phone. Rossi stood even taller and spoke officiously to the operator. Shortly thereafter he was connected to his counterpart in Acciaroli. He had a very animated, rapid-fire discussion with the Acciaroli *Carabinieri*, then hung up the phone and asked Perkin for another cigarette. Perkin gave him the pack.

"Trouble ahead, Tenente. The Germans have a roadblock here." He pointed to a village on the map called Pieta. "It is only six kilometers from here, and my corporal tells me they set it up yesterday afternoon. He was here yesterday morning, spent the day doing paper work, and he saw the roadblock last night while driving home to Acciaroli. I don't know why he didn't call me then." Rossi shrugged. *Allora.* "He says it is a small squad of military police, and they are perhaps looking for deserters from your battle. One light machine gun mounted on a motorcycle and they have a Kübelwagen. You can easily dispatch them."

"My mission isn't to engage the enemy. Can we get around them?" Perkin asked.

"Si, signore. But the path is not on a map. If you like, I will take you to a point in the mountains, show you the path, and then return by foot."

"I would appreciate that. Can we leave now?"

"Si." The Italian turned and pulled what looked to be a carbine off a gun rack on the wall. Perkin looked it over closely and noticed that it had two triggers. Through Fratelli, Perkin asked about the weapon, and was told it was a Beretta 9-millimeter submachine gun. According to Rossi, the rear trigger fired an automatic burst, and the forward trigger fired in a semiautomatic mode. Rossi asked to see the Texan's Thompson, and although he was anxious to leave, Perkin obligingly unslung it and the two soldiers traded weapons for each other's inspection.

"Tommy-gun," Rossi said in English with a big crooked smile. "Sticka them up."

0830 hours
Near Pieta, Italy

The patrol and Sergeant Rossi of the Italian *Carabinieri* had spent nearly two hours working their way on a winding path through the mountains. Perkin had revised his earlier estimate on what constituted a good road in southern Italy. He had truly been on the best road in the area, and as he nearly bounced out of the jeep, he felt a genuine nostalgia for the highway. This, he decided, was a real goat-path. Between the bumps, he took notes in his personal journal, which was doubling as a mission log.

When they progressed several miles, Perkin estimated that at the pace that they were going it would take nearly a year to get to Monty. "That can't be right," he muttered under his breath. "I must have added some zeros." Rather than rework his equation, he gave up and concentrated on the task at hand.

The jeeps were grinding along a path on the seaward side of a mountain ridge several hundred feet below the crest of the ridge. On the opposite side of the ridge and several hundred feet below their elevation, the southbound highway ran parallel to their course, leaving them well protected and their progress hidden. Too soon, the protection of their ridge was lost as the mountain tapered down to the valley floor. Rossi, in the front jeep, halted the procession. He and Private Fratelli trotted back to Perkin.

"Tenente," Rossi pointed ahead. "In a moment, we will be in sight of the highway. Should we walk up to the crest and see if we can sight the German roadblock?"

"Yep." Perkin got out of his jeep and called for Private Pfadenhauer to join them.

"Sergeant, this is Private Roscoe Pfadenhauer. He's our best sniper, and already has a German tank commander to his credit. I'm bringing him along."

Rossi nodded and asked Pfadenhauer through Fratelli, "Are you German?"

"Hell no. Texan." Fratelli rolled his eyes but translated faithfully.

The small party began the climb to the crest a hundred yards away. Although the mountain was covered by small evergreen shrubs, Rossi led them to a small clearing near the crest, where he crouched, then dropped to his stomach. The Americans followed his lead. After crawling another five yards, the view of the valley and the highway opened up before them. Perkin took his binoculars and handed them to Rossi.

"Thank you, Tenente." Rossi looked the glasses over. "These are German?"

Perkin was tempted to tell him that they were also Texan, but nodded and said, "My driver killed a German MG team and took these from the previous owner. He gave them to me. Nice present, aren't they?" Rossi nodded but only half believed the lieutenant. An Italian officer would have simply taken them from the soldier who did the dirty work. For that matter, he had never met an Italian officer who shared his field glasses.

Rossi began from his left, to the north, and then panned right. "There! Tenente. To the south." He handed the glasses to Perkin with an unhappy look on his face. Perkin quickly found the German roadblock but was puzzled by the Italian's reaction. It seemed as Rossi's deputy had described: six soldiers smoking cigarettes next to a wooden barrier. Parked behind them were a motorcycle with sidecar and a Kübelwagen—the German two-wheel-drive equivalent of a jeep. Perkin turned to his right and his eyes followed the ridgeline down to the valley floor; the path they had been following joined the ridgeline and would be visible from the roadblock.

"Shit." Perkin looked through the glasses again. Their path and the highway paralleled only three to four hundred yards apart, and their closest point of approach to the roadblock might be as little as three hundred yards—perhaps less. If the Germans didn't see the jeeps, they would likely hear them as they came down the mountainside. He cursed again and slid away from the crest.

As they walked back to the jeeps, Perkin sorted out his options and found none that he liked. When they arrived, he pulled Sergeant Kenton aside and explained the situation.

"The Kraut roadblock is too far south. We can't get around them on this path unless we are very lucky. The choices as I see 'em are we try and coast down the mountain road with our engines turned off and hope that they don't see us or the dust that we'd kick up. If they do, we lose the element of surprise and we're in a skirmish where they might be able to call for reinforcements. Or we can backtrack to Castellabate and come down a series of coastal roads. Rossi says they're not good, not all connected, and we'd have to try some cross-country driving in between. It'd cost us most of the rest of the day and we'd still only be about ten miles from where we started. Or we kill these sons-a-bitches and push their jeep off in a ravine or the ocean. We can be outta here in half an hour."

"How close can we get to 'em with good cover?" Kenton asked.

"Maybe thirty or forty yards. We couldn't miss 'em."

"Your call, sir, but that's what I vote for."

"Me too. Shit." Perkin took off his helmet and scratched his head thoughtfully for a moment. "Okay, leave three guys behind with the jeeps—make it Pena, Pfadenhauer, and Doc Wagner. They can watch from the crest and bring the jeeps down to the roadblock."

"Yes, sir. What about the Eye-tie?"

"I dunno. Let's go ask him."

Perkin and Sergeant Kenton returned to the jeeps where all the soldiers, including Rossi, were having a cigarette. Perkin instinctively checked the wind. It was blowing down from the mountain ridge, otherwise he would have taken the soldiers to task for smoking this close to the German position.

"Sergeant Rossi, we're going to take out the German squad. I'm leaving three soldiers behind with the jeeps and they'll bring 'em down when we're done. Would you care to join us, wait with the jeeps, or start back to town?"

Rossi thought for a moment before he said carefully, "Signore, I would join you, but despite the armistice, I don't believe that Italy is at war with Germany. It is a matter of time, I am sure, but I don't have permission to fight Germans. I will stay here with your soldiers and then see if I can be of other assistance."

Perkin nodded. "I understand." He turned to Pena and handed him his binoculars, "Be careful with those. You boys watch from up there, and get your butts down there quick when it's over. If it goes south, give us a minute to get back up here, and if it goes far south, then get yourselves back to Agropoli."

0945 hours
Near Pieta, Italy

Corporal Pena started the first jeep and put it in gear. "Follow me," he ordered tersely. *Fucking Anglos*, he thought. As he automatically let the clutch out and began the drive to the roadblock, he mentally ran through what he had just witnessed.

It had not taken Lieutenant Berger's team long to get in position, but of the lieutenant's cautious sliding down the mountain and crossing a small stream, Pena knew nothing. The lieutenant had entered the shrub brush further to the right of the clearing where Pena had taken his team, and was quickly lost to view, so Pena watched the Germans through the binoculars and waited for the attack to begin.

The Italian sergeant might have been the senior soldier present, but there was no way that Pena would entrust a foreigner with his lieutenant's binoculars. So while Pfadenhauer watched through his sniper scope and Pena through Perkin's glasses, the medic and the Italian *Carabinieri* mostly listened for the sound of shots.

Instead of the shots of the gun, a massive boom echoed through the mountains of southern Italy. It was far louder than anything heard coming from the battlefield so far, and as everyone instinctively turned to the north to look for smoke, Pena heard the shots as Perkin's team opened up. Then he heard the lieutenant's Thompson and Fratelli's BAR continue firing. Pena quickly brought the binoculars back to his battle and watched as five Germans dropped simultaneously—almost to a man. One German soldier remained further back than the rest and stared stunned at his fallen comrades. The German soldier dropped his rifle, turned, and began to run down the road.

Pfadenhauer's rifle boomed out, less than a foot from Pena's ear. "You fuck!" Pena shouted and pushed the private away from him. Pena's hearing was still coming back from the battle against the tank two days before, and his ears were ringing again. He put a finger in his left ear—the one closest to the Springfield—and wiggled it several times. It did no good. Neither did yawning.

"What are you complaining about?" Pfadenhauer asked. "I got the son-of-a-bitch, didn't I? Shit, he was on the run and I got him from nearly six hundred yards out." Then under his breath as he bent over and picked up his casing, he added, "Let's see you do that, you fat fuckin' Mexican."

"Fucking white boy," Pena groused as they ran down the hillside to the jeeps.

By the time the deafened and disgruntled corporal led the three jeeps down the mountain and back up the highway, Perkin had the dead German soldiers and their packs and weapons stacked in the Kübelwagen.

"Great shot, Howie!" Perkin said. He was still shaking slightly from the engagement, but he was enthused. There were no casualties on his side, and all the Germans were dead. He had told his soldiers on the way down to make sure they shot to kill—no missed shots allowed. Two of the Germans were killed by shots through the heart and one by a shot to the soldier's forehead. Two others were riddled by Perkin's Thompson and Fratelli's BAR, and all of the soldiers were bringing the fleeing German into their sights when he was killed by the sniper on the mountain.

Perkin was pleased that none of his soldiers had hesitated and that all performed professionally. It was, as Kulis had told him two days before, just like training. Only, of course, it was not training. Except for his medic, a Quaker, who refused to even carry a sidearm, every soldier on this detail, including himself, had now taken a life. Perkin had been brought up to believe that to take a life was deeply morally wrong and mortally inexcusable. At some point in his life, he knew, he would have a reckoning with his conscience over his actions in this war, but now was not the time.

"Sergeant Rossi," Perkin said. "Is there anything here you need or could use?" He indicated the German motorcycle and the Kübelwagen.

"Si, signore." Rossi took a hard look at the motorcycle, a brand-new German-Army-issued BMW R75 with a powered sidecar, and answered, "With your permission, I will take the motorcycle, their machine pistols, and their ammunition. I know a place where I can hide these and they will be available should we need to fight the Germans. I can walk home from there."

"Okey-doke. Kulis and Ewart, load it up for him please."

Through Fratelli, the *Carabinieri* told Perkin where to dispose of the Kübelwagen and the dead Germans. He told Perkin of a very steep cliff over the ocean that would suffice, and it was less than a mile away.

As they were preparing to part ways, Perkin offered his hand. "Sergente, thanks for the help. Don't advertise your assistance until this area is firmly in Allied hands. Best of luck."

The Italian sergeant saluted, which Perkin returned. Rossi offered some final advice, "The same to you, Tenente. One last thing. I am from Orvieto, not this area, so I can say this. Be careful down here—the peasants are primitive and stupid. Many may not have heard of the armistice, and even if they have, they may still support the fascists. Keep a close eye on your belongings while in southern Italy. Theft is the favorite pastime of the locals here, and in the chaos of the war, it will get worse. Arrivederci, signore."

1015 hours
Near Pieta, Italy

As Rossi drove off on his new German motorcycle, which he had no intention of letting fall into the possession of the Italian state, he marveled at the democratic essence of the American military. As an old campaigner himself, he recognized that the American lieutenant was a rare and exceptionally capable officer, even if he was still green. Yet Lieutenant Berger talked to his subordinates in a friendly and joking manner— had he not bought his private a coffee as well as Sergeant Rossi? As a police officer as well as a soldier, he was a pretty astute judge of character, and he could easily observe the respect that went up and down the detail's chain of command, particularly between the big sergeant and the lieutenant. The exception was the incident on the mountain, where the corporal got angry at the private for shooting so close to his ear. *That was a truly fine shot*, Rossi reflected, *but the corporal had every right to be angry*. It was very disrespectful, and in the Italian Army the private would have been slapped for his insolence. How the Americans managed in such chaotic conditions he did not know, but he had to admit that the taking of the German patrol was a neat and efficient little affair.

That the American Army during the war was highly democratic and egalitarian to an unparalleled degree was to become well-known to both its enemies and its allies, but none of the units were more democratic than the National Guard divisions. Those divisions were constituted by friends, neighbors, and coworkers who had known each other for years, and it was not unusual for a unit's command structure to reflect either a peacetime civilian relationship or its obverse, where an officer's subordinate was his civilian boss. Of the country's National Guard divisions, none were more democratic in nature than those with roots in the old army of the Confederate States of America—perhaps the most democratic army ever fielded in history. The southern guard divisions no longer elected their officers, but that democratic essence lingered on.

American democracy and egalitarianism were in play back at the former roadblock where Perkin was now getting his soldiers loaded up to move out. "Come on, sir! We owe it to these guys to bury them decently—it's the law of war." Such was the uninformed legal opinion of Private Wagner, Perkin's medic. It was an opinion held also by Private Ewart, Wagner's best friend.

As Perkin climbed into his jeep, he watched the interaction in the group. Kulis and Pena obviously did not care what became of the German corpses; Fratelli and Pfadenhauer were in favor of disposing quickly of them as the lieutenant intended, but what of Sergeant Kenton?

Kenton saw his lieutenant looking at him, and he remembered the landing craft on the beach where the German gunner had preserved the life of the medic before slaughtering everyone else on the boat. He also thought of the German tanks parading arrogantly back and forth in front of the 1st Battalion shooting anyone who moved.

"Fuck 'em. Let's chuck their ass off the cliff."

"Well said, Sergeant. You make an eloquent, sensitive and, yet, compelling case as always. Move out and follow us."

They followed the directions given to them by Sergeant Rossi, and less than a mile away was a dirt road that ran parallel to the sea. Perkin hopped out of his jeep and scouted what he considered to be the right location—a bend in the road around a promontory into the sea. There was a slight incline to the cliff and it took five soldiers to push the Kübelwagen over the edge.

The German jeep did a half rotation then landed upside down in the waves below. Several dead German soldiers and their packs floated in the surf crashing against the rocks of the shore, while the Kübelwagen sank beneath the waves and disappeared from view.

Perkin watched his soldiers. Oddly enough, for some of the Texans, disposing of the Germans' bodies in such a fashion had a more momentous feeling than the actual killing, and with the exception of Pfadenhauer and Kulis, who were grinning broadly at the fun of pushing the vehicle over a cliff, they had somber looks on their faces. Perkin reflected that he would have liked a little more ceremony, perhaps some words from the Bible, but none came to mind that seemed relevant, and so, after a moment's silence, they loaded up and continued south.

1130 hours
Agropoli, Italy

The morning since Perkin's departure from Able
Company had been a busy one. Captain Spaulding may
have had a troubled night's sleep worrying about Perkin's
personal interaction with the most revered general in
the British Army, but it did not slow him down any that
morning. A normally industrious man, Spaulding had
been restless and bored with the battalion being placed in
reserve. It had been a busy time reorganizing the company,
and he was anxious to be moving and ready to be back
in the fight. Spaulding's officers and noncommissioned
officers had seen to the replenishment of ammunition,
rations, and other supplies, just as they had seen to the
welfare of their soldiers. The sergeants reported back to
the officers that the men were rested and morale was high,
and the officers reported back to Captain Spaulding that
Able Company was ready and just waiting for the order to
go. They did not have long to wait.

One soldier whose morale was not particularly high
that September morning was First Lieutenant Sam
Taft. The previous night's drinking had left him feeling
somewhat bewildered and dim-witted—a rare sensation
for Sam, and one that he despised. Sam's head ached
from too many gin and tonics, and he was beginning to
question the wisdom of asking Perkin to acquire more gin
from the British. Compounding his headache was the
constant noise of battle. Agropoli was only a few miles
from the fighting; the combat had intensified as more
forces, Allied and Axis, flowed into the Salerno plain. To
Sam, it seemed as if the artillery fire never ended; it was
a constant refrain of thumps and booms from the heavy
guns and the incessant rapid fire of automatic weapons.
With his present hangover, the ceaseless near-distant
combat was the worst assault on his senses since he had

visited the first-grade classroom of a teacher he had dated some years before. He broke off the relationship shortly thereafter out of fear that he might have to visit the classroom again.

At the top of Sam's worries that morning was Perkin. Perkin had left on his patrol over six hours before. Theoretically, being on good roads and pushing the jeeps to their limits, he could have already made it through to British lines, but Sam had no way of knowing if Perkin had even made it through German lines or even out of the American lines safely. His anxiety for Perkin gnawed at him, and although he tried to focus on other issues, he was only partly successful. He found himself wishing that he had volunteered for the mission.

"Sir! Sir!" Sergeant Younger's insistent voice pierced through the fog in Sam's mind. Sam turned and looked through bloodshot eyes at his platoon sergeant. Jack Younger was twenty-eight—Sam's age—and had the look of one who had been undernourished his entire life. He was a little less than five feet eight inches tall and wore suspenders because belts could never be tightened enough to keep his trousers up. Younger's looks were deceiving. He was as tough as any soldier in the platoon, and he had become an NCO as quickly as army regulations permitted.

Sam looked over at Younger's cavernous eyes and grunted, "Huh?" It seemed prudent not to be too expansive in his response.

"Are we ready, sir?" Younger was amused at his lieutenant's plight. He had never been much of a drinker because he hated to part with the money, and for the same reason, he never smoked unless someone offered him a cigarette. Although he had no moral objections to either pursuit, he frequently felt morally superior to those who partook—particularly when they had hangovers and he did not.

Sam came mentally back to the present and croaked, "Yep. Lead us out."

Sergeant Younger turned and faced the 2nd Platoon and bawled out in his command voice, "Second Platoon! Forwaarrd march!"

As one man, the fifty-seven soldiers of the reinforced platoon stepped forward and began the four-mile march to the village of Ogliastro Cilento in column formation. More by training and instinct than conscious design, Sam set forth in time and step with his platoon.

At first the march was torturous. Although Sam had been up for hours, his body was not yet fully functional, and Sergeant Younger set a demanding pace. In the warmth and humidity of the late morning, and carrying a full pack and a rifle, Sam began to sweat out the previous night's excess. The road to the village of Ogliastro Cilento, which the soldiers would soon corrupt to "Ugly-ass Children," was yet another winding uphill road, and the soldiers gained over twelve hundred feet in altitude during the march. Within the first quarter mile up the hill, Sam became concerned that he would be sick, but despite the relief that it might bring, he did not want to do so in front of his soldiers. To the great amusement of the troops in the back of the column, he belched loudly several times as his churning stomach protested against his lack of foresight the night before. As he began to sweat profusely, he drained his canteen and belched some more.

Desperate to take his mind off the prospect of vomiting and its attending humiliation, Sam pushed his thoughts homeward. It wasn't hard to do—daydreaming of home or women was the escape of choice for most soldiers during the drudgery of a road march. In his mind, he returned to South Texas in January 1942.

The division had yet to make the move from Camp Bowie in Texas to Camp Blanding in Florida, which would come in another two months, but this January, Sam had a highly coveted leave from the division for three weeks.

He and Margaret had been married for nearly a year at this point, and about half of their marriage had been spent, for her, at Camp Bowie in a small house that Sam had rented off-post in nearby Brownwood. Despite the smallness of the house, the heat and dust of Brownwood, and his demanding training schedule, it was a happy time. They frequently went out with Perkin and one of the many local girls he dated, and through Margaret's patient tutelage Sam came to enjoy dancing—an activity he had previously detested.

It wasn't the house or the days in Brownwood that Sam thought about as he marched up the hill. His thoughts were on the time he spent back on the ranch during that short vacation. They had driven home via San Antonio and spent an evening dancing and dining there. At daylight, Sam bought two bacon-and-egg sandwiches for the road, filled his thermos with coffee, and they drove straight back to the ranch. They would not have stayed over in San Antonio if Margaret had not insisted—it was as close as they'd come yet to a honeymoon.

Sam would recollect nearly two years later in Italy that his return to the ranch with Margaret was one of the happiest times in his life. The ranch was exactly as he remembered; nothing had changed. The house was just a house, and he would get there in time—although he knew if he didn't say hello to Lupé first he would be in trouble. But it was to the stables that his attention was drawn. He had a favorite mare and an old gelding that he wished to get reacquainted with. More than anything, Sam wanted to get out of uniform and onto a horse to ride for the rest of the day. Lupé could wait. Then he caught the faint scent of the sea and the smell of his livestock, and his eyes filled with tears as his throat tightened. Through the tears, and with Margaret holding his hand, he looked around the ranch, saw his ranch hands begin to ride or walk up to say hello, and he watched the ubiquitous low-hanging clouds breeze smoothly by them to the northwest. He was home with Margaret, and if it was even for only a short time, life could not be better.

There were so many memories packed into those happy three weeks—a day out on the bay fishing from a boat with Old Perkin, clearing mesquite from a newly acquired six-hundred-forty-acre parcel of land on the west side of the ranch, hours and hours on horseback—but the thoughts that he came to that day in Italy were of Margaret and a present she had given him.

They had spent no time together as husband and wife on the ranch, and since they had been married she had spent more time there than he had, even though she had not been back to South Texas for months. The changes to his home, their home, were small but pronounced. Some, but not all, of his prized deer heads and mounted trout had been moved from the front room to a study in the back of the house. In their place, Margaret had commissioned the building of bookshelves, and hundreds, if not thousands, of books now filled his house. Some women collected porcelain dolls, but Margaret collected books; Sam's wealth allowed her to indulge her modest hobby. His house could no longer be described as a bachelor's hunting lodge, but it didn't contain many of the usual feminine touches either. It became more like a literary hunting lodge. Sam didn't care one way or the other as long as he was away from the army and at home, and he had his first inkling of what normal married life would be after the war. When evening supper was finished, he would listen to the radio with Margaret, where they followed the grim reports coming from the Philippines and Rabaul and learned of the death of Carole Lombard in an airplane crash. But as all the news in those days seemed bad, he preferred to listen to his favorite country records while Margaret read; when he sang along, his deep bass voice rattled the windows, to her considerable amusement. On the warmer nights that January, they would sit out on the porch, hold hands, and talk for hours of having a large family, of building the ranch together, and of the friends they shared who were being scattered to the winds by the war.

Margaret was a good Southern cook, which was surprising to Sam as her mother was indifferent to food at best. When she and Sam got engaged, Margaret talked to Anna Berger, Old Perkin's wife, and learned Sam's favorite five foods. Her reasoning was that five meals plus leftovers could get a couple through nearly two weeks of suppers. She then read every book she could find on Southern cuisine and sought out the oldest ladies in town for advice. Of course, books and shared knowledge can only go so far with cooking, and even after these steps Margaret was aware of her limitations. So in the weeks before the wedding, she practiced every day on her mother, her neighbors, and quite frequently, her neighbors' dogs until she surmised that she had it about right. Consequently, her fried chicken was the best Sam had ever had, and his ideal dinner was Margaret's chicken with mashed potatoes and milk gravy, green beans cooked to oblivion with fatback, cornbread muffins with butter and damson jam, and pecan pie for dessert. But as good a Southern cook as she was to become, she had no notion at all of Mexican cooking. Sam was very gratified, one day, to walk into the kitchen of the ranch house to see Margaret sitting at the kitchen table with Lupé and her two youngest daughters learning how to make pork tamales—Sam's favorite Mexican food. It wasn't usual for whites and Mexicans to mingle in South Texas, but Sam had no reservations about it and was glad to see that Margaret did not either. Lupé may not have been exactly a mother figure to him, but he had been close to her all of his life, and he valued her cooking above most things on earth. He had harbored reservations throughout his short marriage about how Margaret and Lupé would get along, and it was a pleasant surprise to see that there was no conflict as the four women laughed and joked together while they rolled the tamales. Unknown to Sam, Margaret had resolved any issues the first day she had spent at the ranch. When she told the older Mexican woman about her plans to run the ranch in her husband's absence and to make changes to the house, Lupé had protested and refused to help. Her husband would certainly refuse as well. Lupé was then told in no uncertain terms that Margaret was the mistress of the house, and that Lupé would do things her way, or Lupé and her husband could find new jobs and a new place to live. Stunned, Lupé burst into tears. She was then firmly told that Margaret would not tolerate a whispering campaign against her, and Lupé was either completely onboard or gone, and was that understood? It was.

The greatest surprise of Sam's leave came two days before they returned for Camp Bowie. It was a slow, lazy, sunny day where the temperature reached seventy degrees and Sam had gone fishing early in the morning with Old Perkin. That something was afoot was apparent to Sam as Margaret had asked him on several occasions not to plan anything for that afternoon. He suspected a surprise party, which would not have been to his liking unless it was a barbeque with brisket and ribs—and he saw no indications of that. After a large dinner with his hands and his usual post-lunch nap, his curiosity was further piqued when Margaret led him out to the stables where a ranch hand had two saddled horses waiting for them.

They rode nearly three miles to the north of the ranch house, where a lone mesquite tree stood. It was in a pasture that had been cleared by Sam's grandfather, and the tree had been left for some reason that was lost through the generations. Sam liked it, as it was a twisted old thing with abounding character and was almost dead center in the middle of his ranch. Today it had a large canvas tent standing in the shade on its eastern side.

He looked over at Margaret and asked, "What's this for, sweetheart?" Then he saw a mischievous grin on her face. "Are you thinking of a roll in the wilderness?"

Margaret laughed, her green eyes sparkling in the afternoon sun. "I might be, cowboy, but not quite yet. I'm expecting a visitor."

After Sam helped Margaret down from her horse, he tethered the horses to the tree and shot a salacious grin back at his wife, "Unless someone's waiting in the tent, I think we got the time." He walked over to the tent and pulled back a flap. Inside was a down mattress covered with several heavy blankets and two pillows at his feet. Also in the tent was a large basket—which smelled like fried chicken—and his large metal cooler. When he lifted the lid, he saw it was filled with Shiner beer and ice. Behind Sam, the wood for a campfire had been carefully laid out and prepared—all he needed to do was light it. Two folding chairs were set out by the unlit campfire facing west.

"Oh, Maggie, this is great! Who did all this?" Sam was very pleased. Although he had recently done enough camping for a lifetime, he couldn't think of anything better to do on the ranch before they left.

"Lupé and Ed set it up for us. But this is only part of it," she said in a flirtatious voice.

"By God, it's the best part. Come here. Ain't no one around for miles."

Sam scooped up Margaret and turned towards the tent but she kissed him on the cheek and slapped him playfully on the chest. "Easy there, big fella. I can hear him now. Set me down, I don't want to scare him off by seein' you runnin' around with your trousers down 'round your ankles."

Puzzled, Sam set his wife down and looked around in all directions. His ranch was absolutely flat—there was no one in sight, and he had a clear view for over a mile no matter which way he looked. The only sound he heard was the drone of an airplane.

Maggie unbuttoned her blouse and flashed some cleavage at Sam. As she buttoned her shirt back up, she said, "That's gonna have to hold ya 'til you're done, but I'll make it up to you afterwards."

"After what?" The answer was becoming apparent. The sound of the airplane grew closer and closer; Sam walked out from under the tree until he could see the plane. It was a Stearman biplane with U.S. Navy markings—the type used to train aviators at the flight school at Naval Air Station Corpus Christi. The pilot circled the mesquite tree at what seemed to Sam to be a dangerously low altitude, then headed back towards the ranch house. There was an abrupt and tight turn, the airplane aligned with the mesquite tree and then casually set down in Sam's pasture.

As the aircraft taxied over towards the mesquite tree, Margaret ran over to her horse and, after a struggle, pulled out Sam's only heavy coat from her saddle bag.

"You'll need this," she said with a big smile.

"I'm flying?" Sam looked skeptically over at the airplane, which by now had come to a halt and was idling.

"You are. Happy birthday." Margaret began to push Sam towards the plane.

"It ain't my birthday!" Sam was only beginning to form his protest in his mind. He had never flown before and was uncertain that he wanted to begin this day.

"Come on! I gotta get this plane back before long!" The pilot stood up in his cockpit and waved Sam and Margaret over. When they approached the plane, he leaned over and offered a friendly three-finger salute to Margaret.

"You must be Miss Margaret. I swear, you're prettier than Perkin said. I'm Lieutenant Junior Grade Jim Bob Norris." He looked Sam over and shook his head, "Reckon you're Sam. You're the biggest durn Aggie I ever seen. Perk wrote me that you're a cupcake, though, and won't get in." Sam's protest melted away. "But if you're gonna, get in now. I'm just signed out for a functional check flight, and I can't putter 'round all day." He leaned over and offered his hand to Sam, who shook it and climbed onto the wing.

After climbing awkwardly into the forward cockpit and getting strapped in, Lieutenant Norris said over the headset intercom, "Twenty-three to zero."

The invocation of A&M's shutout the previous fall at the hands of the University of Texas inspired Sam to lift his middle finger up over his shoulder for Lieutenant Norris's benefit. The Navy lieutenant chuckled as he gunned the engine, "That was my comms check. Guess you can hear me."

"Well, I didn't need to hear that. I didn't know the navy entrusted planes to Longhorns."

As the plane began a bumpy departure along Sam's pasture, the naval officer said, "Funny you should mention that. They'd have my bars if they found out that I stopped to give an Aggie a ride today, so this little flight has to stay on the down-low. Here it comes."

The aircraft lifted up on those words, and Sam was pressed back into his seat. In no time at all, the aircraft was leveled off at one thousand feet on a northerly heading. Sam's heart was beating like the drums to "Sing, Sing, Sing," and although he was not a fan of Benny Goodman, the song that Perkin maintained ended the depression ran through his head.

"Your wife said you might like to see the shoreline. Then maybe we'll come back and give your ranch a few passes." The naval aviator's heart rate hadn't changed at all.

"That sounds great! Thank you." Sam couldn't keep the smile off his face.

"Afraid I can't do anymore than that though. But I did promise Perkin I'd take your missus up for about ten minutes."

"You might not get her out if you do. She's read every book by and on Amelia Earhart. How d'ya know Perk?" Sam asked because it seemed polite, but he wasn't really interested. He wanted to concentrate on the flight. Sam had never been so exhilarated—it was like racing a horse and sailing on the bay at the same time. They flew through a cloud; Sam had to stop himself from screaming in delight like a child on a roller coaster.

"We learned about beer together in Austin." Norris offered no more information about Perkin; Sam asked no more questions. He was too busy looking at South Texas from its best vantage.

They made a wide sweep to their right and Lieutenant Norris unknowingly gave Sam a tour of his family's history in South Texas.

"That little village there is Gregory. It was built to support the Coleman-Fulton Pasture Company at the end of the century. They later changed the name of the company to the Taft Ranch and that's the town of Taft way off yonder to your right on the other side of your farm there. Say, did your wife tell me her last name was Taft?"

"Couldn't say," Sam said absently as he looked intently at an oil tanker and a naval escort coming into Corpus Christi Bay from the Gulf of Mexico.

"Well, it's good that I'd do anything for Perk. Hard to get fuel for civilian planes these days."

As they turned south and followed the shoreline, it wasn't long before they passed over Portland. Sam saw Old Perkin's house on its little bluff. He waved at the house with a huge grin on his face, and a minute later, the plane had crossed over the back bay and turned north again over a hive of activity in the new oilfields. In far too short a time, the plane approached Sam's ranch, and Norris dropped the plane down to fifty feet. When they crossed over a herd of Sam's cattle, the animals panicked and stampeded. Norris wheeled the aircraft over and brought it around in a simulated strafing run on the cattle—they scattered in every direction. The pilot brought the aircraft up a little and without warning did a snap roll—Sam screamed this time, then pounded the side of the Stearman and laughed until tears rolled down his cheeks.

When the plane came to a halt, he jumped out of the cockpit, ran over to Margaret and lifted her high in the air before giving her a big kiss. Sam set his wife down, ran back to the plane and offered his hand to Lieutenant Norris.

"If I can ever do anything for you, please let me know. Thank you. That was the best goddamned present I've ever had. And I don't mind sayin' that to either a Longhorn or a squid." He resolved on the spot to buy a plane as soon as the war was over.

Sam was focusing on that thought—what type of plane to buy—when Sergeant Younger brought the platoon to a halt a quarter mile short of their destination. Sam was drenched in sweat, but the climb up the mountain was just what he needed. Although he didn't feel perfect, there was no hangover in Sam's experience that a hard workout and a pleasant daydream couldn't rectify. The fog in his mind was clearly lifting, and the pounding in his head subsided solely to the now-familiar sounds of combat.

1300 hours
Ogliastro Cilento, Italy

The value of Ogliastro to Fifth Army was soon apparent to Sam. The village was three-quarters up a mountain ridge. To Sam's right, a valley opened up to the south where Highway 18 was the main line of communication. The highway passed through Ogliastro and then went down the other side of the mountain onto the Salerno plain. To control Ogliastro meant another control point on the major north-south artery. The 2nd Battalion of the 141st had been in the vicinity of the village since the night of D-day, but they were being withdrawn and placed into a different sector on the plain. Sam's 2nd Platoon was to secure Ogliastro, and then later in the day, the remainder of Able Company was scheduled to pass through en route to the next village up the ridge.

To Sam's left, the view of the battlefield to the north was excellent, and from the ridge of the mountain he could see vehicles moving back and forth through the haze. A dark layer of smoke out to sea marked at least one still burning ship of the fleet—a victim of that morning's Luftwaffe attack.

Sam sent a squad ahead of the main body to reconnoiter the town before they entered, and the report came back that there were some regimental staff officers in the village waiting for him. When he arrived, the American presence in Ogliastro consisted of a tall, handsome captain with a thin mustache sitting in the back of a jeep and smoking a thin, black cigar. Several other Americans were obviously preparing to move out and paid no attention to the newly arrived soldiers. The officer, however, looked at Sam with interested recognition. He smiled inwardly and then settled back into the jeep and affected a lazy stare at the large lieutenant as the platoon came to a halt in the village.

"Why, if it ain't the nigger-lover! And where's your cousin, Pickin' Boogers?" he drawled with evident distain at Sam.

Sam started and then recognized the officer in the jeep. "Hello there, Ronald. I swear, are you drunk already?" Sam was profoundly unhappy with the encounter with Captain Ebbins. He was known to both Perkin and Sam since high school, and their relationship had not improved with age. Sam had heard that Ebbins was newly attached to the regimental staff, and he had not looked forward to the inevitable meeting.

"Sir! You call me sir, and you salute me, Lieutenant!" Ebbins was just preparing to get nasty. He reckoned he had a score to settle with both Sam and Perkin, and he was willing to let it begin by humiliating Sam in front of his troops.

Sam's reaction puzzled Captain Ebbins. He turned and winked at Sergeant Younger, a motion that was missed by Ebbins, and then Sam looked around the village square carefully. He noted the taller buildings and their windows, and took in the village as it rose up on a hill behind the town square. Then he looked at the church and its steeple up on the hill. He seemed to come to a decision and then walked carefully to the side of the jeep so that he would not interpose himself between the jeep and the steeple. Sam came to attention and slowly and grandly knocked out a superbly martial salute—a salute worthy of the Chief of

Staff of the Army himself. He held the salute perfectly—his hand and wrist rigid and straight, his forearm inclined at exactly forty-five degrees. It was a salute learned not in the National Guard Officer Candidate School, but on the parade grounds of the Corps of Cadets at Texas A&M, and Sam held it for a lingering moment past Ebbins' casual return of the salute.

"Damn," Sam said in a low tone to Ebbins with just the faintest of unfriendly smiles. "Wouldn't you know it? No snipers." He leaned in close to the other officer, who had gone pale with the realization of what had just transpired and spoke so only Ebbins could hear: "Don't fuck with me, Ronald, or I'll shoot your dumb ass myself."

Sam stood up straight, took a step backwards, saluted again and in a strong voice said, "Great to see you again, Captain. May we have better luck next time." The white-faced and furious Ebbins ignored the salute, slouched slightly in the back of the jeep, and mentally searched for words for Sam while he looked for his driver. He did not have the chance. Sam did an about-face and looked at his sergeant, who was struggling to keep a straight face. Several soldiers were laughing outright, and Sam waved them on. He walked through the square without sparing another glance for Captain Ebbins, who was still waiting alone in the jeep.

At the other end of the square he saw Captain Waller Finley-Jones, the regiment's British liaison officer, talking to a concerned-looking Italian man in a black suit. Sam headed towards the two men. Finley-Jones excused himself from the Italian in the black suit and walked up to meet Sam.

Finley-Jones gave Sam a sharp look. "What were you doing there, Sam? You know you shouldn't salute in a combat zone . . . oh. Oh, I say, were you trying to kill that twat Ebbins?"

Sam smiled innocently at the Welshman and said, "I don't know what a twat is Waller, but I know my duty, and I did it—I was just rendering the honors that he rightly demanded in the very best way that I know how."

Finley-Jones's sunburned face broke into a delighted grin and he cried, "What can I say, Sam? World class. Sensational." He shook his head in mock sorrow. "Pity it didn't work; he is such an imbecile." Finley-Jones spied Ebbins' driver and waved him over.

"Private Dombrowski, please take Captain Ebbins back to regimental HQ, his work is done here, but I have more to do. Come back and pick me up at 1700 sharp at this square and give this note to Colonel Jamison directly. Do you understand, only to Colonel Jamison." The British officer scribbled a quick note on a small pad of paper, tore the note off and handed it to the American private. "Off with you then."

Sam watched the private run back to the jeep where Ebbins still waited. The private spoke to Ebbins, who looked back at Sam and Waller. Ebbins gave the two men the finger and said something sharply to Private Dombrowski. The jeep set off towards the Salerno plain.

Sam asked of his Welsh friend, "Do you really have work to do here or are you just trying to ditch Ronald?"

"Bit of both actually. What a prat. Anyway, let me introduce you to Mayor Giorgio Magnocavallo, which I suppose translates to George the Superstallion. I'll leave it to you to judge the verity of his name." They walked over to where the Italian had been waiting patiently and Finley-Jones made the introductions in Italian. Over the course of the next twenty minutes, Sam learned that the Italian mayor was concerned about German reprisals, fascist reprisals, running water, rape—to which Finley-Jones said in a sotto voce aside to Sam, "I think the silly bugger's safe,"—food, electricity, German shelling, American shelling, refugees, and German reprisals.

When the circle of concerns and complaints was completed and the cycle began anew, Sam patted the mayor on the back and said he would get back with him later that afternoon. Sam and Finley-Jones set out to walk the terrain and plan the defenses.

1300 hours
Pisciotta, Italy

"Have some more of these, Lieutenant," Corporal Pena said as he handed a basket over to Perkin. They were having lunch in a town square in the mountain seaside village of Pisciotta, which the soldiers called "Pisscutter" after the navy nickname for a garrison cap. Several villagers had gathered by to say hello and inquire about the soldiers and the American Army, but the squad was alone for the moment.

"Thanks. These are great. And unexpected. Okay, Pena, no avoiding it anymore. Tell me the story of these empanadas."

Pena was beginning to question the wisdom of sharing his good fortune with the detail—he did not like having attention focused on him, and right now the entire squad was listening.

"Like I told you, sir, my friend Maria made them for me last night." Pena's partial deafness had not subsided, and he compensated by talking louder than normal. That, coupled with his obvious embarrassment was making the two youngest soldiers, Kulis and Pfadenhauer, snicker. Pena glared at them and then added by way of extra explanation, "She stayed up late." The two young soldiers began to giggle.

Perkin replied, "I don't doubt it," and the giggling increased. Taking mercy on his corporal, Perkin switched to

Spanish. "Let's go check out this village." Switching back to English, he told Sergeant Kenton, "We're going to take a little walk and see if there is a *Carabinieri* post here, and if so, we'll come back and get Fratelli. Have the boys there police up our mess." He indicated Kulis and Pfadenhauer.

The two men slung their rifles and began to mosey through the village looking at shop windows, talking in Spanish, and nodding to the villagers. It turned out that Perkin's corporal had established one of the first friendships with an Italian female that was not on a fee-for-service basis. Her name was Maria, just like his wife back home in Cuero. Pena's extended family consisted of either grocers or restaurateurs, and food was important to the soldier. So he had explained to his Italian friend Maria how to make the dough for the empanadas, and he (preferring meat empanadas to dessert empanadas) had donated canned meat from his rations. All things considered, Perkin thought that they were pretty tasty, and while empanadas weren't necessarily a regular Tex-Mex staple, they made him a little homesick.

"So has the Spanish Army come to Pisciotta to rescue me?" an Irish voice asked.

Perkin started at the unexpected question and the accent, and he turned to his left to see a priest standing in the doorway of the village church. The priest was of medium height, pale with black hair and dark black eyes; he looked about Perkin's age and had a playful air about him. "Well, Padre, he thinks we're the Mexican Army, but we're really from the U.S. Lieutenant Perkin Berger." Perkin held his hand out, which after a short hesitation the priest took. Surprising Perkin, the priest had hard, calloused hands and a viselike handshake.

"Father Patrick Riley. And you are?" This was to Corporal Pena.

"Roberto Pena, Father."

"Perkin Berger?" The priest asked turning back to Perkin. "That's a rather unusual name. What kind is it?" asked the priest.

"Medieval Texan. I've heard of the Rileys before though. We have a branch of your family in my hometown in Texas. They run a restaurant called O'Riley's O'Riginal Irish Pizza. Any kin to you?"

The Irishman laughed and said, "Irish pizza, eh? I'm sure that's interesting. Have you tried the local variety yet?"

"No, but we've been a little busy since we've been here. What brings you to this corner of the world, Father?"

"Why, God of course. How about you?"

"General Eisenhower, of course." Perkin looked at the priest, shook his head and said, "Sorry, Father, I didn't mean to be flippant. I assume that everyone knows by now that an Allied Army has landed on the Salerno plain—we're just the southernmost piece of it . . . ," Perkin broke off and cocked his head, listening. He then looked to the north and said, "You know, I just realized that for the first time today, I don't hear the guns or see the smoke from the battlefield. Thank God for that."

The young priest looked at the two soldiers. Both were dirty with heavy stubble on their faces, and he thought he saw blood mixed with the dirt and grease on the sleeve of Perkin's jacket. Despite a solid five hours of sleep the night before, Perkin had dark circles under his eyes.

"I don't mean to pry, but have you had a rough time so far?" the priest asked.

"Not as rough as some, it's just been a long day. That reminds me—we need to be moving on. It was a pleasure meeting you, Father."

The priest hesitated as if he were trying to make up his mind. He looked at Perkin and then at Pena. "Lieutenant, Berger is French is it not? Are you and your men Catholic?"

"No, Father, we're all Presbyterians—just like Eisenhower. I'm sure you know American military policy is *'Cuius regio, eius religio,'*" Perkin said in mock seriousness.

The priest looked at Perkin in surprise and then laughed again. "I have to admit that I was unaware of that. Lieutenant, this may be the strangest conversation I've had in more than three years in Italy. I'll say good day to you, but first can I have a moment of your time in private? Please?" The priest nodded at the door of the Pisciotta church.

Perkin looked at the priest and saw a compelling sincerity, but he was uneasy about this Irishman in southern Italy. He did not sense ill-intent, but it did not add up either. He turned to Pena and said in Spanish, "If I'm not out in five minutes, get the boys and come down here, safeties off."

He started to follow the Irishman, but the priest turned and said to Pena in Spanish, "You had best give us fifteen minutes, my son."

1325 hours
Pisciotta, Italy

The church of Pisciotta was ancient and dark. Perkin had the sense that the church had been there since Christianity was brought to these shores, although it had not. He followed Father Riley into the church and watched respectfully while the priest blessed himself with holy water at the door and then genuflected before the altar. Perkin followed him to a small office in the back of the church.

The priest flipped a light switch, turning on a dim ceiling light. The light itself surprised Perkin as he expected candles or lanterns or even flaming torches in such an ancient holy building as this church. Father Riley sat on the edge of a shabby wooden desk that might have been considered grand some centuries before and looked at the lieutenant with a somewhat amused look on his face.

After a moment's silence as the two men sized each other up again, Perkin asked, "What can I do for you, Father?"

"Where are you headed, Lieutenant?" asked the priest directly.

"Father, I can't discuss what we're doing or where we're headed. You'll watch us pull out of Pisciotta onto a highway that goes only north and south and draw your own conclusions, but I can't tell you what our mission is. Why do you ask?"

The priest stood up and walked to an interior wall where a large map entitled 'Catholic Italy' in Latin hung. "Take a look at this map with me, Lieutenant. This is the region of Campania, and within Campania, you're in the province of Salerno." Perkin nodded—he knew that already. Father Riley continued, "In Campania, there are numerous archdioceses and dioceses, and more than a thousand churches in Naples alone. Here in the country, in southern Campania, we are farther from the church in Rome than the Neapolitans but closer to God, perhaps." He stopped and smiled, enjoying his last words. He pointed to the map and said, "This is where Campania tapers off, and this area here is where the great three regions of southwestern Italy meet: Campania, Basilicata, and Calabria."

The priest moved his finger further down the map and indicated the town of Nicastro. He started to say something, then stopped. He looked at Perkin again and said, "You are a student of history, are you not?"

"I am, Father; I was at the University of Texas working on my doctorate in history before the war. How did you know?"

"'Cuius regio, eius religio.' Whose rule, his religion— only historians and seminarians know that phrase these days, although I have to question whether your General

Eisenhower has implemented it as policy," the priest said with a smile. "Thankfully, it has had little application in faithful Italy. Ah . . . given the two choices, I judged you to be a historian and not a seminarian. I take it that you are of a low church?"

"Lower than most I reckon . . . Father, don't take this wrong, I would enjoy nothing more than to sit down and discuss history or theology with you, but I don't think that is why you asked me back here. Although since you asked earlier, Berger is French, but my family were Huguenots. Please, sir, what is on your mind?"

The priest smiled. "It is the confluence of history and the present that I thought might be of interest to you. Do you see the diocese of Nicastro here?" The priest pointed to a town on the west coast of Italy above the arch of the boot.

Perkin nodded yes.

"They have a lovely cathedral there dedicated to Saints Peter and Paul. One of the Bishops from there, Paolo Capisucco, sat in judgment of the English criminal Henry VIII . . ."

Perkin interrupted, "No kidding? When he was stripped of the title 'Defender of the Faith'?"

The priest thought for a moment and then shrugged, "Yes, perhaps. Anyway, back to this lovely cathedral—the vanguard of Montgomery's Eighth Army passed by it this morning."

Perkin stared at the priest, looked back at the map, and then looked again at the priest, "How do you know that, Father, and why are you telling me?"

"Unexpected and manifold are His works, aren't they, Perkin?" asked the priest who was obviously enjoying himself. "Do you see this town in southern Campania?" The priest pointed at a town named Policastro. Perkin nodded again.

"There is a diocese there as well. The cathedral in Policastro was built nearly eight hundred years ago. Eight hundred years ago," Riley repeated. "Yet, one day ago, the 29th Panzer Grenadier Division departed Policastro, although I don't know to where. So, if you are to pass through there, caution might be advisable. They might not have gone far because on the eighth of September, the German naval commander at the port of Sapri scuttled his tanker and all of the 29th's fuel. Apparently, he believed that the entire American Army was about to land there. No telling where he got that notion."

"Father—who are you? A Baker Street Irregular? Do you work for Donovan? Why on earth haven't the fascists had you locked up? Between Violet Gibson and the anticlericalism here, I would think that an Irish priest wouldn't be welcome in fascist Italy." Perkin was concerned and curious, but he was asking the questions because he thought that he should. If the priest worked for Allied intelligence as he suspected, or for German intelligence as was possible, he did not expect straight answers.

"Why, there's a kettle full of questions. Let me see if I can put your mind at ease. As to Baker Street, there is one in my hometown of Cork, but the only thing I guess that is irregular about it is that it's Baker's Road, not Street. And I knew a Donovan there as well, but he didn't live on Baker's Road either. I certainly never worked for him." Riley smiled at Perkin, "As for the unfortunate Miss Gibson being Irish . . . well, to paraphrase Wellington, not everything born in a stable is a horse. The Italians know that I am just a simple priest from a neutral country with a history of opposition to the British. Today, I am a member of the community at the Curia of the Society of Jesus in Rome. I just happen to be in Campania because I came down last spring to take care of my friend, Father Carlo. He was very sick, poor man. This was his church, and he just passed away last month. I offered to stay and tend to his congregation until the bishop appoints another pastor. It is just that simple. Oh, by the way, if you're heading south, avoid the inland route around Camerota into Policastro—there were Waffen SS on that road as of last evening. As a soldier, you may subscribe to *'Dulce et decorum est pro patria mori,'* but as a priest I think it's an insult to God. Avoid that road if you can."

1630 hours
Ogliastro Cilento, Italy

It was amazing, Sam thought, that only a few miles away, two armies were locked in a desperate struggle for life with nothing less than the future of civilization at stake. Yet here he was, strolling across a pleasant mountain ridge, with a good friend—both purposely striving to be oblivious to the slaughter of the combatants in the valley to his left. He was not unaware of the pain and suffering on the Salerno plain, but that fight was out of his hands for the moment. So he resolved to focus on his little corner of the war and enjoy what was an otherwise pleasant day.

"I'm sure that you got this from battalion and your company commander, but it bears repeating," Captain Finley-Jones said to Sam. "Your mission here on this quaint little hilltop is the following: one, block Highway 18 and prevent the Germans from using it to reinforce the battlefield from the south. We believe that the 29th Panzer Grenadiers are en route to Salerno from a point midway between Fifth Army and Eighth Army. It would make sense for them to travel inland and then come up the lines of communication that they control. Having said that, it also makes sense for them to probe our defenses on Highway 18 and in its valley to see if we are vulnerable there. Of course, if we are, which we are, then they could strike again on our southern flank. That brings me to point two: aggressively engage German patrols. Defend this territory tenaciously—like a bulldog protecting his turf. Use regimental artillery, call for air strikes, be profligate with automatic fires. We have enough ammunition now and enough tubes to support you—can't speak for the airpower though. Give the impression that there is a battalion on this mountain ridge and not an understrength company. A challenging task I know, but beat your chest like King Kong or mark your territory like dogs, just let Jerry know that this mountain belongs to General Clark. Three, maintain communication with company and battalion. Sounds easy enough, but our communications have been weak since D-day. They're getting better every minute, but they are not what were envisioned. Four, spend some time with the wogs. Reassure the Italians as best you can—I spent plenty of time in Italy before the war, when my father was posted to the embassy in Rome. They are good, decent people, just terribly misled. They are going to be looking to the Allies, you Americans in particular, to be their saviors from this nightmare that has come crashing down on them. I can't sympathize too much as I remember what they did to France in '40, but do try to have some compassion for your average chap and help them along. See if you can identify the fascists, and we'll sort them out later. Anyway, enough philosophy, any questions for me?" Finley-Jones had spent nearly four hours on the mountain ridge walking through the terrain in daylight with Sam and Sergeant Younger. He needed to head back to the village to be picked up.

Not for the first time, Sam was impressed with Finley-Jones. He thought of himself as proficient in defensive warfare, as he had always excelled at defense during the exercises that preceded the 36th's deployment to Europe. But Finley-Jones had a very keen eye, a didactic nature, and a true affection for the Texans with whom he served. His time on the ridge with Sam sharing his insights into terrain and German tactics was well spent as his insights were hard-won. Sam knew that Finley-Jones had earned the Military Cross in Africa and had an O.B.E. tacked to the end of his name, although Sam wasn't sure of what that meant. There was no question but that Sam's position on the ridge was strengthened from the afternoon with Finley-Jones.

"Sure, just a second. Sergeant Younger, please get started with our improvements, I'll join you after the cap'n takes off for regiment." After Sergeant Younger departed, Sam said, "I've two questions for you, sir: what's profligate mean, and are you aware that you have three last names?"

The British officer grinned at Sam and said, "After spending all afternoon with you discussing matters of the utmost importance, literally of life and death, those are the only two questions that you have for me?"

"Yes, sir. I got the rest of it—and thank you for the help. Those were the only two questions that came to mind."

"Okay, I'll make you a deal. I'll answer your two piercing questions, and then you answer two of mine."

"Ah, I show you mine if you show me yours? Fair enough, sir." Sam and Finley-Jones began the walk back to Ogliastro.

"Profligate—think of a sailor on liberty in Sydney. Mind, this is a sailor who has spent nine months at sea and not gambled or wasted a single shilling during his cruise. He pulls into Australia and all inhibitions are gone and his money flows like wine on the beautiful and willing women down under. That is profligate. Be like that sailor with your ammunition and use whatever you need—there should have been a truckload brought up this afternoon for the company. And yes, since you asked, it has occurred to me once or twice that I had three surnames. I've often said that you can never have too many. I shan't tell you about my middle names though—too embarrassing. I suppose that we British tend to go a little overboard with names sometimes. I understand you Southerners do as well." Sam nodded in reply. "Waller is a family name, and the Wallers came over with William in 1066 and later fought at Agincourt, capturing the Duke of Orleans no less. And of course, we British are nuts for combined names. But if you think that Finley-Jones is a questionable appellation, consider my cousins, the Carr family—spelled C-A-R-R— who married into the Parker family. It seems less funny to us since we refer to our automobiles as motorcars, but the name Carr-Parker usually throws Americans into fits."

Indeed it did. Sam laughed out loud for the first time that day and resolved to remember the story so that he could pass it on to Perkin, who always enjoyed hearing about names less fortunate than his own.

Finley-Jones continued, "Now it's my turn. What of your own name—I've heard some say that you are descended from President Taft, and others who argue against that proposition. Is that true? I'll ask my second question after you answer this one."

Sam pointed out an outcropping of rock that they had not seen and remarked that it would be a good place for a machine gun nest. The British officer nodded. Sam replied, "Naw, I ain't descended from President Taft; he was my great-uncle. Great-half-uncle, actually. My granddad Charlie was his half-brother, but they were pretty close."

"Did you ever go to the White House and see him?" Finley-Jones had a gaining appreciation of American history, but it was still a little spotty on timelines.

Sam laughed, "How old do you think I am? No, he was president before I was born. I did meet him once when he was the chief justice—we went to Washington when I was ten or so—but he didn't have much use for me being so young."

"I didn't realize that he was from Texas . . ."

"Oh no. The Tafts and the Sintons, my grandmother's family, were from Ohio. They were all Yankees and got involved in large-scale ranching in Texas after the Civil War. Eventually my father took over the ranch, but it's only a fraction of what it used to be."

Finley-Jones was interested in land—his father had a very nice estate of six hundred acres on the Gower Peninsula in South Wales, which he hoped to own himself some day. "What do you mean by large-scale ranching? What constitutes large-scale in Texas?"

"Well, the ranch was over three hundred thousand acres at the turn of the century. But my ranch is only sixteen thousand acres."

"Good Christ! Are you kidding me?"

"Yeah, I know it's pretty small for a ranch. I'd like to have more, but it got sold off before I got involved." Sam teased his British friend. "I'm just kidding—but although it was huge in its day, it wasn't even close to being the largest ranch in South Texas. I think the King Ranch was at least twice as big. I used to go javelina huntin' down there when I was a boy with Perk."

Finley-Jones wanted to ask what javelina hunting was, but he was fascinated by his picturesque image of the Texas ranch. "What about Indians, and is your ranch just for cattle, or is it also a farm and you grow crops?"

"Well, the Indians were sorted out by the army and the Texas Rangers before we settled down there, although the Bergers have some Texas Indian-fighters in their ancestry. There was a group of giant naked Indians, six to seven feet tall, in that part of Texas called the Karankawas. Evidently pretty nasty—they were cannibals who cooked and ate their victims while they were still alive. I understand that's where Texas barbeque originated. Anyway, they did pull a good one over on the army once. In the last century, the army was fixin' to finish off a tribe of Karanks and had 'em penned in on a little point by one of my favorite fishing holes on Corpus Bay—it's called Indian Point today. The army, being the army, decided that they'd get a good night's sleep and finish off the Indians in the morning—they had 'em trapped on this little point, and there was nowhere left to go, you see. The army woke up and moved in against the Indians after breakfast, and come to find out, all the Indians were gone. They'd waded several miles across the bay on oyster reefs that they knew of, and by morning they were twenty land miles away from the army. I'd hated to have been that company commander and have to explain to the battalion CO how the Indians got away. Think Wranosky would have handled it well?" Finley-Jones and Sam both laughed at the thought of how the explosive Lieutenant Colonel Wranosky might have handled the news.

Sam paused for a second, "What was the sixth part of your first question? Ah, as for farming, we have some crops, cotton and sorghum mostly, but the ranch is primarily a cattle ranch. Oh, and, uh, oil—we don't exactly raise it, but we have a dozen working oil wells going on the ranch these days."

"Good God, Sam. I don't mean to be crass, but you must be as rich as Croesus."

"I might be, but I've never met him so I couldn't say."

Finley-Jones smiled inwardly. "What about Perkin? Is he wealthy too?" Finley-Jones came from a school of thought that believed gentlemen did not discuss money, but he was so surprised to find that his unassuming friend was rich that he forgot the conventions of the day.

Sam normally would have shied from such a conversation as well—he certainly would not have discussed his wealth with any of the Texans. But he suspected, rightly, that Finley-Jones would be discreet, and it was unlikely that they would ever be neighbors. So he answered, "Well, Perkin's comfortable, but he wouldn't call himself wealthy. He's from my mother's side of the family—they had money too, but they're not really in the same league as the Tafts. We both came into a nice inheritance some years ago from our Grandpa Granberry. I signed my share over to Perk, so I reckon he's set for awhile, and he'll get a good remembrance from Old Perkin as well. He's either gonna stay in the army after the war or become a professor at some school—neither are very extravagant lifestyles. Either way, he's got enough now to see him through. You know, Waller, I don't really care about the money, although it's nice from time to time. We came through the depression better than most, that's for sure. I just like being a rancher, and I just wanna get home to Texas. I miss my wife and the ranch so much I can't stand it. The day I get home, take off this uniform, and get on a horse will be the happiest day of my life, and it won't matter if I have a dime or not. Besides, I have another reason to get home—can you guess what it is?

Finley-Jones looked over at his friend in surprise, "Margaret's not expecting, is she?"

"I sure as hell hope not—I ain't seen her for ten months. No, I'm anxious to try your advice." Sam smiled at his little setup of his friend.

Finley-Jones was nonplussed, "I don't remember. What advice was that?"

"Hollerin' 'let copulation thrive,' to the cows and see what they think of it. Maybe quotin' classical literature to 'em like that'd put 'em in the mood or something and I could double the herd. It's easier than wine and candles, and they don't like it when I serenade 'em." Sam and

Waller started laughing, and Sam asked, "What's my second question?"

"Yes, the second question. What is your relationship with Ebbins—how do you know that sod, and why the bad blood?"

"Well, there's a complicated history there, I'm afraid. His family is from Corpus Christi—the nearest city to where Perk and I are from. They got entangled in a lawsuit with us years ago over mineral rights on some property they bought. They knew when they bought the land that they didn't gain all of the mineral rights, but they sued us anyway when we struck oil on an adjacent tract. Of course, they lost the suit but never got over the sense that they were somehow cheated, by us or by the courts, which kind of makes sense, as I understand the leading cause of death in their family used to be five aces. I think they see the worst in people because that's how they are. Anyway, that's been a burr under their saddle ever since, and we don't have any dealings with their family anymore. When we were in high school, Perkin had a run-in with Ronald one night over a girl that they both knew. Ronald and a few of his buddies thought they were goin' to whup-up on Perkin outside of a dance hall, and if I hadn't come along maybe they would have. When I showed up, his buddies all of a sudden weren't quite so enthusiastic; they just stood by while Perk beat Ronald like a rented mule. I learned two things from that fight—Ronald's a coward deep down, and Perkin fights to win." Sam thought back to that fight—he pulled Perkin off of Ebbins after Perkin slammed Ebbins's face into the brick wall of the dance hall several times. Sam ended the fight out of fear that Perkin was going to kill him. An idea struck him, and Sam started laughing, "I realized then that Ronald was like that northern boy in the old story. Have you heard the one about the Yankee that walks into a South Texas bar with a list of names?"

Finley-Jones shook his head but grinned in anticipation—his friend Sam loved jokes but could rarely tell
them without convulsing in laughter before he got to the
punch line. The Welshman had not yet understood one of
Sam's jokes on the first telling.

"Okay, this young fella from Boston walks into a
saloon in Kingsville—that's in South Texas—with a piece
of paper in his hand. On the piece of paper, he'd written a
list of names. After he had a drink or two, the bartender
asked him what the list of names was for and he answered,
'It's a list of fellas I can whip.'

"To this, the foreman on the King Ranch stood up and
asked if his name was on the list.

"'Yep,' said the Yankee, 'it is.'

"So the cowboy says to the fella from Boston, 'Shit,
son. You can't whip me!'

"'Are you sure about that?'

"'I'm damn sure!'

"'Okay,' says the Yankee. 'I'll just cross your name
off then.'"

Sam made it through his story safely, and Finley-Jones
laughed appreciatively. Sam then went back to the subject
of Ebbins. "So Ebbins didn't have as much sense as that
Yankee, but you'd a-thought that was the last we'd see of
him, but we weren't quit of him yet. After the guard was
federalized in '40, we were sent to Camp Bowie, which
by then was in Brownwood, Texas. Some colored soldiers
from a service unit got drunk and got a little outta hand
in a colored neighborhood first and then in a white
neighborhood. The county sheriff couldn't handle it so
they called out the MPs, which is where our buddy Ronald
comes into the story. He was a second lieutenant with an
MP platoon attached to the 36th. They got overwhelmed
from the get-go and ended up gettin' chucked outta the
neighborhood by the nigra soldiers. The MPs called for

reinforcement, and our battalion was called out. We went into the neighborhoods, and there were a few scuffles but nothing serious. Them colored boys were just lettin' off steam—it wasn't too bad, but honestly it could have gotten out of hand. You know how it is. Anyway, it was about over when I heard a fella squawkin' for help, and my squad and I—I was an NCO waiting for my slot at officer candidate school back then—anyway, my squad and I went into an alley, and there was Ronald beatin' the hell out of some colored sergeant with a billy club, and a bunch of MPs standing around cheerin' him on. It didn't seem fair, so I stopped it."

"You stopped it?" Finley-Jones asked.

"Yeah, I took his club away from him. Then I whacked him about five or six times with it, and asked him, 'How do you like that, you dumb son-of-a-bitch?' I didn't know that it was Ebbins or that he was an officer until it was over. So, he filed charges against me for hittin' an officer, and I filed charges against him for abusin' the enlisted soldier. It kind of ended being a draw with us both agreein' to drop charges, and the army was willin' to let it go, as the NAACP—they're a bunch of white do-gooders helpin' out the colored folks—the NAACP was sniffin' around the army's response to the whole riot issue . . ."

The British officer smiled inwardly at Sam's description of the NAACP—based on his exposure to the Texans, he was sure that some white soldiers had used the same description, or perhaps a less complimentary one, for Sam.

" . . . The colored soldier didn't want any part of it either, so that was that. It nearly cost me my commission though, and my OCS was postponed for three months while the case was bein' resolved—that's why Perkin is senior to me even though we joined up together. As for Ebbins, the higher-ups decided that maybe someone of his limited talents shouldn't be a military policeman,

so what did they do? Well, in a perfect world, they'd
a-chucked him out, but they couldn't. His family has ties
to Pappy O'Daniel, the ex-governor of Texas, and you
know the 36th was a state organization . . . so, let's just
say that there are a lot of chits floating around and one
got called in on this. I know it's hard to believe but they
made him an infantry officer."

Finley-Jones snorted and said, "That sounds about
right. I've had my doubts about the good captain since we
landed. I don't think that he would have come this close
to the fighting today other than he met some Italian bint
from this village. I'll give him this much though, he has
an eye for the ladies—she is an incredible sight. She's so
pretty that it makes you ache, which reminds me that I
need to find one of my own—I'm getting so desperate
that I'd roger the crack of dawn if given the chance."

Private Dombrowski was waiting for Captain Finley-
Jones at the appointed place, and the British officer hopped
into his jeep. "Don't hesitate to call for support, and I'm
sure that I'll be by tomorrow. Until then, cheers, mate."

1900 hours
One Mile South of Santa Marina, Italy

It had been a long day and everyone was tired and
ready to halt. That was fine with Perkin—they were high
up in the mountains on roads that had been forgotten
by Mussolini. Perkin had not intended to drive at night,
as headlights make an attractive target for airmen and
soldiers alike, but the unfamiliar mountain roads made
such an endeavor nearly suicidal in any case.

They found themselves on this mountainside near the
village of Santa Marina while they were in the process of
bypassing Policastro and any remnants of the 29th Panzer
Grenadier Divison. That such straggling units were still

in the area was beyond question. As they approached
Policastro, they had seen a small convoy of halftracks and
armored cars heading west-northwest on the road Father
Riley had warned them of. Had they been five minutes
further along, a confrontation with the Germans could not
have been avoided, as their highway crossed with the one
the Germans were using. The Texans had pulled off the
road behind some scrub brush, turned off their jeeps, and
listened. The sounds of the departing armor told them the
Germans had not seen them and were leaving the area.

Perkin and his soldiers had waited another five
minutes, and then they shot across the juncture of the
roads, and within a mile they left the highway and headed
up the mountain road towards Santa Marina. This was
not on their maps but had been suggested to them by
the *Carabinieri* in Camerota. The corporal there had told
them that he would have guided them himself, but he did
not wish to walk back, and besides, Italy was out of the
war. He would, however, draw them a map showing them
how to get around Policastro, and could he please have
some more cigarettes?

Perkin could see Santa Marina in the distance when he
waved the party over into a pasture protected from the road
by trees. Unlike Texas, there were no fences to worry about,
and the soldiers found a secluded spot with relatively flat
ground on which to lie. They ate cold canned rations, the
empanadas being long gone, and Perkin had prohibited
fires. As Sergeant Kenton saw to security assignments in
the dwindling light, Perkin sat in the front seat of his jeep,
deep in thought. When he had come out of the church
in Pisciotta that afternoon, he had seen Sergeant Kenton
waiting instead of Corporal Pena. Kenton had come in
search of the two Texans and had found Pena standing
outside the church smoking a cigarette. He had sent Pena
back to bring the jeeps down to the church.

Kenton had looked at Perkin and seen an unusual seriousness on his face. "What's up, sir? Pena said the priest wanted to talk to you alone," Kenton had asked.

"Yeah, it was kind of odd. He had caught the clap from a nun, and he wanted me to have a look at his pecker. He must have thought I have some experience in these things. I should've referred him to Kulis." Perkin had joked, half in thought.

"What'd you tell him?" Kenton asked with a grin.

"Rub some dirt on it." Perkin said absently as he came to an internal decision and started towards the jeep.

Kenton had laughed but not pressed the issue any further. If the lieutenant wanted to talk about it, he would later, thought his sergeant.

When they left the church, they had loaded up in the jeeps and drove to the highway above the town. After only a hundred feet or so, Perkin had Kulis pull off the road. He had grabbed his binoculars and trotted back to a small clear space of road that overlooked the church. Perkin sighted in on the bell tower and waited patiently. Ten minutes later he was rewarded when Father Riley had appeared in the tower, a small figure standing next to the bell. Wasting no time, Riley had bent his head, said a short prayer and then released a white pigeon out of the bell tower and crossed himself. The bird circled Pisciotta several times before streaking off to the south. Perkin had followed the bird with his binoculars until it was out of sight, and then he looked back to the bell tower. Father Riley was looking back at him with binoculars as well. When the priest saw that he had Perkin's attention, he lowered his binoculars, smiled broadly and acknowledged Perkin with a mock palms-out salute. Perkin had returned the gestures with a wave, and the priest turned and left the bell tower.

As he had walked back to his jeep, his soldiers saw their lieutenant shaking his head with a bemused look on his face. Perkin hopped back in the jeep and sat there deep in thought. After a long pause he had waved his hand forward, and the procession went on until it stopped at Santa Marina that evening.

"Sergeant Kenton?" Perkin asked.

"Sir?"

"Are we set for the night?"

"Yes, sir. I have Kulis and Ewart on security, and they'll be relieved in a couple of hours."

"Good. Come with me." Perkin pulled a bottle out of his pack, and he and Sergeant Kenton walked away from their camp over to an outcropping of rock that overlooked the town and the Gulf of Policastro far below them. They carefully sat down on the edge of the rocks, and their feet dangled nearly two hundred feet above the mountain below them.

Perkin said as he extracted the cork from his bottle of limoncello and passed the bottle over to Kenton, "What an unusual day this has been."

"Yes, sir, I reckon it ain't the last one that we'll have in Italy. Damn that stuff is tart, what's it called?" In the darkness, Kenton made a face that Perkin could not see.

"Limoncello. I guess it's lemon-flavored grain alcohol—pretty tasty though ain't it?"

"I reckon it grows on you, Lieutenant."

"Most drinks do. Well, whaddya think about today?" Perkin asked.

"Well, sir, I think that the boys were shit-hot this morning. The Germans have to be missing their patrol by now, but they may not be in a position to spend time looking for 'em. Hopefully, they'll just give 'em up for lost. I hope our *Carabinieri* friend don't get in trouble for helping us."

"Yep. Me too. I suppose that you're wondering about the priest in Pisscutter today." Perkin had decided to tell

Sergeant Kenton about his conversation with the priest. He trusted his sergeant to keep it to himself, and he wanted Kenton's thoughts on what transpired.

"Yeah, how bad was his clap, and what'd the nun look like?" Kenton grinned in the dark.

"He showed me a picture; she looks like Corporal Pena, only her mustache was fuller." Both soldiers laughed out loud at the image and were shushed by Private Kulis, who was patrolling some forty yards away.

When they quit laughing, Kenton said, "Ah, sir, you're going straight to hell when you die—making fun of a holy man like that."

"That may be, but I ain't sure he was a priest. I dunno." Perkin recounted what transpired as closely as he could remember. Kenton whistled softly when Perkin told him about the warning of the 29th Panzer Grenadiers, and again when he told him about the carrier pigeon. "So, what d'ya reckon was going on?"

"Beats me, sir. I don't see how an Irishman, even a priest, could be in Italy without getting visited by Mussolini's secret police. How do we know that he don't work for the Germans? Some Irish are sympathetic with Hitler—even back home. Maybe that Kraut patrol was looking for us? Maybe that pigeon was to tell them of our presence down here."

"Maybe, but why warn us about the Germans in Policastro?" Perkin asked. "If he's setting us up, he wouldn't tell us about Jerry, would he? I've thought about it all afternoon, except when Kulis was going telling us about his heroics last night—that took my mind off of it." Perkin took another pull from the bottle of limoncello and then handed the bottle to Kenton, who, after some hesitation, took another drink. "By the way, did you ask Kulis if he wrapped his little ranger up, or is he gonna be in the same boat as our priest—except real this time?"

"Well, he said he did. Said he's always paid attention to the V.D. talks and claims he used eight or nine rubbers, but it weren't clear if that was all at once or over the course of the night." Kenton laughed. "I reckon we'll find out the truth in about three days or so. Back to the priest—are you going to talk to the Limeys about him?"

"No. I don't think so. He could be working for us, and I wouldn't want to snitch him out to the British or anyone else. Think I'll wait and talk to Cap'n Lockridge when we get back."

"Yes, sir. What's the plan for tomorrow?"

"More of the same—early departure, and we'll see if we can quickly skirt Policastro and get back on the highway. Outside of the Germans, I'm kind of concerned about our English cousins lightin' us up when we approach their lines. I doubt that they're expecting us."

Chapter Seven

September 12, 1943
0630 hours
Ogliastro Cilento, Italy

"Don't get too attached to this village, Sam. I don't think that you're going to be here for long," said James Lockridge, the battalion S-2.

"Shit, Jim. I ain't had time to get attached. It takes me awhile to develop undying loyalty to an Italian village, and there's not a single gin and tonic to be found in this place." That was bravado speaking. The last thing that Sam had wanted the previous night was more alcohol.

The night had been quiet with no known attempted incursions into the Able Company area of operations, but Sam had stayed up for most of the night, waiting in vain to deal with the crises as they came. It was the first time since D-day that he had spent a night on the line in charge of defending a sector of territory, and he was fairly nervous. It was not that he was not confident—that was seldom a problem for Sam Taft. But he was concerned about night fighting, command and control of his spread-out platoon, and of making mistakes in general. He knew intellectually that this would be the first of perhaps hundreds of nights in such a situation and he needed some sleep, but an odd mixture of anxiety and professionalism drove him to shake awake Private Christian, his radio operator, and travel on foot personally to check on his observation posts twice during the course of the night. What he had seen reassured him. He had been properly challenged and not shot by his soldiers, which he regarded as a good first step. His soldiers were alert, paying attention, and enjoying not being shot at. By daylight, he had managed to accumulate four hours' sleep, which would get him through the day but not restore his normally happy nature.

Lieutenant Colonel Wranosky, the battalion commander, and his intelligence officer had come to Ogliastro on their own rounds and were meeting with the Able Company officers when Captain Lockridge told Sam not to get attached to the village.

"Where are we headed?" Sam asked of his friend.

"We don't know yet, Sam," replied Jim Lockridge. "There is talk at regiment that General Dawley believes that our line is overextended and that we'll be withdrawing some units in the center and on the left to tidy that up. Shouldn't affect 1st Battalion though. But I've also heard rumors that we'll be withdrawn from the right flank and trucked to the left to fill a gap between us and the 45th Division. Bottom line is, I don't know, but I doubt that they'll just keep us here out of the action for long. I expect we'll know by noon."

Despite the universal expectation that they would be pulling out during the course of the day, Lieutenant Colonel Wranosky wanted to take a look at Able Company's positions. They started with Sam's platoon, as his soldiers were spread out closest to Ogliastro. Sam noted that both Captain Spaulding and Colonel Wranosky nodded approvingly as he walked them through his positions, and he was pleased when they offered only minor suggestions. Lieutenant McCarter's platoon fared just as well, mostly because Captain Spaulding had colocated his headquarters the previous night with Lieutenant McCarter's platoon and had helped site his observation posts.

The mountain ridge offered an ideal position to see most of the Salerno plain—at least it would have had the haze from the smoke of battle not obscured much of the battlefield. While the men were walking back to Ogliastro, however, they observed an event that remained with them for the rest of their lives.

Two British Spitfires approached their position on the ridge from the south. The two airplanes were low enough that Sam imagined he could feel the heat and the rush of the aircraft, and he lifted his arms up as if to though to touch them as they flew by. The two warplanes were hugging the terrain at an altitude of only two hundred feet above the ground, and as they passed over the ridge— close enough that Colonel Wranosky's party could see the RAF markings clearly on the fuselages of the planes— they dropped into a sharp approach angle.

"We must have gotten the airfield operational at Paestum," remarked Wranosky. "I wonder if the Spitfires are the first to use it." American engineers had bulldozed a battlefield runway near the beaches at Paestum, and it was hoped that Allied airpower would soon begin to make an impact on the battle. The group watched as the planes quickly and gracefully lined up with the runway, and Sam was carried away in an instant to Margaret's gift of flight over a year before. He began to smile as he imagined the pilots' exhilaration—the sheer joy and freedom of flying one of the premier warplanes of the day—and he felt a friendly wave of envy as he relived the delight of flying over his ranch. *If only I had that kind of mobility on the battlefield today,* he thought.

Without warning, the envy was shattered. Nearly all of the antiaircraft artillery of the 36th Division opened up on the British warplanes, and almost everyone on the ridge ducked as 40mm rounds passed over their heads and into the valley behind. The lone exception was Lieutenant Colonel Wranosky. The stocky officer ran to a precipice of the ridge that overlooked the Salerno plain and screamed at the air defenders to cease fire until the veins popped out in his bull neck, but it was pointless, of course. The American gunners were two miles distant and proved unerringly accurate in their fire. Within seconds, the port wing on the lead aircraft was splintered and the Spitfire went into an uncontrollable roll. Even seeing this, the distant gunners did not let up on the plane and the 40mm rounds continued to pommel the aircraft. It was less than ten seconds from the first shot before the lead aircraft exploded in a large fireball. Seeing the tracer fire track into the lead aircraft, the second pilot tried desperately to peel off and get out to sea but was hit as well. The group on the ridge watched in despair as the smoking Spitfire crashed into the ocean. No parachutes were seen emerging from the downed airplanes—their pilots had no chance to bail out.

"Oh, Jesus, what have we done?" Wranosky looked at his officers with a stunned expression. His emotions were turning from shock to anger, and from anger to fury, and he took his helmet off and slammed it to the ground. "What a pointless fucking way to die!"

Sam shared his colonel's sentiments but said nothing. No one did. Sam was sickened by the shooting, and it made him profoundly sad. Mistakes are made in war, and people die unfairly; Sam reflected that perhaps that is truer in war than in any other endeavor of mankind. But with all the carnage surrounding them, it just seemed more sad when someone died as a result of an accident or negligence—an unnecessary, pointless, meaningless end to a human life. Somehow, Sam thought, it was even worse when friendly fire killed those who were truly friends and allies like the British. Shaking his head, he adjusted his rifle and pack and prepared to move on with the rest.

0705 hours
Vibonati, Italy

The morning started out well. The soldiers had the best night's sleep they'd had since arriving in Italy three days before. Even the soldiers who took turns patrolling the perimeter of their little camp had at least six hours sleep each, and Perkin absolutely thrived in the crystal clear starry night and the cool mountain air.

They began moving slightly after dawn and were through Santa Marina before any of the villagers were awake. Perkin had considered stopping and seeing about mountain roads that would give him a clear passage around Policastro and Sapri, but there were no signs of life when they moved through, so they kept on going. It was Vibonati, the next village, where Perkin knew their luck had changed for the worse.

They stopped in Vibonati when they saw a *Polizia* sign hanging from a single hinge on the corner of a rundown building. As Fratelli explained to Perkin, the sign indicated that this was not a *Carabinieri* post, but a *Vigili Urbani* post—a constable or a village policeman. Although it was still early, a light inside suggested a police officer on duty, and Perkin and Fratelli entered the small stationhouse. For the first time, they found an Italian official not only completely unwilling to help but openly hostile to the Americans. When Perkin walked into his station, a bald but otherwise hirsute fat policeman with porcine black eyes saw the American uniforms, bolted to his feet, and reached for the pistol in his holster.

Perkin quickly walked the few feet to the officer, who was struggling to get his gun out. He put his left hand firmly on the man's right arm and said kindly with a smile, "Hold your horses there, pardner. We're from Texas." Fratelli automatically translated this as, "Please put your pistol down, signore. We're American soldiers."

The police spat on the floor and continued to struggle to get his pistol out. He let loose a hostile stream of words which required no translation, although Fratelli reported in a mocking tone with a fake Texas accent, "It appears he don't dig our chili, sir."

Perkin tightened his grip on the arm of the policeman, smiled grimly at his northern private and said, "It appears he don't. Tell him to leave his gun alone or I'll have to take it away." Perkin held his right hand up with his palm out as if to calm a temperamental child, but neither the gesture nor the order had any effect. The policeman first tried to push Perkin away with his free hand, and then he let go of his pistol and tried an inadvisable and inaccurate punch at the much taller American.

As Perkin took a step back, thinking that he could still calm the policeman, Fratelli walked forward quickly, shouldered his lieutenant aside and rapped the Italian hard in the face with the butt of his Browning Automatic Rifle. The Italian staggered and then dropped sharply to the floor. He sat stunned for a moment and then quickly put his hands to his face—his nose was obviously broken and he spat blood onto the floor. Through his hands and while spitting, he swore loudly at the Americans until Fratelli bent over and spoke softly into the policeman's ear.

The policeman glared at Fratelli through watery eyes but quieted down immediately. What the Jersey private told the Vibonati constable in the Neapolitan dialect, Fratelli's home language, translated very loosely in sentiment to, "Love me, love my lieutenant. Shut up you worthless fat fuck, or I'll cut your goddamned balls off." Fratelli didn't translate this for Perkin.

Fratelli looked up at his lieutenant and said, "Sir, we're gonna have to do something with Andy Gump here, or he's gonna snitch us out to the Germans. He's a fascist. He's gotta be." Fratelli nodded towards a picture of a helmeted and glaring Mussolini on the wall—the policeman had not taken it down since Il Duce's arrest the previous July. The private lowered his BAR and positioned the business end of the barrel an inch away from the Italian policeman's left eye.

Perkin was irritated—not at Fratelli, but at himself for not controlling the situation before it got out of hand. He was becoming unhappy with his options. He looked around and saw that in addition to Mussolini's martial portrait, a desk and chair, a telephone, a gun case, a wall-mounted map, and a small jail cell comprised the totality of the holdings of the Vibonati police station. Perkin nodded to the cell and said to his private, "Chuck him in there. Keep the key." As Fratelli complied with his orders, Perkin walked to the map and looked it over quickly. Fortunately, it showed the local mountain roads. After taking the map from the wall and stuffing it into his jacket, he leaned over to the policeman's desk, where a candlestick telephone stood. He picked up the phone and violently tore the line from the stationhouse wall. "Here's hoping that this is a one-phone village. Tell him to be quiet!"

Fratelli did so, and then he hesitated, " . . . Lieutenant?"

"Yes?"

"Do you want me to run a bayonet through him?"

Perkin laughed, "It's temptin' on general principles, but we ain't at war with the likes of him. Let's get outta here."

The two soldiers left and loaded up in their respective jeeps. Sergeant Kenton, who was in the back of Perkin's jeep, leaned forward and said, "It sounded like y'all had quite the party in there." Perkin raised an eyebrow and nodded sardonically. He waved his hand forward and the three jeeps pulled away from the station, leaving Vibonati and the fat constable behind.

0745 hours
Sapri, Italy

It took the Texas patrol over half an hour to navigate down the mountain road from Vibonati to the outskirts of the larger port town of Sapri. The road that they were on was like other mountain roads they had seen. In some places, the road was reasonably improved with gravel and culverts for the multiple little streams that they crossed. Other areas of the same road were better suited for horses or mules than even the American jeeps. Several switchbacks forced the team to come to a crawl as they navigated through unnerving turns around steep mountain walls on one side and seemingly steeper cliffs on the other. Several times they had to pull too close for comfort to the edge to pass Italians on foot or in horse-drawn wagons. They saw no automobiles. Finally the road appeared to straighten out for a direct run into Sapri—only one more bend, and then Perkin believed that they could work their way around the town on the lateral back roads, emerging on the southbound highway.

The German military police had already been notified by the village of Vibonati. The policeman there was a dedicated fascist, as were his brother, the mayor of Vibonati, and his first cousin (once removed), who was the secretary to a member of the Fascist Grand Council. It had taken five minutes of yelling before the constable was released by a citizen of Vibonati with a spare key kept in the policeman's desk. Three phone calls later from the town hall, and he was talking to the German provost at the port of Sapri. The Germans had to scramble to put together three small teams to cover the various permutations of trails coming down the mountain. The German team on the road used by Perkin's patrol consisted only of a motorcycle with a MG-34–equipped sidecar. They stopped short of the bend at a small crossroads in what seemed a good spot and turned off the motorcycle to listen. It was a good decision, as the engines on the Americans' jeeps were whining loudly as the drivers used the gears to slow their jeeps coming down the steep grade.

As the first American jeep came around the bend, the German gunner opened up at less than fifty yards—point-blank range for the machine gun. The driver opened fire with his MP-40, the submachine gun frequently and incorrectly known to Allied soldiers as a *Schmeisser*. Both Germans fired at the driver of the jeep and Private Wagner, Perkin's medic, was killed instantly. Private Ewart's neck was pierced two seconds later as he stood up to man the Browning machine gun in the back of the jeep. Ewart screamed and clapped his hands to his throat—all thoughts of manning the weapon gone. Corporal Pena was shot by the driver of the German motorcycle as his jeep rolled uncontrollably past the impromptu roadblock and crashed into an ancient stone wall unofficially marking the town limits of Sapri. The impact of the crash threw all three Texans from the jeep—two already dead or dying and the grievously wounded Pena. The corporal hit hard against the stone wall and did not move again.

Although the driver of the German team continued to

fire over the head of his gunner at the jeep as it rolled past, the gunner retrained his MG-34 quickly on the second jeep as it came around the bend. The gunner fired again at the driver, this time Private Kulis. None in the second jeep were hit by directed fire, but the burst from the German gun shattered the windshield of Perkin's jeep, spraying glass onto the private's face. Kulis instinctively swerved the jeep to his left and into the woods lining the road.

Perkin and Kenton jumped out of the jeep before Kulis brought it to a stop. Perkin yelled, "Get the bazooka!" at Sergeant Kenton, and "Flank 'em," to Private Kulis but there was no need. Private Pfadenhauer in the third jeep had heard the machine gun fire from the German motorcycle and was ready at his Browning as his jeep came around the bend.

All soldiers are trained to be proficient with weapons, but some soldiers simply excel with the implements of war—the men throughout the ages that seem born to knives, swords, lances. Pfadenhauer was born to use firearms. If it relied on gunpowder, Private Roscoe Pfadenhauer could shoot it and shoot it well. Over the rapid fire of the MG-34, Perkin heard the slower fire of the Browning M1919 as Pfadenhauer engaged the German motorcycle team. He fired only a short burst, and then it was quiet. By the time that Perkin made it to the road five seconds later, the skirmish was over.

Perkin saw the crashed jeep and ran flat out past the German motorcycle to where Pena lay crumpled up against the wall. A quick glance at Wagner told him the medic was dead, but he did not see Ewart. Perkin looked over the wall—his soldier lay twisted and lifeless against the trunk of a dusty olive tree on the other side. He pulled Pena away from the wall and laid him on his back on the ground. Sick to his heart, he knelt next to the wounded corporal and wrapped Pena's hand around the gold crucifix resting on the corporal's chest. As Perkin reached for Pena's throat to check for a pulse, he jumped as a bloody and fierce-looking Kulis administered the *coup de grace* to the severely wounded German driver with his M-1. There would be no protest from Perkin this time. His shaking hands found a pulse, but it seemed weak.

"He's alive. Kulis, give me a hand here. Kenton, please bring Ewart back over here, and load the dead boys up in my jeep. Get the Browning off this wrecked one and whatever we can scrounge—ammo, gas, food. We leave in three minutes."

Perkin ripped open the leg of Pena's trousers above his leggings and nearly cried as he saw what had happened to his good soldier. "Hang in there, Roberto," he whispered in Spanish to the unconscious corporal. Pena's leg looked as though it had been chopped apart by an angry butcher. The rounds had entered Pena's leg at and above the knee. Some of the 9-millimeter rounds had directly hit and shattered the corporal's knee and femur; others had ripped through his leg and exited on the other side before coming to rest in Wagner's dead body. Between the shredded flesh of Pena's leg, Perkin could see splintered fragments of bone. Worse, he could see blood pulsing from the wound. *Arterial bleeding,* thought Perkin as he whipped off Pena's belt and worked it around the corporal's upper thigh as quickly as he could for a tourniquet. Meanwhile, Kulis frantically dumped a packet of sulfa powder over the wounds and stuffed and wrapped gauze wadding around the corporal's leg.

Perkin looked around to see the progress of the other soldiers, "We're done here! We need to get moving before the Krauts come check out the noise!"

"Sir! Do you want me to burn the jeep and the Kraut bike?" Sergeant Kenton was reaching for a grenade.

Perkin thought for a moment. He hated to leave the Germans with any usable equipment, and an easily repairable jeep would be of value to them. On the other hand, the smoke would lead the Germans directly to this spot. *Well*, he thought, *they'll find it quickly enough anyway.*

"Help me push the bike over to the jeep!" All the soldiers pitched in and they rolled the German BMW motorcycle over to the wrecked jeep. On Perkin's command, they pulled the dead German soldiers off the motorcycle and out of the sidecar and laid them across the road from the stone wall. Perkin quickly unscrewed the cap of the gas tank and they tipped the motorcycle over onto the side of the sidecar and then upside down. There was not much gasoline in the motorcycle's tank, but what there was spilled out onto the road and spread underneath the American jeep.

"Move out!" When his jeep passed the stone wall, Sergeant Kenton tossed a grenade into the gasoline. Both the jeep and the motorcycle went up loudly in a large fireball and the wrecked equipment began to burn fiercely. A dark angry plume of smoke clearly marked the site of the skirmish, and as they drove away, the soldiers could hear what sounded like a string of firecrackers going off as the flames ignited the ammunition of the MG-34.

0915 hours
Acquafredda, Italy

"Si, si, si, signore! I will help, but you must leave Acquafredda quickly." This was from Vittorio Di Biagio, the mayor of Acquafredda.

Mayor Di Biagio was not originally inclined to help the Texans when he was approached by the local *Carabinieri* for guidance. The junior policeman had not been inclined to help either, as there had been German troops all over the area, but he felt he did not have sufficient authority to turn down the Americans. Although he reported to the *Carabinieri* sergeant in Sapri, he had gone to Di

Biagio for guidance because the phones to Sapri were not working. The mayor's ill-considered first response was to tell the Americans that he would like to help but could not do so without permission from his political masters, and he could not contact them because the telephones did not seem to be working. One look at the deep, abiding, anger on the face of the tall lieutenant quickly changed his mind, and Di Biagio began to stammer that perhaps he could be of some assistance. The propriety of his change of heart was further confirmed when the mayor noticed that Sergeant Kenton had indelicately pointed his M-1 Garand at his face and wherever the mayor moved, the rifle still pointed at his face. It was quite upsetting.

"Si. We don't have a hospital, but we have a very good doctor. He can look after your soldier. But you must leave before the Germans come—they have troops in Sapri, and they come out here almost daily. But you know about the Germans in Sapri," he added weakly. The mayor was literally wringing his hands at his dilemma. He believed the Germans would in fact come to Acquafredda again, and all of Italy was hearing rumors of savage German reprisals against Italians since the armistice, but he dared not anger the Americans either. Di Biagio was smart enough to know that a neutral position between the Americans and the Germans was unsustainable and unlikely to win him friends or sympathy with either. These Americans were quite unlike the friendly tourists he had met before the war—both the Americans and the Germans could be, he reflected, very demanding.

Di Biagio looked at the tall American. He had what appeared to be blood on his dirty uniform—quite a lot of it, in fact. He carried a brass-knuckled trench knife tucked into his leggings, and the pockets of his light jacket bulged with what Di Biagio rightly suspected were hand grenades. The American lieutenant carried a German

Luger in an American holster on his web belt and handled the famous Tommy gun as if it were a natural extension of his arm. More concerning to Di Biagio, however, was the look on the American's face. At first glance, the mayor thought that Perkin's deeply tanned face and coal-black hair suggested that he, like so many Americans, could have had Italian blood. Then he looked into Perkin's ice-cold blue eyes and knew he had never seen an Italian with eyes like those. There was no compassion for Di Biagio's dilemma in those eyes, and he knew there would be no arguing with this man.

"Understand me well, Mayor," Perkin brought his face within inches of the unhappy Italian. "I appreciate your help, but I had rather that it had been more forthcoming. If my soldier is dead when we return with the Eighth Army or has been ill-treated or turned over to the Germans, I will hold you personally responsible." Perkin fixed him with his eyes and repeated, "Personally responsible. Do you understand?"

The door to Di Biagio's office opened, and the doctor of Acquafredda walked in. He looked first at the mayor, saw no help or guidance there, and turned to the American officer and said in English, "Signore, I regret to inform you that your man has died. I . . . " He stopped speaking and took a step backwards. The look on Perkin's face was murderous, and the doctor was afraid that he was to become the classic victim of bearing bad news. The doctor had only just arrived after being rushed over to the mayor's office by the *Carabinieri* but the American soldier was already dead. The doctor had looked at the wounds anyway, and thought that Corporal Pena's death would have been inevitable unless he had received immediate and professional care.

Perkin pushed past the doctor and said to Sergeant Kenton and Private Fratelli. "Come on, boys. Let's get out of this goddamn place." He walked out of the office to a small square, where Kulis stood guarding the jeeps. Pfadenhauer had entered the town church with his Springfield and climbed to the top of the bell tower to watch the road coming into Acquafredda.

"Signore. May I have a word please?" The doctor introduced himself as Dr. Giordano. "Your man. There is nothing that anyone could have done. I'm sorry, but his artery was severed. I am sure he died within minutes of being wounded." The doctor touched Perkin's arm and asked, "Is there anything that I can do for you?"

Perkin was about to tell the man to go to hell, but he saw an earnestness on the doctor's face that softened his anger slightly. "Doctor, if you would please look at Private Kulis here, I would appreciate it. He has some glass in his face and might need stitches."

"I'm okay, sir."

"Shut up, Kulis. Please, doctor, take a look at him." Perkin called up to the church bell tower. "Howie, anything?"

"No, sir, no traffic on the road in either direction beyond some of them donkey carts we been seeing."

Perkin wanted to sit in his jeep but did not because of the three bodies in the back. While the doctor put twenty stitches in Kulis's cheek, he walked around the small square thinking about their mission and what to do next. He thought of asking the doctor to take care of their dead, but he knew that should be his responsibility. Besides, he doubted that an Italian Catholic church would bury his two dead Protestant soldiers, and he thought that Pena should be interred with Wagner and Ewart.

Two older Italian women, both fat and wearing black dresses and scarves, tentatively approached Perkin. When they had his attention, they gave the slightest of curtseys and handed him two large baskets. They waited as Perkin

waved Fratelli over, and then indicated that he should
bend over. The ladies kissed him on each cheek and both
said solemnly, "Grazie, signore." One of the baskets was
filled with a large wedge of white cheese wrapped in a
yellow towel, two large round loaves of bread, a canning
jar of small dark-purple olives, two bunches of grapes, and
three bottles of wine. It was a very nice present, and he was
touched by the gesture. The other basket contained clean
white sheets. He looked up at the two women who, seeing
his puzzlement, said something in Italian. Perkin looked to
Fratelli for a translation, but the younger soldier's eyes had
filled with tears. "They're to cover our dead, sir." Perkin
thanked the ladies with tears in his own eyes, and the two
old ladies wandered off discussing the nice Italian-looking
lieutenant with the strange blue eyes.

Although he was deeply touched by the ladies' gesture,
his anger, while slowly subsiding, was not yet gone.
Perkin reviewed the morning's events over and over and
in retrospect, decided he should have allowed Fratelli to
kill the policeman. It would have been nothing short of
murder, and earlier would have been out of the question,
but in the square of Acquafredda only two hours later, he
resolved to stop in Vibonati on their way north to see to
the fat constable.

1015 hours
Ogliastro Cilento, Italy

It had been nearly two hours since Sam said goodbye
to the battalion staff and his company commander. For
the time being, he was in charge, although he could not
claim to be enjoying the experience. He felt that he was in
a holding pattern, waiting for the battalion to be moved
into combat, and while Sam hadn't particularly enjoyed
his first exposure to combat on D-day, he knew that he

had been brought to Italy to fight, and he wanted to get moving. The sooner that the Germans were defeated, the quicker he'd get home, he told himself frequently. Just as he didn't much care for putting up and repairing fences on the ranch, it was a chore that had to be done.

Coupled with his desire to get on with the war, Sam was profoundly disturbed by the friendly fire incident on the ridge. The more he reflected on the deaths of the pilots and the loss of their valuable airplanes, the darker his mood became. Would his end in the war come at the hands of a friendly soldier? Still, he knew the war wouldn't wait until his good nature returned and, while he wasn't in combat, he had duties to attend to—his direction from Lieutenant Colonel Wranosky was to "carry on in Ogliastro until told otherwise."

His platoon was still spread out over the ridge, though he had a handful of troops in the village with him. Those soldiers were doing what soldiers do: they cleaned weapons; checked and rechecked their ammunition; ate delicious Italian croissants, called *cornetti*, by the handful; and drank American coffee; as the Italian variety was hard to come by (although stolen American rations were already beginning to be sold in the Italian cafes). Many soldiers ate the wonderful gelato for breakfast, most smoked cigarettes, and all tried very hard to communicate with the Italian women.

Some American soldiers talked to the straggling Italian soldiers who had, after hearing of the armistice, simply left their posts and headed home—some with weapons and some without. If the Italian soldiers resented the presence of the Texans, they did not let it show. Although many were clearly elated to be out of the war, most seemed lifeless and tired and just wanted to go home without fighting again. If the Americans were going to fight the Germans, well, that was their business, and the Italians would stay out of it.

Sam had spent part of the morning talking to locals and Italian soldiers in the company of an intelligence NCO that Captain Lockridge had sent to the village. Sergeant Scott Taylor was from Boone, North Carolina, and upon his induction into the army in 1940, had been trained in Italian and German after showing an aptitude for languages. All of his acquired languages were spoken very precisely and correctly, albeit with a pronounced and inextinguishable Appalachian accent.

The two men talked to the Italian soldiers to determine whether they had any information on German dispositions and intentions. Taylor made a point of being respectful to all of the Italian soldiers and of being particularly deferential to the officers and chummy with the NCOs, while Sam chatted to the officers. It was a wasted effort. The Italians would have been happy to cooperate, but the problem was that they either did not have any information at all or that their knowledge of German dispositions had been overcome by events since the armistice.

Sam had left Taylor to attend to a meeting with Mayor Magnocavallo at an outdoor table at a café. Sam assured Taylor that his radioman, Private Mark Christian, was capable of interpreting for him with the mayor, but after several fruitless interviews, Taylor wandered over to the meeting to listen and see if he could help.

Christian was a 2nd Platoon rifleman from Houston, who doubled as Sam's Italian interpreter and radioman. His name prior to coming through Ellis Island in 1921 and being Anglicized during their subsequent migration south was Marco Cristiano. Taylor approved of Christian's translation—his training in interpretation had been far less extensive than Taylor's, but he was doing a fine job conveying the essence of the conversation in both directions. Christian spoke with the feeling of a native Italian speaker, and Taylor assumed that either Christian was an immigrant himself (as was the case) or a first-generation American. Still, when he spoke English, he was all Texan.

The mayor was explaining to Sam that the fascists and the Germans had looted all of Italy's wealth and, while parades and marches were fine to watch, unfortunately the fascist militarism had not stopped there. Secretly, like many Italians, Magnocavallo was a communist at heart. He respected how the Soviet Union withstood the Nazi onslaught and, in truth, he did not oppose militarism other than on practical grounds. He thought war was fine as long as the home team won, which pretty much limited his appreciation of Italy's wars to the campaigns against Abyssinia and Albania. Although he felt no need to explain this to Sam, he had been in favor of war with the democracies which he believed were soft and weak. Magnocavallo had then been appalled when Mussolini committed Italian troops to the German war against Bolshevism. Still, these Americans seemed nice, and they behaved themselves better than he expected Italy's erstwhile allies, the Germans, were doing in the territory that they controlled.

Magnocavallo was on the verge of requesting American food supplies for his village, as many food items had been trucked in from Salerno or Naples until that supply route had closed. He did not know how the huge American would react to such a request, but he had noted that the Americans were very generous with their own personal rations—perhaps the American lieutenant would be inclined to help. Ogliastro was not yet in crisis, but Magnocavallo was astute enough to see that crisis was nearing.

"Tenente," he began. "Do you think it possible—" The request remained unuttered. A rifle shot rang out in the village, and Sergeant Taylor dropped to the ground.

The sniper's bullet had not been aimed at Sergeant Taylor, but at Mayor Magnocavallo. Had Sergeant Taylor known that fact, it would have been little consolation, because, although he was only grazed on the chest by the bullet and was essentially unharmed, he was absolutely terrified. He hesitated for an excruciatingly long nanosecond and then, as he had seen cowboys do in the movies, he rolled rapidly to the front of the café's patio and sheltered in the lee of a three-foot-high stone wall. Unlike a singing movie cowboy, though, he covered his head with his arms and screamed obscenities until being told by the lieutenant to shut up.

Sam and Private Christian were already hiding behind the wall. Sam moved surprisingly fast for such a large man, but even so, Christian had beaten both Sam and Taylor to the shelter of the rock wall. The sound of another shot echoed through the village, and a bottle of wine on show in the café's window shattered a foot behind the mayor's right ear. Inexplicably, the mayor slowly raised his shaking hands over his head to surrender to his unseen assailant.

"Oh, for the love of Pete," muttered Sam. He lunged out from his sanctuary behind the wall and grasped the lapel of the mayor's coat with his huge hand and pulled him forcefully to the ground. Just as a shepherd dog will sometimes herd children out of instinct, Sam covered the mayor up with his body. He had not consciously decided to risk his life for the mayor; it was just the instinctive move of a good soldier and a decent man to protect a civilian.

A third shot. This time, the bullet hit the top of the stone wall six inches above Sam's head. Although they were pinned by the sniper, Sam reflected that at least they had chosen the right wall to cower behind. It seemed that his bad day was becoming more disagreeable with every passing moment.

"Jack!" Sam yelled as loud as he could. "Jack!"

"We're working it, Lieutenant! Stay put!" yelled back Sergeant Younger from somewhere to Sam's left. Younger had taken cover at a corner of the square in an open-air blacksmith's shop with two other riflemen at the sound of the first shot. He believed that the shots were being fired over his head as the village wound up a hill behind the town square. Two streets led to the homes, businesses, and the church up the hill, one of which ran past the blacksmith's. Younger took it and sent the two riflemen scurrying along the edge of the square to the other street.

They began to work cautiously up the hill in parallel— Younger on the street to the left and the two riflemen on the road to the right. Although less than fifty yards separated them, he only caught a glimpse of them once as he passed a lateral street. There is no apparent design to most Italian villages and one could be forgiven for thinking that Sir Ebenezer Howard might have had them in mind as an affliction to cure when he sketched out his garden cities for Britain. Younger had no opinion of garden cities, but his anxiety was mounting with every step he took up the hill because he could not see his soldiers. He had not enjoyed his training for urban warfare, or street fighting as he called it, and had been "killed" in nearly every street fighting exercise that he had been in. Complicating his job and magnifying his anxiety was the ubiquitous Italian laundry hanging from almost every window, balcony railing, or line stretching across the streets from one apartment building to another. The flapping of clothes in the breeze made him start more than once and generally obscured his vision as he looked down the streets and up to the rooftops. Two more shots added to his nervousness, and he began to sweat from both the climb and the fear. The sound of the shots at least suggested that he was headed in the right direction, but there were so many buildings in such a small area that he could not be sure as the sound bounced from stone building to stone building.

He was getting close to the church when he heard, "Psssst!" He leapt backwards several yards like a startled cat and simultaneously wheeled around, bringing his Garand up to a firing position. A young Italian man was smoking a pipe in an open window and had been calmly watching Younger work his way up the street. The young man, who was now far less calm than he had been, pointed back down the hill with the stem of his pipe. He gestured silently with his fingers to Younger "two" and then pointed at his own street and then back down the hill. Two streets back. The young man then held his hands two feet apart and then brought one hand in a foot. *The middle of a cross street, two streets down,* thought Younger. The sound of another shot confirmed Younger's thoughts.

"Grazie," he whispered to the Italian, who bobbed his head in reply.

The sergeant turned and began to work his way slowly down the street that he had just climbed. Twice he wiped the sweat off his palms and he paused at the corner of the suspect street to collect his thoughts. He was nerving himself up to look around the corner of an apartment building to see if he could find the sniper when he heard an American voice shouting excitedly, "I got her! Hey Sarge, I got her! I got the sniper!"

Younger breathed for what seemed like the first time in minutes and then thought, *Her?*

1105 hours
Ogliastro Cilento, Italy

Even though he had heard the all-clear call from Sergeant Younger, Sam hurriedly shuffled his party to the most sheltered part of the square. He checked the mayor over himself for wounds, as Magnocavallo was nearly catatonic with fright. The mayor had not been hurt. Sam looked over at Sergeant Taylor.

"Sergeant, are you okay?" he asked.

"I don't know, sir. I think so." Taylor was opening his bloody shirt with shaking hands. The wound was high enough on his chest that the short-necked soldier could not see for himself, so Sam looked it over for him. The bullet had left a shallow crease on the soldier's chest like a tear from a barbed wire fence. It probably stung like hell, assessed Sam, but wouldn't require stitches. Had the bullet been up one or two inches and in a little, though, it would have taken out Taylor's throat.

The wound had already stopped bleeding, but Sam sprinkled sulfa powder on it anyway to keep it from getting infected. While he did that he asked, "Christian—you okay?"

"Good to go, Lieutenant." The Italian boy from Houston was taking it all in stride. Christian was already looking forward to telling the story to his friends in the company how the lieutenant actually said "For the love of Pete" before saving the mayor's life. Those were not the words that came to Christian's mind as he watched the mayor surrendering to the sniper; he would not have risked so much as a carpet-burn to save Magnocavallo.

The radioman said nothing further—the normally loquacious soldier was struck silent by the arrival of Sergeant Younger, his two riflemen and the enemy sniper. Sam was equally taken aback. The sniper, who was being pushed along by the muzzle of Younger's rifle, was a woman—and a beautiful woman at that. For a moment he said nothing as he looked at the would-be assassin. Sam had met a broad range of women in his life, and he recognized that the woman standing before him was in a category by herself.

She carried her five feet, three inches with a haughty arrogance that somehow made her appear taller. She had black hair and black eyes, like every other Italian woman Sam had seen so far, but there the resemblance ended. Unlike the dark, coarse complexions of the peasant women Sam had seen in Agropoli and Ogliastro, the woman before him was pale and perfect in her complexion. Had Sam met her in America, he might have been tempted to believe she was of Irish origins but for the slightest of Mediterranean tints to her coloring. She wore an expensive silk blouse and a tight tailored skirt but no rings or jewelry other than an elegant string of pearls and matching pearl earrings—the necklace and earrings looked identical to the pearls he had given Margaret as a wedding present. Either the woman came from money, or she had donned her best clothes and jewelry to shoot at the Americans. Sam guessed she was only twenty—perhaps younger. *Could she really be the sniper?* he asked himself.

Sam turned to Sergeant Younger. "What happened? Are we sure she is the shooter?"

Sergeant Younger had regained his composure and had stopped sweating, but the fear that he felt and the awful memory of walking up the street would revisit him in his sleep many times. "Sir, Private Froman caught her single-handedly."

Sam looked over at the soldier—a sniper, originally from Perkin's platoon—who was grinning from ear to ear. *He is as proud as Lucifer,* thought Sam, and despite his black mood, he grinned back at the soldier. "Okay, Froman, what happened?"

"Sir, me and Private Woods split up, with him working on one street and me another. I heard her fire, looked up and saw the muzzle of her rifle poking out over a three-story balcony, but she couldn't see me. Her flat was unlocked, so I just went up and got her.

Almost tossed a grenade, but thought you might need a prisoner."

"Damn fine job, just wait until you've got someone to support you next time. Good work, everyone. Are you sure she was the shooter?" Sam asked again.

Froman nodded. He reached into his pocket and pulled out a handful of casings. "She was moving to another part of the balcony. Ya know, see if she could get a better angle. When I walked up behind her, she was still trying to scope you in. Oh, here's her rifle, sir. Pretty swell."

Sam took the rifle from Private Froman and examined it: a modern Winchester Model 70 that was chambered for the ultra high-velocity .270 Winchester round. The fact that Sergeant Taylor had been shot with an American-made rifle only added to his irritation. The Winchester was a rifleman's rifle with a beautiful polished walnut stock and a great balance and feel to it. Sam had its predecessor, the Model 54, and had considered acquiring the Model 70 when it came out in 1937. He looked at the scope—it was nicer than any of his at home and of far better quality and greater magnification than any he had seen in the army. Given the tariffs in effect during the pre-war era, it must have been an expensive hunting rifle for an Italian to own— and the cost of the scope alone might have challenged the cost of the rifle. Sam worked the action and ejected one last round. The weapon was very well maintained and in great condition, and he would have loved to keep it for himself. He took the scope off and tossed it to Private Froman.

"Do you want that?"

"Do you mean it, sir?" Froman's eyes lit up.

"Reckon so. I definitely think that you earned something—or would you rather have a medal?"

Froman didn't hesitate, and his choice was apparent. "I'll take the scope. Hell yeah . . . sir. Thank you, sir." He set to work immediately to fit his new scope on his Springfield.

Sam turned his attention back to the woman and all smiles left his face. He did not know how to deal with the woman, so he moved on to another issue. He picked up the Winchester, motioned to Christian to follow him, and walked over to the blacksmith's open-air shop. The blacksmith moved out of Sam's way; he had witnessed the morning's events and thought it best to give the huge American a wide berth.

Sam grasped the rifle by the barrel, raised it high behind his head and swung the weapon down, much as Perkin had swung the sledge hammer three days earlier, with as much force and violence as he could muster. He slammed the stock against the smith's anvil. When it shattered, most of the stock flew up high and then clattered down on the stone floor of the shop. Sam slammed the barrel down again, smashing the action against the anvil. He tossed the barrel to the blacksmith, turned to Christian, and said, "Tell him to bend that barrel in half and show it to me when he's done."

Sam walked out, his mood even blacker. His fury had not abated from the destruction of the weapon. It was only growing now as he thought about the stupid girl putting everyone's life at risk. And for what? He intended to find out.

"Mayor!" Sam spoke with absolute authority. "Do you know this woman?"

Magnocavallo was obviously uncomfortable and through Taylor he said, "Si, signore. Her name is Antoniette Bernardi. She comes from a very prominent fascist family."

"I don't give two shits about her social standing," Sam said. He turned to Taylor, "Ask her why she did this."

Taylor was the sole American unimpressed by her beauty—she had, after all, shot him. He opened his mouth to ask the question, but the woman spoke first.

"I speak English, Tenente." She had a deep husky voice, which was noted by all the men present, including Sergeant Taylor.

"Thank you, Miss Bernardi," Sam said. "What the hell were you doing?"

"Isn't it clear, Tenente? I was trying to kill this collaborator," she said in a slightly mocking tone. Antoniette Bernardi was not afraid of the big American and, in fact, thought that perhaps she would seduce him later to see if he was as talkative in bed as the other American officer. Maybe this American would not be as easy, she thought, but she was not concerned. The democracies were so weak, so decadent, and this was such a delightful game. As she had done with many men, she would challenge this weak American and push him to the brink. Then she would lower her voice, maybe touch his hand or share a long look, but always give him a glimpse of her cleavage, and he would eat out of her hand as long as she allowed. Men always did. Magnocavallo was no worry. He would do nothing. He was afraid of her father, and she would be out of this unpleasantness by noon.

"Are you telling me, Miss Bernardi, that the mayor is collaborating with the Germans?" Sam was getting a headache now, and was angry and tired with the banter.

Seeing his frustration, the woman laughed mockingly—her tone was not nearly as subtle this time. It was time for another little push. "Of course not, Tenente. He is collaborating with the enemy. Not the Germans. You. You asked what was I doing today? Dealing with him." She gestured contemptuously at Magnocavallo, and then looked at Sam with all the arrogance she could muster, and said, "I am a fascist. That is how we treat collaborators in Italy, but . . ." She was about to offer a small olive branch by explaining that perhaps she had gone too far and that she was sure this could all be worked out—the first step on the road to her planned seduction of Sam.

Sam stopped her planning process. He had had enough talking, and it was time to conclude the chatter. His great rage which had been simmering all morning came close to boiling over—a rage built upon fatigue, anxiety, and homesickness. It was an anger that fed voraciously on a single question: *Is this why I left home?*

With the greatest restraint that he could muster—he wanted to hit the Italian woman so badly that his hands were trembling—Sam interrupted the beautiful woman, returning her sarcasm.

"Fascist eh? Well, in Texas, we'd just as soon shoot ya as look at ya, and I won't have no truck with fascists. I reckon your kind's as thick as fleas on an old coon dog down here, but you're the only one I've met." He glanced over at Magnocavallo. "So, what do I do with her?"

Sam then learned an Italian mannerism that the Texans would see many times in the months to come. The mayor tilted his head to one side, pursed his lips, lifted his eyebrows, shrugged his shoulders and held his hands out palms up. The meaning didn't require translation—it was evident that the mayor didn't want to deal with the issue himself.

Sam took a deep breath, his growing anger reflected in more sarcasm, "Thank you, Mayor, for your assistance. You've had a rough day so far, why don't you send for your police or your constable, then go home and catch your breath." Sam dismissed the mayor with a contemptuous wave of his hand, and the mayor scuttled away, very pleased with what he considered a masterful dodge of a difficult decision. After all, Mr. Bernardi was a very powerful man.

Sam looked at the beautiful young lady again, who had clearly enjoyed the Mayor's discomfiture. "Miss Bernardi, we have a saying back home: 'Ya can't get lard unless ya boil the hog.' I imagine that sums up your situation pretty well."

At the blank stares from Bernardi and his soldiers, Sam tried to come up with a more appropriate aphorism but failed, "Uh . . . tie her hands and chuck this young . . . lady . . . into that stable. Let her enjoy nature's finest aromas while we wait for the cops—we'll let the Eye-ties sort her out."

The blacksmith served as the village farrier and, although horses were being slowly replaced by automobiles, many people in southern Italy did not have the means or the desire to make the transition. He maintained a small stable next to his smith so customers could leave a horse with him for shoeing without having to wait. There were no stabled horses at that moment, but the stable boy, the blacksmith's youngest son, had been conscripted two days before the landings, so there was an unusual amount of filth in the stable.

When the vociferously protesting Bernardi was shoved into the stall by a scowling Sergeant Taylor, and the lower half of the Dutch door was closed, Bernardi stepped in manure, and her expensive shoes slid on the stone floor of the stable. With her hands tied in front of her, she was unable to balance and after trying unsuccessfully to regain command of her footing, she lost the fight and landed hard on her side on the stable's filthy floor. The resulting torrent of abuse was in Italian, but Sam was under no illusion that it was directed at anyone but him. Taylor and Christian went back into the stable to pull Bernardi to her feet and immediately they became the subject of her wrath. A snarling Bernardi twisted free of their grasp and tried a kick at Taylor's knee, but slipped again on the stable floor. Christian caught her before she hit, getting manure on his uniform for his troubles, and his reward was spit in the face from the red-faced young woman and another river of obscenity.

"By God, that is enough!" Sam roared. His huge, angry presence in the door stunned the two soldiers, who took a step back from their captive, but it had no effect on the humiliated Italian fascist. Her threats were in a mix of Italian and English and she kicked again at the soldiers.

Sam finally reached his breaking point. Knowing that he could not face Margaret if he ever hit a woman, yet not being the type of man to walk away from a confrontation, he settled for the next best thing. He stormed back to the blacksmith's shop, picked up a tin bucket off the stone floor and dunked it in the horse trough next to the stable. As Bernardi continued to scream obscenities at the soldiers, Sam opened the Dutch door, strode in angrily, and flung the bucket of horse water as hard as he could directly into Bernardi's face. She lost her balance once again, and this time no one caught her.

Lying prostrate on the floor of the stable, her soaked white blouse suddenly transparent, Bernardi looked up at the three angry foreign soldiers standing over her, and her vulnerability and the seriousness of her situation finally sunk in. As she started weeping and struggled unsuccessfully to get up, she choked out, "I'm sorry, Tenente."

Sam knelt down and pulled Bernardi up to a sitting position by her tied wrists. His anger replaced by weariness, Sam said with calm distaste to the young woman, "Sister, I'm glad to hear that, and I hope you mean it. You seem to think this is a game of some sort, but I'm here to tell ya, it ain't. I don't have time to waste on spoilt girls, and I won't tolerate no more guff from you neither. Bad-mouth my soldiers or me again, and I'll either gag you or shoot you. I ain't decided which, but one thing's certain. If I see you with a rifle again . . . well, it'll be the last goddamned day of your sorry life."

1215 hours
One Mile South of Acquafredda, Italy

There had been no German pursuit of the patrol, at least as far as Perkin could see. They had left Acquafredda shortly after the Italian women had presented their gifts and driven down the coastal highway. After only a mile, Perkin had pulled the jeeps off the highway and driven the groaning vehicles through the trees up the mountainside to a small clearing. This was the hardest country that they had been in yet. The highway was literally carved out of the mountainsides and generally edged against a cliff that ran some forty or fifty feet above the rocky shore.

The clearing was about as good as Perkin could hope for—there was a beautiful view of the Gulf of Policastro and the clearest ocean waters that Perkin had ever seen. Despite its purpose that day, the clearing seemed remote from the war, and when he died, Perkin thought that he wanted to be buried in such a place. The mountain vistas were spectacular across the bend of the gulf, and the mountain directly behind the clearing rose sharply up to several thousand feet. In addition to a fantastic view, the small clearing provided just enough dirt to bury his soldiers—though it still required back-breaking effort to carve the burial site out of the rocky mountainside. One soldier remained on security with Perkin's binoculars, while Perkin, who dug the entire time using the spade from the jeep, and the other four soldiers spent nearly two hours digging three graves deep enough for their dead comrades. The Texans respectfully wrapped their friends in the sheets given to them by the women of Acquafredda, cleaned their faces and hands, then laid them to rest. The bodies were covered with dirt and the soldiers piled the graves high with rocks, as there was no shortage of those. Corporal Pena's and Private Ewart's graves were marked by driving their Garands into the ground by bayonet-point and hanging their helmets over the stocks of the rifles. Private Wagner's grave, in the middle, was marked by placing his red-crossed helmet atop the rocks.

"'Our Father, which art in heaven,'" began Perkin. "'Hallowed be thy name. Thy kingdom come. Thy will be done in earth as it is in heaven. Give us this day our daily bread and forgive us our debts as we forgive our debtors. And lead us not into temptation, but deliver us from evil. For thine is the kingdom, the power and the glory forever. Amen.'" There was some shuffling and confusion among his remaining soldiers as that was not how they had all learned the Lord's Prayer, and a couple of "trespasses" were heard as they recited the prayer with their lieutenant. They waited expectantly to see what the lieutenant would say next—he paused, unsure of what he should say.

Perkin looked at the small circle of men around the burial site then at the sun high above the mountains. If it had not been such a tragic morning, it would have been a spectacular day. Perkin closed his eyes against the sunlight for a moment and collected his thoughts before he began.

"Gentlemen," he said, "we are here to say goodbye to our friends, our comrades-in-arms—our fellow Texans. These good men have been our friends since we left home so many months ago. We soldiered together in Texas, Louisiana, Florida, Massachusetts, Africa, and now Europe. It is a journey we began together as American soldiers nearly three years ago, and today that journey came to an end for Roberto Pena, Travis Ewart, and Paul Wagner. It is just a sad thing that these boys won't be with us to see the journey's end—whether the end finds us in Italy, Germany, Japan or, most appropriately, back home in Texas."

Perkin took a moment to steady his voice, then continued, "Travis and Paul joined us at Camp Blanding, and they were two of the best young men you could ever hope to meet. Travis was from Peaster, way up in Parker County, and leaves behind a young wife named Missy and a young boy whose name, I think, is James. I hope that you will remember them in your prayers. Paul had come to us from near Galveston. We all know that because of his beliefs Paul didn't hold with war—expected better of mankind in general—but he still volunteered to serve his country as a medic. I can't think of anything nobler than that. He leaves behind no wife, but his mom and dad back in Friendswood. Roberto came from Cuero, not far from my home. I had been with Roberto in the 141st since I joined the National Guard four years ago. He was a damn fine man and a good soldier. He leaves behind his wife, Maria, and four children. Please pray for them as well. Bobby, Travis, and Paul's journey began in Texas, but now they lay 'at rest on a distant shore.' We know that, given their druthers, they'd rather be home in Texas with their families, but, as I look around, it strikes me that the distant shore where they lay is the most beautiful place I've ever seen. I hope it brings them peace. Ashes to ashes, dust to dust. May God pardon their sins and save them. Let's have a moment of prayer for our friends . . . amen."

1545 hours
Paola, Italy

Private Kulis set the jerry can down and said, "That's it, sir. We should have plenty in each tank. At least more than ten gallons each, and I'd guess that we can top off when we get to the Eighth Army."

Perkin nodded, silent. He was thinking about what to do next. There was at least another three hours of daylight and only another thirty miles or so to the British lines. If war were a vacuum, he could be there in less than an hour, but ever since the mission began, Perkin had been anxious about how to get through to the British side. At the beginning of the patrol, the romantic part of Perkin's mind had envisioned blasting through the German lines—machine guns blazing—into the welcoming arms of the British Eighth Army. After Sapri, his romantic and heroic notions were quiescent. Perkin considered going to ground and waiting for the combatants to pass him by, but he knew that could add days to his mission. He wanted desperately to be back with Sam and Able Company.

Of the two problems he had—the Germans and the British—he was not sure which concerned him the most. The Germans knew that he was in the area, and they could easily speculate about his intentions and radio ahead to forward units. During the drive from Acquafredda, he had expected an ambush at every turn, and there were a lot of turns on the coastal road. As for the British, he could not even be sure that they knew he was on the road, and it had occurred to him they did not know the British password. It would be better to come in during daylight.

Perkin expected that the Germans would be falling back in good order, and the focus of their defense would be in the central valley running up the Italian Peninsula rather than on the coastal road. Still, it was reasonable to believe they would fight a small delaying action in this little sideshow of the campaign along the coast. The odds of confronting the Germans were rising with every mile.

"Sergeant Kenton!"

"Sir?"

"Let's load up and get moving. I'll drive this jeep. You drive that one. Fratelli rides with me in the back with the BAR, and Kulis rides shotgun. You take Pfadenhauer to man your .30 cal. I want him on the gun all the way until we reach British lines. When we reach Eighth Army, we'll see if an armorer can weld us an MG stand for this jeep and our extra .30 cal for the return trip." Even though he had a watch, Perkin looked up at the sun to gauge the remaining daylight. "As we get closer to where I think the German lines are, we'll pull off periodically to look and listen. I'd like to get out of no-man's land and behind English lines today, but I'm taking no chances." Perkin looked at his small collection of soldiers and offered a wan smile. "Speaking of which, you go first."

"Thank you, sir." Kenton returned his lieutenant's smile and then looked for around for Private Kulis. "Kulis!"

"Yes, Sergeant?"

"Clean your fuckin' glasses, you goddamned killin' machine! I don't want the greatest alliance in history derailed because Edwin Kulis greased a Limey by mistake."

Kulis automatically reached for his glasses, and then said in a sarcastic tone, "Thanks, Sarge, I was a little unclear 'bout killing our allies. Anyone else you don't want me to kill?"

Sergeant Kenton grinned at his rifleman, "Me and the lieutenant. Other than that, it's weapons free." Kenton turned away and started to look for things to do, but he was ambiguous about moving again. He was running through the same calculus as his lieutenant, and did not see any clear-cut way to go other than to just go. He understood the appeal of approaching British lines in daylight, but of course that complicated things with the Germans. Sergeant Kenton would have approved of Lieutenant Berger's flirtation with the notion of hiding out until the warring armies had passed them by, had he known about it. He had not been asked, and he did not have a good opinion to proffer, so he squeezed his huge frame behind the wheel of the jeep and started it up.

Sergeant Kenton led a slow pace along the winding highway. He stopped before crossing several bridges to check for mines or booby-traps and to see if the bridges had been wired for demolition. None showed any signs of German attention, but Kenton's soldierly instincts told him that they must be approaching the vanguard of the withdrawing German Army, even though the Italians they queried on the road reported seeing no Germans for days.

Perkin was cycling through the same thoughts, but his reflections were dominated by the loss of his three soldiers, and he wanted something to take his mind off the inevitable question of whether he had done something wrong. He looked over at Kulis riding shotgun next to him and asked, "What are you reading these days, Kulis?"

"It's that book that I traded you for back in Africa— *The Fountainhead*."

"You're not done with it yet?"

"Shit, sir, it's the biggest book I ever seen, and you don't give us a lot of time to read. I was gonna finish up last night and then see if the English want to trade for it, but we didn't have any campfires."

Perkin smiled inwardly. He had always been impressed with the diamond-in-the-rough intellect of his rifleman, and he frequently encouraged Kulis to consider college after his service was complete. It was true that the soldiers had not had much spare time, but Perkin had watched over the months as his young soldier read *Moby Dick* thoroughly before trading it to Captain Spaulding for *Ulysses*—a book the rifleman had struggled with. When Kulis could not make much sense of it, he traded it to a soldier from Dog Company for Steinbeck's new book, *The Moon is Down*, and Perkin had taken that book in trade for Ayn Rand's new novel. As Kulis told Perkin as they drove, he found Howard Roark to be both admirable and annoying at the same time. He didn't believe that uncompromising people like Roark really existed, and, if they did, he reckoned it was likely that they'd be treated as shabbily as Roark was.

"They most likely would," Perkin agreed. "Kulis, if your book is handy, why don't you read to us while we drive? Private Fratelli and I can keep an eye out."

Kulis twisted around and found his pack in the back of the jeep. He dug into the pack, pulling the large book from its depths and spilling out a half-dozen condoms in the process. Fratelli laughed as Kulis blushed and stuffed the condoms back in his pack. Kulis asked, "Do you want me to start at the beginning, sir?"

"No—just wherever you left off. I don't need any setup. Just read."

"Yes, sir." Private Kulis squinted and thumbed through the book until he found the passage where he had stopped reading on the *Thomas Jefferson* several days before. But his face was too swollen from the glass and the stitches, and the jeep was bouncing around too much for him to be able to read smoothly. Despite his best efforts, Kulis couldn't manage more than a slow halting narration.

After a rocky three minutes, Perkin ended the private's embarrassment. As the jeeps continued slowly southward, the two soldiers in the front discussed Rand's concepts of individualism and the role of ego in greatness. They talked of this for a moment and Perkin offered up his thoughts based on the Turner Thesis that the original "great" Americans were the frontiersmen. He told Kulis of the role that the individual on the frontier played in developing American exceptionalism and why the United States was so culturally distinct from Europe.

Fratelli was on the verge of asking Kulis to begin reading again, not out of interest in the book but to stave off the boredom that the egghead discussion in the front of the jeep was causing, when a fragment of the conversation caught his attention. Perkin was saying to Kulis: "The great frontiersmen were the wilderness versions of Howard Roark—men like John Finley, Daniel Boone, George Rogers Clark. One of the greatest was the great-great-great granddaddy of our Sergeant Kenton; his name was Simon Kenton. These men were the Roarks of their day: unbending individualists who built a country, not skyscrapers."

The discussion drifted back to Howard Roark, and Fratelli lost interest again, and despite being bored, Fratelli didn't resent being left out of it. Fratelli thought highly of his lieutenant, and he had liked Kulis since he had seen the small Texan take on a much larger soldier from the 1st Division who had been picking on him at Camp Blanding. That Kulis hadn't won that fight didn't matter to Fratelli— he and another soldier from Able Company later resolved the dispute on Kulis's behalf by beating the soldier from the Big Red One senseless out of principle. What counted, in Fratelli's book, was that Kulis the shy bookworm was not afraid to play in the big boys' games. Fratelli came from a rough neighborhood, and he respected courage. He had been particularly impressed with the little rifleman when the Italian doctor stitched up his face. It must have hurt like hell, but Kulis had not complained—then or afterwards. He shared courage with the Texan, but unlike Kulis, he didn't have much use for books. A passage about how controlling men's happiness leads to the control of men sparked his interest, and the South Jersey rifleman was about to jump into his first literary discussion with the observation: "Ain't that the fucking truth."

Sergeant Kenton's jeep slowed, then came to a halt. Perkin brought his jeep to a stop about thirty yards behind the front jeep and watched intently as Kenton reached for his rifle and Pfadenhauer trained his machine gun at a small copse of trees on the left side of the road. Both Pfadenhauer and Kenton signaled back to Perkin: enemy in sight.

Perkin opened his mouth to tell his soldiers to get ready when a vaguely Irish voice boomed out, "British Army! Come forward one vehicle at a time and be recognized!" As Sergeant Kenton looked back to Perkin for guidance, Perkin put his jeep into gear and came even with Kenton.

"What'd you see?" Perkin asked of his sergeant.

"A soldier ran across the road and ducked into them trees there. I couldn't identify his uniform at that distance, but I figured we'd meet Germans first. Maybe not."

"Maybe not." Perkin started the jeep again and rolled slowly forward until he was almost even with the copse of trees.

"That's far enough!" the Irish voice called out. "Identify yourself!"

"Lieutenant Berger, 141st Infantry Regiment, United States Army!" Perkin called out in reply. "Who are you?"

"Sergeant MacKenna, Royal Inniskilling Fusiliers. I'm coming out."

A short, stocky man rose up from the bushes and walked warily towards the American patrol. MacKenna had a darkly tanned face on what would have normally been a fair complexion, and he carried a Lee-Enfield bolt-action rifle that remained pointed at the Americans. He had the air of a professional soldier about him, and he looked alertly at Perkin before walking around the jeep. Kulis and Fratelli watched him closely in turn. MacKenna said nothing as he circumnavigated the jeep, but he paid close attention to its condition, noting the blood in the back, the shattered windshield, Kulis's stitched-up face, and the weapons and the uniforms of the three soldiers.

MacKenna walked around to Perkin and said in the harsh accent of Belfast, "What is your purpose here?"

Perkin looked up into the British soldier's eyes and said mildly, "I'm an Allied officer, Sergeant. You address me as 'Sir' or 'Lieutenant.'"

"Yes, sir. Sorry, sir." MacKenna did not look very contrite. "What is your purpose here? Sir."

"We're a reconnaissance patrol from the Fifth Army," and, in an excellent dead-pan imitation of Gary Cooper's Sergeant York, Perkin added, "And we're a-lookin' for Germans. Seen any?" Perkin asked with a tired smile.

For the first time, Sergeant MacKenna relaxed and offered a small smile back. "You're on a long reconnaissance, Lieutenant. Salerno must be two hundred miles away."

"Two hundred miles? Christ! I thought it was just over this hill. I told you we were lost, Kulis!" On seeing the confusion on his private's face, Perkin laughed. Despite the pain of his day, he was beginning to relax as well, and the laugh was more the release of nervous tension than genuine humor. It was becoming apparent that the first half of their patrol was nearly complete. "No, Sergeant. We're here to establish contact with the Eighth Army. How far to your lines and what's the disposition of enemy troops in between?"

The British trooper smiled grimly at the American lieutenant, "Is it enemy troops you're looking for now? Why, sir, you may be disappointed. I haven't seen any bleedin' Germans since Sicily. Of course, if you do see any as you head south, we may all be in trouble. You've been inside our lines for about three miles now."

1930 hours
Ogliastro Cilento, Italy

"Okay, Sam, here's the deal," said Captain Spaulding as he shoved another bite of pizza into his mouth. "We're not moving until tomorrow morning at the earliest, but I want us to be ready to go by then. Try and get a good night's sleep, because I reckon we're going into the fight tomorrow or the next day."

Captain Spaulding had never had pizza before in his life, but he was a fairly open-minded man. He found the round flat bread with olive oil, tomatoes, cheese, and purple olives to be an ingenious culinary delight that was competitive, in his mind, even with a barbequed baloney sandwich. He was ravenous, having spent the day walking between platoons and squads and ensuring that his company was prepared for whatever might come its way. Spaulding had managed to time his inspection of Sam's platoon in Ogliastro with supper, and he, Sam, and Jim Lockridge dined together.

Lockridge had also planned to arrive in Ogliastro for supper. He had been through Ogliastro in the afternoon to pick up Sergeant Taylor and had heard an almost accurate version of the morning's events from Taylor and Private Christian. He came back that evening to have dinner with Sam and to check on his friend.

The only variation on the truth in Sergeant Taylor's account was a brief addendum to the story where Sam pulled the huge Bowie knife that he carried and said to the prostrate Bernardi, "Don't fuck with me and my boys again or else." In a separate accounting to other members of Sam's platoon, Christian added that Sam had placed his boot on her neck and was preparing to crush her windpipe when Christian dragged him off. He wouldn't have saved her, he said, except for her beauty and her wet, see-through blouse.

Unknown embellishments aside, Sam was cheerful for the first time in several days—just like the morning after a great Texas thunderstorm over the plains, all the clouds in his visage had passed. True, he was concerned about Perkin, and there was the underlying guilt about having treated a woman as severely as he had. Compounding that, many of the Italian citizens of Ogliastro had given him a wide berth for the rest of the afternoon. During those instances, he felt more like a conquering barbarian than a liberating American. But there were other citizens, mostly women, who went out of their way to indicate their approval of his interaction with Miss Bernardi.

Mrs. Magnocavallo, for instance, approached him soon afterwards and thanked him profusely, through Private Christian, for saving her husband's life. She was obviously nervous around the large Texan, but insisted on laundering his uniform—he was already wearing the spare that he carried in his pack. Two young ladies, almost in Antoniette Bernardi's league of beauty, were also approving of his actions that morning. Holding hands, they boldly walked up to Sam on the street that afternoon and while kissing him on either cheek, they said together, "Grazie, Tenente." In moments like those, he felt more like Sinatra the pop-star than Alaric the Visigoth.

His notions of celebrity status came crashing down with Captain Spaulding's next words: "Now, Lieutenant Taft, it is my sad duty to inform you that there have been two serious charges leveled against you since your occupation of Ogliastro, and before I proceed further, I reckon I need to hear your side of it."

Sam glanced over at Captain Lockridge whose face indicated nothing. In the background, he saw Sergeant Younger sitting at the next table over with two of Sam's soldiers. Younger's back was to the officers' table and he had obviously caught a word or two of the conversation. Younger sat bolt upright at his own table, motioned to his dinner companions to hush and then leaned backwards in his chair with a casual air. Sam didn't have to think long about his conduct in Ogliastro—Ebbins and Bernardi.

Sam turned to his company commander and said coolly, "Sir, what two charges are you referring to?"

"Oh for God's sake, Sam! Are ya telling me that ya don't know what I'm talking about? You're not a six-year-old, so don't play innocent with me. Be a man, and tell me what happened." Spaulding's face was stern and his tone unforgiving.

Sam hung his head. "Which do you want to hear about first, sir? Me threatenin' Cap'n Ebbins or me chuckin' the bucket of water on the woman?"

"What?! You threatened Ebbins and did what with a woman? I didn't know that—Jim, no one tells me anything! What else have you done?" Spaulding's tone had changed, and Sam looked up. There was a playful look on his face. Sam looked over at Jim who was grinning at him.

"Uh . . . nothin'." Sam began to relax. "What charges were you talking about?"

"That you're a Republican and a nigger-lover, of course." With a wry grin, Spaulding rocked back in his chair and ordered another pizza. "How d'ya answer to that?"

"Guilty to one and *nolo contendre* to the other, I reckon. I'll let you figure out which is which. You assholes, you scared the shit out of me." He offered a weak smile, "So, what'd ya hear?"

Spaulding took a drink of his Italian beer, grimaced from the taste, and said, "I guess the most concerning part is that you're a Republican. I never would've guessed. I mean, I know that they exist, just never met one in Texas. But you're missin' the tail and horns that I expected. I swear, the things you learn about a man in a combat zone. Don't tell me Perkin's one as well?"

"Oh, hell no. He's the founding member of the Roosevelt for King Society of South Texas. Naw, I'm pretty sure I'm the only Republican in San Patricio County, maybe in the Coastal Bend. Even my wife and dogs are Democrats. But surely you didn't think I could be a Taft and be one too, did ya?" Sam ordered even more pizzas and a final round of beers—figuring, rightly, that food and drink at his expense would trump political adversity.

Jim, who had been silent during dinner, said, "I understand that you had a run-in with the idiot, Ebbins. Did he really call you a nigger-lover in front of your troops?"

"He did. He also referred to Perk as 'Pickin' Boogers.' He'd have gotten beat again for that if Perk had heard. He hates that name even worse than his own." Sam recounted for Jim's benefit the story of the race incident in Brownwood in 1941. Bill Spaulding was already aware of it, as he had been with the battalion since '38.

"That's the guy? Some time ago, Perk told me the story of you breaking up what he described as a lynching in progress. I didn't know it was our own Captain Ebbins."

"Yeah, lucky me. You know something? Probably like your part of Texas, South Texas don't have many colored folks. I suspect that he ain't ever met one in his life before the army. I know I hadn't met many—less than a dozen maybe—so I guess he decided to capitalize on it and beat up the first nigra he came across. As for being a nigger-lover, I don't have much opinion one way or the other about them folk, but I did learn a great lesson in college about toleratin' others. It sure changed my perspective on how I look at other people; do you wanna hear about it?" Bill and Jim nodded.

"It was my junior year at A&M, before my dad died, and I'd gone to Austin to spend the weekend with Perk. I don't know if he knew you back then, Jim." Jim thought for a second and then shrugged. He was too tired to think back that far. "Anyway, I was to meet him at a bar after he got out of school, and I got there early after havin' a couple of road-sodas on the way. I walked in and just knew that I was in the wrong kind of place. I thought it was Perkin playing a gag on me 'cause I mean it was the wrong kind of place—ya know what I mean? I walked in and saw two of 'em holding hands, and tipsy dumbass that I was, d'ya know what I did? I walked right up to 'em and said, 'Which one of you sucks the meaner dick?'"

At this Bill and Jim broke up laughing, and a guffaw from the next table indicated that Sergeant Younger was still listening in.

Sam laughed, "Well, they didn't take it too good. I mean, I ain't had a beatin' like that in my whole life. I got a black eye, got kicked in the balls, and my nose got broke. The worst part was that my balls swelled up to the size of grapefruits afterwards—well, you know, bigger grapefruits. But I learned a valuable lesson about toleratin' other people, and those two and their kind earned more than a little bit of my respect that day."

Jim, who was laughing so hard at Sam's parable of tolerance that he could barely speak, croaked out, "Respect? For queers? Really?"

"Queers? Who said anything about cornholers?" With a wink at Bill, he said, "I was talking about Longhorns—you and your dumb orange sweaters. Shit, she was meaner than he was—that's who kicked me in the balls and broke my nose."

2030 hours
2nd Battalion HQ, Royal Inniskilling Fusiliers

Sergeant MacKenna had directed them back to the headquarters of the 2nd Battalion of the Royal Inniskilling Fusiliers, and Perkin had been invited to dinner by the battalion commander, Lieutenant Colonel Maurice Fox. In a large tent and over a dinner of canned Australian beef, fresh sliced Italian tomatoes (the best of Perkin's life), and canned American peaches, Fox listened closely to Perkin's report of their patrol. He nodded approvingly when Perkin told him of the ambush of the German patrol and shook his head sympathetically when told of the German ambush of his own patrol.

Fox was a professional soldier who had been a company commander that had survived the fighting in France in 1940 and the evacuation at Dunkirk. His battalion was attached to the 5th Division, and he had seen service in Syria, Persia, Madagascar, and India before being sent to the Mediterranean theater. Despite the hard times since the war began, Fox had a lot of sympathy for the young American lieutenant. He remembered vividly the loss of every soldier under his command until he had risen in rank to the point that the soldiers were mostly faceless, as he commanded so many of them. Fox was pleased that Perkin maintained his composure as well as he did. Although Perkin's pain over losing his first soldiers was written clearly on his face, he had not wept or sobbed as many officers in the same position had done over the countless centuries of warfare. Fox found such displays of emotion embarrassing.

Upon finding out that Perkin had been a history student before the war, Fox told Perkin about his battalion and regiment. "The Royal Inniskilling Fusilier Regiment is sadly dispersed right now. The 1st Battalion is fighting in Burma; we are here; the 6th Battalion is attached to the Irish Guards, etcetera, etcetera. The regiment has been renamed several times, as have most British regiments, but we date back to the plantation of Ireland in the early 17th century. Most of our original soldiers in the current war were Irish-born, including many from Southern Ireland, but the nature of the war and conscription has changed our makeup."

"I understand, sir. The same is happening to our division, which started out as entirely Texan, but now is maybe two-thirds or three-quarters Texan."

Lieutenant Colonel Fox passed the plate of beef over to Perkin for a second helping. "Are you familiar with the Peninsular Campaign?"

Perkin nodded. "Yes, sir. It was the primary British effort on the ground until Napoleon's abdication in 1814. It was where Wellington cut his teeth."

Fox nodded then shrugged, "Well, not quite. Wellington cut his teeth in India, but I know what you mean. By the way, did you know his great-great-great grandson, Captain, the Duke of Wellington, is engaged in your battle in Salerno? I've met him several times. He's a good lad—leads one of the commando teams there. Anyway, the regiment saw action under Arthur Wellesley, later ennobled as Wellington, at Badajoz, Salamanca, Vitoria, and countless other battles." Fox reached over to a box on his field desk. He opened it up and offered a cigar to Perkin, who declined. Fox set the box down without taking a cigar for himself. "When Napoleon returned from Elba, it was the 1st Battalion of this regiment which held the center against Marshal Ney's charge at Waterloo. It was the most glorious page in our history, but at what a terrible price—nearly everyone in the battalion was killed or wounded. If you're interested, you'll meet one of our officers tomorrow: Lieutenant Colonel Russ, on the division staff as the intelligence officer. He is a true source of knowledge on the Napoleonic era. Anyway, after Napoleon's exile at St. Helena, and for the rest of the last century, the regiment fought in South Africa, India, Afghanistan, and South Africa again in the Boer War. During the Great War, the regiment saw action in Flanders, France, and Gallipoli. This battalion was disestablished between the wars, but the 1st Battalion saw imperial service in India and Singapore. Thank God they left before that mess in Singapore began." Fox poured out two small brandies for the officers and winced inwardly as Perkin downed it in a single shot. "Tell me of your regiment."

Perkin, after catching his breath, was on the verge of telling the British colonel that his regiment was originally known as the Amazon Brigade, as it had been formed by large-breasted women, but he remembered Captain Spaulding's admonition to behave himself only the day before. "Sir, we rename our units as well. My regiment, the 141st Infantry, is the lineal descendant of the 1st Texas Regiment, which predates when America threw in with the Texas Republic. Elements of the 1st Texas fought at the Alamo, which, as you may know, was not a commendable success for Texas arms, but since nothin' motivates people like an ancient grudge, our regiment is known as the 'Alamo Regiment.' I think it had more success durin' the War of Northern Aggression, where it was part of Hood's Brigade. The 1st Texas fought at the Second Battle of Manassas, and then Sharpsburg— although you may have heard that battle called Antietam, the Yankee name for it. It was at Sharpsburg where the regiment held the center of the Confederate line against General McClellan's troops—he was no Marshal Ney though—and took the highest casualties, 82 percent, of any regiment north or south during the entire war. Following Sharpsburg, it fought at Fredericksburg, Gettysburg, Chickamauga, the Wilderness, and Cold Harbor. The 1st Texas was with General Lee at his surrender at Appomattox but was so decimated at that point that, accordin' to legend, it consisted of four soldiers, three dogs, and a camp follower."

Fox laughed at the image and poured himself and Perkin another drink. Although it was not his policy to drink with officers as junior as Perkin, he was an enthusiast of history as well, and he liked the young Texan. "I've always thought of your civil war as a transition war—a transition between epochs, if you will, between old warfare like the Napoleonic wars and modern warfare, which truly began with the Great War. Did your family fight for the 1st Texas?"

"No, sir. On my father's side, the war fell between generations, and they kind of sat it out. On my mother's side though, my great-grandfather was General Hiram Granberry, who was a brigade commander in Hood's Army of Tennessee. He was killed at the Battle of Franklin in '64. There were several Texas regiments under his command, but the 1st Texas wasn't one of them. In gratitude for his sacrifice, the people of Texas immortalized Old Hiram by naming a pretty little town on the Brazos River after him, but they spelt his name wrong. Who knew immortality could be so ironic?"

Chapter Eight

September 13, 1943
0930 hours
Ogliastro Cilento, Italy

The large truck, known as a deuce and a half to the soldiers, groaned as the left front wheel eased into a large pothole, and the soldiers in the back swayed with the motions of the truck as it bounced over the rough Italian roads. Sam and Jim Lockridge sat in the front of the truck, while a Transportation Company private from Cuero, Texas, drove. When Sam asked the private if he knew Corporal Pena, who was also from Cuero, the private nodded and then amused the officers by recounting a claim made by the Pena family years ago about an animal-vampire that sucked the blood out of goats.

The trucks and some members of the battalion staff had showed up over an hour earlier to pick up Able Company and move it, along with the rest of the battalion, into the line. Sam's platoon was recalled and rushed back to Ogliastro to be loaded onto the trucks, while other trucks rumbled further up the mountain ridge to pick up the rest of Able Company. Lieutenant Colonel Wranosky rode in another truck with Captain Spaulding and briefed him on the mission, just as Jim was doing for Sam.

After learning about the goat-sucking vampire of Cuero, Jim spoke in low tones so the driver would be excluded from the conversation—it didn't matter to the private in any case, as he had not slept since coming ashore at Red Beach seventy-two hours earlier, and his focus was solely on staying awake and not wrecking his truck.

"Things aren't where we would like them to be," Jim began. "The 142nd RCT got bogged down in a battle for a village called Altavilla yesterday and spent the whole day taking the village before getting chucked out by the 2nd Panzer Regiment and then retaking it again. I don't know where in the cycle of taking and chucking we are right now, but they pretty much lost a battalion in the process. Do you remember where Altavilla is?"

Sam nodded, "It's on that little complex of hills overlooking the Sele-Calore corridor, right?"

"Yeah. I've got a buddy in VI Corps G-2. I saw him this morning about 0400, he said that Clark is pushing Dawley to abandon the fight for Altavilla and focus on two things: controlling the corridor proper and closing the gap between us and the Limeys. I'm no fan of Clark's, but he may be on to something. That corridor is like a dagger pointed at the heart of our beachhead. But my buddy said that Dawley wants to control the high ground over the corridor."

Sam felt a twinge of guilt about Jim's comment on meeting his corps counterpart at 0400—Sam had had his best night's sleep since coming to Italy. While his guilt quickly dissipated, Sam digested what Jim had told him.

"What about the corridor? What's happening there?"

"One of General Middleton's regiments from the 45th Division was in a hell of a scrap in there yesterday, and I think one of their battalions got chewed up pretty bad by the Krauts fighting around Persano. The corridor is v-shaped, with the point of the V headed to our beaches." Jim used his hands to illustrate the geography. "Persano is in the center of the corridor, and that road going down the corridor cuts right through it. I reckon controlling Persano is more important than Altavilla. We're sending the tanks in as we speak, and then I think the plan is to move part of the 143rd RCT into the corridor to support Middleton's troops."

"You think?" Sam was surprised. Jim Lockridge had the sharpest mind in the battalion, perhaps the division. Lockridge seldom made mistakes and was a stickler for details. Sam was surprised at the generalities of what he was being told by Jim.

"Yeah, Sam . . . I think. The whole goddamn thing is fluid, and what they were planning at 0400 is likely O.B.E. by now.* To make matters worse, there's no cohesion at the top. Clark wants to do one thing, Dawley another, and Walker's caught between them. My buddy told me, and please don't repeat this, that Clark and Dawley aren't hardly even talking."

"Don't that strike you as odd? It's Clark's battle. His ass is on the line. If he's had a fallin' out with Dawley, then why doesn't he relieve him and make Walker or Middleton the acting corps commander? Walker can do it—shit, up until a few months ago, he was senior to Clark."

Jim shrugged. "I don't know, Sam. Clark told Dawley that he wanted the focus to be on the corridor, but he didn't order Dawley to break off the attack on Altavilla, so I think that Dawley is going to pursue both. That's

*Overcome By Events.

where we come in. Our battalion is being placed in corps reserve to support either the fight in the corridor or Altavilla."

Sam was appalled. "Jim, can that be right? A battalion as the corps reserve? Not the regiment? What if they need to support both Altavilla and the fight for Persano? Do they break the battalion up and send two companies here and two companies there?"

Again Jim shrugged, "I don't know. The other two battalions of the 141st are being trucked to the far side of the Sele River. I understand that the plan is to put 'em in the gap between us and the British, but as of this morning, no one knew exactly where they're going to go. I heard Colonel Jamison was apoplectic. He's pissed off that the regiment is being divided like this and I think he's concerned that they are either going to be rushed into battle or that they'll sit on their ass all day."

"What do you reckon will come of us?" Sam was getting more alarmed as the truck came off the mountainside and entered the Salerno plain along Highway 18, and they drove past the carnage of the landing sites at Paestum. Sam had essentially been away from the fight for three days and was shocked at the sight. Burned-out hulks of American tanks and tank destroyers mixed with the burned-out hulks of the German panzers on both sides of the highway. The carrion eaters, vultures and ravens, had found the battlefield, and Sam watched in sorrow as wounded soldiers shot at the birds to keep them away from the dead that hadn't been collected yet.

"Well, if you had a three-sided coin, the even odds would be like this: we get thrown into the fight for the corridor, we get thrown into the grinder at Altavilla, or we sit around all day with our thumbs up our ass, waiting for something to do."

0945 hours
British 5th Division HQ

Perkin stood outside a large villa that had been commandeered by the British 5th Division as their headquarters. He was drinking British tea with canned milk and heaps of sugar out of his canteen cup and listening to British and German artillery casually trading fire in the distance to the northeast. It was far less intense than he had experienced on the Salerno plain. Perkin's attention turned back to the tea. He was surprised at how good it was. Just as the British always seem appalled at the thought of iced tea, Perkin had been convinced that hot tea with milk bordered on heresy. He freely admitted to himself now that he had been wrong. Perkin did not know whether tea would ever supplant coffee in his morning ritual, but he was certainly open to considering the prospect.

Colonel Fox had sent word back to division of Perkin's arrival in the Eighth Army area of operations, and at Perkin's request, Fox had stressed that the coastal road to Agropoli was open and unguarded. Fox sympathized with the young lieutenant when, after a few brandies, Perkin said he hoped his presence would spur a faster advance by Montgomery's forces. Fox wanted to be moving as well, but he privately thought that it would not happen quickly.

At 1000 sharp, a British orderly brought Perkin into what had been the living room of the villa, although it was now the operations center for the British 5th Division. "The colonel will be right with you, sir," the orderly said as he left the room.

Looking around the room, Perkin saw two British non-commissioned officers standing at a very large mahogany dining table, which had been brought into the living room and covered with a huge map of southern Italy. The floors were sparkling white marble, and ornate trim circled the floors and ceiling. Beautiful paintings of country life hung on the wall amid painted portraits of the owner's ancestors, and luxurious chairs and sofas had been moved to the sides of the room out of the way. Perkin thought of General Walker's headquarters in the dirty tobacco barn, and Perkin's ceaseless anxiety for his comrades at Paestum flooded out of the compartment in his mind where it had been relegated.

Other than the two British sergeants, who were evidently updating the operations plot, there were no other personnel in the room, although Perkin could hear other people talking and moving throughout the house. Perkin walked over to the soldiers, nodded to them, and looked down at the table. Small wooden markers represented the disposition of British, Canadian, and known enemy forces. Perkin noted the route he had taken—it was clear of any enemy markers.

A small officer with a clipped moustache and short-cropped graying hair walked into the room, followed by several junior officers. "Ah, here is our American," he said with a trace of a Scottish accent. As he saw Perkin was preparing to salute, he quickly stuck out his hand and the two officers, British and American, shook hands. "We're like your navy, we don't salute uncovered. Welcome to the Eighth Army. I am Colonel Alexander Foster—the 5th Division operations officer. These young men here are my deputies, and in a moment, I expect our intelligence officer to join us."

"I'm pleased to meet you, sir. I'm Lieutenant Perkin Berger of the 36th Division."

"Perkin . . . Berger?" the British officer asked slowly, unsure of what he had heard.

"Yes, sir. It's Melungeon," Perkin added brightly.

"Oh . . . uh, quite. Yes. Not familiar with . . . uh, hmm . . . how did you come to have this mission, Lieutenant? Are

you from the reconnaissance troop of the 36th?" Foster
was obviously making small talk until the intelligence
officer arrived.

"No, sir—Able Company, 141st RCT. I think the
battalion commander sent me as punishment for having
my hands in my pockets." The words were out before
Perkin could stop himself, but there did not seem to be
any damage done.

Foster brightened up immediately. "Quite right! I have
done the same on many occasions. I never hesitate to
send a slouching subaltern into harm's way if I think it
might help his military bearing. Ha-ha! Ah, there you are,
Russ. Come here and meet our Yank. Lieutenant Berger,
this is Lieutenant Colonel Michael Russ—the divisional
intelligence officer."

Perkin turned and stared at the newly arrived
intelligence officer. Aside from a few gray hairs, the
ubiquitous British officer's moustache and the uniform of
the Royal Inniskilling Fusiliers instead of a cassock, he
might have been looking at Father Patrick Riley.

The British intelligence officer extended his hand, as
the operations officer had done, and looked steadily in
Perkin's eyes as they shook hands, but Perkin could not
divine anything from the look. Russ's hands were hard
and calloused, like the Irish priest's, but he was taller than
Father Riley. The resemblance was unmistakable, and
Perkin realized that Riley and Russ were either brothers
or he was witnessing an uncanny coincidence.

"Congratulations on your journey, Lieutenant. I can't
wait to hear about it." Russ said in a public-school English
accent—no trace of Cork at all.

"Thank you, sir. I'm ready as soon as y'all are."

"Fine. Let's get started." Russ turned to Colonel Foster
and said, "Sorry that I was late, Sir Alexander. I was
attending to something unexpected."

"Quite alright. Lieutenant, if you'd be so kind, let's go over to the map. Pray walk us through your patrol."

"Yes, sir. Let me get to the bottom line up front. The coastal road is open. The lines of communication are intact and lightly guarded—if at all. We covered two hundred miles and encountered only two German patrols. It is my opinion that a battalion-sized link-up between the Fifth and Eighth Armies could be accomplished in less than twenty-four hours using the coastal road." Perkin realized his mistake as soon as he said it, and he hoped fervently that it would not be caught by the British officers. His hope was not realized.

"*Your opinion?*" Foster all but sneered at Perkin, and the instant transformation in the British officer surprised the Texan. "Young man, I don't know how things are done in the American Army, but in the British Army subalterns do not proffer unsolicited *opinions*. Furthermore, the Eighth Army does not move on the *opinion* of a First Lieutenant rifleman who was exiled on this mission for slouching. The only *opinion* on this subject that will matter to General Montgomery are those of his own reconnaissance teams, who can give him a valued assessment of roads, bridges, and above all, enemy dispositions! These men are professionals who can support or refute your claim that this road can manage and sustain a link-up between the armies."

Perkin felt his anger rising and said as neutrally as he could manage, "Of course, Colonel. It's just . . . well, I didn't see any of those professionals on our journey down. I understand that they must be occupied elsewhere, like looking for bridges that haven't been blown yet. Perhaps they could take a look at the bridges that I drove over and give General Montgomery a valued assessment as to whether they are intact or not. The point that I evidently failed to make was that we could've made the trip in only a few hours, but being lightly armed, it took me more time than I anticipated to destroy the first German patrol that we encountered and dispose of their vehicles and bodies. We could've breezed in yesterday, except it took us several hours to bury my dead soldiers after we were ambushed by the second patrol that we encountered. We were eight soldiers, now five, but we killed every German we encountered and—amateurs that we are—we still managed to get here. Perhaps a battalion would not be slowed as much as we were by a single squad of the enemy. I understand that the *opinion* of an American rifleman may not count for much, sir, but as I'm on orders from General Clark and General Walker, and as I'm the only Allied officer who's been on that fucking road in the past two days, I thought my *opinion* might carry some weight!"

There was absolute silence in the room. Colonel Foster looked as though he had been slapped, and he was turning a very deep shade of red. Perkin, who although not Melungeon was normally very dark complexioned, was turning a deep shade of red as well. The tall American lieutenant and the much shorter British colonel glared at each other, and Foster took a deep breath as he prepared to take a verbal wire brush to the insolent Yank.

"Gentlemen," Lieutenant Colonel Russ intervened smoothly in a calm voice—the neutral voice that Perkin had striven for unsuccessfully. "No need to refight the Battle of Bladensburg just now. Let me see if I can sum up where we stand so far. As clearly articulated by our American cousin here, the road is demonstrably open and appears to be lightly guarded. We know that because he is here. Lieutenant Berger, Colonel Foster was not calling your competence or experience into question, but rather stating that we'd all be best served to have further examination of this route to ensure it can support our needs."

Foster shifted uncomfortably as he realized that was a very generous interpretation of what he had, in fact, said. He remained silent.

Russ looked pointedly at Perkin and said, "Lieutenant, I suggest that an apology is in order to Sir Alexander, as I'm sure that junior officers don't speak thus to senior officers—even in the Texas Army."

Perkin did not hesitate, "Of course, sir, refighting the Battle of . . . New Orleans was not my intent. Colonel, I apologize if my words were abrupt or disrespectful."

The colonel nodded to Perkin and said curtly, "Very well." Foster was not yet prepared to be gracious to the American. Seeing this, Russ pulled Foster aside and, while Perkin looked at the map, said in a low voice, "Sir, one last word on this subject. I passed the lieutenant's soldiers on the way here to the villa and stopped to chat with them. That is why I was late. They were washing the blood out of their jeeps and getting prepared to head north again—they are anxious to get back to their own fight. His soldiers regard him very highly; they told me he single-handedly attacked a Panzer IV at Salerno and drove it off the battlefield . . . with a sledgehammer." Foster looked skeptical and Russ shrugged. "I don't know how you could make something like that up, sir." Foster stared at Perkin who was talking with one of the British NCOs at the table. Russ continued: "Lieutenant Berger and his men paid a price to demonstrate that the coastal road is viable to us. I think that they've earned the right to be heard, so I recommend that I take Lieutenant Berger to my office and do a proper debrief. If I am satisfied, I shall make a recommendation to Eighth Army intelligence that we conduct a reconnaissance in force along that road no later than tomorrow."

1100 hours
British 5th Division HQ

The intelligence center was set up in the servant's quarters on the villa grounds. *Even the servants have it nicer than General Walker,* Perkin thought. He had calmed down considerably, although he still resented Foster's attitude. That he knew senior officers took a dim view on unsolicited recommendations from junior officers, and had offered his opinion anyway, did not help his mood. He resolved to do a better job holding his tongue in the future.

Perkin and Lieutenant Colonel Russ had walked across the compound without saying a word. When they entered the building, Russ called out to the various junior officers and enlisted men working there, "I have an uncleared foreign national with me. Be on your guard that he doesn't steal any of our paper clips."

When they entered the bedroom that had been converted to Russ's office, he offered a chair to Perkin and said, "Do you normally talk to a colonel and a Knight Commander of the Order of the British Empire like that?"

Perkin hung his head and then shook it. "Well, sir, I appear to be batting a thousand on knights, but I'm mostly polite to colonels. I'm glad there wasn't any royalty around though, or I'd have probably chapped their ass as well."

Russ smiled at the embarrassed soldier—his first smile since Perkin met him. "Don't beat yourself up too much. The colonel was rude to you, and you put him in his place very directly. He's a good man and a good operations officer, but he comes from a different generation of soldiers. An unsolicited word of advice to you, Berger: in life, you either control your emotions or they end up controlling you—it's that simple. Don't let your anger show, and be careful with words because words matter." He walked to the door and called for two cups of tea. "Now, let's get to business. Please show me on the map the precise route you took, exactly where you encountered Jerry, and feel free to offer opinions, observations, and suggestions—I don't mind."

The next hour was filled with an accounting of Perkin's patrol with Russ asking numerous questions about virtually every subject from the helpfulness of the *Carabinieri* to estimated load capacities on the bridges. The intelligence officer was impressed with Perkin's observations and memory for detail. When his memory failed him, Perkin referred to the journal that he had kept; when he could not answer a question, he said so, and when he expressed an opinion, he qualified it as such. Every aspect of the patrol was covered in detail—except for Pisciotta. Perkin waited to see if the British officer would bring it up.

He did not have to wait long. They were discussing the route that Perkin took when Russ asked him why they took such a long detour around Camerota.

"I was advised against it." Perkin replied.

"By whom?"

"I don't know. Maybe your brother? A cousin? The Irish priest at Pisciotta." Perkin replied, watching Russ closely.

"I don't know what you're talking about, Lieutenant. My brother—an Irish priest? I'm not Irish." Russ seemed amused.

"Well sir, I understand Wellington said something along the lines of 'Not everything born in a stable is a horse.'"

Russ grinned widely and then couldn't contain himself as he laughed out loud and slapped his thigh. "Did Patrick say that? I used to tell him that every time he reminded me of our Irish heritage. Ah, Lieutenant Berger, I have to trust you to not discuss this further. Patrick is what he said he is—an Irish priest assigned to the Jesuit Curia in Rome. It's kind of complicated, but the short version is that we were born in County Down, that's in Northern Ireland, eight years apart. Our father was in this regiment, 9th Battalion, 36th Division. He died on the Somme, and our mother soon remarried a Catholic man from the south named Patrick Riley."

Perkin interrupted, "My father was killed on the Marne. Did you know that my division is also the 36th?"

Russ nodded, "Yes, that's what your squaddies told me. Anyway, it was very scandalous for my mother, you know—marrying a Catholic so soon after my father died. Riley adopted my younger brother, whose birth name was Richard Russ, and Patrick took his adopted father's name and religion. Maybe it was better that way—after the Easter Uprising and through the days of the Black and Tans, it was not a good thing to have an English name in an Irish neighborhood. I tease him that he has been pretending to be an Irishman ever since. I was much older, chose not to be adopted and went away to public school in England. That's why we have different surnames."

Perkin was silent for a moment as he digested the information. "But how did he come to work for you in Italy, how did he get to Pisciotta and how did he get the information to you? I mean, I know he used pigeons, but I thought pigeons were trained to specific places. I've been thinking about this for two days. How did he send a pigeon to a mobile army?"

"He didn't. He sent them to . . . "

"Churches?" Perkin interrupted again.

"Yes. My brother has a conspiratorial side to him—probably why he became a Jesuit. He would send information about the state of Italy back to me in England or friends of mine in the trade—he's been here for three years and he has quite a network of like-minded associates in Italy that oppose fascism. The bishop here in Nicastro is one and has been our conduit since we landed at Reggio. So you can see the reason for confidentiality: there is a lot at stake. Not just for Patrick and his circle of friends, but for the Church as well. As for Pisciotta, he was there taking care of a friend, as I'm sure he told you. It is unfortunate as he was more use to us in Rome, but it worked out well as he was able to help you." Russ pulled out a pack of cigarettes, offered one to Perkin who declined, and lit up and inhaled deeply. "I would ask you to refrain from stopping at Pisciotta on your way back north. He does not need the attention you would bring."

"Sir, that brings me to another subject if you don't mind."

Russ nodded, "Go ahead."

"My mission was to see if the route was open and to gently encourage its use to the Eighth Army if it seemed viable. Is there any chance of my seeing General Montgomery?" Perkin knew the answer but had to ask the question.

Russ smiled and shook his head. "There is no chance, whatsoever, of seeing General Montgomery. His staff protects his time more jealously than a nun guards her chastity, and they will not be able to find time for an American lieutenant—or a British lieutenant colonel, for that matter. I think it's fair to say that the goals of your mission are met, however. Based on our discussion here, I shall report to the Eighth Army staff of your arrival and that the line of communication between Eighth and Fifth Armies appears open. I'll then recommend that they conduct a reconnaissance in force along that LOC to confirm and protect the bridges. Good enough?"

"Yes, sir, I would appreciate that. We should be heading back then, sir. Do you know how the Salerno battle is progressing?"

The smile left Russ's face, and he shook his head. "I've only heard bits and pieces, and it's not all good. The

Germans have decided to contest the landings and are rapidly withdrawing forces from our front and sending them to Salerno. Fifth Army is no longer expanding its beachhead but is hard-pressed to hold on to what it's attained. I'm heading to Eighth Army HQ to see about orders for the reconnaissance that we were talking about just now. Why don't you come with me? We'll get some lunch, and then we'll talk to their staff. I'm sure they have a more complete picture."

Perkin nodded but said, "I need to see how my soldiers are gettin' along. They're lookin' to get a machine gun mount installed in one of the jeeps and scroungin' for gas, uh, petrol, and rations. If they're not yet ready, I'll go over with you. If they are ready, we're leavin' now for Salerno."

When Perkin and Lieutenant Colonel Russ walked out of the small villa into the heat and sunlight, Private Kulis was waiting for him.

Kulis's standard greeting would normally have been a casual salute and "Hey, sir," but as they were in the presence of a foreign officer, he came stiffly to attention, then produced a parade ground salute. "Good afternoon, gentlemen!"

"Good afternoon, Private Kulis. At ease!" Perkin suppressed a smile.

"Sir, Sergeant Kenton found a welder who'll get us that mount. The welder is finishing up another project, then he'll take of it. He said they'll be back here about 1600. Sarge arranged to top off the tanks of the jeep and get a little to spare. He gave 'em the flask of that terrible tequila from Pena's pack in exchange for the MG mount, and we took one of the pints of bourbon outta your pack for the gas." Kulis looked over at the British intelligence officer. "Your boys said they couldn't spare any gas, sir, but after some negotiating they found it in their hearts to share a little. We felt it was a good deal—a pint of the lieutenant's hooch for several gallons of His Majesty's gas. Hope that's okay, Lieutenant."

"Let's see . . . you traded something that wasn't yours for somethin' that wasn't theirs. I think that shows outstanding initiative—just the kind of business that made Britain and America great." He gave Kulis a friendly shove and then turned to Russ. "Sir, that reminds me. I was supposed to trade some bourbon for gin. We found a stock of tonic water in Agropoli but ran outta gin. Assumin' that Kulis didn't trade my remainin' bottle to the chaplain for a naked picture of the queen, do you know of someone who might be interested in tradin' some gin for good Kentucky bourbon?"

Russ nodded and said, "You're in luck. I know just the chap, and he's at the HQ. By the way, Private Kulis—this is for you." The British officer reached into a leather satchel he was carrying and pulled out a thick black book. "It's a collection of Rudyard Kipling's stories. I look forward to reading *The Fountainhead*. Private, you are welcome to accompany us, but you won't be able to attend any briefings or discussions, I'm afraid."

"Sergeant Kenton told me to stay here, although I plan to press my luck and sit in the shade over yonder." Kulis pointed to an apple tree—the nearest tree in the small orchard on the villa's grounds. The private requested his leave of the officers, found a comfortable seat under the tree, and opened his newly acquired book to *The Man Who Would Be King*. As a piper in the distance played "The Minstrel Boy," he began to read.

1545 hours
Mount Chirico, Italy

The trucks had dropped off the four companies of the 1st Battalion and then sped off to their next assignments.

The battalion was placed in an olive orchard on the west side of a small mountain called Mount San Chirico. It was, Sam thought, a good site; the mountain shielded the battalion from the view of German artillery spotters in the mountains ringing the Salerno plain.

Those same spotters had seen the convoy of trucks moving along Highway 18 through patches in the haze caused by American smoke pots placed all over the battlefield, and the German gunners had taken shots at the battalion as the convoy occasionally presented itself. Certainly, the Germans had the range and location of the highway down cold by this point, but they also had more pressing fire support missions to execute; German fire was sporadic and was never pressed home to its full potential.

When it comes to artillery fire, however, sporadic is in the eye of the receiver. From Sam's personal vantage, it seemed that the Germans were making a dedicated effort to kill him. Despite his perception that the convoy of trucks would most certainly be destroyed before reaching their destination, it passed through the gauntlet of occasional fire unscathed but for a few close calls. Consequently, both Sam and Jim were sweating but relieved when the big trucks came to a halt and the officers and sergeants began yelling for the soldiers to dismount.

As was becoming his habit after a scrap, Sam looked around at his platoon and took in the gamut of emotions: some soldiers were angry at the Germans for the shelling— *they'll get angrier soon,* thought Sam—others were pale and sweating, and Sam suspected this was how he looked to them. Yet another group of soldiers were laughing, as if being shot at by some of the best field artillery in the world were the greatest lark imaginable.

"Morons," Sam muttered to himself. He knew that he was in danger of having his black mood return, but the platoon's laughter became infectious as the men realized no one had been hurt. Momentarily, he found himself smiling and laughing with the rest.

Captain Spaulding had quickly put the company to work establishing defensive positions. They were perhaps four miles behind the forward line of troops. Though Spaulding did not expect a German breakthrough where they were, he hated to see soldiers standing around. The men sited machine guns and mortars and the new 57mm antitank guns of the battalion's antitank platoon. Lieutenant Colonel Wranosky had seen to arranging A-rations instead of the C- and K-rations that the troops had been on since the landings; they would be glad to have a good hot meal before any fighting. As always, the soldiers cleaned weapons, smoked cigarettes, and talked of women, food, and baseball or football—depending on their inclinations.

At Captain Spaulding's direction, Sam had left the concerns of the platoon in the capable hands of Sergeant Younger. In company with Jim Lockridge, Sam and a squad of riflemen had climbed Mount Chirico to its crest, where a large wooden cross stood. Although he had a flatlander's perspective on mountains, Sam recognized that Mount Chirico barely rose to the mountainous standard; after the walk, however, he was willing to concede that it was a damn big hill. It gave his party a good view of the battlefield from the hill's crest: to his right, the south, was Mount Soprano, one of the division's D-day objectives. There was a small flat valley on the plain below dotted with villages between the two mountains, and a large body of soldiers on foot moved through the valley to the east. Through the haze, Sam estimated that there were three or four companies on the march, and Jim, who had a better understanding of the Allied dispositions, reckoned that it was the 1st Battalion of the 142nd Regiment en route to Altavilla. For both men, it was moving and majestic to watch the hundreds of soldiers move through the valley. After a moment of silently watching the columns of men, Sam broke some soldiers out of his squad and established an observation post to cover the valley to the south and east of Mount Chirico.

As they moved around the hilltop to the eastern slope, they saw a low but wide mountain complex topped by several small crests. Jim pointed out the left side of the mountain where Altavilla would be, although they could not see the village for the smoke that hung over the fighting. They could hear the sounds of combat, though, and it seemed possession of Altavilla was being contested again, and Sam hoped the 1/142nd might make the difference in the fight. Below them was another valley between Mount Chirico and the Altavilla mountain complex, and weaving its way through the valley was a large creek. Jim told Sam that was La Cosa Stream and that it flowed northerly into the Calore River. On the other side of the creek, before the rising complex, was another large village that Jim identified as Albanella.

As they walked further towards the northeast corner of the hilltop, they saw a black cloud of smoke over the Sele-Calore corridor. Yet another fierce battle was being waged for the finger-shaped wedge of land between the two rivers.

"Do you know who's out there?" Sam asked.

"One of the battalions of the 143rd, I think, but it's hard to tell." Jim took off his wire-rimmed glasses and squinted at the corridor as if he could tell which battalion was in the fight by looking over the miles. "The battalions have been moved around so much to plug holes here and there that I don't think a single regimental combat team is fighting as a coherent body. You know, we had the roughest time on D-day, but we're probably the most intact regiment left. Let's head back and see what the colonel has in mind for us."

It seemed a lifetime before Jim and Sam returned to the battalion. German forward observers had caught sight of the battalion of soldiers on foot as a strengthening afternoon breeze cleared the smoke from the valley. The course of the soldiers was plotted, and the fire mission was called in and prepared. Fifteen minutes later, as the two Texans were returning to the observation post and the entire 1st Battalion of the 142nd Regiment was exposed in the valley, the German artillery fired a single spotting round. It was dead-on target in the center of the columns. All other fire missions became secondary for the Germans, and within seconds, every howitzer tucked away in the mountains within range opened fire at the exposed soldiers. It was a terrible and destructive barrage that lasted for an eternally long fifteen minutes. The slaughter was horrific, and only the few soldiers who broke and ran back to the relative safety of La Cosa Stream emerged physically unscathed. Sam and Jim watched in agony from Mount Chirico, tears flowing down Sam's cheeks, as a battalion of American infantry virtually ceased to exist.

1800 hours
Eighth Army HQ

After a ten mile drive, Perkin and Lieutenant Colonel Russ arrived at a larger villa which was the Eighth Army HQ. They found an improvised officer's mess and had lunch. Since the jeep would not be ready for some time, Russ took Perkin into the room housing the operations staff, where Perkin recounted his mission for several other officers. No opinions were put forth by Perkin this time, and a good technical discussion ensued about the coastal road.

It was much later in the afternoon when they walked out of the villa housing operations, and the two officers followed a sign to the building housing the intelligence directorate. The afternoon with the British had eaten up most of his daylight, and although Perkin had resolved to begin the journey back that day, it was increasingly unlikely that he would do so. Still, the afternoon with the Eighth Army staff fulfilled his mission, and there seemed genuine interest in the route. One more day was regrettable but was looking necessary.

"Lieutenant, I know a sharp subaltern who can speak your language and bring you up to date on the battle in Salerno. I'm going to find my counterpart on this staff and talk about a reconnaissance of the coastal road. He may have some questions for you, and if so, I'll send for you. Your jeep is probably ready by now, so I won't be long." Russ led them into the small house and looked around until he found the officer that he wanted.

"Lieutenant Rose! Can you spare a moment?"

"Certainly, sir. What can I do for you?"

Perkin studied Rose, intrigued by what sounded like an American West-Coast accent coming from the officer wearing a British uniform. On closer examination, he saw the "Canada" tab on the officer's sleeve.

"This is Lieutenant Berger of the American 141st. He's completed a link-up from the Fifth Army along the coastal road—he heads back today or tomorrow and wanted an update on his battle before he goes. I thought you might be able to help. While you do that, I need to speak to your boss. Is he about?"

"Yes, sir. He's in there." Rose pointed to a doorway. Without another word, Russ headed to the back of the house.

Perkin looked at Lieutenant Rose—about five feet nine inches tall, pale complexion, and pale blue eyes with blond hair in a severely short buzz cut. Rose looked back and offered his hand, "Bob Rose, Seaforth Highlanders."

"Perkin Berger, South Texas Flatlanders." Perkin thought that Rose was preparing a question and decided to preempt him. "I'll make you a deal, Bob—if you don't ask me about my name, I won't mention your haircut."

Rose, who was actually preparing a retort to Perkin's mimicry of his regiment, instead frowned thoughtfully and said, "I don't know that I want to commit to that. You might want the name of my barber some day. Besides, what if I told you I know a Perkin Berger back in Vancouver?"

"Really?" Perkin was astonished. He had never heard of another Perkin Berger outside of his own unfortunately named ancestors.

"No. I just think we should keep our options open." Rose waved Perkin over to an army table that had a map of the Salerno battlefield on it. "My task is to track Fifth Army's battle so that we will be prepared when we approach your area of operations. This should be an operations job, but as there is very little formal communication between Clark and Montgomery's staffs, it has been given to the intelligence fellows to sort out. It's probably best; we're able to add Jerry's perspective on the fight as well. When did you leave the Salerno plain?"

"Saturday."

"It's been a pretty rough dust-up since then, and I believe Clark's asked for your 82nd Airborne to be dropped either tonight or tomorrow to firm up the VI Corps lines. He must be pretty nervous—the 82nd was only given a day to prepare this drop. Let's begin with the maritime picture: we maintain control of the seas. The fleet has pulled in close to the shore and used their guns quite effectively; although the Jerries have made some actual runs at the beach, the navy and ground fire has turned them back. They actually had a tank make it to the water's edge in the British sector before some ship destroyed it. However, the Luftwaffe has had several goes at the fleet in an attempt to push them further out to sea. We are hearing reports of radio-controlled rocket bombs that have sunk or damaged a number of ships."

Perkin interrupted the Canadian officer, "No kidding? That's amazing—I'd sure hate to be a squid."

"Me too. On the morning that you left, they hit your cruiser *Savannah* with one, maybe two, of these damned things and detonated some of her onboard ammunition. I don't know how, but she remained afloat. You must have heard the explosion."

"I don't know. We heard explosions until we were way south of Agropoli . . . but there was an exceptionally loud one, just as we assaulted a German roadblock." Perkin thought back to that morning. He could still remember the tension and the excitement of creeping up on the German position, the loud explosion, his team firing and the shaking, nausea, pride, and shame afterwards.

"Maybe that was it. I'd like to hear about your attack when we're done with this. Maybe over a drink this evening, if you're around. Anyway, we have sea control, but the Germans are challenging it as best they can."

Perkin asked, "What about air?"

Rose smiled sardonically, "Well, you'd think that wouldn't be an issue, would you? We were supposed to have air supremacy over the Fifth Army from D-day onwards, but sadly, that is not the case. I guess no one told the Germans that their air force is combat ineffective. We have patrols that are up and over the Salerno plain, but the Krauts keep sneaking raids in. They have been able to conduct bombing raids, almost at will, against both the ground forces and the fleet. Damn flyboys. I don't know your feelings on the subject, but I think I'd rather have a sister in a whorehouse than a brother in the air force."

Perkin laughed—he was beginning to like the Canadian lieutenant. "That goes without saying. It could be worse though—my cousin is an Aggie."

"What?"

"Never mind. Are the troops getting any air support?"

"Nope—not much, anyway. They are supposed to be redirecting strategic air to the battle, but I don't know when that will happen. The ground forces could use the help; the Rangers and Commandos are holding on to the key passes to Naples, but they've been severely pressed to do so. One interesting thing is that your regiment of Rangers has been so effective that our radio intercepts suggest the Germans believe at least an entire division is holding the Chiunzi Pass. The British Corps, X Corps, has taken Montecorvino Airfield, though, until they get the German artillery cleared out from the surrounding hills, they aren't getting much use out of it. VI Corps is getting the worst of it, I'm afraid. I've heard, but I can't confirm, that at least one battalion of the 36th has been virtually destroyed."

"Jesus Christ! Which one?" Perkin asked intensely. There were only nine rifle battalions in the 36th.

Rose picked up a piece of paper and looked at it. "The 2nd Battalion of the 142nd. They have been caught up in a back-and-forth battle for the past day with the Germans for a mountain village called Altavilla—looks like good high ground overlooking the Sele-Calore corridor. I gather that VI Corps has committed more troops to the battle of Altavilla today, so I hope that they get it in check quickly. Also, your General Walker had to give one battalion, uh . . . to . . . ," he checked his paper again, "to those Rangers at the other end of the battlefield in the British sector, so he's probably feeling the loss of all that combat power."

"My God," Perkin interrupted again. "That brings him down to seven out of nine battalions. Do you know anything about the 1st Battalion of the 141st?"

"Nothing other than they had a rough go of it on D-day, but I guess you know that already . . . " Rose broke off as a British noncommissioned officer walked into the room. The corporal started to speak, looked at Perkin, and instead bent over and whispered at length in Lieutenant Rose's ear.

Rose asked of the soldier, "Are you sure? Who else knows?"

The soldier nodded and said, "Just you, sir. You'll have to tell the senior staff." He waited a moment until he saw that there were no further questions and then left.

Rose looked at Perkin and shook his head, his anguish clear on his face, "Perkin, I'm afraid that I have some very bad news for you—for all of us. It looks like your division lost two more battalions in today's fighting. We've just gotten word that General Clark has directed his staff and the fleet to prepare for the evacuation of the Salerno beachhead. I hadn't thought it was this bad, but it sounds like another Dunkirk is in the making. I'm very sorry."

1900 hours
Mount Chirico, Italy

The regimental commander, Colonel Jamison, looked dog-tired as he looked over the small group of 1st Battalion officers assembled before him. He had a terrible message to convey to these young men, and he did not know how to break the news. He had always believed in a straightforward approach.

"All right, boys, listen up. The division got beat like a westbound hobo today, and we'll have to make some quick adjustments to our line if we're to prevent a successful run against the beachhead. This is important, so I'm going to repeat it. I want everyone to understand where we are: we're at D+4, the day we expected to enter

Naples, and instead we are in danger of losing the beach. While that soaks in, let me tell you what happened today and what we're gonna do about it. In the past three days, the division has effectively lost four rifle battalions out of nine. Three rendered combat ineffective and a fourth, Fred Walker's team, was sent to bolster the Rangers in the X Corps sector.* So we have five beat-up battalions left to cover twenty-two miles of front. We all know that is an impossible task, and we'll have to shorten our lines. I'll talk to that in a minute, but I want to tell you what happened to the 2/143rd. There was a hell of a fight in the Sele-Calore corridor yesterday, and one of the 45th's regiments got kicked in the balls by the Germans and then kicked out of the corridor. This morning, General Dawley sent a battalion of ours into the same ground that a regiment got kicked out of yesterday and didn't tell Walker about yesterday's fight. Why Walker didn't already know, I can't say, but he evidently didn't know we were going onto ground where the Germans had already cleaned our clocks. Today, the other regiment from the 45th Division was supposed to protect our left flank but withdrew without telling our boys. So the 2nd Battalion got fixed in front and then flanked on its left. It was a short fight, and it ended with most of the battalion surrendering—looks like they even got the battalion commander. I don't know where the fault lies—Clark, Dawley, Middleton, or Walker—but I think that we can agree that battalion commander deserved better. Let this serve as a lesson to you, young gentlemen: always, always, always talk to each other!"

Jamison's already florid face was turning dark red as his passion began to show. "We lost six hundred men in the

---

*This was Lt Col Fred Walker, Jr., the division commander's son and battalion commander of 1/143rd. Colonel Walker was kind enough to write the foreword to *The Texas Gun Club*.

corridor today because of a simple failure to communicate. It was a dumb, amateurish performance today. Oh, and we also lost Altavilla in the process."

Jamison stopped talking, wiped his forehead with a handkerchief, and then scratched at the red and white stubble on his chin. "So, what's this mean for us? It means our lives just got a little more complicated. The Germans have to smell blood after today's fight, and they will seek to put an end to this tomorrow—maybe tonight, but most likely tomorrow. Expect them to throw everything into this, including the kitchen sink, and I mean everything. Gents, it's no exaggeration to say that the next day determines the outcome of the fight for Salerno—if we win, we resume the offensive in a day or two, and we march into Naples in a week or so. If we lose, well, we lose big. But I think that there is a good plan in place to recover from 'Black Monday' today. First, Walker is establishing three defensive sectors, each under the command of a brigadier general." In response to murmuring among the assembled officers, Jamison smiled wanly and said, "No, I hate to disappoint you, but that does not mean I'm being relieved. Nor are any of the regimental commanders. Except for us, the regiments really don't exist anymore and the brigadiers are taking command of a sector where the rifle battalions are only one element. They'll be in command of artillery, armor, and the antitank forces in their sector as well, and the regimental commanders will be their deputies. The three sectors are planned along a defensive line based on the La Cosa Stream and the Calore River. We're gonna dig in like ticks on a coonhound and wait for the counter-attack. Y'all, and by that I mean your battalion, are gonna establish a defensive line along La Cosa Stream between Mounts Soprano and Chirico. The 2nd Battalion'll be to your left, in front of and on Mount Chirico. Second, if the weather holds, Clark is having the 82nd Airborne drop the 504th PIR from Sicily into our sector tonight, and they'll be on the line by daybreak. There is a discussion underway at corps where they'll go, and they might take over your positions as you move closer to the corridor. I don't know for sure, but we have more heavy stuff than the airborne guys, and they'll probably want you at the confluence of La Cosa and the Calore tomorrow. Because of what happened to the 82nd at Sicily, no one, and I mean no one, shoots at the sky tonight for any reason."*

Jamison stopped talking and reached for his canteen. It was empty, so he took a drink from Lieutenant Colonel Wranosky's canteen while a second lieutenant from Charlie Company refilled his from a battalion HQ water trailer.

Jamison cleared his throat and began again, "Three other things that I want to impart to you: First, we have no reserves. I understand that Old Dawley told Clark that all he's got left is a prayer. That might be helpful, but unfortunately, those Germans are praying to the same God as us. I assume He don't listen to 'em as much, but let's take no chances. Second, there can be no falling back, or we're all goners. No reserve, no defense in depth. Everyone fights where he is placed, and that is that. In spite of all of this, I want to share something I overheard this afternoon: An artillery commander supportin' the fight for the corridor was concerned about being overrun. He told his boys, 'No one gets past us, and if we have to, we'll fight with the goddamned rammer staff!' Now, I don't know about you young gentlemen, but if the artillery is going to stand up to the Wehrmacht with a fuckin' tampon, then I reckon that we in the infantry can't do any less." When the laughter subsided, Jamison said in a serious voice, "Finally, you might hear some rumors that Clark is ordering an

---

*Transports carrying the 82nd into battle at Sicily were mistaken for German bombers by the Allied fleet. Twenty-three transports were shot down by friendly fire, killing over eighty paratroopers and wounding hundreds more.

evacuation. Gentlemen, I'm going to ask you to disregard those rumors and stop your troops from spreading them. A rumor like that would spread among the soldiers like contagion and be far more deadly in its consequence. An evacuation just ain't gonna happen."

Jamison knew they were more than rumors. General Clark had directed his planners to coordinate with the combined fleet to prepare three plans—an evacuation of both corps to Sicily; a seaborne transfer of the VI Corps into the British sector; and a seaborne transfer of X Corps into the American sector. *What a goddamn goat-rope,* Jamison thought—it really couldn't be done. Jamison had heard that the British X Corps Commander, General McCreery, had flatly refused to even consider any such evacuation, and Jamison wholeheartedly agreed. It would be a slaughter and, unlike Dunkirk, he didn't think that German armor would stand by and wait for the Luftwaffe this time. His other worry was if Clark was stupid enough to order the evacuation, the 141st, as the only intact regiment, would be left to fight the delaying action. The thought that all his boys would be killed or taken prisoner made him nauseous. He shuddered involuntarily. Rumor or not, he did not want the soldiers talking about it or it would lead to panic. *More panic is closer to the truth,* he thought worriedly.

1915 hours
British 5th Division HQ

Sergeant Kenton had the jeeps and the soldiers ready to depart when Lieutenant Colonel Russ dropped Perkin off at the 5th Division headquarters. "Be careful moving through our lines," Russ counseled Perkin. "As you have so clearly demonstrated, Jerry hasn't given us any indication that they are opposing us along the coastal road, but things change. As soon as they recognize the danger that road poses to their flanks, they'll try to block our movement just as they've done in the center of our advance. I understand why you want to return, and while I think you should stay with Eighth Army, I shan't try to talk you into it. Don't be in such a hurry that you compromise your safety."

"Yes, sir. Thank you for your help. I hope we meet again," Perkin said with genuine feeling as he shook Russ's outstretched hand.

"It's a small world, Perkin; I wouldn't be surprised if we do." Privately, Russ doubted they would meet again. He feared the young American would likely be killed or captured during his return journey or soon after he made it back to his regiment. Still, one never knew. As the tall Texan had proven his worth on his southbound journey and impressed the British intelligence officer with his command of details, Russ resolved to do him a small favor. The first chance that he had, Russ would draft a classified message to the intelligence officer of the 36th Division and recommend that Perkin be retrained and reassigned to a reconnaissance command. *No sense allowing such talent to be wasted as infantry cannon fodder,* he thought. "One last word of advice: don't drive too long tonight. Headlights are almost irresistible for airmen—they'll strafe the blazes out of you and then report that they destroyed Hermann Goering's staff car."

"Don't worry, sir." The tall, lean lieutenant said with a grin. "I'm used to it. Most people mistake me for the field marshal."

"No doubt they do. Good luck." The British officer climbed behind the wheel of his jeep, and without a further word drove off to the small quarters housing his intelligence center.

Perkin called his men together and they all took a knee, as if they were a football team and Perkin their coach.

He laid the situation out as clearly as he could to his four soldiers, but it truthfully wasn't a complex story: VI Corps was in danger of being driven back into the sea. Perkin further stated his intentions to return that night, and although some officers might have offered their soldiers the opportunity to stay behind with the British rather than run the risk of returning to a disintegrating battle, Perkin did not. He intended to take everyone else back to the Texas Army alive, and the matter was not open to discussion. To a man, they were all for departing the Eighth Army's hospitality and returning to Paestum; no one believed in their hearts that their return would matter much to the fight—after all, what contribution could five soldiers make—but they could not sit the fight out in the relative safety of Eighth Army while their fellow Texans were being evacuated from the beach under fire. Their response reinforced Perkin's pride in his small detail—this was one of the defining moments of the war for all of them, the time when they all truly entered the brotherhood. If the division was going down, they would go down together.

1945 hours
La Cosa Defenses, 1.5 Miles WSW of Albanella,
Italy

The valley through which the 1st Battalion of the 142nd RCT had marched to its destruction was littered with the wreckage of war. Rifles, destroyed jeeps and trucks, burned packs, and bodies covered the landscape east of the La Cosa Stream. The occasional buildings, farmhouses, and barns had long been destroyed by artillery seeking out infantrymen who had sought cover. Discarded equipment on the western side of the stream was evidence that many Texans had dropped their rifles and ran—even when out of the German artillery fire. It was a sobering sight to the soldiers of Able Company, who had largely been out of combat since D-day.

Sam and Captain Spaulding reviewed their defenses. It was a hasty defensive line based on the stream—obscured from the watchful eyes of German observers in the foothills and mountains by hundreds of smoke pots on the battlefield—and the new defenses were a tacit admission that the battle was being lost. This line was at least three miles behind the perimeter marking the farthest advance of the Americans of VI Corps. It did not even encompass all the objectives of D-day, and the new situation was particularly concerning to the soldiers of Able Company, who knew there was no one standing behind them. As General Dawley had said of his reserves, all they had was a prayer.

As Sam was well aware, there were pluses and minuses to defending a stream or river. The La Cosa Stream offered a depth below ground level that surpassed a foxhole, which at least gave a soldier a sense of protection from enemy fires. The stream was also easy access to water, now in short supply for many of the soldiers who were filling their canteens in the stream and then dropping in water purification tablets. Still, Sam knew the protection of the stream was illusory. It had been registered by German artillery—evident by the few remaining shattered trees along the creek bank. Sam's frontage was four hundred yards, meaning that his platoon was responsible for defending almost a quarter mile of the American defensive line. The defensive line itself was simple in the Able Company sector and in many ways less sophisticated than defenses in the Great War. Concertina wire, called "bob-wahr" by the Texans, had been strung two hundred yards in front of the stream, and a second single wire adorned with tin cans, known as a jingle line, had been strung a dozen yards inside of the concertina wire to give an advanced warning of an infiltrating patrol. Sam divided a squad up and established two small outposts between the stream and the jingle line; and telephone lines had been dropped from his command post behind the stream to his outposts. All along the creek, soldiers established firing steps on the bank of the stream while others dug foxholes on the American side of the stream. Interlocking machine gun fire was planned, phone lines were run back to company and battalion command posts, and fire support missions were prepared. As night began to settle in, so did the men of Able Company.

As Captain Spaulding left to check on the remainder of the defenses with the company top sergeant, Master Sergeant Hawkins, Sam stood on a firing step on the La Cosa bank and took out a small notebook and a pencil—he would move to his command post, a foxhole, later. Sam had already written what he thought might be his last letter to Margaret, and he wanted to wait on the battle's outcome before he wrote her another intentionally mundane letter about wet socks, his hatred of leggings, and the inadequacy of army chow. In truth, Sam did not want to think too much about Margaret; he was afraid he would tear up, and he did not want tears in his eyes in front of his soldiers. So, instead, he set to writing a letter to Old Perkin.

> *Dear Pop: First off, we're well. By now you'll have heard that the division's entered combat. Although the censors won't allow us to discuss where we are, I'm sure that it will be in the Corpus paper before you get this letter. Perkin and I've seen a little bit of the fighting and we're doing okay. Perk is off in another sector of the battlefield, and I haven't seen anything of him for two days, but I haven't heard anything either. No news is good news.*

I don't want to overly concern you, but this is a tough fix. You made us promise to give you the straight skinny and not a white-washed accounting of what's going on, so here goes. Our arrival was greeted with great fanfare, but instead of a band and cheerleaders, we were met by 88s and panzer grenadiers. We've been shelled by the Krauts several times since. It was more exciting than when the oil well exploded out by the Midway gin in '38 (and I'll say again for the record that neither Perk nor I were involved in that mess). Perk and I already had some casualties in our platoons, and I hate to tell you that Lt. Ed Brown was killed in the first minute of the war. Trust me, though, I haven't done anything more heroic than dousing a fascist with a bucket of water. It was pretty satisfying, but I'll save that story for when I get home, as there are nuances involved. I also had a nice 500 yd shot through peep sights, but I'll also save that for in person (you would've approved of it, though).

You should be terribly proud of Perkin, who is a natural leader. I am jealous, as he is better at these things than I am, but I'm proud just the same. I don't know how he arranged it, but he was the first soldier on the enemy's shore, and he is such a talker that his boys bought into it as well (certainly more impressive than when he led his failed charge to change the school mascot to howler monkeys). He is respected by the officers and the men, and the average G.I. knows that he can talk to Perk and get a fair shake. He will make a great company commander or battalion commander, for that matter, when his time comes (although in the meanwhile we are both blessed to have Bill Spaulding).

I don't know what runs in the Berger blood, but it has more than its share of bravery. Perk earned the right to tell the whole tale, but he turned the tide in a little skirmish that we were in. All I'll say is every soldier who witnessed it said they had never seen anything like it. The good news is I don't think it'll inspire him to further acts. It scared the s—t out of him, and I'm sure that he'll lie low in the future . . .

Sam wasn't sure of that at all, but even though they had promised Old Perkin to tell him the details, he didn't think the old boy could bear to hear about Perkin attacking a tank with a hammer. It still gave Sam chills.

. . . I've written to Maggie and will again in the next day or two. I know you go out to the ranch every few days to visit, and I appreciate it more than I can say. I know that Maggie's tougher than a nickel steak, but I still worry.

Despite Sam's intentions, his eyes got watery and he got a lump in his throat. He took a deep breath and looked out over the darkening battlefield. He wondered if they would hit tonight or wait until tomorrow. "Let it be tomorrow," Sam said under his breath. Everything was quiet, and he went back to his letter to Old Perkin.

Next time you go out, please ask her to send me some horse liniment. I'm stiff as hell from sleeping on the ground, although I slept in a bed a couple days ago. Other than that, tell her I'm thriving out here and I have a terrible farmer's tan, which is more ridiculous because of this g—damn helmet. She'd think it's a hoot and a half. Speaking of ridiculous, I ran into that c—ks—ker Ron Ebbins the other day, and

I wouldn't put it past their miserable lot to stir up trouble at the ranch just because she's a girl. I feel sorry for them if they try.

I've also written to Mr. Bob at the King Ranch and arranged to buy another prime S. Gertrudis bull calf, so we're set when old Igor goes (why Dad let Perk name his prize bull, I'll never know). Tell Maggie I've thought about it and to go ahead with her idea and try breeding Igor with Hereford and Red Angus heifers. Hope it don't kill him, ha-ha.

I'm running out of light and will close now. Don't worry about us too much. Perkin lives a charmed life, and I'm too smart to poke my head up much. Please give my love to Anna. Your grandson, Sam.

2005 hours
Ogliastro Cilento

Major Douglas Grossmann picked his teeth and impatiently took another sip of espresso. She was late. Always late. *Goddamned prima donna,* he thought. Grossmann desperately wanted another cigarette, but American cigarettes were still hard to come by for anyone but an American soldier. Despite the unit patch on his uniform indicating he was a member of the 5th Army staff, he was not an American soldier. Despite having spent sixteen of his twenty-seven years in Coronado, California, he was not even an American.

Grossmann nodded to two enlisted men who walked past his table at the outdoor café, rifles slung on their shoulders. He looked away and forced a casual laziness which he did not feel. It was not that he was concerned about his ability to pass for American, but he did not like the public meeting place—she had insisted through an intermediary that they meet here. *Prima donna,* he thought again. Grossmann's stomach tightened as the two soldiers stopped and began to turn around, but they weren't interested in him. There she was—walking as if she had no cares or worries in the world.

She smiled brightly at the soldiers who continued turning as they watched her walk up to Grossmann's table. The soldiers stared for a second then walked away, complaining to each other about how the officers always get the pretty ones. Grossmann stood as she approached, pulled her chair out for her, and watched appreciatively as she sat down. Although Grossmann had been informed of yesterday's incident—he knew much of what was occurring in the American sector of the battlefield—it wasn't until he was seated across from Antoniette Bernardi that he saw the intense anger burning in her eyes. No amount of acting could cover that entirely.

"My dear, what in God's name has happened to you?" Although solicitude exuded from the German intelligence officer for her benefit, Grossmann asked the question with a hidden degree of personal satisfaction. It was an unnecessary question, as he not only was aware of the incident and its origins, he had even made the effort to identify the officer who humiliated Bernardi. He asked another unnecessary question for fun: "My goodness, you seem to have a small limp. Have you walked into a door or fallen down a flight of stairs?" He asked her in English, although he spoke passable Italian as well as fluent French and, of course, his native German.

"Shut up, Douglas, and give me a cigarette." Despite her deep anxiety and irritation—her looks and her pride were everything after all—she smiled prettily at the officer for the benefit of anyone who might be watching and intimately touched his hand with her fingertips. "An American officer . . . hit me. I want you to kill him for me," she said acidly with the same sweet smile.

"Certainly, my dear, I shall put it at the top of my list and attend to it immediately." Grossmann replied with the slightest of inward sneers and just a trace of outward sarcasm. Antoniette Bernardi may have been the most successful of his agents since he had been stationed in Rome as a case officer eleven months before, and she was without question the most beautiful woman he had ever known, but he couldn't stand her. The truth was that as much as he admired her looks and her capabilities, he despised and distrusted Bernardi. Part of his attitude stemmed from the fact that he had not recruited her—she had been passed to him by his predecessor at the Rome *Abwehr* station. Her information had been unerringly accurate, she was a devoted fascist and cost far less for her services than her abilities merited; still, there was something about her that he found both unnerving and contemptible. Overlooking the subtle contradictions of his own situation as an *Auslandsdeutsch*e—he was more American than German—Grossmann despised those who would inform on their own countrymen, and Bernardi had established her bona fides by providing information about Italy to German military intelligence. Over the past two years, the young lady who was considered to be Germany's best agent in Italy, had provided considerable and verifiable information about senior Italian officers, wavering politicians, and antifascist clergy. As her primary means of collection was seduction, he wasn't entirely sure how she gathered information on the clergy, but she did. Now she was turning her skills—honey traps—against the Americans.

"Don't patronize me," she replied with a lover's smile on her lips. "I want him to pay."

Grossmann thought her smile was more suitable for a shark, or maybe a jackal, than for a beautiful young woman. Jackals were known to lead lions to their prey in order to scavenge off the remains—*she is a jackal*, he concluded. "My apologies," he said smoothly. "But how exactly should I do that? I understand that there are currently more than twenty thousand Americans in your country."

Bernardi accepted a glass of wine from the café's owner without acknowledgement, waited until he had moved out of earshot, and then said, "My source says he's in Company A of the 141st regiment of foot." Grossmann smiled at her use of the antiquated British term as she continued. "His name is Sam Taft. I would kill him myself, but he ruined Papa's favorite rifle. After Papa paid so much to get me out of trouble, he won't let me have another one." She said it with the same petulance that a girl her age, under normal circumstances, might have used after being told of an early evening curfew after a date.

"What a shame about your father's rifle. I don't suppose that you know where Taft's unit might be; maybe I could ask my friends in the artillery branch to pay him a visit." It was more patronization. Despite being an *Abwehr* officer, tactical military intelligence wasn't exactly Grossmann's forte, nor had Bernardi reported on it before. He really doubted that Bernardi could provide him with any useful information on the American divisions, let alone about the soldier that struck her. Their combined efforts in Rome and Naples had been of a more strategic nature, and although Bernardi was extremely talented, it was a long shot to bring her down here after the Allied landings in Sicily. It was fortuitous that Bernardi's family had property in the area—in addition to extensive holdings in Rome and Tuscany, they also maintained a villa near Amalfi and apartments in Naples and Ogliastro.

"Yes, of course I know. The American commander is panicking, and they are going to shorten their lines tonight. I don't know exactly what this means, but they are going to set up a defensive line on the La Cosa Stream between Mount Chirico and Mount Soprano. Do you know it?"

Grossmann nodded. Shortly before the Allied landings on the Salerno plain, Grossmann had taken a one-man staff ride on horseback on the likely battlefield. "What else do you know?" Grossmann asked with renewed interest.

"Will you do your best to kill him?"

"I promise," Grossmann said sincerely. He was an honest and conscientious man—at least as honest as one could be in what was known as the world's second oldest profession. As Grossmann admitted to himself sometimes, however, the second oldest profession lacked many of the scruples of the first.

Bernardi took another cigarette from the pack and held it up to her lips as Grossmann lit it for her. "The Americans have been hurt badly, and they are preparing evacuation orders," Bernardi spoke confidently and precisely. "My source doesn't think that they will follow through with the evacuation, as a regiment of paratroopers are coming in tonight or tomorrow, and more reinforcements are scheduled to arrive soon. He told me that things were 'touch and go,' whatever that means. They are abandoning the fight for Altavilla, and he said his boss is very concerned about the La Cosa defense, particularly of that little bridge on the road from Albanella. The defenses there are weak, and the Americans won't be able to . . . what's the phrase? 'Shore it up' before tomorrow. Do you know which bridge?"

Grossmann closed his eyes, visualized the battlefield map and saw the importance of the bridge immediately. The *Abwehr* officer replied positively and asked, "Are the parachutists American or British? Do you know when they are coming and where they will land? When will the bridge be reinforced?"

With a cold smile but a voice like honey, she said, "There are limits to pillow talk, darling."

"Yes, I would imagine. Does he suspect anything?"

"No, of course not. He's an idiot. Most men are. They want to tell you how important they are, so he doesn't listen to my questions, he just answers them."

Bernardi inhaled her cigarette deeply, savored the smoke for a moment, then blew it into Grossmann's face. She stood, picked up the cigarettes from the table, and tossed them in her handbag, closing it with a crisp snap. She leaned over the table placing her left hand on Grossmann's shoulder and with her right hand she caressed his cheek. Smiling again, she brought her lips close to Grossmann's ear—the image of two young lovers saying goodbye for the moment with, perhaps, the promise of more to come. Her closeness and presence provoked an involuntary arousal in the German officer, but the words she whispered were not a lover's endearments, "Do what you promised. Kill the American." As she walked away, every eye in the café and on the street following her, she turned and said flirtatiously over her shoulder, "Ciao, darling."

Grossmann watched her walk away as she had walked in—seemingly without a care. He waited until he could stand without embarrassment then picked up his M-1 carbine—a trophy from the American disaster at the Kasserine Pass—dropped the appropriate amount of lira on the table and walked away from the café and into the growing darkness of the village. He had a report to draft, encode, and get into the hands of his runner—his headquarters needed to know about the airborne soldiers. There was no time to lose, and his courier would have to navigate the goat paths through the mountains within the hour while the information was still of value. Maybe, just maybe, his army could arrange a greeting not just for the paratroopers but also for the soldiers of Company A of the 141st regiment of foot.

2005 hours
Paola, Italy

The detail had cleared the British lines with no trouble and entered the uneasy territory that was controlled by neither side but might be watched and patrolled by all sides. On leaving Eighth Army Headquarters, Lieutenant Rose had reminded Perkin that nature abhors a vacuum, cautioning Perkin to watch out for German patrols, or possibly British or American patrols that might be unaware of another Allied presence in the area.

That friendly forces might "shoot first and ask questions later" was bad enough, but it was a possibility that Perkin had considered before. Something else Rose mentioned concerned him more and had not occurred to Perkin since the armistice with Italy had been announced: "Keep an eye on the former Italian soldiers," he said seriously as they parted ways. "Most of them have not been disarmed by either the Germans or us. Many have kept their weapons and faded into the villages and countryside. Most have simply gone home, but there are some who can't make it home because either the Allied or German armies are in the way. They're afraid of being imprisoned by us or conscripted or shot by the Germans, so they're roaming the countryside looking for food, shelter, or money. I saw one radio intercept from a German patrol which mentioned Italian soldiers taking over a mountain village in the center of the peninsula. I wouldn't have paid much attention to it, but it caught my eye because the village was named Rose. Brigand soldiers robbed the shops and the church, and the villagers wanted the Germans to do something about it. I suspect that they'll be disappointed."

It was rain that forced Perkin's decision to call a halt for the night. He had internally decided to ignore Lieutenant Colonel Russ and Lieutenant Rose's well-intentioned advice and instead press on through the night. He reasoned that even with the slower pace forced by driving with black-out headlights, they could arrive in the Fifth Army area of operations by daylight. The rain began less than twenty miles past the last British checkpoint, and it was such a rain Perkin had never seen before. He and his soldiers were no stranger to storms, but this strange rain was as much dirt as it was water. At first it splattered lazily on the hood of their jeeps and on the lenses of Kulis's glasses, leaving a residue of thin mud. It was unpleasant to drive in, but they pressed on. Half an hour later, and ten miles further along the coastal road, the rain began in earnest.

The winds coming off the sea whipped up to gale force almost instantly, and the temperature began to drop precipitously. It reminded Perkin of a Blue Norther that struck once when he and Sam were fishing off the bank of the Brazos River near Granbury, Texas. The warm seventy-degree day suddenly turned black, and the temperature dropped by fifty degrees as the storm blew in at fifty miles per hour. The memory of that distant storm in Texas, which he recalled as a tremendous day of fishing, prompted Perkin to start looking for shelter. He contemplated returning to the small town they had just passed through, the village of Paola, but decided the countryside was better than the risk of being trapped in a town.

He might have pressed on through the rain anyway, but the winds were beginning to push the light jeeps across the road and darkness was setting in rapidly. In the back of Perkin's mind, he also rationalized the decision to seek shelter as being of military necessity. The palpable grit carried in the water would eventually find its way into the nooks and crannies of the machine guns on the jeep and into the rifles of his soldiers, possibly leading to jammed weapons just when they were needed. As it began to rain harder, the cold and gritty water blowing into the hood of his poncho and rolling down the back of his neck reinforced his decision. When he saw a small sign on the highway pointing to the Sanctuary of St. Francis of Paola, he had Kulis put the wheel over and they began a winding drive up a mountainside.

At first glance, the Sanctuary of St. Francis, or San Francesco as it read in Italian, looked uninhabited. There were no exterior lights and no indications of occupation, but as they drove closer to the monastery, Perkin noticed that the bushes were trimmed and well-kept. The outer buildings were solid and had been white-washed, and the road leading to the monastery had been recently graveled. Perkin drove over an ancient stone bridge, high over a stream filling with the muddy rainwater, to an impressive collection of buildings whose construction had obviously spanned many centuries. To his left, a broad rectangular building with a red tile roof was built on a high arch over the muddy stream; it was connected to another broad building at a right angle—Perkin guessed that those were likely monks' quarters. At the apex of the two buildings stood a taller building topped by a cross and fronted with a Renaissance façade with impressive arches and columns. It reminded him of a picture he had seen once of the treasury building carved out of rock in the desert village of Petra in Transjordan.

Perkin directed the two jeeps to drive down a long rectangular piazza and park before the entrance to what he assumed was the church building of the monastery. Even as he and the detail were running for the shelter of the church, he noticed the architecture and craftsmanship of the buildings. They date back, he guessed, at least five hundred years—perhaps even further.

Sergeant Kenton was the first to get to the entrance— it was sheltered somewhat from the rain by a high, arched portico. Kenton glanced at Perkin who nodded, and he knocked sharply on the heavy wooden door. There was no answer. Kenton paused for a moment then pounded heavily on the door. This time, the sound of running footsteps reached the soldiers outside.

The large door opened and Perkin saw a tall, heavy-set man dressed in a faded white shirt, black pants, and work boots. The man looked up at Sergeant Kenton and seemed surprised to find a man larger than himself. He addressed himself to Kenton, "Si?"

Perkin turned to Private Fratelli and said, "Tell him we're American soldiers, and we were wondering if it was possible to come in from the rain for the night." As Fratelli complied, Perkin looked past the man at the door and into the entryway of the church. Inside, he saw what looked to be an anteroom lit by candles on a narrow table, which were dangerously close to being blown out by the wind.

"Please wait, signori," the man said to Fratelli. He closed the door on the Americans, and Perkin could hear his footsteps retreat. After a few minutes, while the soldiers became progressively colder and wetter, the steps returned and an ancient wisp of a man, dressed in a faded black habit with the hood pulled over his head, answered the door. The weight of the heavy cloth seemed as much as the old man could bear to carry, and he stooped under the burden. The monk studied the Americans. Even Kulis seemed to tower over him, and he took a step backwards when he grasped the size of the red-headed Sergeant Kenton, who taken off his helmet as he attempted to clear the mud from his eyes.

He mumbled to himself—Perkin thought he heard the Spanish words "Normans" and "again," but when he eventually addressed Perkin, he spoke in Italian. "I am Friar Immanuel—how may I help you?"

"Sir, I am Lieutenant Berger of the United States Army. I don't mean to intrude, but we were wondering if we could stay here overnight." Perkin turned to allow the friar to see the savagery of the storm that was building—the gale continued to build, and the rain took on a horizontal orientation. "We'll be on our way by daylight, and we'll try not to disturb you and your folks."

"Lieutenant," the friar said through Fratelli. "You are welcome to Italy. Most Italians have said since the beginning that the war would not end until the Americans come to Europe again, so it is this that I have prayed for. I have prayed for years for an end to the evils of this war, and I keep praying," he said again. He looked at Perkin through dark, wrinkled eyes that were framed by wispy white eyebrows. "But, I'm sorry; this is not a hostel. This is the *Sanctuario di San Francesco di Paola*—a place of pilgrimage and a monastery of the Order of Minims. We do not allow soldiers, combatants, to stay here. There is a hotel in the town on Via San Francesco that many pilgrims use. Perhaps you should try there." The old man looked up at the dark scudding clouds and said, "You should go before the sirocco gets worse."

Before the monk could begin to close the door Perkin said, "Sir, we're soldiers. We are prepared to ride out this storm—what did you call it? The sirocco? But I'd like a dry night's sleep if possible, and we can't use a hotel in town. If there are German forces in the vicinity, I would not want to bring that kind of attention to the town of Paola."

Friar Immanuel said nothing as he contemplated Perkin's concern. As the wind sprayed muddy water onto his robes, the old man sighed and said, "You should come in while I think about this, but you will have to leave your swords outside. This house is a place of peace—there are no weapons allowed in here."

Perkin thought of what the friar demanded. Asking himself if the old man had been here since the Centurions ruled the land, he put aside the issue of the soldiers not having swords and contemplated the monk's condition— it was out of the question that the soldiers would abandon their weapons. "Sir, perhaps it would be best if we were to stay in a stable or a barn, if that would be possible. We can't leave our weapons in our jeeps."

At the mention of the jeeps, the old man's eyes lit up. Astonishing Perkin and the rest of the detail, Friar Immanuel pushed past Perkin and walked up to one of the jeeps. Ignoring the rain and the mud, which had been picked up as dust by the winds over the Libyan Sahara, the monk slowly walked around the jeep, took in all of the details and tentatively kicked at a tire. Perkin looked over at Kulis who grinned at his officer. Intuitively, Kulis said to the friar, "Sir, would you like a short ride in the jeep? It'll climb your mountain here faster than any mule you've ever seen."

A boyish smile lit up the old man's face. "Since America came into the war, all we have heard about in Italy is the marvelous jeep of the Americans that can swim the streams and climb the mountains." Friar Immanuel pronounced the word "geeep-uh." "We have a small shrine at the top of the mountain. It is the most peaceful place to pray in Italy, but I can't walk there any longer, and it hurts to ride a mule or burro. I've dreamed of a jeep, knowing that as His humble servants we will never have one, but I am glad to see it for myself." He turned to Kulis and said through Fratelli, "No, young man. Thank you, but we need to get you out of this storm." Friar Immanuel walked over to Kulis and looked closely at his face, and surprising everyone, he stretched up as tall as he could and sniffed at the stitches on Kulis's face. "No corruption. That is good. Follow me."

2100 hours
La Cosa Defenses

The sun was down and the soldiers were set for the night on the line. Sam had concluded his letter to Old Perkin, debated about accepting a cup of coffee from the company cook, and took it, knowing it would make sleep difficult. *Little chance of that in any case,* he thought.

His mind wandered. As ashamed as he was to admit it, fear seemed to dominate his thoughts: fear of the unknown, fear of the known, fear of failure, fear of the darkness, fear for Perkin. Where was he anyway? Probably bedded down for the night in the arms of an Italian beauty.

The notion that his opportunistic cousin might get laid while he was facing sixteeen thousand German soldiers directed Sam's thoughts away from his fears as he eased himself onto his back with his lower legs dangling in the foxhole. He tuned out all the background noise of the war— he didn't sense any action within a mile of the company— and he stared at the stars emerging from the battlefield smoke. The stars led his thoughts back to the ranch.

Even knowing that the stars were the same in Italy as they were in Texas, he felt like they were different somehow—they were weaker, lesser stars than those of home. He had last seen those stars from his ranch the night that Margaret and he had camped next to the gnarled old mesquite tree.

What a starry night that was, he thought, half a world distant and nearly two years later. He missed Margaret so much that his heart ached, and sometimes, uncharacteristically, he despaired of ever seeing her again. If it had been within his power to do so, he would have stood up and walked home from Europe just to spend another night with her like that night on the ranch. Sam kept a picture of Margaret in his wallet and another set in the inside cover of an antique pocket watch that had belonged to his father, but he seldom looked at them. He didn't need to. Margaret's face was crystal clear in his mind: her red hair, her green eyes, the light dusting of freckles on her face, her easy smile.

That night in Texas, they'd lain under the covers and talked about matters of great import and of no consequence and, as they watched the fire die down to embers, they whispered in the darkness, even though there was no human within miles to hear them. When the light died down completely, they had rolled onto their backs and stared straight up into the heavens.

"D'ya know anything about the stars?" Sam had asked.

"No, baby, tell me about them."

Sam had rolled back over and pointed to a constellation just off the horizon to their right, "That's the constellation Ursa Major."

"I thought that's the Big Dipper."

"It's part of it, but the constellation includes those stars to the right and just above the dipper. Now, if you follow the edge of the box it points you to Polaris, which is the end of the handle of the Little Dipper, see? It's really called Ursa Minor—the little bear."

"That's the North Star?" Margaret was puzzled and then pointed out a very bright light directly above them. "I thought that's the North Star."

"No, honey, that's Jupiter, and it's stuck between the horns of Taurus the bull right now, but it'll wander all over the sky tonight and be gone by morning. I think Taurus's my favorite constellation, and right next to it is Orion the hunter. Maybe those two are meant to be me and Perkin."

"I don't think so, baby. Now you've pointed it out to me, I think you belong to the little bear."

"Why's that?"

"In *Julius Caesar*, Caesar said, 'I am constant as the northern star.' So are you." She had hesitated, then continued, "Baby, war changes people, and so many lives are going to be ruined by this war. A lot of these boys you know now won't come home the same as when they left. But like that star there, you'll always be the same man that I love. You're steady, dependable, a constant truth, an absolute. And like the bear, you're courageous and tough and not afraid of anything."

Margaret had struggled to find the right words and a rare tear trickled down her cheek in the dark. "I know that I can count on you to do the right thing when you're over there, wherever 'there' is. You'll take care of your boys, you'll take care of Perkin, you'll kill every goddamned German or Jap you see, and you'll just do right. You'll do right by me . . . by the country . . . by your family's name. And baby, I want you to know that I'm so proud of you. I know this isn't what you want to do, but I know you'll do it well. I'm worried, of course, but I believe deep in my heart that you're coming back just as you are. That's why you're the northern star to me."

"Well, I reckon it's better than bein' your Little Dipper." Sam had laughed in the dark.

Margaret laughed as well, the serious spell broken. "No girl would call you that."

"Well, I sure hope not! So, you think me and Perk are gonna come out of this okay?"

Without hesitating, she had said, "Absolutely . . . show me some more stars, Little Bear."

Everything Margaret had said about Sam she believed to be true. Although she was more afraid than she let on to Sam, deep down in her heart, she truly believed that the love of her life would come home to her unscathed from the war. Margaret was an intelligent, intuitive woman; she never mentioned it to Sam, but it was Perkin who worried her. He was Jupiter to Sam's northern star—he might appear to burn brighter, but she had no idea where he would be at the end of the war.

2130 hours
The Sanctuary of St. Francis of Paola

Friar Immanuel had taken the Texans to a large outbuilding far behind the monastery that was used as storage for the monks, and the soldiers quickly lit two lanterns and moved aside crates and unused furniture to make room for their bedrolls on the stone floor. Not long after the departure of the monk, the soldiers heard the splash of running feet through the rain, and a young monk nearly tripped through the heavy oak doorway of their warehouse.

"Hello! I am Brother Giuseppe, but my American friends always called me 'Joey,'" the round-faced, beaming young man said in American-accented English. "I've brought you something to eat and drink."

"Well, hello yourself! Thank you very much, Joey. I'm Perkin Berger, the leader of this muddy group of cowboys. This is Bill Kenton, Vince Fratelli, Roscoe Pfadenhauer, and Ed Kulis." Perkin indicated each soldier in turn, and Giuseppe enthusiastically shook each man's hand up and down. It turned out that Giuseppe had lived with relatives in Frankfort, New York, as a child before he returned to Italy to take his vows in the Minim Order. He told the soldiers that he loved America, but he thought it unlikely that he would see its beauty again.

As he passed around fruit, cheese, and bread, Giuseppe told the Americans about St. Francis of Paola, "He was one of the greatest of the saints—a very humble man who performed many miracles and prognostications. St. Francis served God in Italy and in France, where he was much beloved by the French King Charles VIII, and I think that so beneficent were his works that God granted him an extremely long life. He died in France in 1507 at the age of ninety-one. Yet, after all the good and kind things that he had done in his life, wicked Huguenots raided his tomb fifty years later and scattered his bones." Perkin listened with interest and asked the young monk if any of the bones had been saved.

"Yes! Yes! Fortunately, some were saved and stored at the Cathedral in Tours for centuries. By the Grace of God, his relics were returned to the place of his birth eight years ago and reside in the sanctuary here at the monastery." Giuseppe was obviously proud of the fact, and his eyes lit up as he turned to Kulis and Pfadenhauer—the two youngest of the soldiers—and said, "Some of his bones are in a reliquary in our beautiful altar, but one of his ribs has been enclosed in a large statue of St. Francis. I'll show it to you tomorrow." Brother Giuseppe was an instinctive story-teller—the young soldiers' interest had been flagging, but the news that a holy bone had been incorporated into a nearby statue was a welcome and intriguing twist to the story. Giuseppe turned back to Perkin as he said, "His enduring legacy is our order—he created the Minim Order, the least of all the brethren, in 1435." At the blank looks on the faces of the Americans, he explained, "We are a mendicant order." Realizing that his explanation was not helpful, he added, "Think of the Minims as very humble Franciscans. We have taken a vow of poverty and endure through the charity of others. In turn, we serve God by serving the poor."

"But what of all this?" Perkin asked, referring to the beautiful monastery.

"This place of pilgrimage was built through the gifts of the followers of St. Francis, including the King of France, and maintained through the contributions of pilgrims. Some of our monasteries supplement their existence through the sale of beer or wine, although we do not. Which, by the way, brings me to this." Giuseppe reached again into his basket and pulled out several large dark brown bottles. "Our brothers in Germany . . . no, no, not all Germans are bad," he counseled in response to visible stiffening in his audience. "Our brothers in Germany make an excellent kind of beer which is called a *doppio malto* here in Italy, but there in Bavaria it is called a *doppelbock*."

"A bock?" cried Perkin as he eagerly grabbed the bottle. "I haven't had a bock beer for ages. It's my favorite kind, but I've only seen it during Lent." He looked at the label on the bottle—it featured a smiling monk holding a flask over the name 'Paulaner.' "Is Paulaner a reference to this town?" he asked of a smiling Giuseppe.

"Yes it is. Isn't it wonderful? But the beer's not always for Lent—sometimes we have it for other special occasions, like tomorrow. As I'm sure you know, September 14 is the *Exaltatio Sanctae Crucis*—the Triumph of the Holy Cross. Tomorrow will be the Feast of the Cross—the remembrance of finding the true cross of our savior Jesus Christ by St. Helena." Giuseppe looked at Perkin and smiled shyly, "As I understand from Brother Immanuel, you're leaving tomorrow. I thought maybe you would like to celebrate a little early."

Perkin smiled back and said to the young monk, "Joey, you've truly surprised me, and we're very grateful. Should we open this up and share it together?"

Giuseppe's surprises weren't over yet for the evening. He shook his head, stood up, and said wistfully, "I would like to, but I need to get back to the sanctuary—I've work to do to get ready for the feast. Between us though . . . sometimes I wish I was going home to Maggie's Bush."

Private Pfadenhauer, who was taking his first taste from the bottle of Paulaner's, snorted as the first trickle of beer went down his throat and then started coughing sharply as the liquid went down his windpipe. Kulis, who was sitting next to Pfadenhauer tried to slap him on the back, but was laughing so hard that he couldn't move.

Giuseppe looked at all of the Americans in puzzlement—Perkin appeared to be trying to keep a straight face, and Kenton and Fratelli were grinning broadly—and he asked uncertainly, "Did I say something wrong?"

"I'm sorry, Joey, but who's Maggie?" Perkin asked kindly. He didn't want to embarrass Giuseppe, who had been very kind and friendly to the Americans.

"Maggie's not a person—Maggie's Bush was the neighborhood where my uncle lived in Frankfort. I doubt that I'll ever go there again. What did you . . . ?" The realization that he had treaded into unfamiliar territory dawned on the monk who stopped himself, blushed deep red and stammered, ". . . oh. Oh! That is not what I meant!" Giuseppe wasn't sure whether to defend his intentions and his uncle's neighborhood further or whether to run from the situation altogether when the enormity of his error fully registered. Surprising the Americans once again, the monk's habit started to shake as a belly laugh began to build deep within the young friar. Laughing so hard that he could barely speak, he croaked out, "Oh dear. I'm afraid that's another neighborhood I can't go to either. Ha ha ha! I have to leave before you wicked men get me into trouble—as it is, my confession this week might be the end of Brother Immanuel." With that, he backed out of the door bowing, to the amuse-ment and applause of the Americans.

The soldiers were still laughing when, two minutes later, Giuseppe stumbled through the door again—his face contorted with agony and his eyes comprehending of his fate. The genial monk collapsed into the circle of his newfound friends, his slit throat spilling blood onto the stone floor.

2200 hours
La Cosa Defenses

Sam was trying to take a catnap but couldn't doze off. It was the coffee. If there was to be any enemy activity along his lines, it would likely be around 0200–0400 hours when the defenders were at their sleepiest. At least that's what he was trained to believe, so he tried to get twenty minutes here and twenty minutes there to be wide awake in the early morning hours. On Captain Spaulding's orders, the men were on fifty-fifty—50 percent getting some sleep and 50 percent awake and alert. He hoped.

The platoon command post was set back fifty yards from the creek bank. Sam thought of the doctrinal approach to defending a stream or small river, and he knew that both he and his troops were too close to the stream. The La Cosa creek was on every German map, and it was obviously preregistered. If he were to defend this line by the book, he would actually establish his main defenses far behind his current position, but in this case, that might take him to the beach itself. "Oh well. You play the cards you're dealt," he said to himself.

Without warning, an American machine gun opened up to Sam's left in the Able Company sector. Instantly, another machine gun further down the line opened fire, and Sam leapt out of his foxhole to get a better look. By the light of the tracers, the gunfire was converging on a point in the middle of Lieutenant McCarter's sector, and Sam could hear the popping of rifle fire as the infantrymen fired into the dark.

"Ceasefire! Ceasefire, goddamnit!" Sam could hear both Captain Spaulding and Lieutenant McCarter's shouts from his position, and shortly the fire from the nervous machine gunners dropped off to nothing. Less than thirty seconds later, the growling on Sam's phone indicated an incoming call—from Spaulding, he assumed.

"Able Hammer Two," Sam answered. Hammer had become the new company call sign.

"Hammer Two, Hammer Six." Sam had been right. It was Spaulding. "Sam, make sure your gunners hold fire unless the outposts fire first! They're testing our line to determine the location of our . . ."

Captain Spaulding's sentence was cut-off as a salvo of German 88-millimeter artillery fire came crashing down on the Able Company positions to Sam's left. The German rounds found the creek bed on the first salvo, and then the rounds began to rain down on both sides of the stream. The German gunners tried for several minutes to find the sources of the tracer fire they had seen from their mountain vantage points, but they could have no confirmation of striking their targets in the dark. The attack was short-lived, as the German gunners put themselves at risk if they fired for too long at once.

Sam sent runners out to his two machine gun nests and his two outposts on the other side of the stream—he didn't want to risk the noise of the phone if there was a German patrol in the vicinity—but there was no need to warn his soldiers. They were aware that their company-mates had committed an amateurish mistake, and his gunners would wait until they had an identified target. The night was becoming unnerving. There was sporadic gunfire all along the Gulf of Salerno, and who was to say that Able Company would not get attacked again? Their eyes strained into the darkness, and their ringing ears tried hard to discriminate between all sounds, real and imagined.

2210 hours
The Sanctuary of St. Francis of Paola

The killer of Brother Giuseppe was also named Giuseppe and also belonged to a brotherhood. Lance Corporal Giuseppe Colucci was a Blackshirt, the feared Camicie Nere, and a self-proclaimed elite and hardened irregular soldier of the fascist state. Colucci frequently told his fellow countrymen that the famous German SS had been modeled on the Italian Blackshirts but always bragged that the SS failed to rise to the standards of their model. In fact, Colucci had served alongside the SS during service on the Eastern Front and greatly admired both their dedication and their brutality. Colucci had been a member of the Blackshirts since before the Abyssinian Campaign, and although he did not shy from combat, he much preferred the spoils of war to the act of war. Twice Colucci had made it to the rank of First Sergeant, and twice he had been reduced in rank back to private—once for theft in Spain and the second time for the rape of a teenage girl during the occupation of Greece. The ongoing war with the democracies and then with the Soviet Union had widened his opportunities for savagery, and acts that would have brought a prison sentence when he joined the force were now widely tolerated or even encouraged.

His squad had been serving with the Italian Army retreating before the Eighth Army when the armistice was announced. Armistice brought a new confusion to the war, and many soldiers were uncertain what to do after Badoglio's capitulation to the Allies. Colucci had no doubts however—he would continue to fight, or rather, he would continue to exploit the war for its opportunities. At the orders of his squad leader, Sergeant Millesi, Colucci had quickly reestablished order in the disintegrating squad by executing the few soldiers who seemed to waver in their dedication—including Corporal Sardo, the second-in-command of the squad. Things were looking up, and as soon as the fascists reassumed power, he would be promoted again. If the fascists never came back, well, he had at least increased his share of the spoils.

It was the laughter of the monk that brought his wrath. No one had doubted that the church would be easy pickings—and it was rumored to have a fantastic silver collection and maybe some gold—but it was irritating to have been ordered to patrol the perimeter of the monastery after he had knifed the large porter in the faded white shirt. It was more than irritating, he thought, it was insulting. Why had Millesi shouted at him to control himself in front of the other soldiers? Control himself? What did Millesi think they were doing here anyway?

And so, his mood was exceptionally black when he had crossed paths with the laughing monk coming out of the large building. "Turn adversity into opportunity" was Colucci's personal motto, and he thought that perhaps this would be a good opportunity to get a jump on the silver. He walked swiftly out of the darkness and the rain and punched the monk sharply in the solar plexus. Colucci reached for the doubled-over monk's hair to pull him up, found none to grasp, and straightened Brother Giuseppe up by the collar of his robe.

"Where is the silver, maggot?" Colucci snarled in Giuseppe's face. Before the monk had the opportunity to answer, or even catch his breath, Colucci struck him again. Hard. This time the younger man collapsed onto the stone walk. Colucci reached down and effortlessly lifted Brother Giuseppe back to his feet.

"I asked you a question, priest. Where is the silver?" *Terror is such a unique and effective tool,* thought Colucci. The priest, which is what Colucci believed the monk to be, would soon tell him where the silver was. Colucci pulled his razor sharp knife and pushed its point into Giuseppe's shoulder and twisted the blade, but Brother Giuseppe was too terrified to even scream from the pain. It had taken him several seconds to comprehend what was happening, and even then he could not truly accept that he was being assaulted like this by another human. The thought never crossed his mind to fight back—that was not his training in life, and he knew instinctively that he could do nothing to stop this animal. There was only one hope for survival: the Americans would know what to do. He turned towards the warehouse door and, in the last conscious act of his life, he tried to call for help but could make no sound.

Colucci misinterpreted the monk's movement. Ah, he thought, that's where they keep the silver. With a casual swipe of his arm, he sliced open Brother Giuseppe's throat and sent the man of God to God. Colucci laughed and then shoved the dying friar towards the warehouse.

"Show me, priest."

The monk staggered through the wind and rain and leaned heavily against the door. His arm pushed down on the latch, the door swung open wildly, and before he died, Brother Giuseppe staggered again and fell among the soldiers sitting on the floor.

Colucci sheathed his knife and was only a few steps behind the monk as he strode expectantly down the stone walkway to the open door of the warehouse. Perhaps it was the rain or maybe the dim light coming through the doorway, but the fascist soldier failed to identify the two jeeps parked at the side of the building for what they were. His expectation of an empty and uninhabited warehouse was shattered when he crossed the threshold of the building and took several arrogant steps towards the twitching body of Brother Giuseppe and said caustically, "Now where's that silver?" Staring up at him in the dim lantern light he saw five shocked American soldiers.

Colucci was equally stunned—this was bad news, but nothing he could not handle. None of the soldiers had weapons in their hands, and they had been sitting on the floor staring at the dying friar. His adrenaline was already pumping, and he was more experienced and more alert than the Americans. All he needed to do was unsling his Beretta submachine gun and the fight would be over. In fact, he believed that there would be no fight, only a slaughter, if he acted quickly. He moved first and began to back away from the soldiers and pull the Beretta off his shoulder. Out of the corner of his eye he saw one of the Americans, an immensely large, helmeted soldier, starting to get to his feet. The American's speed surprised Lance Corporal Colucci, and Colucci reacted instinctively by backing up even faster. He recognized that if the big man were to grab him he would be dead, and he was beginning to think that perhaps it would have been better to have run back to his comrades in the monastery.

It was Brother Giuseppe who brought him down. In the last movement of his life, Giuseppe's foot slid unconsciously to the right and caught the retreating Lance Corporal Colucci's heel. The fascist soldier stumbled as he went backwards, and he stumbled again as his other foot caught on the threshold of the door. Colucci was still moving backwards and he landed hard on his back halfway though the door. The Beretta flew off his shoulder, clattering on the stone walkway, and Colucci abandoned it as he crab-walked away from the Americans for several steps before scrambling to his feet and sprinting towards the monastery. Even now, Colucci was not panicked as he believed there was a hope of getting lost in the dark and the rain. If not, he was a brawler and a street fighter, and he had overcome bad odds before.

2215 hours
The Sanctuary of St. Francis of Paola

Lance Corporal Colucci was not the only street fighter at the warehouse, and to his great detriment, he was not the fastest runner either. Private Vincent Fratelli may not have reacted quicker than Sergeant Kenton, but he reacted *faster*. As Colucci was springing to his feet outside of the ware-house, Fratelli was already moving past his sergeant towards the door. Fratelli never lost sight of the fleeing lance corporal, and before Colucci had taken ten steps, Fratelli brought him down hard with a tackle from behind. The Blackshirt was on his feet in an instant and was pulling his knife as he stood. He was a second too late. From the ground, Fratelli lashed out hard with his foot, catching Colucci in the leg from the side—there was an audible crack from Colucci's knee as his leg buckled. The corporal dropped onto his fractured knee as he screamed in pain, but the brawler held onto his knife and prepared for the next attack.

Fratelli stood up and whipped out his own knife— the private had grown up in a hard neighborhood in the shadow of the Camden shipyard and it wasn't his first knife fight either. He was preparing to move in and finish off Colucci when he heard Lieutenant Berger saying in a low and intense tone, "Don't shoot him!" The puzzled Fratelli looked over in time to see Sergeant Kenton reversing his rifle and grasping it by the muzzle as he came running up like an enraged bull. Kenton swung his Garand like a baseball bat, narrowly missing Fratelli, and the comb of the stock hit the Italian soldier squarely in the mouth. The blow shattered most of Colucci's teeth and knocked him onto his back. Tossing his rifle back to Perkin, the large sergeant from Texas knelt and pinned the stunned fascist with his knee while he gripped Colucci tightly by the throat with his left hand. He reached up with his right hand and grasped the front lip of his steel helmet lifting it high over his shoulder and then Kenton crashed the heavy helmet down hard as if it were a hammer and Colucci's forehead the anvil. Then he did it a second time. Then a third. When Perkin caught Kenton's arm as it lifted up for a fourth swing, the Blackshirt irregular was already dead—his brains mixing with the mud and rain from Africa.

Perkin was breathing hard, and his heart was pounding as he tried to comprehend the rapid events of the past few minutes—less than five minutes had passed since he and his soldiers had been laughing and joking with the monk. He had recognized the Italian soldier's sodden uniform, but at first it didn't make sense. Then, as he began to calm down and realize that the immediate danger was over, he remembered Lieutenant Rose's warning about rogue Italian soldiers. Was that what he was dealing with? A diehard fascist, or maybe a thief? Or thieves?

"Fratelli," Perkin kept his tone low and tried with some success to keep the fear out of his voice. "What was he saying when he came in back there?" There was no answer from Private Fratelli, who was staring at Sergeant Kenton and the dead Italian soldier. "Fratelli! Vince! What was he saying when he came in?"

Fratelli turned his head and looked at Perkin and then back at Colucci. "Silver. He was asking Joey where the silver was." Fratelli said nothing else as he too began to get his bearings. Private Pfadenhauer walked up to him and handed Fratelli his BAR and then squeezed him on the shoulder.

"Has anyone looked to Joey?" Perkin asked of Pfadenhauer, although he knew the answer.

"Yes, sir. This fucker cut his artery." There was nothing else to be said of Giuseppe.

"Where's Kulis?" Perkin turned and looked around. Pfadenhauer nodded to the far corner of the building. Perkin could barely make out Private Kulis in the dim light from the lanterns in the warehouse. He was crouching with his rifle in the darkness—standing sentry over their small party. Even before his lieutenant, Private Kulis suspected that there might be more than one of the rogue soldiers.

"God bless that boy," whispered Perkin to himself. He turned to Sergeant Kenton. "Are you okay?"

"Yes, sir." Kenton didn't feel okay, but there really wasn't another answer that he could think of. He paused for a long moment and mentally came back to his duties. "What are your orders, sir?"

"There were reports of rogue Italian soldiers. He must be one—Howie, go through his pockets and see what he's carrying." Perkin was temporizing—he really didn't know what to do. If there was one fascist soldier here, there were likely more in the monastery. Perkin intellectually recognized that may be the case, but at the same time he did not want to get involved in anything that was not part of his mission or would keep him from getting back to Sam. But he could not leave Friar Immanuel at the mercy of animals like this. That thought decided his internal debate.

"Sergeant Kenton, Private Kulis! Get our packs loaded in the jeeps. We'll be pulling out . . . ," Perkin stopped and hesitated while he thought through his embryonic plan further.

Thinking his lieutenant intended to abandon the monastery; Sergeant Kenton started to object and then realized that Perkin was not done.

"Howie, you and Fratelli are with me. Kulis, trade me weapons and give me your ammo belt." Private Kulis passed over his Garand, and in turn, the delighted private received Perkin's Thompson. Perkin looked at Sergeant Kenton. "Sergeant, get a .30 cal ready to go. You and Kulis back a jeep away from the warehouse and cover that back entrance to the monastery." Perkin pointed to a covered door that was barely illuminated by two storm lanterns. "Be quiet and get in position quickly, we're gonna work our way to the front. Kill anyone with a weapon who ain't us."

2220 hours
The Sanctuary of St. Francis of Paola

It had taken Perkin longer to work around to the front of the monastery than he had expected. The warehouse was at least fifty or sixty yards to the east of the main buildings; it was not all smooth ground, and visibility was limited at best between gusts of wind and rain. Perkin wanted to make sure that he didn't lose contact with Fratelli and Pfadenhauer in the dark, so they walked slowly up to the three-story rectangular building that formed the southeastern side of the piazza they'd seen when they arrived. When he reached the building that he had guessed were the quarters of the monks, Perkin turned his soldiers to the left and led them towards the entrance to the piazza by keeping his right hand on the exterior wall of the building. When he reached the corner, Perkin squatted for a moment and looked down to the road coming up the mountain. If there were more rogue soldiers, he could not see any sign that they had posted guards on the road—maybe they had killed the sole guard or even the sole thief. Perkin shook off such notions as wishful thinking and edged around the southwest corner of the building. He and his soldiers walked slowly over to the piazza side of the building.

As Perkin peered around the corner into the piazza, he saw a large covered truck with Italian Army markings backed up to the entrance of the church—the same doorway where he had first met Brother Immanuel only a short time before. Perkin took an initial step into the piazza and then quickly stepped back. Two uniformed men walked out from shadows of the portico of the church, each obviously carrying a heavy burden. They struggled up to the rear of truck and unceremoniously dumped their loads onto the truck bed. They didn't waste time, hurrying back into the church.

Perkin's stomach was churning and he hesitated, shivering in the rain. Summoning up more courage, he whispered back to his soldiers, "Fratelli, come with me. Howie, you cover us, then I'll wave you up." Perkin and Private Fratelli ran crouching across the piazza and knelt in front of the Italian truck. Perkin had Fratelli stay at the front of the truck and then soft-stepped the remaining distance to the portico. When Perkin reached the shadows, Fratelli waved Pfadenhauer forward, and after Pfadenhauer scudded over to the truck Fratelli ran to join Perkin under the arches of the portico.

Perkin waved Pfadenhauer over and the three men huddled in the shadows of the church's portico. Perkin peeked around the corner of the door and looked into the entrance of the church—it was a large anteroom with another set of open double doors at the other end. In the anteroom, the candles on the old table had been supplemented by the Italian soldiers with a battery-powered lantern. Looking through the double doors, Perkin guessed that they opened into the back of the church's nave. On the floor of the anteroom, rolled neatly to one side, was the body of the large porter.

Perkin silently took a deep breath, and the three soldiers crept into the anteroom. Uncertain of what to do, Perkin reached up and switched off the lantern; the soldiers moved into the shadows of the door. The light inside the church was dim, but there were enough oil lamps burning for Perkin to see to the other end of the church. He identified several Blackshirts escorting a handful of monks who had been forced to carry silver plates from the dining hall and the monastery altar to a collection point in the middle of the nave. Bodies in front of the altar marked where two friars had fallen after resisting the desecration of their holy relics. Stepping over one of the bodies, two Italian soldiers taunted a young monk who looked barely older than a boy. One grinning soldier used the muzzle of his rifle to lift up the robes of the monk, who shrank away from the soldiers to their great amusement. Perkin was puzzled by the relative lack of monks in the nave—there were likely dozens at the monastery. Where were they, and where was Friar Immanuel?

Sitting on the altar, smoking a cigarette, and swinging his legs back and forth, another soldier had his arm casually draped over the gold and silver sculpted reliquary, which had been raised up from within the altar. Although this soldier had no apparent rank, he seemed to be in charge. He occasionally barked out orders to the other soldiers; one such order put two very wet soldiers heading to the collection point of the spoils. It was time to carry another load out to the truck.

Perkin and his soldiers glided back outside to the portico, where Perkin directed the other two soldiers to the opposite side of the outer door. Perkin leaned against the wall of the church and laid Kulis's rifle silently on the ground and pulled his trench knife from the scabbard tucked into his leggings. The trench knife was his father's and had been shipped home to Perkin's grandfather after Captain Berger had been killed in 1918. It was a formidable weapon, with a dagger's blade set into brass knuckles. Perkin watched as Fratelli handed his rifle to Pfadenhauer and pulled his own knife—an eight-inch Bowie knife that he had won from a Texan in a card game during the crossing to Africa. It was the second time that night that he had pulled his knife.

The two Blackshirts walked out into the portico—both carrying heavy loads of silver plate and chattering back and forth with cigarettes dangling from the corners of their mouths. Seeing the heavy rain, one soldier mumbled something to his comrade, and they walked to the edge of the portico and set down their loads. It was apparent that they wanted to finish their cigarettes before going out into the rain. They didn't have the chance.

While Pfadenhauer stood guard at the door, anxiously watching over his shoulder, Perkin and Fratelli walked up simultaneously behind the two fascist soldiers. As they were trained, both clapped their left hand over the mouths of the Italians. Perkin wrenched the soldier's head over towards his left shoulder, and with his right hand, Perkin pushed in the dagger's blade of his trench knife into the vulnerable spot behind and below the struggling man's right ear. As the knife slid between the vertebrae and blood sprayed out onto his arm, Perkin angled the knife upwards and pushed hard again. The Italian soldier collapsed without a sound. Fratelli grasped his man's mouth and pulled his head back exposing his neck—the razor-sharp bowie knife penetrated deep into the neck, slicing open the windpipe of the soldier. Unlike Perkin's man, Fratelli's soldier stayed upright and Fratelli ran him to the edge of the piazza and flipped the mute body over the railing into the muddy stream below.

The killing of the Blackshirt was the worst moment of Perkin's life. With perhaps the exception of strangulation, knifing is the most personal of all forms of killing—Perkin loathed it. At that moment, he did not care what the Blackshirts were doing to the monks, nor did he care about the war. He felt his gorge rising, and he walked away from the church into the rain and stood next to Private Fratelli. He abruptly vomited over the railing and then vomited again. Fratelli turned away and kept his eyes on the door to the church. He said nothing until Perkin spat the bile out of his mouth and returned the knife to its scabbard with shaking hands, and then the younger soldier said to his lieutenant in a quiet voice, "Sir . . . let's finish this and get back to the boys."

Perkin nodded silently and then walked back to the portico. He picked up Kulis's rifle and noticed that his hands were steady again—the shaking subsided much quicker than it had days before when he climbed on the tank back at Fort Rosebud. Unlike then, he felt no pride in his work. He was utterly appalled at what he had done, and he felt an intense disgust within himself. Perkin looked at his two soldiers. Pfadenhauer was breathing rapidly and his eyes were wide as he looked back at his lieutenant. Fratelli grimly nodded his head towards the door and started to walk in, but Perkin pulled him back and walked into the anteroom first.

2225 hours
The Sanctuary of St. Francis of Paola

Perkin put the Garand up to his shoulder as he walked into the anteroom and looked through the doors into the church. Brother Immanuel had been brought into the nave, and the head soldier had gotten off the altar and was alternately shouting at Immanuel and then slapping him across the face. Whatever the soldier wanted was denied to him by the old friar, and he screamed even louder at Immanuel. The frail old man took each slap with a look of defiance as he straightened himself upright. The soldier reached over to the altar and picked up the last piece of ceremonial silver plate and waved it in the monk's face, who disdainfully pushed the soldier's arm away. The nonsensical thought crossed Perkin's mind that Friar Immanuel was no Monseigneur Bienvenue, and there would be no purchase of this man's soul with the silver. The soldier was no Jean Valjean, for that matter— without warning, he hit the old man hard across the side of the head with the silver plate. As Immanuel dropped to the floor and lay unmoving, Perkin walked into the nave and shot the angry soldier, Sergeant Millesi, in the head. He turned quickly and took aim at another soldier who was standing near the collection of stolen silver. Perkin shot him in the throat and a second time in the head as he collapsed. Next to him, Pfadenhauer's Springfield cracked, and another Italian soldier fell, and as the boy from the hill country worked the action of his rifle, Perkin killed his third Blackshirt in the church. The final three Italian soldiers sprinted for a side door used by the monks to come to prayers. Fratelli opened up with the BAR and killed one as the other two escaped through the door. As Fratelli and Pfadenhauer started in pursuit, Perkin heard the chatter of the jeep's machine gun and the stutter of his own Thompson.

Chapter Nine

September 14, 1943
0430 hours
La Cosa Defenses

Sam had been awake since midnight. Since the first incident six hours before, they had been shelled four more times along the company's frontage. Sam wasn't entirely sure of what the German intent might be, other than denying sleep to the defenders. If that was their motive, he thought, then job well done. Other than that, it didn't make much sense—it just seemed to be harassing fire. Although he couldn't be sure, there appeared to be no attempt by the German patrols to penetrate past the concertina wire to really determine the strength and disposition of the American defenses. Several patrols sent out by Captain Spaulding indicated that the wire had not been cut in any places and the jingle line was still intact, but it was undeniable that the Germans were interested in this sector of the La Cosa defenses. As far as Sam could see, no other unit on the line was getting shelled like this; perhaps, Sam thought in shameful hope, they were trying to draw attention to this part of the line while they prepared to attack elsewhere.

Twice during the early morning hours, Sam left his command post and checked on his outspread platoon, including the outposts established on the far side of the stream. During one such inspection, the drone of aircraft overhead provoked the most intense German antiaircraft barrage of Sam's experience. The 82nd Airborne Division was landing its first battalion. Soldiers at Paestum had made a huge T on the beachhead with buckets of sand doused with gasoline. When the buckets were lit, just prior to the arrival of the transport aircraft, the light of the fires reflected off the cloudy skies. It was the first time Sam had seen a night drop, and he was awed by the inherent power and mobility of the airborne division, though he shivered as he imagined what the paratroopers must be envisioning as they descended into the hell of the battlefield. Several paratroopers landed off course inside the Able Company sector, and Captain Spaulding's soldiers watched in the dim light of the battlefield as the wayward troopers shrugged off their parachutes and jogged back to assembly areas. Sam also watched helplessly as at least one stick of paratroopers drifted over the American lines and into German territory; he prayed that they would be able to find their way back before daylight.

Half an hour after the drone of the airlift ceased and the antiaircraft guns grew silent, this prayer was still on Sam's mind as he was at his forward-most outpost when a southern voice called out loudly from the far side of the concertina wire, "Able Company?"

Sam stiffened, and the three soldiers in the large foxhole instinctively pointed their rifles in the direction of the voice. No one answered, but the soldier on the far side was persistent. "Able Company? Where's Able? I'm coming in." One of the soldiers at the outpost, Private Martinez, took a breath to answer, then exhaled quietly as Sam put his hand on the soldier's shoulder.

"Able Company?" The voice on the other side of the wire sounded plaintive and lost to Sam; it also seemed as if he were moving from left to right. "Where's Able? I need to find Able Company."

Sam whispered in the ear of Private Martinez, "Challenge."

The San Antonio private called out tersely in a voice that carried across the wire, "Texas!"

The countersign was "Tornado," but what Sam heard instead sent a chill down his spine.

"Where's Lieutenant Taft? Is that Able Company? Sam? Help me, Sam. I'm wounded out here. Where the hell are you?" The voice continued to drift to the south, to Sam's right.

Sam had to resist the impulse to get out of the large foxhole and walk to the wire. His mind raced as he tried to place the voice. It was clearly a southern accent, but it wasn't from Texas—maybe Georgia or one of the Carolinas. Sam could not attach that voice to a face, but he examined the possibilities. No enlisted man would call him by his first name. Although Sam occasionally breached protocol by calling his soldiers by their first names, he did not permit his troops that familiarity, and he knew that the voice in the darkness was not one of his soldiers. What officer might be out there? There were no missing officers from his company—Ed Brown's body had been identified—and it certainly was not Perkin's voice. There were some missing battalion officers from the D-day landings, but that made no sense either—they would not have called for Sam. His mind turned to the paratroopers that landed on the enemy side of the line, but he did not know anyone from the 82nd. Who on earth was out there?

Sam remained silent, even though he knew his soldiers were looking over at him in the dark. He could not imagine either possibility: that the voice belonged to a friendly soldier on the other side of the wire—a soldier who evidently did not know the password—or that he had somehow come to the enemy's attention.

It was at least ten minutes before Sam heard the voice again. This time it was far to his right along Baker Company's frontage. It was the same call for Able Company and Lieutenant Taft. The soldiers from Baker Company who had heard the previous exchange also challenged the unknown soldier, who repeated his call for Sam without offering the countersign. Baker Company showed less restraint than had Sam's troops, and a soldier from Baker shouted out over the lines, "Shut up, goddamnit!"

Sam's straining ears picked up the voice calling out, "Sammy? Is that you, Sam? Help me!"

"Yeah, Mac! This is Sammy! Your fuckin' Uncle Sammy! Come on in, we left the door open!" A West Texas drawl could be heard across the distance. Then a startling light climbed out of the darkness as Baker's West Texan fired a flare. For a second, Sam thought he could see several shapes receding into the darkness at the edge of the flare's illumination, but as he blinked from the unexpected brightness, there was no one ahead of the wire. The Baker Company riflemen had a clearer view and opened fire into the darkness. Before the flare died, German artillery shifted fire to Baker Company and shelled Able's sister company for several minutes. Then the guns and the voices were silent along the line, and all that could be heard were the cries of the wounded.

0520 hours
Sapri, Italy

The two jeeps slowed, and Perkin stopped at the crossroads. They were on the southern outskirts of Sapri, and Perkin had a decision to make. To his right lay the road that led to the mountain route they had taken to avoid Sapri and Policastro on their way south. Straight ahead, the highway led through the town and continued up the coast to Agropoli.

It was not the threat of the Germans that gave Perkin pause. Since leaving the monastery, all indications were that the Germans had begun to evacuate southern Italy before the advance of Eighth Army. It was likely that they were withdrawing their scarce forces along the coastal road before the Allied armies linked up and the German forces along the sea were cut off. Two bridges that the American patrol had crossed only two days before had been blown by the retreating Germans; the first time, the jeeps had been able to ford the stream, but the next time they had been forced to head into the mountains and find a path around the little marsh the bridge crossed.

No, it was not the Germans who occupied Perkin's thoughts, it was the fat constable at Vibonati, and his soldiers knew it. He spun the knob on the steering wheel idly as he thought darkly about the events the night before, the murder of Giuseppe and their battle with the Blackshirts.

When the fight was over, there had been a terrible silence in the monastery. Perkin had stood in the nave of the church, his ears ringing from the gunfire and tears momentarily obscuring his vision. His cheeks, ears, and neck were burning hot as he walked through the church and looked at the desecration of the altar. The reliquary had been forced open in the search for more gold and silver, and upon finding bones, Millesi had emptied it on the floor. The reliquary and the remaining silver plate were staged for movement to the truck next to a diptych of Saint Francis and a sixteenth century Madonna by Antonello de Saliba. Amid the scattered bones of St. Francis, Brother Immanuel lay unconscious but stirring, while the remaining monks were in a state of shock.

It had taken several minutes for Perkin and Fratelli to convince the terrified monks that the American soldiers were not of the Blackshirts and meant them no harm. It was not until Immanuel regained consciousness that order began to take form in the monastery. Despite his age and his injuries, the old monk immediately began to collect and reestablish the relics of the sanctuary, but his anguish over the news of Brother Giuseppe's death was heartbreaking. Perkin could not bear to look at the tears streaming down the cheeks of the wizened old friar, and Perkin found himself, once again, faced with a difficult choice. There was no point in remaining at the monastery any longer—no one would sleep now, no one wanted to stay, and other than dealing with the bodies, there was nothing further they could do to help the monks.

Pfadenhauer and Kulis unloaded the treasures of the monastery from the Italian Army truck then helped Fratelli and Kenton load the dead fascist soldiers in the back; there was no argument from Immanuel about the bodies of the Blackshirts as there was no discussion about turning them over to the Italian authorities. Lance Corporal Colucci's body had been dragged to the truck at the front of the monastery behind one of the jeeps— further disfiguring the corpse—and two of the watching monks crossed themselves involuntarily as they witnessed the unfathomable hatred, violence, and destruction marked on the face of the Blackshirt. He, too, was loaded in the back of the truck.

Fratelli had driven the truck, and he followed the two jeeps down the mountainside; he was even more grateful to leave the monastery than he was that the rain had stopped. There were no words of farewell from the monks, and Perkin would wonder for the remainder of his life if the monks blamed him for the catastrophe that befell them that night.

The first blown bridge of the night was less than two miles on the highway from the turnoff to the monastery, and Perkin had decided it was a good place to dispose of the truck and the bodies of the Italian soldiers. While Sergeant Kenton scouted the stream for a ford, which he found in the form of an overgrown Roman road of stones, Perkin and his remaining soldiers went through the truck. In addition to the packs of the fascist soldiers, they found weapons and ammunition and small tools of the engineers who had been the original owners of the truck before its commandeering by Millesi. The engineer's possessions, which included paint and brushes for signage, were pulled out on Perkin's orders and set aside. In the packs of the soldiers and on the soldiers themselves were thousands of dollars worth of lira—the proceeds from the spoils of the sack of Rose. Perkin was tempted to take it back to Brother Immanuel, but could not bring himself to return to the monastery.

Perkin had Colucci's body pulled from the truck, and he dragged it to a still-standing support of the bridge and pushed, prodded, and kicked the stiffening body into a sitting position with Colucci's back to the stanchion and his mutilated face to the bridge's approach. While his soldiers watched, silently horrified, through the dim blackout lights of the truck, Perkin took a bundle of baling wire from the engineer's equipment and wrapped it tightly around the bridge support and the dead man's neck, ensuring the dead fascist soldier would not fall over. Perkin ripped open the soldier's shirt, exposing Colucci's bare chest. As Perkin picked up a pot of paint and a brush from the engineer's supplies, Private Fratelli finally understood and knelt by his lieutenant. After a quiet conversation Fratelli spelled aloud the Italian word for "fascist" as Perkin painted it on the dead man's chest.

Sixty miles and several hours later, as the jeeps sat parked outside of Sapri, Perkin was still not sure why he had made a display of Lance Corporal Colucci's body. His hatred of the fascists had become so visceral and atavistic that the deaths of the Blackshirts had limits in appeasing his appetite for vengeance—a vengeance that he felt necessary for Pena, Ewart, and Wagner as well as for Brother Giuseppe. Although Perkin was tired—physically and mentally—he was also angry, and his anger gave him energy to keep going, to complete his mission. Below his anger, a strong undercurrent of disillusionment and sadness flowed. This journey had shown him a side of war that his training never could, and the personal unfairness of war and the randomness of its violence would remain with him always. *If this is what the first week is like,* he wondered, *what will the next year bring?*

Perkin remained at the crossroads, silent, for five full minutes as he contemplated the murder of the Vibonati constable. His soldiers were silent as well—they knew what he was thinking and would follow him without complaint or reservations, whatever he decided.

He knew that he could do it, but it was the question of whether he should do it that preoccupied his thoughts. Through the medium of his anger he felt the compulsion of vengeance, and he sensed that the revulsion that had sickened him earlier had faded. Perkin tried to put this compulsion into a historical context, to see abstractly and academically what the act of murder would be like, but he could not. Surely, in all of history there was a precedent that would somehow make the constable's death permissible, but he found that every example of a revenge killing he could recall from the Romans to the American frontier left him with a shaky moral foundation. As he could not find a historical justification or a just precedent for what he wanted to do, he allowed his thirst for vengeance to trump his intellect and morality, and he told himself that killing the constable was no different than killing the soldier at the roadblock or the Blackshirts at the monastery. It was war, and the constable was the enemy. Even that rationalization was weak—it didn't answer Perkin's questions, and he knew it. Something was missing, it was on the fringe of his thoughts, but he couldn't quite grasp what it was.

Perkin hit the starter and put the jeep into gear. He hesitated, made up his mind, then let the clutch out and swung the jeep to the right and up the mountain toward Vibonati. Sergeant Kenton inwardly shrugged and let out the clutch on his own jeep. Perkin had gone no more than a hundred yards when movement out of the corner of his eye caught his attention. Seagulls were flying along the road catching the updrafts as the emerging sun warmed the mountainside. At first he could only see the birds from a distance, then they flew closer to see if the strange vehicles offered the promise of food. Their harsh, familiar squawking had always annoyed Perkin, but today it brought forth a memory of home and happier days spent fishing in Portland with Sam.

As he watched the birds circle the jeeps, he thought of Sam and Able Company. He remembered why they left the safety of Eighth Army and were heading back to Salerno. Sam and his friends were in trouble, and he was wasting time and risking more soldiers' lives on a vendetta. He finally found the piece of the equation that, in his fatigue, had escaped him. Sam was in trouble. Murder was an indulgence he could not allow himself.

He hit the brakes, the jeep slid to a halt in the gravel, and he pounded the steering wheel in anger and frustration before turning the jeep around and heading back down the mountain road.

0630 hours
Pisciotta

Corporal Gerhard Wagenbach hated early morning operations, but that was the way of the Wehrmacht. He was an intelligence NCO who had recently been detailed to Major Grossmann's unit in southern Italy—he liked working for the major and enjoyed the comforts of Italy, but he hated to get up early. Wagenbach's orders had been specific: arrest the priest in the early morning before the Italians were awake to witness the arrest. They were to raid the church long before daylight, but their Kübelwagen had hit a sharp pothole on the back-road trip down from their station at Eboli, and it blew out the German jeep's front right tire. It had taken more time to change the tire and negotiate the remainder of the bad roads to Pisciotta than the corporal had allotted. The pothole might have been, Wagenbach reflected, an act of God, as such inadvertent accidents were known, but such an explanation would carry little weight with the major or his deputy, Captain Gerschoffer, who would mark it down as an act of carelessness on the part of the corporal.

The good news for Corporal Wagenbach was that the Italians were largely still asleep. His driver turned off the engine of the Kübelwagen and coasted down a small hill behind the Pisciotta church and came noiselessly to a halt in front of a small door that led into the back of the church. The corporal yawned from a mixture of fatigue and nervousness, and he thought back to his mission briefing. Wagenbach's information was that the priest was Irish, was suspected of supplying the Allies with information on German activities in Rome, and had been in place in southern Italy for some months—most likely to facilitate the invasion. It had been reported back to Major Grossmann's office that the priest had talked to an American patrol on the same day a German MP section in the area had been reported as missing. There was speculation in the *Abwehr* office that perhaps the priest had assisted the Amis in eliminating the German roadblock, but Wagenbach held no opinion on that. Nevertheless, the report of the American patrol spurred Captain Gerschoffer's decision to bring in the priest.

The *Abwehr*'s local Italian man reported to the Eboli station that the priest slept in a small office at the back of the church while the parish priest lay sick in his residence next door. After the Italian priest had died, the Irishman remained at the church, sometimes dining there alone or with parishioners. Wagenbach's instructions were to arrest the priest, search the church and the official church residence, and return with the Irishman and his pigeons (Captain Gerschoffer had laughingly told Wagenbach that he had some messages he wanted to forward to the British).

Wagenbach was Austrian and Catholic, just like the Führer, only a little more devout. He did not want to barge into the church and arrest a priest, but orders were orders. If the priest was an enemy of the Fatherland, then arrest was the right thing to do, but Wagenbach would knock first.

He slung his machine pistol, but both of his soldiers kept their rifles ready. He pounded on the door three times and waited. Nothing. He pounded again and put his ear to the door. Nothing. Swearing, as he recognized his mistake, he tersely told one of his soldiers to cover the front of the church, and the soldier set off at a run around the church down an alley.

The soldier, Private Hahn, had known that they should have covered the front of the church from the beginning, but Wagenbach did not take kindly to suggestions from privates, so he kept his mouth shut. Let the corporal take the heat if the priest escapes. Although Private Hahn was not running hard as he turned the front corner of the church, his impact with a large man in uniform planted him squarely on his back. As he looked up at the huge soldier with red hair under his helmet, Private Hahn heard the large man say in English—as he deftly reached down and took away Hahn's rifle—"Hey, Lieutenant! Looky what we got here!"

0635 hours
Pisciotta

With unintentional irony, Perkin groaned to himself, "Oh Christ. Not again." *What was it about this mission and churches,* he wondered. The sight of the German soldier running around the church had sent a bolt of adrenaline through the young officer, whose body had been pumping out adrenaline nearly nonstop for four days—it seemed to have less and less effect each time it happened.

"Pfadenhauer, Ewart . . . ," Perkin realized his mistake and then said, ". . . sorry, Kulis. Around to the right— where this guy came from . . . ," Perkin stopped and thought for a second, "Wait . . . ," Perkin bent down and pulled his trench knife from its scabbard and walked towards where Sergeant Kenton was holding Private Hahn against the church wall. The German looked at the tall lieutenant and the blood-encrusted knife. His eyes darted to the American's grim face and then down to his arm and the hand holding the knife. The right arm of the officer's jacket—the one holding the knife—was covered in dried blood. As he shrank back against Sergeant Kenton, the German soldier lost control of his bladder.

Perkin saw the spreading stain on Hahn's trousers, and not for the first time in the last twenty-four hours, Perkin was ashamed of himself. He had provoked that reaction in another human, and again he was sad deep within himself, but he didn't have time to lose in sorrow. He pulled his arm back fast and then hit the German hard on the side of the face with the brass knuckle handle of the trench knife. The *Abwehr* soldier dropped unconscious to the ground, his jaw broken and his face torn open from the spikes on the knife's knuckles.

"Goddamn, Lieutenant. That's gonna hurt." Kenton said admiringly as he grabbed a bundle of the baling wire from his jeep and quickly twisted Hahn's hands behind his back.

"Well, it'll work out better for him than Plan A would have, although I don't expect a thank-you note or a Christmas card from him. Okay, boys. Get movin.' Sergeant, you go to the left. For God's sake, don't get caught up in a cross fire. Fratelli, you're with me."

The soldiers began to move out along the designated sides of the church, and Perkin softly tried the door to the church. It was locked. He tried again. The door would not budge. Perkin shrugged and waved Fratelli over to the left, and he headed around the right. He caught up to Kulis and Pfadenhauer quickly, and when he had their attention, he moved past them to take the lead. Ten seconds later, he was peering around the corner. There were two German soldiers; one, a corporal, was pounding on the door. The corporal's machine pistol was slung over his shoulder, and the other soldier was staring disinterestedly at the door— they were less than thirty feet away.

Perkin motioned to Kulis and Pfadenhauer to follow him, and as he walked quickly out from the side of the building, he heard Pfadenhauer call out loudly, "Hands up!" in German. Both soldiers started as if they were little boys caught with their hands in the cookie jar; neither soldier went for his weapon. Perkin had taken three prisoners without a shot being fired, although he reflected that Private Hahn would be in intense pain for some weeks to come.

"Ask them if there are others!" Perkin ordered Private Pfadenhauer.

Corporal Wagenbach was on the verge of answering with his name and rank when he saw Sergeant Kenton and Private Fratelli walk around the other corner of the building. Wagenbach, distracted, said nothing.

"Fratelli, go back to the jeeps and keep an eye on our other prisoner. Kulis, go with him. See if you can find the priest. Coming running if you see any more Krauts. Sergeant Kenton, pull this guy's arm off and beat him to death with it—we'll see if that motivates the private to talk."

There was actually a hint of a smirk on the private's face, and on a hunch Perkin turned to the corporal. "You speak English?"

"Yes, sir. I speak English." Corporal Wagenbach didn't take the arm threat literally, but the American sergeant was huge, mean looking, and like all the Americans, looked as if he had been drenched in blood.

Perkin was surprised—Wagenbach's English seemed to be spoken in an American accent. "Are there others? Why are you here?"

As far as Wagenbach knew, there was not another German soldier for thirty miles, but he saw no need to pass that information to the Americans. He shrugged, and then said, "We're deserters. We were seeking sanctuary at this church."

It was a calamitous improvisation on the part of Corporal Wagenbach, and the words deserter and sanctuary took Perkin back over a personal line that he had not wished to cross again. He slammed his knee into the groin of the corporal and then kicked his legs out from under him. Perkin walked up to the stricken soldier and kicked the helmet off of his head so hard that it slammed against a stone wall behind the church and then spun down the street like a top. Perkin stomped his boot down on Wagenbach's neck and hissed, "There's no sanctuary for you here, motherfucker. Tell me what your mission is or I break your goddamned neck!" He turned to the private, who had lost the smirk, and said in an ice-cold voice, "You're next."

"Sir." It was the private speaking, and in an imploring American accent. "We have orders to arrest the priest here and take him to Eboli for questioning."

"The priest? Why?" Perkin knew the answer, but had to ask anyway.

"I don't know, sir. We were just told to pick him up." The private was shaking involuntarily—he was now terrified of the Texans and afraid of saying too much or not enough. He had never been this afraid in his life. Everyone had heard that the Americans were taking almost no prisoners in the war against Japan, and they had heard that the 45th Division was executing German prisoners at Salerno, but he, like almost everyone else, believed the rumors to have been propaganda. Like all of the men in his unit, he had spent time in America before the war—he had spent a year in Milwaukee as part of his gymnasium studies—and he had always found the Americans to be generous and friendly. This American just seemed angry—maybe there was some truth to the rumors.

"Put them up against that wall. We'll shoot the private first. Wait for my command!" Perkin ordered Sergeant Kenton. As Kenton and Pfadenhauer pushed the soldiers to a high stone wall behind the church and Perkin pointed his Thompson menacingly, he snapped at Pfadenhauer, "Ask them in German what their interest is in the priest—make sure they understand what I want and what the consequences are if they don't answer."

Without waiting for the translation, the corporal answered, although with difficulty. "The priest came to the attention of military intelligence headquarters in Rome. We suspected he was providing information to the Allies, and that suspicion was validated when our people here reported he met with an American patrol last weekend. Was that you, sir?"

Perkin was going to ask who their unit commander was and who their "people" were—maybe that would be of interest to Jim Lockridge—and then load them up in the Kübelwagen. There was really no sense in wasting the opportunity of the moment, but as he opened his mouth to shout at the soldiers still lined up against the wall, he heard "Perkin! Stop! Stop! Oh, please, God, stop!"

As Perkin turned, he saw Father Riley running along the back road leading to the church at full bore. He was covered in sweat and wearing black shorts, leather running shoes with black socks, and a long-sleeved red and white jersey, which Perkin saw was embroidered with the words "Corcaigh—1941 All-Ireland Hurling Champions."

"Father, what on earth are you doing?" Perkin asked as the priest pounded to a halt in front of him. Father Riley was bent over with his hands on his knees, breathing hard. It had never occurred to Perkin that priests might find enjoyment in exercise, and he was astonished to see the Irishman going for a run so early in the morning.

"Fer fuck's sake, what are you doing? Perkin, you can't just kill these men." Riley's Irish accent was very much more pronounced than the last time he had talked to Perkin, and he had reverted to the vernacular of his pre-church youth. Then the realization that there were

German soldiers at his church finally came home to the priest. "What . . . what're they doing here?"

"They came to arrest you, Father. They work for German intelligence and it seems that they have informers here who reported that we asked you for directions the other day." Father Riley stiffened at the mention of informers—it was a dark word with an insidious history in Ireland. Perkin continued, "Seems that because you were cordial to us, they deduced you're working for the Allies. I hate to say it, but you'd best come back with us. They won't stop now, they'll just send another team when we leave, and we can't wait here until Eighth Army arrives."

Father Riley was appalled. It was not only the thought that he had come to the notice of German intelligence, but also that he might have compromised other like-minded priests who were assisting the Allies in whatever manner they could. He knew that what Perkin said made sense, but he was internally convincing himself to stay—that it would be all right—when Perkin poked the German corporal hard in the ribs with his Thompson and said, "Tell him. Tell him what happens next."

Gerhard Wagenbach hesitated and, after taking another poke from the Thompson, said, "Father . . . it is true. The lieutenant is correct. They will send another team to find out what happened to us and to complete the mission. You would be arrested, taken back to German lines and interrogated. If the *Abwehr* so chooses or the Gestapo demands, you might be turned over to the Gestapo and then interned in a camp—or worse. It's not in your best interests to stay here." The corporal, with his aching testicles and tender ribs, had decided that it was in his own best interests to be forthcoming. He wanted the priest to stay with him as long as possible to keep this butcherous Ami from following through on his threats.

0943 hours
La Cosa Defenses, 1.5 Miles WSW of Albanella,
Italy

"First and second platoons! Form up on me! Come on and move it, for Christ's sake. Let's go!" Sam bellowed in a deep booming voice that could be heard from back home in Texas.

They could see the trucks finally coming up the road to pick up the battalion. Lieutenant Colonel Wranosky had received their fragmentary order, known as a FRAGO, directing them to move to a different sector over three hours previously, but the promised transportation had not arrived. This would be the second move for the battalion in thirteen hours.

It had been a long, hard, frightening night without much sleep for anyone. Twice more since the disconnected voice had disappeared, Able Company soldiers had been shelled by German artillery, and Sam's platoon took its first casualties since D-day, although none of the wounds were life threatening. Even through the artillery attacks, Sam thought hard about the voice but was unable to reach any conclusion that made sense.

Captain Spaulding had no answers either, and after the much-anticipated break of day, Spaulding had sent a patrol out on the other side of the wire. Nothing out of the ordinary was found—there were no bodies and no cuts in the Able Company wire. In any case, Sam had more pressing things to worry about. Charlie Company had captured a German patrol after a brief fire fight early in the morning. Interrogation of these and other prisoners had indicated the Germans were preparing a massive counterattack, but the German prisoners did not know where the *Schwerpunkt*, or focal point, of the attack would be. The prisoners seemed confident that the counterattack would be overwhelming and that the Battle of Salerno was winding down toward a successful conclusion. They did note, however, that the fighting was worse than what they had experienced on the Eastern Front, and many of their comrades would prefer to be back fighting the Russians over the Americans. The Russians, they said, were predictable, but these crazy Texans were not.

The highlight of the morning was the arrival of two battalions of the 504th Parachute Infantry Regiment of the 82nd Airborne Division. Sam met the first platoon of paratroopers around 0700, as they moved into his area to take up position. Sam was reassured by what he saw: tough, confident soldiers who would be a match for anything that the Germans could throw at them. As the T-Patchers moved out of their positions and the paratroopers into them, Sam was irritated to note that they were making changes to his defensive dispositions. Still, he watched and paid attention as machine gun positions were resited by the airborne troops. Grudgingly, he admitted to himself that they were improvements, but he consoled himself with the knowledge that his defenses were established in the dark and the airborne troops had the benefit of daylight.

When the trucks finally arrived, Sam moved quickly to load his platoon up on the heavy trucks, but then they sat without moving. To everyone's great frustration, evidently no one knew where exactly the battalion was headed other than toward the Sele-Calore corridor. After half an hour of waiting, Sam allowed his troops to dismount to stretch their legs and walk around.

Eventually, leadership arrived in the form of Colonel Jamison and several of his staff officers. Jamison was joined at his jeep by Lieutenant Colonel Wranosky, and they bent over the hood of the jeep to pore over a map of the battlefield. Much to Sam's delight, he saw Captain Waller

Finley-Jones in the party. Finley-Jones was heading over to talk to Sam when he was called back over to the jeep by Jamison. Instead, Sam was approached by a widely smiling Captain Ronald Ebbins.

Sam immediately shot to attention and gave the captain a razor-sharp salute. Seeing this, those of Sam's platoon who had heard of the incident in Ogliastro jumped to their feet and saluted Ebbins as well. "Good morning, sir!" barked several of the soldiers, and Ebbins's smile faltered slightly, but by the time he lazily returned the salute, he had regained his brimming confidence.

"Come with me for a moment, Lieutenant. I have some wonderful news to share with you," Ebbins drawled with his Hollywood smile.

Sam shrugged, and the two of them walked out of earshot of the platoon. After a few more paces, Ebbins stopped, turned, and faced Sam. The smile was replaced with a nasty grin. "If you touch my woman again, Taft, I'll kill you. She said that you hit her. I should press charges, but she wants to put this past her."

Sam was stunned, and for a brief moment he was not sure of whom Ebbins was speaking. Then he realized, of course, Ebbins's woman had to be Antoniette Bernardi. Now it was Sam's turn to smile nastily, and he said in a patronizing tone, "Oh, Ronald. Don't you know better than to believe everything you hear? I suppose that she forgot to tell you that she was shooting at us. And as for you killing me? Ain't that a little out of character? I mean, we both know you're all hat and no cattle, and I don't see any boys 'round here who'd help ya out. But if it'd make ya feel better, I'm willin' to take my helmet off and we could go a few rounds. Is that the wonderful news you have for me—that you'd like some boxin' lessons?"

Even Sam's taunt had no effect on Ebbins's smile. If anything, it widened even further. Ebbins turned and headed back to his jeep. Over his shoulder he said, "No, that's not it. Enjoy your next operation, Taft. I worked hard to get it for you—best of luck out there, cowboy."

0840 hours
Near Pieta, Italy

Perkin and Father Riley rode alone in Perkin's jeep and behind the rest of their little convoy. In the front was a jeep with Private Kulis and Sergeant Kenton. They were followed by Pfadenhauer driving the Kübelwagen, which was flying a small Lone Star flag from its whip antenna. The three German soldiers were tightly trussed up in the back seat, and Private Hahn and Corporal Wagenbach both found their situation exceedingly uncomfortable. However, they did not complain, not with Private Fratelli sitting twisted around in the front seat with his BAR pointed at Corporal Wagenbach's chest.

Father Riley had taken more time to get ready to depart than Perkin wished, but the roads were largely free of vehicular traffic again. Occasionally, the procession would swing out past horse-drawn wagons or groups of people on foot, but it did not slow the Americans down an appreciable difference. Some Italian soldiers on foot stared at the jeeps and the Kübelwagen as they passed; the Americans got a friendly wave from some of the soldiers, and the Germans once got the evil eye. Perkin noted the friendly waves, but he did not return them.

For the first quarter of the hour drive between Pisciotta and Castellabate, the last village on their road through no-man's-land, Perkin and Father Riley did not speak. Perkin finally broke the silence. He felt the press of conscience to confess to the priest, although that was not in his tradition. As he didn't know how to begin, he said instead, "I met your brother. He's a good man. He asked me not to stop to visit on our way north—he didn't want us to bring more attention to you."

Patrick Riley soaked that news in and then said pensively, "Why did you stop then? Mind you, I'm not complaining . . ."

"I wanted to warn you." Perkin then recounted the incident at the Sanctuary of St. Francis of Paola. Father Riley sat silently aghast as Perkin told him of the vicious attacks on the monks and the desecration of the sanctuary. Perkin did not describe his role in stopping the attack; he only noted that they had intervened. Riley looked at Perkin, and he could see the intense anger still burning in the American.

It had occurred to Riley that there were fewer Americans now than when they had passed through previously. He had not wanted to ask the question, but he felt that he should. "Perkin . . . ," Riley hesitated and asked softly, "Where's Corporal Pena? Did you lose your men there at the monastery?"

"Roberto's buried about a hundred miles south of here with two of our other boys. It's a beautiful little spot," Perkin said bitterly. He was unsure how, or if, he should talk about the ambush or the details of the monastery; yet, prompted by astute questions from the young priest, he did. Bit by bit the story came out—how Fratelli had warned him about the constable at Vibonati and how he had ignored it and his men had died. He told the priest of the two kind old ladies at Acquafredda and of the total inadequacy of his words at the boys' funeral. His voice was strained when he told the story of Brother Giuseppe and the savage deaths of the peaceful monk and the violent Blackshirt, and when he told the priest of the knifing of the Italian soldier and of the bravery of Friar Immanuel, his voice broke altogether. It took several tries to get through the story, yet he wasn't done.

Perkin saw the horrified look on Father Riley's face as he told him of wiring the dead fascist soldier to the bridge, but he kept telling his tale, including how he later headed up the road to Vibonati to murder the constable only to change his mind.

"Thank God he stopped," whispered the priest to himself. He could see the torment on Perkin's face and hear the fatalism in his voice, and he could sense, somehow, that Perkin wanted an explanation for the things that had happened to his men and for the things that he had done. There was not an easy answer.

"Perkin, how did you come to be in the army?" Father Riley asked.

"Excuse me?" It was a simple question, but Perkin was tired. He understood the question, but he did not know where it was leading him.

"You're not a career officer, if I remember correctly. Did you come in after the war began? Were you conscripted? Do the Americans even conscript officers?"

"No, Patrick." Unconsciously, Perkin had moved to the priest's Christian name. "I was not conscripted. I came into the service in '39."

Father Riley smiled and said, "My Protestant friends, both of 'em, God bless their souls, call me Pat. Please do that." He resumed his questioning of Perkin. "What was your reason for joining? Patriotism? Adventure? Money?"

"Maybe a bit of the former two." Perkin thought back to that day long ago where he had argued with Sam on Corpus Christi Bay. "I saw what was goin' on in Europe in the spring of '39, and I believed that the U.S. would eventually get dragged in. I've always thought that if you enjoy the bounty and the freedoms of America that you should be prepared to serve it." Perkin paused as he downshifted the gears of his jeep to slow down for a turn on the highway. "Colonel Russ told me that your father was killed in the Great War. So was mine, and my family have been Indian fighters or soldiers on or off for generations," Perkin shrugged. "Maybe that also influenced my decision."

"What did you see in Europe in 1939?"

"I saw Hitler in the process of dismembering Versailles and destroying the security regime that had been established at the cost of millions of lives."

The priest thought carefully before he asked his next question. "Did you not recognize those actions for what they represent, Perkin?"

"What do you mean?" Again, Perkin did not know where the question was heading.

"Evil. This war's origins and conduct are engulfed in evil, Perkin." Seeing a protest from Perkin, Father Riley interrupted, "Don't get me wrong, I am not implying criticism of your conduct. With your permission, I'll talk to that in a minute. Don't you want to know why you're here? Why God, not your General Eisenhower, has brought you here? It is to oppose evil. Your Texans are here to oppose evil. America is here to oppose evil. Even Winston Churchill and the whole stinking, rotten British Empire are the tools of God in opposing this evil. And don't mistake it for anything else . . ."

Perkin interrupted, "No, Pat, I don't believe that. It's not that simple. This conflict can't be sketched out in black and white terms that easily."

Speaking softly, the priest replied, "It may not appear to be simple, Perkin, but it is. It truly is. In this modern year of our Lord, 1943, this may sound a bit medieval to you, but good and evil still define our lives. This war is defined by good and evil. We should never lose sight of that."

"Now you sound more like a Baptist minister from South Texas to me than a Catholic priest—even one from the Middle Ages." Perkin said with a tired attempt at a smile.

"Even the Proddys get it right from time to time," replied Father Riley with a smile in return. He had been concerned that Perkin might not smile again. "One thing that this war will teach you over and again is that evil seldom manifests itself in simplicity. There are always variables and nuances . . . always other explanations and different points of view, which Satan uses to confuse us and muddle the issues. The world, our conduct, and our role in it, is black and white—it's just that he would have you believe that there are shades of grey in between. In 1939, were we not told that there were complex problems that dictated our actions, but were we not given complex excuses for why the whole sorry mess ended in war? Was Germany not just righting the wrong of Versailles, and did not the people of Central Europe need the great powers to make their decisions for them? But this war isn't about righting boundaries or destroying your security regimes. It is about extending the dominion of Satan and the exercise of evil over us all. Make no mistake, my friend. America and Britain and the rest of the Allied nations are the only things that stand between us and a future of unspeakable barbarity where the light, love, and freedoms given us by God are collected like cigarette cards and then doled out by the state when or if it chooses. It's my belief that the true Dark Ages were not a thousand years ago, but they are the growing shadows just around the corner! Do you remember what Hindenburg called America during the Great War? That 'thoroughly hellish, inexorable machine'? He was wrong, of course—that description only fits his own country." The priest hesitated, took a deep breath, and continued, "With their ruthless efficiency, the Germans have already begun to round up the Jews in Rome, just like they have throughout Europe. Think about this, Perkin: they've been in control of Rome for less than a week, and there are two Allied Armies marching their direction, and they've decided this is a priority? Why? To what end?" The priest thought of the messages he had seen from his network within the Church. "My friend, I'm going to tell you something, which you should believe and never forget. There are reports coming from priests—good priests—in Germany and Poland that the Nazis have invested in the wholesale slaughter of European Jewry. First the German Jews, then the Polish Jews, then those of Western Europe and Eastern Europe and now Italy are simply disappearing. I'll say that again—they are simply disappearing."

Perkin looked over at the priest and asked incredulously, "What are you saying, Pat? That the Germans are murdering all of Europe's Jews?"

"Yes! Exactly that. Their intentions were spelled out before the war, but no one listened, and the war gives the Nazis a medium through which to act: the people are rounded up like cattle, their property is appropriated by the state, and then it's sold to so-called Christians. What does that tell you, Perkin? It says that the Jews are not coming back." Riley paused and thought about it a second and then repeated, "The Jews are not coming back. And it's not just the Jews. Priests who have opposed National Socialism have disappeared, and political opponents are tossed into concentration camps. So, too, have the Romanis disappeared—the Gypsies. The Nazis sterilize their feeble, they euthanize the old and the weak, and now they make their opponents disappear. I'm telling you that there is no other explanation—evil has gripped this continent!" The priest angrily clenched his fist to emphasize his last point.

Perkin was silent as he digested this information. He looked over at Father Riley who now appeared to be waiting, and he nodded. Father Riley continued, "Since I've been in Rome, I've met scores of German soldiers. Most seem like you or me—ordinary men—but more than a few seem to have unbounded arrogance, as if they know this is their time, that this world, right now, will be their kingdom. But what you must understand is that it doesn't matter because, humble or arrogant, they serve the same master. Perkin, I ask you again. Why are you here?" The priest answered for him. "It must be to oppose this. That must be God's plan for you, just as it's his plan for me. Has it occurred to you that the things you do serve a higher purpose? And I'm not talking about your noble service to America. Will not your trip to see my brother shorten this war in some way? Did you not save my life and the lives of those poor monks? Why were you there at just the right moment in time? A day later, and that beautiful monastery would be burned to the ground with all the monks inside. Many soldiers in your place would have simply left the monks to deal with the fascist soldiers on their own, but you did not. You witnessed horrifying acts, and you conducted horrifying acts, but you saved them—at terrible cost to yourself, I'm afraid." Father Riley paused and thought for a second. "Why didn't you leave?"

"After what happened to Joey, I couldn't leave. I don't think anyone could." Perkin thought back—part of him had started to rationalize skulking out in the cover of darkness, but of course he could not.

"You'd be surprised at how many would have. Perkin, I don't know, but perhaps the descendant of Huguenots atoned for the ancient sins of his ancestors last night. Think about what you did. You saved the holy relics of St. Francis and the lives of the men entrusted with preserving them."

Both men thought silently about that prospect, but Perkin had neither sought nor offered atonement. Father Riley had one last point to make, and it struck at the core of Perkin's inner turmoil. "A word of caution, my friend. It does not serve God to use the tactics of the adversary. While some of the ancient founders of my order may disagree, only in Machiavelli's world do the ends justify the means. While I understand the driving force of revenge, I was so happy to hear that you didn't go to Vibonati. No good would have been served by that man's death, but the cost to your soul would have been paid over eternity. As a friend—not just a priest—let me tell you something: do what you need to in this war, but don't allow it to destroy you in the process. You've a good heart, Perkin. Make sure that when you go home to Texas, you still do."

1115 hours
Ogliastro Cilento

It had been a long morning. The good news was that the Americans were not evacuating. Not yet. That was the impression Perkin had as his party, minus Father Riley, crossed over the bridge from Agropoli and headed down to the beach near Paestum. The priest decided to stay in Castellabate where he would be outside of the combat zone. The decision carried risks, which were now clear to the priest, but he believed it would also give him the freedom to return to Pisciotta when Eighth Army controlled what was currently no-man's-land. As with Father Riley's brother, Perkin had enjoyed his company and welcomed his counsel, but the priest's words on the drive had eased his conscience little. They parted with a handshake, as friends, with the mutual hope to meet again.

The battlefield was completely different than it had been less than a week earlier. The sounds of battle and the smoke and the thunder of the guns were the same, but vast amounts of supplies had been built up on the beaches, and more continued to be offloaded from the landing ships in the Gulf of Salerno. Out to sea, scores of ships extended as far as the eye could see. Were they there to pick up the remnants of Clark's army? It was not clear how things would turn, and in Perkin's state of mind, he feared the worst. This unnatural pessimism—his guilt of losing soldiers and of taking lives—gave him a sense of urgency. A sense of fatalism had set in after the momentary lift of speaking with Father Riley. He would likely die at Salerno, just like his soldiers had. Just like the soldiers he had brought back would. Another poor decision. More guilt.

He had to see Sam. He had to make sure his cousin was safe, and if he were to die this day, it was to be at his cousin's side and with the company.

They had entered the VI Corps area of operations two hours earlier, but the true crossover into friendly territory was slow. The bridge that Perkin's patrol had crossed four days ago was gone, blown to keep the Germans from advancing into the battlefield from the south. It now created the same roadblock for Perkin.

It had taken a back track to Castellabate and Sergeant Rossi's assistance to find a ford. Perkin and Fratelli found him in the same café having an ersatz coffee. The Italian *Carabinieri* sergeant, while happy to see his American friends, was shocked at the changes in the Texans. He noticed that they were missing three soldiers, including the irritable Mexican corporal, and Perkin and Fratelli both seemed to be covered in dried blood and mud. Unlike last time, Perkin offered no easy smiles and no cigarettes—he just walked in and asked for help. Rossi had been in the same hard, miserable, execrable place before, on the Eastern Front, and he wordlessly picked up his Beretta submachine gun and nodded to Perkin. Rossi saw them across a small ford that involved all the soldiers virtually carrying the jeeps across a mountain stream, then he headed back to his coffee with a fresh pack of American cigarettes in his pocket, a gift from Private Fratelli.

Perkin's first stop was a prisoner collection point, where he turned over the three *Abwehr* soldiers. He wanted to take them back to his friend Jim Lockridge, but there were more qualified soldiers to interrogate these men. If he had the opportunity, he would bring Captain Lockridge back with him for a visit, and at a minimum, he would make their presence known to Fifth Army intelligence. Before leaving, Perkin walked up to the German soldiers and said, not unkindly, "I suspect you sons-of-bitches will make it to Texas before I do. I've heard the prisoner camps there are decent, and you'll be well treated." He turned to Private Hahn and said, "Private, sorry about your face. Good luck to you boys."

His second stop was to talk to a white-haired top sergeant of a company of Negro soldiers who were off-loading ammunition from landing ships. Neither the outposts at the edge of the American line nor the MPs at the prisoner collection point knew where Able Company was. Nor did the Negro soldiers, but they were certain that Able had been at Ogliastro as they had sent an ammunition truck to the company just days before. It was the best answer that Perkin received yet. The old sergeant, who had the look of regular army, told Perkin that few below regiment or division knew where any given unit was, and even then the information could be out of date. Perkin appreciated that but wanted to avoid entering regimental or division headquarters. He was not ready to deliver his mission report yet, and he did not want the delay. He would find Sam and the company first. The report could wait.

Ogliastro was a disappointment. The town center was occupied by a squad from a different regiment. Those soldiers looked ragged. One exhausted second lieutenant, who had been laying down on a stone bench, stood up at Perkin's arrival and gave him the *Reader's Digest* version of the battle. It sounded grim, but perhaps not all was lost. Morale was buoyed by the arrival of the paratroopers and the rumors that the 3rd Division, Rock of the Marne, would be landing within a day or two. While the second john was helpful in bringing Sam up to date on the general state of the battle, he had no knowledge of where Able Company was.

"Maybe he could help." The second lieutenant pointed to a short, slim, fair major walking rapidly across the square toward the eastern side of town. "He's a Fifth Army staff puke, who has one hell of a good lookin' dame here. She seems to have more than one boyfriend, but I reckon she's reached her allotment. She wouldn't even talk to me. See, there she is. Goddamn! Thinking of her keeps me awake at night—that and the shelling of course. Why is it the senior officers get all the good lookin' blanket wives?"

Perkin stared off across the square and watched as the young lady kissed the soldier on the cheek in the European style. He agreed with the lieutenant's assessment about her beauty, thanked him for the help, and then hopped into his jeep, now driven by Private Kulis. The small three-vehicle convoy pulled around the square and as Major Grossmann and Antoniette Bernardi watched arm-in-arm, Perkin hopped out of the jeep as it rolled to a stop.

"What is it, Lieutenant?" Grossmann sounded exactly the way a field grade officer who was talking to a pretty girl would sound when interrupted by a company grade officer.

"Sorry to bother you, sir. Ma'am." Perkin nodded to the young woman—a stunning young lady. "Major, the fellas back there said you were army staff and might be able to help us. I'm lookin' for Able Company of the 141st. Do you know where they might be?"

Major Grossmann had been planning to give his last set of instructions to Bernardi—he was crossing back to German lines as soon as it was dark and would not return. Grossmann had noted the arrival of the German Kübelwagen with interest and was intrigued by this tall lieutenant covered in dried blood. The consummate opportunist, Grossmann considered how he might make his answer work to his advantage or that of the Fatherland, which were not always the same thing, as he frequently reflected.

"What's your name, Lieutenant, and what's the story of the Kübelwagen?" Grossmann was careful to pronounce the German word as an American would: with a "w" sound instead of a "v."

"Perkin Berger, sir. We captured a German patrol in a little town about thirty miles south of our lines. This is their jeep. I'm taking it back to Able Company with me as a war trophy."

At the mention of the patrol, Grossmann stiffened. It may have been his soldiers. His reaction was missed by Perkin but noted by Antoniette Bernardi who tightened her grip on his arm. Her touch was oddly reassuring to the German officer who asked, "No kidding? Where were you?" Unconsciously echoing Father Riley, he asked, "What were they—what were you doing down there?"

"I'll discuss it with you in private over there if you like, sir." Perkin nodded to the Kübelwagen. He was surprised that the major would ask such a question in front of the Italian lady.

Grossmann smiled at his young Italian spy and said, "Miss Bernardi, if you will excuse me for a second." She nodded and smiled fetchingly at Private Kulis, whose face looked worse as the days progressed. Bernardi walked over to the jeep and started talking to the shy private. You never know what you might learn, she thought.

Grossmann walked over to the Kübelwagen and immediately recognized it as the vehicle he had ridden in when he came down to the Salerno plain from Rome. The blood in the back was a new addition though, and while Grossmann kept his feelings tightly controlled, he was angry at the thought that these Texans might have hurt or killed his soldiers.

"So what happened?"

"Sir, we were on a long range patrol to make contact with Eighth Army and scout out the coastal road. It's open to Eighth Army's advance, by the way. We ran into the Kraut patrol in a town called Pisciotta. They gave up without much of a fight, so we got three good prisoners. They're *Abwehr*—we turned 'em over to the intel guys for interrogation."

"Swell," Grossmann said without conviction. "If they didn't put up a fight, where'd the blood come from?"

Perkin was getting tired of the conversation; he didn't know this major and thus felt no need to explain himself to the officer. "We had a fallin' out. Can you tell me where Able Company is?"

Grossmann smiled inwardly. He could make this work out to his advantage and maybe exact a little revenge for his wounded soldier—whichever one it was. He would tell this troublesome lieutenant the truth and send him to the *Schwerpunkt* of the German attack—the La Cosa defenses.

"Do you have a map?"

Perkin nodded and pulled it out. Grossmann unfolded it along the hood of the Kübelwagen and said, "Now there are no guarantees, but Able, I believe, is deployed here along the La Cosa Stream in the valley between Mount San Chirico and Mount Soprano. At least that is where I believed they were last night. If they aren't there, look for 'em at this bridge." He pointed to a bridge on the north side of Mount San Chirico and then smiled to himself again. "I had actually sent a messenger to Able last night to find them; I don't know if he did."

A few minutes later, the American patrol pulled out of Ogliastro. Bernardi and Grossmann continued their walk up the streets of the mountain village. Grossmann wanted to be away from this woman—she attracted too much attention—and lay low for the rest of the day.

"My dear, you will have to use your best judgment, but we will need you up north if the battle turns against us—Naples, if possible. Let me know your whereabouts through the usual channels. I think . . . continue exploiting your source with the Texans as much as possible. They will be key to the fight in Italy for months to come. Should the battle go in our favor, stay here and we'll get you back to Rome as soon as possible. Now, if you have no questions for me, I must say goodbye."

Bernardi looked up at the German intelligence officer without any acknowledgment of his instructions. The beautiful face was devoid of passion as she said, "The ugly little soldier told me that Berger, the lieutenant you were talking to, is the cousin of Sam Taft. He said they are like brothers. You may kill him instead—whichever is easier."

Grossmann suppressed a shiver and said, "That is very considerate of you, Miss Bernardi. If Taft wasn't killed last night, he likely will be today. Maybe for good measure, we'll get both of them."

1115 hours
La Cosa Defenses, 1 Mile South of Calore River

"Yea, though I walk through the valley of the shadow of death, I will fear no evil: for thou art with me; thy rod and thy staff they comfort me." Such were the words of Psalms 23:4 as spoken by the battalion chaplain, a

Methodist lieutenant. The chaplain was walking through the new battalion area and praying with the soldiers even as the trucks disgorged their cargoes of men, weapons, and ammunition.

Sam didn't have time to pray with the chaplain, but he did anyway. He had been praying nonstop to himself since Captain Finley-Jones had explained Captain Ebbins's taunt. The 1st Battalion was charged with plugging the last remaining gap in the La Cosa defensive line at a spot that was vital to the tattered integrity of the beachhead. Lieutenant Colonel Wranosky's troops, specifically Able Company, were to cover the last remaining bridge over the upper Sele-Calore–La Cosa waterway not in German possession. If the Germans gained control of the bridge, the Germans would have a clear shot from their positions past Eboli down to the beach. As Finley-Jones explained, it was as certain as the sun rising in the east that the Germans would commit heavily to taking the bridge. "My cup runneth over indeed," thought Sam wryly, as the chaplain concluded the psalm with the platoon.

As recounted by Finley-Jones, Ebbins's role at a 0300 meeting was instrumental in getting the battalion assigned to that sector of the La Cosa defense. As they were already in defense, it was a significant effort to move the battalion even a few miles, but Ebbins had forcefully argued that the 1st Battalion was best positioned to move to meet the expected counterattack, and that Able Company itself should be emplaced to defend the critical bridge. As Finley-Jones explained, Ebbins's contribution may have been motivated more by animus than by military genius, but given the relative strength of the company and battalion, his reasoning was sound. The regimental operations officer began drafting the FRAGO, and Colonel Jamison made the recommendation to General Walker to move 1st Battalion.

Sam also learned from Finley-Jones that Jamison was now the acting sector commander. General Walker had found the previously appointed sector commander, Brigadier General Lange, sound asleep that morning on the side of a road. The exhausted general had been without sleep for several days, but a furious Walker informed him that everyone was tired and then relieved Lange of his duties on the spot.

Praying had the Bible on Sam's mind as he went through his lengthening list of tasks, specifically the story of Daniel in the lion's den. As he dug his foxhole, Sam pondered that although Daniel was tossed into the lion's den on the order of a friendly king, in the aggregate it probably felt no better than being chucked in by enemies. He prayed a final time, this time asking the angels to come and close his lions' mouths, and for good measure prayed for the same end for Ebbins as the satraps of Darius. He was in an Old Testament frame of mind, and charity and forgiveness were not in his way of thinking that morning.

After digging hard for what seemed like ages, he climbed out of his foxhole and looked around. He was two and a half miles from his last foxhole, which he had dug only the evening before—and there was more rock here. It was a critical lesson learned from the debacle at the Kasserine Pass that lackadaisical effort in preparing fighting positions in the desert rocks had led to high casualties. He had long ago learned that as the largest man in the company, followed closely by Sergeant Kenton, he had to dig faster and deeper than anyone else to have a fighting position that fit his frame. Next to his foxhole, he had ordered Private Froman to dig in as well. He would have liked a better place to put his sniper, but as Sam was directly in front of the bridge, he wanted another sure shot available to take out the infantry that would accompany the German armor.

The company position was at the base of the northeast slope of Mount Chirico, directly fronting the small wooden bridge. The road, as it faced him, crossed the stream from the east then curved quickly to his left and around the northern base of Mount Chirico. As was to become a familiar process for the Americans in Italy, he was on the mountain, then off and now back on—without firing a single shot. The last time that he had been on Mount Chirico—the afternoon before—he had watched a fine battalion of Texans destroyed by German artillery fire. He hoped they would be able to return the favor today.

Sam's reinforced platoon was at the edge of a tree line that began about twenty yards up the slope of the mountain. There was very little room between the bridge and the beginning of the slope—Sam estimated fifty yards. He watched as engineers used bulldozers to push down trees near the bridge, yet more engineers and available infantrymen were busy sowing mines in the eastern approach to the bridge. When the bulldozers finished knocking down trees, they began to dig out pits that Sam assumed would be for tank destroyers or Shermans in a hull down position—a notion that gladdened Sam greatly.

After Sam had seen to his platoon's defenses, he and Bill Spaulding jogged to the other side of the bridge down an unmined avenue that was marked by white tape. "I'm surprised that they ain't here yet," Sam commented as they carefully crossed the small wooden bridge.

"Me too," said Bill. "Maybe they're done for the day. Colonel Wranosky told me he just received word that the Krauts had their heads handed to 'em this morning by our armor in the corridor. It appears the Germans didn't pay enough attention to our new positions and one panzer-grenadier battalion crossed right in front of our lines and got chewed to pieces by our boys. They kept pushing, trying to get to a ford they'd found over the lower Calore, and the 636th Tank Destroyers ate those panzers for breakfast. I understand that one M-10 alone in Charlie Company, named Jinx, got five Panzer IVs and an ammunition carrier, and B Company claimed another five Panzer IVs."

"Good for them," Sam said. "Any chance that Jerry ran outta tanks this morning?"

Bill gave a short laugh, "I thought Perk was the optimist in your family. Naw, Jim says to expect more Panzer IVs supported by Stugs and infantry. The good news is that although there have been reports all along the line of Tigers, not one has been found destroyed on the battlefield yet. It's kind of like that goat-sucking vampire of Pena's that you told me about last night—I'll believe it when I see it. Speaking of Perkin and Pena, I wish I knew where them boys were and if they made it through to Eighth Army."

"Me too." Among all of his other cares, Sam was extremely anxious about Perkin. Although he knew better than to hope, he wished that Perkin had found a way to send word back to Able Company that he had made it through. "You don't think that he and Kenton have found some señoritas and are drinking gin and tonics on some beach down south do you?"

"If it was any officer other than your cousin, I'd say hell no. With Perkin, the odds are about even. But at least with him, he'll have some girls and cocktails saved for us. I wouldn't mind either one about now."

The geography on the other side of the stream was different than the Able Company territory. It was flat pasture, although Sam could not see any livestock. *Either the farmer has brought them in to a barn, or one army or the other has had a hell of barbeque,* he thought. About one hundred yards from the stream, the road crossed over a small drainage ditch which emptied into the stream a few hundred yards to the north. Bill stood on the edge of the ditch about five yards in from the road, turned and faced the American lines and waved his arms over his head until he saw Len Anderson wave back. He was marking a target for mortar fire, and he did the same about five yards in from the other side of the road.

They walked carefully along the ditch, waving periodically to Len, and talking about the likelihood of an assault on this position.

"After this morning, d'ya reckon they'll be back for more?" Sam asked. *Hope springs eternal,* he thought.

"Yep. They won't try fording the lower Calore again. So that leaves this route, unless they want to try bridging further upstream. But why do that when there is a standing bridge left? Besides, Jim was telling me that the third regiment of the 45th finally lands tonight at Red Beach and more of the airborne boys are to drop tonight as well. The 3rd Division is supposed to land soon too. The Germans probably know more about our reinforcements than you or me, so by their lights, it's to the beach now or never. I was thinking about a line to use on our historians about this, but they ain't ever around when you want 'em."

"What line is that?" Sam asked.

"Remember General Forrest's dictum to 'Get thar fustest with the mostest?' Well, although I might be the only doggie in Fifth Army that thinks so, it strikes me that maybe we did. But I was thinking that the other side of the dictum may be more true for the Germans."

Sam thought for a moment and then asked, "What's that?"

As Bill stuffed a huge wad of tobacco into his cheek, he said, "Get thar lastest with the leastest."

Sam laughed and said, "They turn 'em out eloquent at that teacher's school you went to."

"That they do. So, you show up last to this little dance here, what do you do?"

Sam turned and looked down the road toward the northeast. At the other end of the pasture, the road emerged from trees on either side, and the tree line extended north and south for several hundred yards in both directions. "Depends on how many troops they're bringin' to the dance, but I'd reckon tanks down the road, move the Stugs out through the woods—they don't look dense—and fire on us from the tree line. Or put the Stugs in that farm down yonder and shoot at us from there. They'll have infantry in support and armored vehicles throughout. Don't matter though—they all have to show up here at some point, don't they?" Sam nodded back at the bridge.

"Yeah, they all have to show up here. I'd rather they try to bridge the stream upriver in front of 2nd Batt, but as you said, if they want this bridge, it doesn't matter. Well, let's—what's he doing?" Bill had caught sight of Frank McCarter running full bore out to the bridge. He was blocked and stopped by a sergeant of the engineers, whereupon he started frantically waving Sam and Bill in.

"They're coming! Fire support mission's all called in! We got less than five minutes!"

1255 hours
La Cosa Defenses, 1 Mile South of Calore River

It was a fortunate circumstance that the expected five minutes were underestimated. It took over a minute for Sam and Bill to run back with packs and rifles to the company positions—both red-faced and breathing heavily. The engineering sergeant grinned wildly at them as they pounded over the bridge, and then scurried to pull up the white tape marking the safe lane through the minefield on both sides of the bridge.

Five minutes later, Sam was in his foxhole. His breathing was normal again, but the Germans had not materialized. Bill walked up to Sam and knelt down beside him. "A P-38 saw an armored column crossing that bridge on the upper Calore, not far from Altavilla, and the call was made that it was coming our way. Jim's estimate is a battalion-sized task force with two companies of panzers. Wranosky's trying to get the plane over the area again to take another look, but I reckon we'll know where they've gone before we get a-holt of the flyboys. Although they may be headed over to our right in 2nd Battalion territory, my guess is that they're using that wedge—that island of trees—to cover their movement, and they'll come out when it suits 'em," Bill pointed to the tall trees at the far end of the pasture on the south side of the road.

If Bill was right, thought Sam, they would have a quick run to the bridge only four or five hundred yards or so distant. No sooner had the thought crossed Sam's mind, than a platoon-sized body of soldiers emerged on the road from behind the wedge of trees. The soldiers were formed up in two small columns, and Sam could see a large white flag flying from a pole held by the lead soldier in the left column. Damn, they march well, he thought.

"Hold your fire!" Bill had seen the white flag at the same time as Sam. He pulled out his binoculars and looked hard at the German soldiers. Magnified, he saw big strong men with no cause to surrender marching resolutely towards the bridge. All of the soldiers carried their rifles at shoulder arms, and at least two of the soldiers looked like they were carrying MG-34s or 42s on their shoulders.

Bill looked over in disbelief at Sam, who had gotten out of his foxhole for a better look himself, and said, "What kind of dumb sons-of-bitches do they think we are?"

"Exceptional, by the looks of it." Sam turned and hollered back at Lieutenant Anderson, whose mortar teams were in a clearing behind him, "Lenny, target the ditch fifteen yards on either side of the road! I meant to pace off the distance, but I can't run like a little girl and count at the same time. I estimate 175 yards." He looked over at Bill, who nodded.

Bill said to Sam, "I'm going to the center of the company line. Good luck." As he walked, he raised his arm in anticipation and called out, "Able Company! Stand by!" All of the soldiers along the line of Able Company who could see him looked back and forth between their company commander and the approaching Germans.

Sam looked over at Froman and said, "He's gonna drop that flag in another ten yards and bolt for the ditch. Get him; don't wait for an order." The young private from Chicago nodded and put the crosshairs of his new scope on the heart of the German sergeant leading the detail.

As the enemy platoon neared the ditch, the platoon leader dropped his flag and the German soldiers scattered to both sides of the ditch. Simultaneously with the drop of the white flag, Bill's arm dropped as well, and Froman's Springfield cracked as the German sergeant became the first casualty of the battle.

The rest of his men were not far behind him as they ran to the exact positions that Bill had marked less than half an hour earlier, and the mortar rounds began falling on the German soldiers before most of them had their rifles ready.

It was a guilt-free massacre: an exciting thirty seconds for the Texans, an agonizing lifetime for the Germans. Able Company fired nearly a thousand rounds, the Germans four. When the last living German soldier, a wounded private from Karlsruhe, tried bravely to surrender by raising his hands over his head, he was hit by no less than a score of bullets in the chest and face.

"Yeah! Who's the dumb son-of-a-bitch now, you dumbass mother-fuckers!" Private Froman had evidently been listening in on the conversation.

Sam looked at his sniper with amused affection and then lifted his head sharply as another soldier called out, "Here comes the rest of 'em!"

The German attack had been poorly timed, but the intent was for the "surrendering" party to be a diversion: while the focus was on them, the assault task force was to emerge from the cover of the trees several hundred yards distant. The timing needed to be near perfect if the diversion group was to have a chance to survive. It was not. That party was dead before the first half-tracks, infantry carriers, entered the pasture from the direction of the farm. More importantly, the Americans had been alerted both by the P-38 and the diversionary attack, and the main body of the German attack would pay the price.

Sam ducked involuntarily as the first spotting round from USS *Boise* (CL-47) screamed past the Texans to the north. *Boise* had moved into position onto the firing line that morning when she relieved USS *Philadelphia* as duty cruiser—*Philadelphia* had fired just under a thousand six-inch rounds in support of the beleaguered ground troops of the 45th Division overnight and needed to replenish her depleted magazines.

Although only five years old, *Boise* was a veteran warship with a veteran crew. She had been in the fight from the beginning of the war and had six Japanese flags and warship profiles optimistically painted on her pilot house from the Battle of Cape Esperance eleven months before. There, she had been nearly sunk during the battle and had limped home to the yards in Philadelphia for repair.

She had since had been assigned to the Mediterranean, was also a veteran of the Battle of Sicily, and had been on the firing line since Salerno began—naval gunfire support was not new to her crew.

From her position on station, *Boise* was firing northwest to southeast, and her spotting round was over the distant tree line by several hundred yards. The artillery forward observers on Mount Chirico called in the adjustments, and her next spotting round landed fifty yards short—she had straddled the target area; the last adjustments were made, and the call was made to fire for effect.

Boise was not the only veteran at play that afternoon though, and the German troops of the 29th Panzer Grenadiers that made up the battalion combat team had been on the receiving end of American artillery and naval gunfire support since Sicily. The 29th Panzer Grenadier Division facing the Texans was the second division to bear that name; the first was destroyed at Stalingrad, but not before it and another division had joined to defeat twelve Soviet divisions in a single day, and the current troops of the 29th keenly felt the press of history to be as lethal in combat as their predecessors. The lethality that was on their minds at present, though, was American artillery. Even the veterans of the Eastern Front had never experienced artillery fire as accurate and deadly as they had received in Sicily and repeated again at Salerno. The moving column of vehicles and troops stretching back to the upper Calore River crossing staggered as the forward-most troops balked at entering the pasture—an American artillery kill zone—but knew that to remain in one place was a death sentence as well.

German officers, sergeants, and corporals screamed at their soldiers; the fantastic discipline of the Wehrmacht reasserted itself, and the assault carried forward along a ragged line stretching across the 1st and 2nd Battalion boundary. German divisional artillery back in the mountains began to hit the eastern slope of Mount Chirico. Mortars began to carpet the battlefield with a thick layer of smoke, and half-tracks disgorged infantrymen into the pasture and quickly returned to infantry assembly areas to pick up more soldiers.

As the artillery began to plaster his hillside through the gaps in the smoke screen, Sam watched the German plan unfold. The Germans were attacking across a narrow front of several hundred yards, and it looked as though two armored thrusts were underway: an armored column was approaching along the road to the bridge with infantry support spread out to the north, and another column was emerging from behind the trees to the right about three hundred yards south of the road. They would either angle north in a moment or continue on to the stream to support an infantry crossing in the Second Battalion area. If so, Sam thought, they would try to seize the bridge from both sides. So far there was nothing for Sam to do but watch, and it was the show of a lifetime.

The lead vehicles of the German column had advanced no more than one hundred yards past the tree line, when naval and shore-based fires came screeching to the battlefield simultaneously. Sam grinned madly, his hands cupped over his ears, as the ground literally shook underneath them when a rippling broadside from the fifteen six-inch guns of *Boise* tore through the back third of the pasture. Arriving simultaneously were the coordinated fires of two divisions' artillery—the 36th's and the 45th's—and the combined effect brought the entire German effort to a halt. Nothing could move in that pasture, and those who were foolish enough to try and stand were torn apart. The panzer grenadiers who survived clung to the earth, their hands over their heads, screaming and praying for the artillery fire to stop. It did not for a long time.

For the next fifteen minutes, the ground shook, and the sky filled with smoke and dust as the combined fires continued unabated. *Boise* alone fired ninety rounds in that period, and the forward observers worked her fire to the east into and past the unlucky Italian farm into the trees. The divisional artillery was directed at concentrations of armor at first, then against any single vehicle that was identified. Company-level mortar and machine gun fire worked over the German infantry severely, and most of the two platoons of grenadiers that had made it onto the field were dead or wounded.

But the battle was not over. German Stugs, armored assault vehicles that resembled tanks but were really mobile artillery, had rolled back in the woods away from the naval fire, and when the opportunity presented itself, they rolled forward and opened fire at Mount Chirico. It was not a precision attack—it was brute application of force in a manner more reminiscent of a Napoleonic cannon barrage than of modern twentieth-century warfare. Sam noticed the difference from the howitzer fire from the mountains immediately; unlike those rounds which seemed to come down vertically on top of the target, the flat trajectory of the Stug round gave Sam the sensation of being personally shot at. He noticed that the 75mm rounds of the Stugs gave little notice before they slammed into the slope of the mountain and exploded. Just as the grenadiers curled up tight and sought whatever shelter they could find, Sam and his fellow Texans hunkered down in their foxholes to wait out the assault.

Sam, who had a strong constitution and was not intimidated by much, was terrified. The show of a lifetime had turned into a nightmare. His terror was a fear that was far worse than childhood terrors in the night, and it was worse than any fear of the unknown. It was a fear that fed on knowledge and certainty—the knowledge and certainty that he was going to die. Each round seemingly came closer to his position, and he believed that the walls of his foxhole would collapse from the quaking of the mountainside.

Crouched down in the foxhole and certain he was about to die, Sam urgently prayed, "Father, please watch over Maggie, and take care of Perk." He prayed again for Maggie, then fixed an image of her in his mind. She was in her wedding dress and laughing—it was the first dance at their wedding reception. She was looking up at Sam, her eyes alight, and she was obviously enjoying herself as Sam struggled mightily to remember the dance steps. She was laughing, gently teasing, whispering counts in his ear that were deliberately one or two off from his own. She had laughed as he lost what little sense of rhythm he had, stepping on her foot in the process. Sam had believed ever since that Margaret knew before he did that he would give up on the dance, sweep her up into his arms, and kiss her passionately before all their guests. The soldiers had applauded and wolf-whistled, while Margaret's friends clapped delightedly and the children covered their eyes. On the mountain in Italy, Sam vowed that his last thought would be of her on that day.

The impact of the shells moved closer. Around him, trees shattered from the explosions. The splinters mixed with the white-hot shrapnel and crashed down on the cowering soldiers. The earth itself—the giver of life— seemed to conspire with the Germans to become the bringer of death. Dirt moved in tons in a blink of an eye and what little air Sam seemed able to find reeked of acrid chemicals, dirt, and smoke. One final round detonated so close behind Sam that he was slammed violently to the bottom of his foxhole, the air sucked from his lungs as he tried to scream from fear and pain. Even after the German fires adjusted to the north and the cruiser began to attrite the Stugs, he stayed crushed in the depths of his foxhole. It was not until the cries for help and the calls for medics overpowered the ringing in his ears that he thought of moving. At first, he could not. He found that he had no strength in his legs, and he planted the stock of his M-1 hard into the ground in his foxhole and pulled himself up as if the Garand were a playground pole.

Through the smoke, all he could see was utter devastation. The illusory protection of the trees around him was gone, and the hillside was cratered and torn apart. He looked to his right and saw soldiers beginning to lift their heads over the rim of their foxholes, and Sam leaned slowly over to Froman's foxhole to see if he was still alive. He was, but the sniper was not yet prepared to commit himself to movement.

Sam started to pull himself out of his foxhole to see to the wounded, but he heard Lieutenant McCarter's distinctive East Texas accent, "Stay down! Stay in your foxholes! Here they come! Hold the line, Able Company! Hold the line! Give 'em hell!"

"What . . . ," Sam was puzzled. He could not think clearly, but he knew that something was wrong. Why was Frank giving orders to the company? Where was Bill? He started once again to climb out of his foxhole to find out, and then he saw what Frank had seen—the Germans had come in under the artillery barrage and while armored flamethrowers were shooting burning fuel over the stream onto the Texans' positions, half-tracks were disembarking grenadiers only yards from the bridge. The gunners on the German half-tracks frantically began sweeping the hillside with MG-34s, and the scream of soldiers to his left told Sam that they had found their targets. Sam moved in a fog, unable still to think clearly but knowing that he had to act. He turned back to call to Len Anderson to get machine gun fire on the dismounted infantry and mortar fire on the vehicles, but Len was no longer behind him. He saw Sergeant Hernandez, the weapons platoon NCO, on his knees next to a red smear on the mountainside. Hernandez was struggling to remount a .30 caliber machine gun with one arm—his other one was hanging limply at his side, his sleeve drenched in blood. "I should help him," thought Sam, and he started again to climb out of his foxhole, then he felt a sharp tug as a bullet slammed into the head of Perkin's hammer in his pack and disintegrated. Sam didn't know what happened, only that it felt and sounded unnatural, and he turned around to see a panzer grenadier with a bolt-action Mauser on the other side of the stream take aim at him again. Froman's rifle fired and the grenadier dropped straight down. *It doesn't look like that in the movies,* Sam thought.

Sam dropped back to his fighting position and raised his Garand and took aim at the gunner on one of the half-tracks and squeezed the trigger. Nothing. His safety was on. *How could I make that mistake after all these years?* he wondered. He pushed the safety off and shot at the gunner. He missed. Froman shot him instead. Through his fog he watched as a squad of German soldiers rushed the bridge. When the soldiers came to the engineer's minefield, the squad went down in a violent tangled mess. Another squad of soldiers ran over them, deliberately stepping on their wounded comrades' bodies as they went. The lead soldier, a sergeant, leaped from the bridge over what he assumed was another minefield and made it to the momentary safety of the other side. Sam focused hard and shot the sergeant. Froman shot the next soldier, and Sam fired at grenadiers until his Garand ejected his empty clip. Sam fumbled getting another clip out of his cartridge belt, and he heard Froman shouting at him to hang on. "Why would he say that?" Sam asked himself stupidly.

"We need to get a machine gun going!" Sam yelled at Froman slowly, struggling to form his words. Froman did not acknowledge him but kept firing at Germans on the bridge. Sam looked back again to see if he could help Sergeant Hernandez with the M1919, but he saw that Private Pfadenhauer was rapidly setting it up instead. Sam turned back to the bridge and, as the machine gun began to fire, said to himself, "Good old Howie, where'd he come from?"

Sam did not have time to think through it further—two Panzer IVs had approached the stream, and the first was only thirty yards from the bridge when it exploded. Sam looked slowly to his left—the source of the killing shot. It had been fired by an M-10 tank destroyer that was hull down in one of the excavated pits. The events of the last half hour had unfolded so quickly that Sam was unaware that American armor had arrived on the battlefield. The second panzer was rapidly traversing its turret to deal with this new threat when a loud whoosh over Sam's head made him wince in pain. He watched dumbly as the bazooka rocket flew over his head and streaked through the hundred yards to the panzer, striking it on the thin armor of the closed commander's hatch.

The exploding tank signaled the end of the threat to Sam's bridge and to the Allied beachhead. The German task force had no choice but to withdraw under unrelenting fire from *Boise* and *Philadelphia,* which had rejoined its sister cruiser on the firing line. Aided by spotting aircraft, the cruisers harried the task force until it had withdrawn past Eboli. Although it would not become apparent to the Allies for several days, the Germans had gone permanently on the defensive at Salerno as a prelude to breaking contact with Fifth Army before Eighth Army arrived. The German window of opportunity to defeat the Allies on the beach had closed.

It was certainly not apparent to Sam, but he was glad to see the Germans withdraw from the shredded and burning pasture. He wiped the blood from his nose—he was unaware that it had been bleeding for the past ten minutes. He put a finger to his ear to wiggle it to see if the goddamned ringing would go away, and he found that his right ear was bleeding as well. Concussion, he thought in a moment of clarity. "I must have a concussion," Sam said thickly to Private Kulis who was kneeling in front of him.

Kulis looked up behind Sam with concern, and Sam turned and saw a tall, thin officer with black hair and piercing blue eyes looking down at him. The officer handed the bazooka tube he was holding over to a large sergeant with red hair, and then the officer knelt down next to Sam as well and gently pulled Sam's helmet off.

"Hey, Sam." The officer was smiling.

Sam blinked hard to clear his eyes, smiled back and said, "Hey yourself. What took you so long?"

"I had to stop and look for a priest. He'd gone out for a run." Despite the smile, Perkin looked very, very tired, and something, maybe his fatigue, made him look much older.

Sam slowly digested this answer and nodded, still smiling, as if it made perfect sense. "They ain't ever around when you want one. Say, Perk, what was that story you were tellin' me about the nun and them two Aggies?"

Epilogue

October 24, 1943
0415 hours
Naples, Italy

They came about the same time every morning, the dreams—earlier than he would normally wake up. Early enough to rob him of sleep. Dreams of Roberto Pena, whole, alive, and surly—or dead in the back of Perkin's jeep. This morning, the dream was of Brother Giuseppe's death. He had this dream often as well, and he always awoke with a sense of utter helplessness. Even as he lay asleep and dreaming of the murder of the young monk, oddly conscious while he slept that it was a dream, he had the urgent sense that he had to help the monk. In many of these terrible nights, he tried to get out of the warehouse to warn the monk but he never made it in time. Giuseppe always stumbled through the door and fell among the circle of soldiers while Perkin sat there unable to get to his feet. In another frequent dream, which he had this night, he made it through the door, except instead of running into the darkness at the monastery, he came through the door into daylight over the graves of his three dead soldiers. He saw Colucci with his knife at the throat of the monk, and he struggled to pull his pistol. As he pointed it at the Blackshirt, while seagulls circled overhead mocking him, Colucci grinned an evil smile at him and cut the monk's throat. Perkin pulled the trigger, and then pulled the trigger again and again. The gun never fired, and he awoke on these nights clenching his right hand as if he could pull the trigger in his sleep.

He awoke with a start and a shudder as he slowly gathered his bearings. As his heart settled down and his breathing returned to normal, his hand reached over and touched the naked back of the woman next to him. Her name was Gianina, and meeting her had been a gift from heaven. She was a young war widow who worked as a restoration assistant at the *Museo di Capodimonte*, the Neapolitan National Art Gallery. Perkin had met her two weeks prior when he had been sight-seeing with Jim Lockridge. Most of the great art, including the Caravaggios that Jim had wanted to see, were still hidden away in the caves and secret vaults of Italy; some priceless Italian art had already been looted by the occupying Nazis further north. There were only a few minor works available for viewing for Perkin and Jim, but it didn't matter to Perkin, as he had met Gianina that day.

In a very short time, Gianina brought a feminine balance and sympathy that had been missing from Perkin's life. Unlike most of the women that he met in Italy, Gianina was neither shy nor brazen—she matter-of-factly said "yes" when Perkin had asked her out the first day that they met. Perkin wasn't the first American soldier to ask her out, but he didn't flirt with her like the others. He simply sought, he needed, the companionship of a lady, and she liked what she saw deep in the eyes of the tall, serious American. She spoke fluent English and was perhaps the sole optimist left in Naples during those dark days. Gianina had a teasing personality and was a good listener, and she had cried when Perkin had told her, after a few drinks, of the monastery at Paola. He had not cried himself, but it was a "close run thing," as Wellington had once said. Slowly but surely, Gianina was teasing, coercing, and leading Perkin away from his personal heart of darkness in a way that even Sam and his friends could not.

Perkin stared up towards the ceiling and thought about the day to come. He wanted to spend the day with Gianina, but he would not be able to. Even though he was on the fourth day of an authorized week of leave, Kulis had been sent as a runner to his hotel room the night before to tell Perkin to report to the division commander's office in a clean uniform at 1100 sharp—which meant be there at 1045. Kulis had no further information for him and was distressed at the concern that passed over the face of his lieutenant at the news. "He can't think that he's in trouble can he?" the private asked himself later in the evening after he had given it some thought. The private declined the offer of a glass of wine with the lieutenant and his lady; mission completed, Kulis was planning on spending more of his share of the lira taken from the Blackshirts, and if he didn't meet Fratelli and Pfadenhauer on time, they would hit the brothels without him.

It was in the darkness, after the dreams, that Perkin most frequently took the counsel of his fears. Surely, he thought, he was to be held to account for the deaths of his soldiers. God knows he was guilty enough, he thought. Perhaps Colonel Foster had sent a complaint through to American channels, or maybe he was even in trouble for the assault of the Italian constable in Vibonati. Why hadn't he posted a guard at the monastery? If he had taken that most basic step of soldiering, Giuseppe would still be alive. The truth is that they seemed safe at the monastery under the cover of the sirocco. He sighed.

"Did you have the dream again?" Gianina stirred and rolled over. She placed her head on Perkin's shoulder and her arm protectively across his chest. She knew the answer to her question—she could tell by the tenseness of Perkin's body. Intuitively, she asked, "Are you worried about today?"

"I don't know enough to be worried." Belying that assertion, he said doubtfully, "I don't know. Maybe this will cost me my commission."

"What? Don't be silly. They can't blame you for the things that happened in Paola. You should be rewarded, not punished. Stop worrying. You'll be a general before you know it, and then I'll be a Texas contessa."

Perkin heard the smile in her voice in the darkness and relaxed. She was teasing him again. "We don't have contessas in Texas—just matronly women. Is that what you want?"

"Would I have to get fat and give you bunches of cowboys for your ranch?"

"Bunches? Well, that's the way it's usually done, except it seems you're mistakin' me for Sam. I don't have a ranch."

Gianina laughed in the darkness and kissed Perkin below his ear. "Oh, am I mistaken? I forgot who I was with tonight. Are you the skinny, serious one? I do like Sam though. He tells terrible jokes and laughs at them himself." She stretched up and kissed Perkin on the lips and said, "You should get to sleep—everything is better with a good night's sleep."

Perkin said nothing for several minutes as he thought about the girl in bed with him. She was tall and thin, with stylish black glasses and long, glossy black hair which had been pulled back in a severe bun when they met. He had dated many beautiful women before, but he could not think of one with as beautiful a soul as this one.

"Do you want to come to Texas with me?" he whispered.

There was no answer, she had gone back to sleep and her steady breathing on his chest calmed him down, and soon he fell asleep as well.

1045 hours
Naples, Italy

Perkin had been worried about getting to the general's office at the Italian Army base in time. Security was pretty tight, and it took him longer to clear through the guards at the gate than he expected. Still, he arrived at the building which had once been the office of an Italian brigade commander and was now the temporary property of the Texas Army. The American and Lone Star flags flapped in the cool breeze at twin flagpoles outside of the headquarters building, and under the American flag was a smaller red flag with two white stars—the flag of a major general.

As Perkin walked up to the headquarters building, a collection of his friends were standing there outside: Sam, Bill Spaulding, Jim Lockridge, Waller Finley-Jones, Frank McCarter, and Sergeant Kenton. Perkin looked for Len Anderson, even though he knew Len had been killed at the bridge and was buried at the temporary American cemetery at Paestum. Perkin looked quizzically at his cousin and asked, "What's going on, Bear?"

Smiling broadly, Sam said, "What d'ya think numb-nuts? The general's fixin' to have you address the divisional Aggie association. Didn't they tell you?"

Perkin looked to Bill Spaulding whose face had been shredded by shrapnel during the battle at the La Cosa bridge. Two medics working together had frantically stitched his face back together while under fire when Perkin arrived and took command of the company. "What about you, Frankenstein? What's happening here?"

"It's Frankenstein's Monster, you moron. Frankenstein was the doctor."

Captain Spaulding gingerly stuffed some tobacco into his cheek and started to say more, but was interrupted when a very young looking captain walked out the door, looked around, and settled his gaze on Perkin. The very young captain asked impatiently, "Are you Berger? Yes? I'm Captain Walker. Let's head on in. Lieutenant, Sergeant—sorry, but there's no room for you." The lieutenant in question was Lieutenant McCarter. He and Kenton shrugged and walked over to a stone wall and sat down to wait.

1100 hours
Naples, Italy

The very young captain was the general's aide and was also his son. Captain Walker barked "Ten-hut!" and the small assembly stood at attention in the general's office. It was less dramatic than in the movies because everyone was already standing at attention as Charlie Walker had given them all a fifteen-second heads-up with the customary warning "stand-by" before the old man walked in.

"Good morning everyone. Please stand at ease." Walker strode into his office and studied the collection of officers. General Walker knew most of the soldiers there—Colonel Jamison was one of his three regimental commanders and Lieutenant Colonel Wranosky was one of the few surviving battalion commanders. Behind Colonel Jamison was the

British liaison officer who seemed totally at ease in the company of the Americans. There was a captain he did not know personally—his face was stitched up in an angry jagged line running from his left temple across his nose to the right corner of his mouth—but he had been told the captain was the Able Company commander. Walker thought that the captain had to have been in terrible pain, yet the officer looked very happy as he switched a huge quid of tobacco from one side of his mouth to another. A second captain was also squeezed into the small office. The balding captain was thin and athletic, and he beamed at the general through wire-rimmed glasses. Walker looked over at a very large soldier, a first lieutenant who was tall and heavily muscled. The lieutenant had more than a passing resemblance to Lieutenant Berger, and the large man also looked very pleased—this would be the cousin that he had been told about.

"Good morning, General," the response from the assembly was in unison.

There were no airs to the general, and Walker introduced himself to the few officers that he didn't know and shook hands with the rest. While he would have enjoyed sitting down over an afternoon of beers with everyone present to hear the stories of their battle, he had work to do. He nodded at his son and said, "Let's get to it, Charlie."

"Yes, sir. We'll begin with the award. Attention to orders!" Captain Walker began to read the citation accompanying the award in a monotone voice:

> *First Lieutenant Perkin Warbeck Berger, Infantry, United States Army National Guard, State of Texas, distinguished himself by gallantry in action as a platoon leader of Company "A," 141st Infantry, on two occasions in Italy. On 9 Sep 1943,*

Lieutenant Berger's company was pinned and unable to move to its objectives by enemy armor and artillery. While under enemy machine gun fire, Lieutenant Berger climbed onto a German Panzer Mark IV tank. Finding the commander's hatch secured, Lieutenant Berger assaulted the tank and drove it off of the battlefield with a submachine gun and the panzer's sledge-hammer, while also directing the destruction of a second tank by M1A1 rocket fire. From 11–14 Sep 1943, Lieutenant Berger led a mission over two hundred miles behind enemy lines and back to establish contact with the British Eighth Army. During this successful mission, Lieutenant Berger's patrol sustained heavy casualties yet engaged and killed thirteen Axis soldiers and captured three additional intelligence personnel of the German Army. Lieutenant Berger's actions saved countless civilian lives and preserved an historic site of religious significance while facilitating the link-up between Fifth and Eighth Army. His daring, bravery, determination, and devotion to duty bring great credit to his regiment and were in keeping with the highest traditions of the United States Army National Guard and the State of Texas.

Perkin stood at attention while Captain Walker read and General Walker pinned the Silver Star on Perkin's clean but stained jacket. He had recognized by now that this day was going to be better than he had anticipated, and he secretly wished that Gianina was there to see the medal. He was also conscious of the eyes upon him. Perkin felt that if he had to be the center of an awards ceremony, he was grateful that the general had directed this small and intimate one, although he could not understand why he was being singled out—the division had been notified that the first battlefield citations would be handed out by Thanksgiving at a large divisional formation. Perkin's thoughts wandered momentarily from Gianina and the words that were being read by Captain Walker, and he thought of the Texans who had been recommended for the Medal of Honor for their actions at Salerno. One of those soldiers, Corporal Charles Kelly, had earned the nickname "Commando Kelly," and among many other heroic acts that he committed on Black Monday at Altavilla, Perkin had heard that Kelly had dropped live mortar shells onto German soldiers from the balcony of a building where he had taken shelter. As Perkin wondered if Kelly would get "The Medal," and he began to wish for the ceremony to be over, the general spoke again.

"Okay, Charlie. What's next?"

Charlie Walker placed the award citation to the bottom of a stack of papers and picked up the next sheet and began to read in the same monotone, "From the Commanding Officer, 36th Division, United States Army, to First Lieutenant Perkin W. Berger: Effective immediately, you are hereby promoted to the temporary rank and title of Captain, Army of the United States. You are required to discharge carefully and diligently the duties of the rank to which promoted and to uphold the traditions and standards of the Army."

Walker looked over at Sam and with a wave of his hand indicated that he was to join Walker standing in front of Perkin. As he walked up to the general and the newly appointed captain, Walker said, "Help me out here, Lieutenant."

Sam grinned and said, "Yes, sir. I'm very happy to."

Sam reached up to Perkin's right collar tab and removed Perkin's old lieutenant insignia. Walker handed Sam a brand new set of captain's bars, and as Sam attached them to Perkin's collar, said, "Congratulations, Perkin. I think your father would be very proud of you. I am. I wish I had some of my own bars to pass down to you since you don't have your father's, but I'm afraid my own boys have cleaned me out. Thank you, Lieutenant." This last was to Sam, who then joined the other officers assembled in the office. Walker smiled and said, "I remember being promoted to captain. You think, 'Thank God, I'm not a looey anymore,' and then you immediately start fretting that your new bars look too new. Don't worry though, these will get broke in quickly enough. Charlie, tell 'em what's next."

"Yes, sir." Captain Walker picked up a third sheet and slid Perkin's promotion orders under the larger stack and hesitated as he skipped through the preamble of the orders. ". . . Effective immediately, Captain Perkin W. Berger is detached from Able Company, 141st Infantry, and will assume acting command of the 36th Cavalry Reconnaissance Troop."

"Sir?" Perkin's surprise was obvious. He was an infantry officer, not a cavalry officer, and while it was not unprecedented for an infantry officer to command cavalry units, it was rare. He would not be welcome in that community, he was sure.

"Ah, yes." Walker smiled at Perkin. "Let's have a quick round of applause for Captain Berger. Then, let's all come into the next room for some coffee and I'll try to shed some light on this." After shaking Perkin's hand and slapping him on the back, the group followed General Walker into a large conference room where maps of Italy covered the wall, and a large table had several pots of coffee and a tray of sandwiches waiting. As he took a cup of coffee from an orderly, Walker explained, "I'm sorry, but it's an acting command. You see, I had a bit of a dilemma with you. I have more company grade infantry officers who need a company command than I have company commands available. Unfortunately, we know that a lot of opportunities opened up at Salerno, but we still have an overage. By the time the war ends, I suspect that most companies will be commanded by first lieutenants or even butter bars, but as it stands now, I have captains stashed at regiments and elsewhere who are ahead of you for a command position of a rifle company. I could put you into one of those stash billets or into a unique platoon command elsewhere, but either way I run the risk of Big Army coming in and ordering you to another division that needs company commanders— probably one that is still forming in the States. We have a terrible fight ahead of us in Italy, and I need as many combat-experienced officers as I can beg, borrow, or steal for my rifle companies. Although I have my doubts about your sanity after hearing about the panzer . . . ," Walker smiled at Perkin, "your chain of command assures me that it is in my best interests to keep you in the Texas Army. This is my solution: I'm putting you into the 36th Reconnaissance Troop for the time being. They lost their XO and their senior platoon leader in combat at Altavilla, and their CO has just had a relapse of the African ague compounded by fatigue. He's an excellent officer, but he'll be out of commission for a long time. I can put you there in command temporarily—either until he is fit for duty again or until the cavalry mafia gets another qualified officer for me. You may be there for as short as six weeks or as long as next year. In the meantime, I'll keep you in the rotation for an infantry command. Now, you may have noticed that I don't do personal award ceremonies for lieutenants and captains . . . ," Walker trailed off.

Perkin nodded and remained silent.

"Well, I made an exception for you. I have a bit of a Machiavellian motive, I'm afraid. I say this only partially in jest, but you're going into a hostile environment. Your well-deserved Silver Star for a long-range reconnaissance patrol might mitigate the hard feelings that the cavalry will feel to your appointment and give you some credibility with your platoon leaders and NCOs. But, here's the main reason: I wanted to do this for your father. Again, I think that he would be very proud of you. Now, let's sit down. While we have some of these sandwiches, I have some stories to tell about the first Captain Berger of my acquaintance. Before I get started, do you have any questions for me about your new command?"

Perkin looked at the smiling face of Sam—his broad smile was reflected on the faces of his friends—and it seemed that the nightmares of the night before were only a distant memory. He smiled back at his cousin and turned to the general, "Yes, sir. When can I start?"

Author's Note

The battle at Salerno continued well after the ending of this book, and while there was plenty of desperate fighting ahead for the 36th Division and the other soldiers on the Salerno plain, the German counterattacks of September 14, 1943, were the last serious threat to the beachhead. On September 18, the Germans broke contact with Fifth Army and withdrew from the Salerno battlefield, yet Allied soldiers did not enter Naples until October 1. As bad as "Bloody Salerno" was, there was far worse fighting for the boys of the Texas Gun Club in Italy to come.

Although this is first and foremost a series about Texans just trying to get home, I want to add a note about the British—the X Corps fight at Salerno was as significant, as desperate, and as difficult as was the fight of the American VI Corps. British casualties at Salerno were higher than American, but I felt I couldn't do their fight justice while remaining within the boundaries of my own story. The British divisions at Salerno had more experience than their American counterparts, though not a great deal more. Some events in the British sector are very compelling—the role of the Commandos and the Rangers in particular. I became an admirer of General McCreery, whose composure served to shore up General Clark when he needed it, both at Salerno and later in the campaign.

In my novel, one of my fictional heroes is portrayed as a relative of an American president and part of a real and enduring family in American politics, but coincidentally, there were actually three Churchills at that battle, including the Prime Minister's son Randolph. Both of my heroes are portrayed as descendants of a real American (Confederate) general, while again coincidentally, the great-great-great grandson of the Duke of Wellington fought and died at Salerno.

A less noble side of the British experience was the infamous mutiny of September 20, 1943, when replacement soldiers brought in from Africa refused to fight. Some had been led to believe that they would join their regiments in Eighth Army; some believed that they were headed home to Britain, but instead they were sent as individual replacements to the British divisions in the Fifth Army. It was a shameful affair that could have been avoided. Ultimately, charges of mutiny were filed and sentences were handed out ranging from several years imprisonment to death (which were commuted).

With the exception of Captain, the Duke of Wellington, Captain Charlie Walker, and Lieutenant Colonel Fred Walker, Jr. (the latter two the sons of the division commander), none of the military characters in this book below the rank of Brigadier General are real. In many cases, their positions correspond to certain historical figures or their actions to historical events. For example, Colonel Richard Werner was the actual commander of the

141st RCT at Salerno, while in my novel, the commander is Colonel Tony Jamison (whose namesake at the time of this writing is a lieutenant in the world's finest navy).

I would like to thank Colonel Walker again for writing the foreword to *The Texas Gun Club*. I had the privilege of meeting him in the summer of 2009, and he graciously agreed to read my manuscript. Those readers who are familiar with today's military might be surprised to know that as a lieutenant colonel, he was a twenty-eight-year-old battalion commander at Salerno. I was ten years older when I reached the equivalent rank in the navy.

I tried to stay as faithful to the real story as possible, using some of the real pearls of history when I could. One example was the call to surrender as the landing craft approached the shore. The veracity of this incident has been called into question by some historians, but it is part of the lore of the division. Another example is General Dawley's lament to Clark that he had no reserves, only a prayer. Dawley was relieved by Clark on September 20, after the end of the battle (and not long after his corps received a commendation from Clark on their performance), and it is not entirely clear to me whether it was for genuine mismanagement of his corps, the need for a scapegoat for Black Monday, or whether it was because on September 17, Dawley ill-advisedly called Generals Eisenhower and Clark a couple of "boy scouts" to Clark's face. Perhaps that was a valid comment from Dawley's perspective, but the usual protocol is to make a remark of that nature behind their backs, instead of to one of the boy scouts in question. That particular boy scout (Clark) did order his staff and the fleet to prepare an evacuation as described by Colonel Jamison, and the rumors spread like wildfire, further undermining already shaky morale.

Another pearl was the German ruse of the white flag, which occurred on the same day as I wrote of, but to another unit (2/179th). I gather it was as successful in real life as I portrayed it here. I would like to credit two other incidents taken from the pages of history which I incorporated into *The Texas Gun Club*. The first was the story of the medic who was waved aside by the German gunner before opening fire on his landing craft. It was such a compassionate and yet chilling story that I wanted to adapt it for my use. The medic was Ike Franklin (3/143rd), and unlike the soldier in my story, Franklin kept working his way inland. He had another terrible incident only a couple hours later when a bursting artillery shell mutilated two companions, decapitating one, while Franklin escaped without a scratch.

Finally, the coastal road was open and only lightly patrolled by the Germans. Two separate convoys of journalists who were bored by the pace of Monty's advance traveled along that road, only in the opposite direction. I agree with one historian's assessment that Eighth Army could have sent a battalion along that road and linked up with Fifth Army by the 12th or 13th (I read his assessment some weeks after I wrote Perkin's ill-fated recommendation to Colonel Foster, so it looks like Perk was on to something. His timing needs work though, doesn't it?)

I think it is fair to say that the value of Salerno has been slighted somewhat by history. Had the landings there been a failure—and it was a close one—the landings at Normandy almost certainly would have been postponed. In other words, had we failed at Salerno, the course of the Second World War would have been dramatically changed. Perhaps the Soviets would have sought a separate peace, or perhaps advanced all the way to the English Channel. Either way, our lives would be different today. In addition, there were a great number of lessons learned at Salerno about amphibious warfare and combined warfare that carried over into Normandy to help make those landings successful.

It was a very tall order for the two National Guard divisions that carried the load for VI Corps—the 36th and the 45th—and all things considered, the boys from Texas and Oklahoma did pretty well. It is a testament to the high regard in Army circles for the untested 36th and its commander that they were given an assignment of this magnitude and responsibility. Both the troops and their commander made mistakes, but they both recovered quickly. There were very few divisions in World War II that were in combat longer than the 36th, and the Texas Gun Club had many more battles ahead of it in Italy, France, and Germany.

CDR Mark Bowlin, USN (Ret.)
Flower Mound, Texas
September, 2009

About the Author

Commander Mark Bowlin, USN (Ret.) is a somewhat opinionated former naval intelligence officer who believes that the Dallas Cowboys will win this year's Super Bowl, that Texas is truly God's country, and that good Texas barbeque and a cold beer is superior to champagne and caviar in every respect.

Mark was a soldier in the Texas National Guard before being commissioned as an ensign in the United States Navy. Mark has lived in Wales, Japan, and Italy and served in a variety of billets—ashore and afloat—in the United States and overseas. His awards include the Legion of Merit and Defense Meritorious Service Medal, among other personal, unit, and campaign awards.